RIVEN KNIGHT

USA TODAY BESTSELLING AUTHOR

DEVNEY PERRY

RIVEN KNIGHT

ISBN: 978-1-950692-77-4

Editing & Proofreading:

Elizabeth Nover, Razor Sharp Editing

Marion Archer, Making Manuscripts

Julie Deaton, Deaton Author Services

Karen Lawson, The Proof is in the Reading

Kaitlyn Moodie, Moodie Editing Services

Judy Zweifel, Judy's Proofreading

Cover: Sarah Hansen, Okay Creations

OTHER TITLES

The Edens Series

Indigo Ridge

Juniper Hill

Garnet Flats

Jasper Vale

Crimson River

Sable Peak

Christmas in Quincy - Prequel

The Edens: A Legacy Short Story

Treasure State Wildcats Series

Coach

Blitz

Clifton Forge Series

Steel King

Riven Knight

Stone Princess

Noble Prince

Fallen Jester

Tin Queen

Calamity Montana Series

The Bribe

The Bluff

The Brazen

The Bully

The Brawl

The Brood

Jamison Valley Series

The Coppersmith Farmhouse

The Clover Chapel

The Lucky Heart

The Outpost

The Bitterroot Inn

The Candle Palace

Maysen Jar Series

The Birthday List

Letters to Molly

The Dandelion Diary

CONTENTS

To Jennifer
For that day we drove around Texas
and plotted this book

CHAPTER ONE

GENEVIEVE

"I'm disappointed."

I'd take a slap across the face any day over that statement. It was especially sharp and painful today of all days, coming from Mr. Reggie Barker, a man I'd considered a mentor and professional hero.

"I'm sorry, Reggie."

My boss—former boss—sighed on the other end of the phone. "Given the way you chose to leave the firm, I'm unable to give you a reference."

I winced. "Oh, um . . . okay."

Reggie felt that giving one week's notice instead of two was a snub. It didn't matter that I'd worked as his paralegal for the past four years, that I was the first person to arrive at the firm each morning and the last to leave each night. It didn't matter that, while paralegals in the firm could study for their LSAT exams during work hours, I'd saved all my studies for home, ensuring every minute of my workday was dedicated to helping Reggie.

I'd pushed taking the exam four times because he'd

cautioned me to be *ready*—stated in a way he didn't think I was.

I'd trusted him. I'd valued his opinion above all others at the firm. I'd given him all that I'd had to give, and apparently, it wasn't enough.

I was disappointed too.

I'd only called this morning because I'd forgotten to leave my office key behind. Now I wished I'd simply mailed it with a note.

"Best of luck, Genevieve."

"Thank—"

He hung up the phone before I could finish. Twenty-seven was already shaping up to be a disaster.

Happy birthday to me.

I set my phone aside and stared through the windshield at the store ahead. I was parked in front of a small clothing shop on Central Avenue. It was the only store in Clifton Forge, Montana, that sold women's clothing besides the farm-and-ranch-supply warehouse.

Clifton Forge.

My mom had gone to high school here. My grandparents, two people I'd never known, had been killed in a car accident and were buried here. Six weeks ago, the town of Clifton Forge was nothing more than a footnote in my family's history.

Then Mom came for a visit and was viciously slaughtered at the local motel.

Now Clifton Forge wasn't only a black spot on the past, it was also my home for the foreseeable future.

I longed to be at home in Denver, driving on familiar streets to familiar places. The allure of the highway had a strong pull. On the drive from Colorado, I'd been tempted more than once to turn around and never look back. To run and hide.

Except I'd made a promise to a perfect stranger, a man I'd known only hours. I wouldn't break my word.

Not after what Isaiah had done for me.

So here I was, in Clifton Forge.

For months. Years. Decades. *For as long as it takes.* I owed Isaiah that time.

The queasy feeling I'd had for days surged, the bile rising in my throat. I swallowed it down, not wanting to think about a lifetime condemned to Montana. I didn't have time to dwell on the possibilities—the consequences—of what was about to happen. I was supposed to meet Isaiah at noon, which only gave me two hours to get ready. So I steeled my spine, pushed the nerves away and got out of the car to do some shopping.

I refused to wear jeans today.

In the past week, I'd packed up everything in my condo in Denver, much like I'd done with my mother's home, though this time not quite as soul shattering. Still, it had hurt and I'd cried every time I'd taped a box shut. All this change, all this loss—I was drowning.

Most of my larger belongings had gone into storage. Some had been packed to ship. And the rest had been crammed into my gray, four-door Toyota Camry, which I'd driven from Colorado to Montana yesterday.

Too frazzled, trying to pack and finish up my last week at work, I hadn't thought to pack a dress. Maybe it was my subconscious protesting today's nuptials.

But, like it or not, this wedding was happening, and I was not wearing jeans.

Especially on my birthday.

I'd taken extra care with my makeup this morning. I'd washed and styled my thick, brown hair using the expensive curling wand Mom had bought me last year.

It was the last birthday gift she'd ever give me.

My God, I missed her. She wouldn't be here today to stand by my side as I made arguably the biggest mistake of my life. She wouldn't be here for any more birthdays, because a vile and vicious human had snuffed out her life. It wasn't fair.

Mom had been murdered, stabbed seven times, left to bleed out in a motel room alone. She'd died, leaving behind a trail of secrets and lies that were ruining her beautiful memory.

Why? I wanted to scream it to the heavens until she answered.

Why?

I was so angry at her. I was furious she hadn't trusted me with the truth. That she hadn't told me about my father. That I was here in this shitty little town because of her bad choices.

But damn it, I missed her. Today of all days, I wanted my mom.

Tears welled behind my sunglasses and I blinked them away before walking into the clothing store. I put on the fake smile I'd been wearing for weeks.

"Good morning," the clerk greeted as the bell chimed over my head. "Please feel free to look around. Is there something in particular you're looking for?"

"Actually, yes. I need a dress and heels."

The heels would hurt. The soles of my feet were wrecked from running through the mountains with bare feet, but I'd suffer through it today.

"Oooh. I might have just the thing." She came from around the counter where she'd been folding a sweater. "We just got this deep-green dress in yesterday. I'm *obsessed* with it. And it will go beautifully with your hair."

"Perfect."

Just as long as it isn't white.

Thirty minutes later, I was home—a term I used loosely —because my temporary residence, this shitty apartment located above a shitty garage in a shitty town, was definitely no *home*. I pulled on my new sleeveless green wrap dress, adjusting the deep V-neck so not too much cleavage was showing. Then I stood on my tiptoes in the bathroom, trying to see myself in the mirror. Whoever had furnished this place didn't seem to care what they looked like from the waist down.

I strapped on the nude heels I'd bought today too, wishing I'd had time for a pedicure. Was there even a place for pedicures in Clifton Forge? Instead, I rifled through my purse for the bottle of hot pink polish I'd tossed in there weeks ago for emergency touch-ups. I applied another coat and let it dry. There were so many layers now, it would take a jackhammer to chip it all off.

I fluffed my hair once more and swiped on a fresh coat of lip color. Noise from the Clifton Forge Garage carried up from the floor. The clang of metal on metal. The hum of a compressor. The muffled voices of men working.

Crossing the studio apartment, I stepped up to the only window that overlooked the parking lot below. A row of gleaming black motorcycles was parked against the edge of the property, lined up and equally spaced against a chain-link fence.

My half brother owned one of those bikes.

So did my father.

He was Mom's biggest secret, one I'd only learned about because of her death. Would she have told me about him eventually? I guess it didn't make a difference now. Except for a few times as a kid and then a bratty teenager, I hadn't asked about him. I hadn't needed a father when I'd had her as a mother.

She was everything I'd needed and more. And now she was gone, leaving me to deal with this family of strangers. What other secrets would I uncover in Clifton Forge? They seemed to be seeping from the boards of her coffin.

A man walked out from the garage, striding to a black bike that didn't gleam like the others. It was the only motorcycle in the row I'd ridden.

Isaiah. A name that had been haunting my thoughts for days.

His stride was long and confident. He had a grace about his steps, an ease in the way those strong thighs lifted and his narrow hips rolled. But then came the thud, a heaviness each time his boot hit pavement.

It sounded a lot like dread.

I could sympathize.

He glanced over his shoulder, his eyes landing on my car parked by the stairs leading to the apartment. He stared at it for a long moment, then turned his gaze to the window.

I didn't bother trying to hide. If he could see me past the dirt and water spots, it didn't make a difference. Soon, there'd be no escaping his gaze.

It was impossible to see the color of his eyes from this distance, but like his name, they'd been a constant part of my dreams. And nightmares.

Green and brown and gold. Most would classify them as

hazel and move along to his other mouth-watering qualities—
the long legs, rock-hard stomach, chiseled arms decorated
with tattoos and an ass that didn't quit. But those eyes, they
were exquisite.

The spiral of colors was ringed with a bold circle of dark
chocolate. And though the pattern was intriguing, what
made them so heartbreaking were the demons beneath.

There was no sparkle. No light. They were empty.

From his time in prison? Or from something more?

Isaiah gave me a single nod, then went to his bike, strad-
dling the machine as it rumbled to life. It was time to go.

My heart jumped into my throat. *I'm going to be sick.* I
swallowed down the wash of saliva in my mouth and
breathed through my nose, because there wasn't time to
puke. It was almost noon.

I pulled myself away from the window and returned to
the bathroom, tidying up the few things I'd left on the
counter. While the rest of the studio was wide open, the
bathroom had a door, which was good since I'd be sharing
this space tonight.

Then with all my things put away in a travel case, I
risked one long look in the mirror.

I looked pretty today, a fancier version of my normal self.
In a way, I looked like Mom.

*Damn it, Mom. Damn you for not being here. For making
me do this alone.*

I sucked in a breath, not allowing the threat of tears to
ruin my mascara. I shoved those feelings deep, to a dark
place where they'd stay until I could afford the breakdown
needed. Now was not that time, no matter how fucked my
life had become.

First, there was my job. By quitting, I'd killed my dream

to one day become a lawyer and work alongside the great Reggie Barker. Did Clifton Forge even have lawyers? If so, I doubted any specialized in pro bono work for abused women. There certainly wasn't a law school nearby. Which meant if I did find a job, I'd be stuck as a paralegal.

Goodbye, dream job.

Next, there was my condo, the one I'd picked out meticulously. The one I'd drained my savings account to buy. The one I'd been slowly decorating, taking care and patience to pick things that were perfect, not just things that filled empty spaces.

Goodbye, home.

It was agony to think of selling my condo, especially while I was stuck in a studio apartment, and not the swanky kind. No, this was the bachelor kind with white, cracked walls and old tan carpet.

Goodbye, life.

I trudged out of the bathroom, grabbed my purse and headed for the door. My heels clopped down the metal stairs as I gripped the handrail to keep my balance. When my shoes hit pavement, I hustled for the car, not risking a glance at the garage.

I'd been avoiding my half brother, Dash, and his girlfriend, Bryce, since I'd arrived yesterday. They had questions about what I was doing here. Why I was living in Isaiah's apartment. How long I was staying.

I had answers but wasn't ready to give them yet.

When I pulled out of the parking lot undetected, I breathed a long sigh, then followed my phone's navigation toward downtown Clifton Forge.

I passed a wide river along the way. It meandered along the edge of town, bordered by trees that swayed in the breeze. The sun gleamed off its flowing currents. The mountains stood proud and blue in the distance. It was . . . picturesque.

Maybe I'd been a bit harsh in my judgment of Clifton Forge. It actually had the same country, quiet feel as some of the rural areas in Colorado, places Mom had taken me for weekend getaways. The garage wasn't all that shitty either but fancy, like the garages you saw on car-resurrection shows.

Maybe, in time, I'd get to know the town and its people and not feel like a prisoner.

Today was not that day.

Today was day one of my sentence.

The closer I got to my destination, the faster my heart raced. Parking in one of the few open spaces in front of the Clifton Forge courthouse, I dug through my console for a handful of change to slot into the meter. I couldn't remember the last time I'd used change instead of my credit card to pay for parking.

With it maxed out at two hours—I really hoped this didn't take that long—I walked up the stairs that led to the red brick building. When I reached the door, my eyes caught sight of a familiar form waiting, and I stuttered a step.

"Hey." Isaiah pushed off the wall.

"Hi," I breathed, wiping my sweaty palms on my dress.

He was in a black button-up shirt and a pair of jeans, the same as he'd been in at the garage. They were clean jeans, a bit faded, and they fit him nicely. Still, they were jeans. I wasn't sure why that bothered me. Maybe I should have just worn jeans too.

"What?" He glanced at himself.

I snapped my eyes away from those long legs, waving it off. "Nothing."

"You look nice." He ran a hand over his short brown hair, avoiding my eyes.

"Thanks. So do you."

His black shirt was buttoned down to his wrists, covering the tattoos on his forearms. The one that ran behind his ear trailed down his neck before it disappeared under his collar. I wasn't sure if he had any on his back, legs or chest, but each of his fingers had a different design. Ten small tattoos made of lines and dots, all situated across his knuckles.

"Ready?" I asked.

He nodded. "Are you sure about this?"

"We don't have a choice."

"No. I guess we don't."

Isaiah opened the door for me, but inside, he took the lead, guiding us through the courthouse hallways by the wooden signs hung on the walls. The floors had been freshly polished and the overwhelming smell of lemon filled my nose. We disappeared down a series of turns until we reached the door emblazoned with *Clerk of the District Court*. Underneath was a judge's name. Below that was *Justice of the Peace*.

We were here. We were really doing this. I was marrying a stranger today. I was marrying the man who'd saved my life.

It was my turn to return the favor and save his.

Isaiah greeted the clerk at the front desk, speaking for us both because I'd forgotten how to work my tongue. I stood by his side, frozen and dazed, waiting as he filled out the marriage license application. When it was my turn, my hand shook as I filled in the blanks.

"Do you have your IDs?" the clerk asked. She took them both along with the application, then pointed to the row of chairs behind us. "You can have a seat."

I clenched the arms of the chair as I sat, taking a few long breaths to stop my head from spinning. This was not how I'd imagined getting married. This was not special. I was in a green dress because I didn't want to wear white when this marriage was a farce. I didn't know my fiancé's middle name or how he liked to be kissed. I didn't know if he drank coffee or what side of the bed he slept on.

My mom wasn't here to walk me down the aisle.

Blood pumped loud in my ears and the hammering in my chest hurt like crazy. I'd never had an anxiety attack before. Was that what this was? I'd gotten kidnapped just over a week ago and hadn't flipped out then. If I could survive that experience, then this was a piece of cake.

It's temporary. It's only temporary. Eventually, we'd get a divorce and I'd be free to move home to Colorado. A few years here and then I'd get my life back. I could do this for Isaiah.

"We don't have to do this," he whispered.

"We do," I insisted, finding the same determination I'd had when I'd suggested marriage in the first place. "We do."

"Genevieve . . ." My name sounded so smooth in his deep voice. Each syllable was evenly spaced. He didn't rush through it like a lot of people did.

I looked up at him, meeting that gorgeous gaze, and my heart softened. Isaiah was a nice man. A good man. He didn't deserve to suffer because of my mother's mistakes. "We're doing this."

"Isaiah and Genevieve?" The clerk waved us up, sliding

a marriage license across the counter. "You're all set. Just go right through there."

We followed her finger through a door to our left, finding a man shuffling some papers on his oak desk. His glasses were perched low on his nose. His head was bald except for the ring of gray hair that ran from ear to ear.

"The future Mr. and Mrs."—he scanned a paper on the desk—"Reynolds."

Mrs. Reynolds. I gulped, then forced a smile. We were supposed to be in love—a couple who'd met and fallen in love on the same day—so I slipped my hand into Isaiah's, tensing as the heat and calluses from his palm hit mine.

He didn't flinch but his frame tightened.

"Shall we?" The judge motioned us to the middle of the room. We stood in front of him as he took up his position and gave us both a kind smile. If he could sense our fear, he didn't comment.

"Do you have rings?"

Panic hit hard. In everything I'd done this past week, I hadn't thought to get rings. "I, uh—"

"Here." Isaiah fished two rings out of his jeans pocket. One was a simple band. Not gold or silver but a dark gray, like titanium. And the other was a thin platinum band with a halo of small diamonds in the center.

My mouth fell open.

"It's not much." Isaiah swallowed, embarrassment coloring his cheeks.

"It's beautiful." I squeezed his hand, then took the ring. Beautiful was the truth. The diamonds weren't huge, but I didn't need huge. He'd already done enough. "Thank you."

"Excellent." The judge smiled. "Isaiah, Genevieve, please join hands."

We did, facing one another. Direct eye contact was fleeting at best. Mostly, I focused on Isaiah's nose and its wide bridge. It was an admirable nose, strong and straight, set perfectly between those haunted eyes.

"By joining hands, you are consenting to be bound together. Husband and wife. You are promising to honor, love and support each other. Do you, Isaiah, take Genevieve as your wife?"

His eyes found mine. "I do."

"Do you, Genevieve, take Isaiah as your husband?"

"I do."

Two words and it was done. I was married.

"Then by the authority vested in me by the great state of Montana, I pronounce you husband and wife. I wish you the best of luck in your marriage, Mr. and Mrs. Reynolds."

Marriage.

It was done.

Isaiah was safe. No one in the world could make me tell them what had happened at that cabin in the mountains. Because now, I was his wife.

I turned to the justice, ready to say *thank you*, then make my escape. But he opened his mouth for one last statement that made all the color drain from Isaiah's face.

"Isaiah, you may now kiss your bride."

CHAPTER TWO

ISAIAH

The last woman I'd kissed was the woman I'd killed.

Not exactly the thought a groom wants flashing through his mind as he's standing across from his bride.

Genevieve looked about as terrified of this kiss as I did. Her eyes were wide and full of apprehension. Her lips were pressed into a firm line. *No entry.* Got it.

Fuck. The judge was waiting. Genevieve wasn't making a move and I just wanted to get this over with.

I dropped my mouth to hers, closing my eyes on the way. It wasn't . . . horrible. Genevieve didn't have on sticky gloss. Her lips were soft and full. I held there, pretending to be her loving husband for ten seconds. Was that enough?

It was going to have to be. I pulled away and dropped my eyes to the floor. Guilt gnawed at my insides. I hadn't eaten in two days. I hadn't slept in three. Everything about this situation was wrong, but what the hell was I supposed to do? Genevieve thought this would work and that this marriage could keep me out of prison.

And I'd die before spending another day in a cell.

"Thank you," Genevieve told the justice of the peace. We were still holding hands. She squeezed mine tight, forcing my gaze up, then practically dragged me out of the room. The clerk at the front desk was all smiles as she tossed out congratulations.

I grunted. Genevieve nodded.

We walked in silence, our hands linked loosely, until we got outside, then she dropped my hand like a hot plate and we both took a step apart.

"So, um"—she touched her lips—"that's done."

"Yeah." Done.

We were married.

What the fuck are we doing? If this blew up, it wouldn't only be bad for me, it could ruin her life. The corner of our marriage license poked out of her purse. Doubts or not, there was no turning back.

"I'm going to head back to work."

"Okay. Good idea. I guess I'll just . . ." She blinked a couple of times, then shook her head, walking down the stairs toward the street where she'd parked.

My bike was five spaces ahead of hers. I waited long enough to make sure she was in her car, then hustled to my bike and got the hell away from the courthouse.

I knew Genevieve would head for Central. It was the fastest way across town and to the garage. I took the side streets, needing some separation—*from my wife*—to get my head on right.

Why were my lips still burning? No matter how many times I wiped them, the feel of hers remained. Maybe because I hadn't kissed anyone in a long time.

Six years, one month, two weeks and four days, to be exact. Memorial Day. That was the last time I'd kissed a woman. I'd planned to marry Shannon, but then . . .

Thinking about her was painful. Each beat of my heart pricked. My lungs burned. I'd married Genevieve when my soul was held captive by a ghost.

Genevieve and Shannon were like night and day. Shannon had been a happy, softly spoken person, her voice a chime and her face set in a perpetual smile. Genevieve had a husky, resonating voice. Even her whisper was bold. Her dark hair and dark eyes didn't blend with the sunshine or float on the breeze. Genevieve was a force, one who had changed my life forever.

The metal band on my ring finger bit into my palm as I gripped the handlebars. It was cheap metal, the only thing I could afford after buying Genevieve's ring.

She'd saved my life today, and for that, she deserved much more than the chip I'd slid onto her finger. But she'd seemed to like it. She'd stared at the halo of diamonds in awe.

Genevieve spoke with her beautiful eyes. Every emotion, every feeling, flashed in her rich, coffee-colored gaze.

I'd do right by her. I'd be respectful and honest. Fake marriage or not, I wasn't a guy who strayed. I'd do my best to make this easy for her.

And I wouldn't fail Genevieve—not like I'd failed Shannon.

The garage came into view and my stomach knotted.

I'd come to care about the people at the garage. They were my coworkers, maybe even my friends. They'd given a fucked-up ex-con a chance to build a new life in a new town. I might not have been forthcoming about my past with them, but I had been honest.

Starting today, I'd look them in the eye and tell them lie after lie.

But it was the only choice. After everything that had happened on that mountain, in that cabin, Genevieve and I had to lie.

The day of the mountain, after taking Genevieve to the airport in Bozeman so she could fly to Colorado and pack up her stuff, I'd returned to Clifton Forge and been assaulted with questions. My boss, Dash, asked questions. His girl-friend, Bryce, who'd been kidnapped with Genevieve, asked questions. Draven, Emmett, Leo—they all asked questions.

I had no truths to give.

So I left town without a word, hiding in Bozeman at my mom's house for a week, until Genevieve was due to arrive in Montana. It would be easier to lie with her here, wouldn't it?

Dash was pissed that I'd ditched work. I was lucky he hadn't fired me on the spot. Because, damn it, I needed this job. I *liked* this job, and there were few things I genuinely liked these days. I didn't deserve his grace, but I'd take it.

That was only yesterday.

The blur of the past week made my head spin.

Ever since Genevieve Daylee had entered my life, the order and simplicity I craved and found had vanished.

I parked at the garage and walked toward the open bay doors. The shop was bright and spacious. The tools were a dream. Maybe one day Dash would let me move beyond oil changes and tune-ups so I could work on the custom rebuilds that this garage was becoming famous for.

"Hey, Isaiah." Bryce waved from a chair beside a truck. Dash was under the raised hood. "We just saw Genevieve head up to your apartment."

"Yeah." I glanced over my shoulder to where Genevieve's

gray Toyota was parked in a spot beside the office, one of three spaces near the stairs to the apartment above.

"She's living with you?"

"Uh . . . yeah."

Damn it. Genevieve and I should have talked about this. Were we telling people we'd gotten married? Should we keep it a secret for a while? Eventually we'd have to share, but I didn't trust myself to deliver the news today and not fuck it up. They had to believe we were in love. There was no way I could sell love at first sight right now.

If I kept quiet, then maybe the questions would stop. That had worked for me in prison. I hadn't talked unless absolutely necessary. It had been the best way to make sure I didn't say something stupid and get my ass kicked for nothing.

Dash stood from under the hood with a socket wrench in his hand. "Hey."

"Hey. Thanks for the break," I told him, avoiding Bryce's narrowing gaze.

She was a reporter, and a damn smart woman at that. She was likely sniffing out the unspoken lies at the moment, but there was no way I'd talk. She could glare at me all she wanted, fire question after question. I'd spent three years in prison shutting people out. Bryce didn't stand a chance.

"What would you like me to work on?" I asked Dash.

He jerked his thumb at the truck. "Finish up this oil change if you want."

"Sure thing."

I walked over to the tool bench, glancing down at my jeans. They were the nicest pair I owned and the only ones without grease stains. I'd bought them in Bozeman specifically for today because I hadn't wanted to get married in dirty jeans.

Genevieve had taken me in from head to toe at the courthouse, and though she'd said I looked nice, I realized jeans had been a mistake. I'd felt like trash standing next to her, this stunning woman in a green dress.

She deserved better than jeans. Genevieve deserved better than me. But selfish bastard that I was, I'd let her hitch her wagon to mine.

I was probably going to crash us both.

"You good?" Dash came up to my side and clapped a hand on my shoulder.

"Yeah, man. I'm good."

How would he react to the news that I wasn't just his employee now, but his brother-in-law? Or half brother-in-law? This family dynamic was weird.

I wasn't sure what was going on with the Slater family. I'd only moved to Clifton Forge this summer to take a mechanic job at the garage. I'd been desperate to get away from Bozeman, where memories haunted every road.

A guy who'd been inside with me had connected me with Draven, Dash's father. He'd interviewed and hired me, though I officially reported to Dash. The pay hadn't been much at first, but it must have been probationary, because they'd quickly bumped up my hourly wage. That, and when my landlord had screwed me over, Dash had given me the apartment above the garage rent-free.

Had moving here been the right choice? If I'd stayed in Bozeman, I wouldn't have gotten married today. I wouldn't have gotten mixed up in a fucking kidnapping. I wouldn't have tangled my life with a former motorcycle gang.

The Tin Kings had closed their clubhouse doors, but that hadn't kept trouble away, had it?

Six weeks ago, Genevieve's mother, Amina, had been murdered at the local motel. She'd been brutally stabbed to death. Draven, the first person I'd met in Clifton Forge and a man who I'd deemed decent, had been pinned for the crime.

Draven had been the president of the Tin Kings until he'd passed the title to Dash. They didn't wear their patches or leather vests any longer, but the targets remained on their backs.

I didn't know all the details about the club—didn't want to. Dash and Draven kept quiet about it. So did Emmett and Leo, two of the other mechanics who worked at the garage and had been part of the club.

They'd all sheltered me from the details, but I'd picked up on a few things. Mostly, that Draven was innocent. He was being framed for Amina's death. I'd stayed out of it until Bryce had been kidnapped.

Everything changed that day.

I'd gone with Dash and the guys to rescue her. I liked Bryce and I'd wanted to help. We'd found her in the mountains, frozen and scared. That's where I'd found Genevieve too.

In the middle of a hell that had already broken loose.

Genevieve and I needed to get our stories straight. We had to work out what lies we were telling and what truths we'd use to fill in the gaps. I didn't have the energy to hash it out today.

For now, I needed the reliability of work.

As I pulled on some coveralls to save my jeans, Dash put his tools away in a drawer. When they were stowed, he gave me a nod. "Glad you're back."

"Appreciate the second chance."

He shrugged. "Around here, we believe in second chances. Third and fourth, actually. Just ask Leo how many times Dad has fired him over the years."

"I won't let you down again," I promised.

"Good." Dash nodded, then disappeared into the office with Bryce.

I opened a drawer on the workbench and the ring on my hand caught the overhead florescent light. Shit. I checked over both shoulders to make sure the other guys weren't close, then I slipped the ring off and into my pocket where it would stay. At least I had an excuse as to why I wouldn't wear it. Rings at work were a good way for mechanics to lose fingers.

How had this happened? I'd come to work one day, gone on a motorcycle chase to rescue my boss's girlfriend and now had a wife.

Mom always said trouble found me no matter where I went.

I grabbed a handful of tools and got started on the oil change. I hadn't been a mechanic for long, but I was a fast learner and auto mechanics came naturally. Gears fit with other gears. Bolts threaded through nuts. A screw tightened with a turn to the right and loosened with a turn to the left. I soaked in the simplicity that one part was designed for another and blocked out the chaos of my life.

I spent the rest of the day on oil changes and one bumper-to-bumper inspection. Even after Dash and Bryce went home, followed soon by Emmett and Leo, I kept working.

The last place I wanted to go was upstairs where Genevieve waited.

"Isaiah? Are you still here?"

I turned from the shop sink as Presley's voice carried through the garage. "Yeah."

"Okay. Want me to lock up?"

"Nah. I got it." I shook my hands dry.

Presley left the doorway to the office and walked deeper into the shop. Her hair was like snow, cut short at the sides and swooped long on top. She tucked her hands in her overalls as she approached, the denim baggy around her small frame. Emmett always teased that she was no bigger than a fairy princess.

"I know I said it this morning, but I'm glad you're back."

"Me too. How are things?"

"Good." She shrugged. "I'm just going home for the day. You should too."

I'd drag myself upstairs soon enough. "Yeah."

Presley had to know Genevieve was in the apartment, but she didn't ask. She was the one person at the garage who didn't have questions. Maybe because she knew I wouldn't talk.

The two of us had formed a fast friendship. She hadn't been part of the Tin King world either, something that had paired us together as outsiders. We fit in the garage family, but while the others whispered about secrets, Presley and I bonded over coffee in the office.

She didn't ask me about prison. She didn't ask me about my past. When we talked, it was mostly about her or life in Clifton Forge. She told me the best place in town to get a cheeseburger and where to go for haircuts. Presley had been my sounding board when my landlord had jacked up my rent.

"How's it coming along upstairs? Did you get it all cleaned out?" she asked.

I nodded. "For the most part. Needs paint and some updates, but I want to run those by Dash before I go making major changes."

When I'd moved to town, I'd rented an apartment not far from here. The landlord hadn't liked my record—no one did, including me. Still, he'd let me rent a place on a month-to-month lease. Not two weeks later, right about the time Dash had given me a raise, he'd come over to tell me he was doubling my rent.

Maybe it was because I was an ex-con and he knew I wouldn't find another place to live. Presley's theory was he'd learned I was working at the garage and knew Dash paid his mechanics a fair wage.

She was a good one to have in your corner.

Pres had gone to Dash, unasked by me, and talked to him about letting me move into the upstairs apartment. All it had cost me was some time cleaning it up.

Even after hours of scrubbing the walls and shampooing the carpet, it wasn't good enough for Genevieve. It was an apartment made for a bachelor, not a classy, poised woman who walked into a room and captured everyone's attention.

"Is everything all right?" Presley asked. "I know you and Genevieve are keeping to yourselves right now and that's fine. You don't have to tell me details. I'm not trying to butt into your love life. But . . . are you good?"

"Yeah," I answered honestly. Thanks to Genevieve. She might be out of her mind with this marriage idea, but if it worked, I'd be more than good. I'd be free. "Thanks, Pres."

"Anytime. See you tomorrow?"

I nodded. "Tomorrow."

Presley left through the office as I shut down everything in the shop, turning off the rows of florescent lights and closing each of the large bay doors. I locked up the side door, loitered on the asphalt for a long minute and, when I couldn't avoid it any longer, forced my feet up the black, iron staircase that led to my apartment.

I paused at the doorknob. Should I knock? I lived here. My bed, my belongings were all inside. But with Genevieve having moved in yesterday, it didn't feel like my home anymore.

My knuckles tapped on the door before I pushed it open.

Genevieve was on the couch, sitting cross-legged with her laptop balanced on her thighs. Her back stiffened as I entered. "Hey."

"Hey." I shut the door behind me and went to the kitchen to my left, grabbing a pop from the fridge. "Working on something?"

"Trying to find a job."

"Hmm." The can hissed as I popped it open. I chugged three gulps, letting the fizz and sugar slide down my throat.

Genevieve closed her laptop and set it aside. Her dark hair was piled on top of her head, the waves from earlier in the day trapped in a white ribbon. The dress was gone. She'd traded it for a pair of maroon leggings and a T-shirt that dipped over one shoulder, showcasing her collarbone.

Just that little sliver of skin and my heart galloped. My fingers itched to graze her smooth, creamy skin. I took another drink of Coke, shoving my reaction to Genevieve's beauty away.

The urge to touch her was simply physical. Today's kiss had stirred up some pent-up sexual frustration that had been absent for years. After a few days, it would be buried again

24

and forgotten. I'd learn how to live with this gorgeous woman who was far too beautiful to be in this dingy room, even in her loungewear.

Her outfit was hot, but not as sexy as the green dress from the courthouse.

"We didn't get a picture," I muttered.

"Huh?"

I went to the couch, sitting as far away from her as the piece would allow. "A picture. We didn't get one today. Do you think that'll be suspicious? People are going to expect a picture from the wedding, right?"

"Oh." Her shoulders fell. "I didn't think of that either. Maybe we could say we're getting them done later or something."

"Yeah."

An awkward quiet hovered over the couch. It was the same silence that we'd endured yesterday after moving her boxes and suitcases in from her car. I'd stuck it out for a few hours, but it had become uncomfortable, so I'd excused myself for the night and rented a room at the motel.

"So." I drew out the word.

"So."

How were we supposed to convince people we were married when we couldn't speak more than one word to each other?

My eyes darted to the bed at our side and I gulped. *Christ.* It was our wedding night. She didn't expect us to consummate this thing, did she?

Her eyes followed mine, then widened with fear.

That's a no.

"Um . . . where's your ring?" she asked.

"Oh. I wasn't sure if we were telling people. Or how you

25

thought we should handle this." I shifted to dig the ring out of my pocket, then slid it back on my finger. The damn thing was heavy.

"What are we going to do?" she whispered. "People need to think that we're in love, but I don't have a clue how we're going to convince anyone when we just met last week."

Thank fuck. "Me either."

"This is awkward and horrible and—shit." She waved her hands in the air, erasing the words. "I don't mean you're horrible, just this whole situation. You're great, and I owe you so much."

I lifted my left hand, wiggling my ring finger. "Think we're even as of today."

"No." Her shoulders fell. "You saved my life, Isaiah. I realized after the ceremony that I haven't said thank you."

"You don't need to."

"Yes, I do." She put her hand on my knee. "Thank you."

I'd do it again, over and over if it meant saving her. "You're welcome."

"It's not forever." She gave me a sad smile. "A few years, maybe. We'll make sure it all dies down and then we can call it quits."

Years. That seemed like a long time to be married to a stranger. "I'm not ready to tell people."

"I'm fine waiting a few days. We're getting enough questions at the moment, so let's not add this on top."

"Sounds good," I agreed. "Did Bryce come up from the garage earlier? I saw her when I got back from the courthouse."

"Yeah." Her eyes dropped to the floor. "I didn't answer the door. Or her texts. I feel so bad. I haven't known her for long, but she feels like a friend."

"It's hard not to like her."

"Try getting stuffed in a trunk with her, then dragged up a mountain and tied up by a tree together. Bryce kept it together. She made *me* keep it together. I'll never be able to repay her for that. She deserves the truth but . . ."

Our safety was in the lies.

"I hate lying," she confessed.

Genevieve Daylee was a good person who'd been thrown into a fucking awful situation. Or was it Genevieve Reynolds now?

Would she change her last name? Was it strange that I wanted her to?

"Do you think anyone is going to buy this?" I asked.

"No." She laughed. "But maybe if we stick it out long enough, they'll come to accept it."

The silence returned. I finished my Coke. Genevieve stared blankly across the apartment. The goddamn bed kept catching the corner of my eye.

I stood from the couch, taking my can to the recycling bin in the kitchen. "I'm going to head to the motel for another night."

"Are you sure?" she asked, though there was relief in her voice.

"I think getting married is enough for today. We'll save the wedding night for another time."

Her face paled.

Oh, fuck. "No, that's not what I meant. I mean a wedding night as in us both under the same roof. Not, you know." I tossed a hand toward the bed. "We don't have to, uh . . . do that. Ever."

She gulped.

"See you tomorrow." I marched to the door, leaving her

wide-eyed on the couch. I jogged down the stairs and ran to my bike. Only when it was on the road did I start to breathe again.

Wedding night? What the hell had I been thinking? Genevieve and I wouldn't have a wedding night. Pretending to be married to Genevieve didn't mean we had to sleep together.

No, today's kiss had been enough.

Especially since it still lingered on my lips.

CHAPTER THREE

GENEVIEVE

"Genevieve! I'm so glad you're here."

I froze as Bryce's voice hit my back. *Shit.* So much for my plan to sneak in and out of the apartment today.

My forearms were looped with grocery bags and I was bent over the trunk of my car, retrieving a gallon of milk. I should have gone to the store first thing this morning instead of waiting until lunch. Except Isaiah had been up this morning, showering and getting ready for work. I'd stayed in bed, pretending to be asleep so we wouldn't have to talk.

When he'd left, I had dragged out my normal routine, listening to the muffled voices drift up from the office below. Everyone at the garage seemed to congregate downstairs in the mornings, drinking coffee for half an hour before finally getting to work.

I'd waited until the chatter had died before tiptoeing down the stairs and racing to my car so no one would notice me. The getaway had been easy. Except I'd gotten caught on the return.

It was Friday, two days after Isaiah and I had married, and I'd barely set foot outside the apartment. Fear had turned me into a recluse. If not for the empty refrigerator and final scoop of coffee grounds, I would have delayed my trip to the store even longer.

I stood, hefting the bags and milk, and turned away from the trunk. Bryce and Dash walked my way. They were both smiling, leaning into one another with their fingers laced. The perfect couple, so happy and so in love. With them around, Isaiah and I would seem exactly like what we were.

Pretenders.

"Hey," I greeted. "How are you?"

Bryce smiled up at Dash. "Great."

Dash kissed her forehead. "Got some news to share in the garage."

They seemed too happy for it to be bad news, but I wasn't buying it. In the past six weeks, anyone with *news* had only delivered heartache.

I definitely should have stayed inside.

"I need to run these upstairs." I nodded to the groceries. "I'll, uh . . . meet you down there."

Or lock the door and hide.

"It can wait." Bryce let go of Dash's hand, coming to the trunk. She picked up a case of Coke and the last two bags. "I'll help you carry these up. Lead the way."

"Oh, um . . ." *Double shit.*

Isaiah had been sleeping on the couch. He'd stayed the wedding night at the motel, but neither of us wanted to arouse suspicion or rumors, so he'd returned to the apartment. This morning, he'd folded his blanket and stacked it on top of his pillow, but both were on the couch.

Bryce would spot them instantly and know one of us had slept on the sofa.

With my hands full, I couldn't exactly take the groceries from her. I was about to attempt it though, carrying an entire shopping cartful of bags myself, when a deep voice came from the garage.

"I got it."

Bryce turned to Isaiah, handing off the Coke and sacks. "Okay, great. See you in a few."

I forced a tight smile, then headed up the stairs and unlocked the apartment door as Isaiah's footsteps echoed behind me.

"What's that about?" he asked, putting the milk in the fridge as I took out the perishables.

"They have news." I handed him a carton of eggs. "I don't know what news, but I'm just glad she didn't come up here."

We made short work of the groceries, and before going to the garage, I hid Isaiah's bedding. His maroon blanket got draped over the back of the couch, covering up some of the tan corduroy. The pillow got tossed on the bed with the others, like it had been there all along.

"We have to tell them." Isaiah stood by the door. "The guys have been asking what's going on with us. Not often, but enough. I can't keep grunting or they'll think I have a brain injury."

Normally, I would have laughed, but the anxiety was sobering. "Today?"

He dug his ring from his pocket and slipped it on his finger.

Ugh. "Let me get mine."

I trudged to the bathroom and retrieved my ring from the

31

medicine cabinet, sliding it on my finger. The metal was cool, but it didn't feel as foreign as it had two days ago. There'd be no more taking it off after today's announcement.

"All right." I joined him by the door. "I'm ready."

"How do you think this is going to go?"

"Not great."

"Yeah. Me too." He hung his head. "I'm sorry."

"So am I." I gave him a sad smile. "How about we stop apologizing to one another? Neither of us is at fault here. Let's just stick together and . . . be."

Some of the worry eased from his face. "I can do that."

We'd survive this. We'd coexist and bide our time. At some point, the days wouldn't feel so long and heavy, right?

"We need to look like we're married," I said. "Next to Bryce and Dash, everyone will see right through us if we stand three feet apart."

He held out his elbow. "Let's go tell everyone you're Mrs. Reynolds."

A strange thrill ran through my veins at the name. Was it pride? Or excitement? Terror? Maybe it was a mixture of all three.

I looped my arm through Isaiah's and my heart stuttered. A tingle shot from my wrist to elbow where his bare skin touched mine. His arm was hot, scorching even, and the heat seeped into my bones.

We stepped outside, connected as we walked down the stairs, and I risked a glance at his profile. The sun caught the gold flecks in his eyes and their beauty stole my breath. He was truly mesmerizing, this stranger. And for the moment, his world was linked to mine. Another thrill ran the length of my spine.

The more time I spent around Isaiah, the more I caught

myself staring. Yesterday, he'd come out of the bathroom only wearing his jeans. I'd been feigning sleep but had sneaked a look as his bare feet padded to the closet.

There were so many defined and honed muscles in his back, my mouth had watered. Even the strength of his forearms was amazing. Holding on to his arm was akin to gripping the steel railing down the apartment's stairs.

Which was a good thing. I'd need to borrow some of his strength to get through this.

We found everyone in the garage, huddled by the row of toolboxes against the far wall. I dropped Isaiah's arm to follow him, single file, through the maze of cars and tools. Each of the bays was occupied with a vehicle today. Things in the garage always seemed to be busy.

"So what's the news?" one of the men asked. *Emmett.* I was pretty sure his name was Emmett.

He wore a pair of coveralls, the same faded blue as the ones Isaiah had donned yesterday morning over his jeans. Emmett unzipped them, peeling off the sleeves to reveal two bulky arms covered in tattoos. The white T-shirt he wore barely contained his barrel of a chest. Then he tied up his shoulder-length dark hair and shared a look with Leo.

Leo was the blond one. *I think.* None of us had been properly introduced but Isaiah had told me about them. Clearly, they all knew who I was. Leo, like Emmett, was handsome and also sporting some colorful tattoos. He shot me a devilish grin that was pure sex and sin.

I shuffled closer to Isaiah. We were the only two people in the group not smiling.

Come to think of it, I'd never seen Isaiah smile.

Why didn't he smile? Was that because of our situation? If he was this handsome now, solemn and serious, he'd be godlike with a smile. I wouldn't mind earning one or two, just to find out.

Dash's smile faltered when his eyes landed on me. It stung. My half brother hated my existence. He did realize I didn't exactly have control over who my parents were, didn't he? That I hadn't made his father impregnate my mother?

The numb feeling I'd had for weeks settled over my skin, erasing the sting.

None of this would matter. One day, I'd leave this town and this family and never look back.

"Where's Pres?" Dash asked. "She needs to be here."

"Coming!" Past Isaiah, Presley was rushing through the door that linked the office and the garage. Behind her was Draven.

Oh, hell. This was not my day. But at least all of them were here and our announcement only had to be made this once. Isaiah and I would rip off the Band-Aid, then I could return to hiding.

Draven came to stand beside me in the circle. I felt his gaze but kept my own on the array of tools hanging on the wall.

I'd met my father for the first time this week, on the day I'd arrived in Clifton Forge.

My mother was buried here. I'd held a memorial service for her in Colorado, but according to her will, she'd wanted to be buried in Clifton Forge. I'd honored her wishes and made the arrangements. On the trip I'd taken to visit her grave, I'd been kidnapped instead.

So when I arrived in town this week after driving from Colorado to Montana, my first stop in Clifton Forge was at the cemetery. Before I did anything else, I wanted to see her resting place. Except fear and loneliness stole my courage. I parked at the cemetery and wasn't able to get out of my car.

I called Bryce, my new friend.

She met me without hesitation.

Except, these days, where Bryce went, Dash followed. He was worried, for good reason, that the man who'd kidnapped us was on the loose.

Dash came with Bryce to the cemetery. Draven followed.

We had an awkward introduction, at best. Thankfully, Draven didn't try to hug me or shake my hand. He waved, introduced himself as Draven and said, "Guess I'm your dad."

Then we stared at one another—until I couldn't stand the sadness and regret in his gaze any longer and ran back to my car. He hadn't attempted to contact me since.

Draven cleared his throat and stepped closer.

I inched toward Isaiah until my arm brushed his and I begged the universe for strength.

"So? What's the news?" Presley asked Dash.

He looked down at Bryce and his smile was blinding. His face was so full of love it made my heart hurt. Never had I seen a man look at a woman that way.

"We got engaged this morning." Bryce held up her hand.

I smiled, instantly delighted for my friend. She was marrying the love of her life. After our near-death experience, I was glad to see she and Dash weren't taking life for granted. They deserved a happy day.

And I wasn't going to ruin any part of it with my lies.

Isaiah was staring at Dash and Bryce, not paying me any attention. I nudged him with my elbow, mouthing *no* while shaking my head.

Today was not the day to announce our marriage. I wouldn't steal an ounce of Bryce's joy.

His eyebrows came together, so I mouthed *no* again. Understanding washed over his face and he nodded, tucking his left hand into his pocket.

"What's that?" Dash asked.

"Huh?" My gaze whipped in his direction. "Oh, nothing. I'm just happy for you guys. Congrats."

"Thanks." Bryce tucked herself into Dash's side.

"And . . . we're having a kid," Dash announced, practically floating.

The group erupted in cheers. Draven crossed over and held out his hand. It took Dash a minute to shake it. Their tension was palpable. What was that about? Me?

I felt like I had stepped into the middle of the story and was racing to catch up on all the chapters I'd missed. My list of unknowns was three times longer than my list of knowns.

Draven was my father, but I had no idea how he'd known my mother. She'd come to Clifton Forge and been murdered. For weeks I'd thought Draven was her killer, but now I knew he was innocent. So who'd killed Mom? And why? Was it the same man who'd kidnapped me and Bryce?

Would he come after us again?

He'd have a hard time finding Bryce alone, given the way Dash hovered.

She snuck away from his side, coming our way.

I pulled her in for a hug. "Congratulations."

"Thanks." She beamed.

"Happy for you guys," Isaiah said.

"Me too. So . . . how are things?" Bryce asked me. "Would you like to go to coffee one of these days? Catch up?"

"That would be nice." It would be much easier telling her about Isaiah and me over coffee than in a crowd. "I'm free any day next week. And the week after that. And the week after that. I'm still hunting for a job."

"What kind of job?" Draven appeared at Bryce's side.

I shied back a step. It was his eyes that unnerved me the most because I saw them in the mirror every morning. "I was a paralegal in Denver. I was hoping to find something with a lawyer but the firms in town aren't hiring at the moment, so I've applied for other jobs, but most everything open is part-time."

He ran a hand over his salt and pepper beard. "I'll give Jim a call."

"Jim?"

"My lawyer."

Right. He had a lawyer because he was being prosecuted for my mother's murder. I wasn't sure I wanted to work for his attorney—that was hitting awfully close to home—but I simply said, "Thanks."

I wasn't holding out hope. When Bryce and I went to coffee, I'd ask if they needed a new barista with no barista experience.

A car door slammed, and all eyes turned to the parking lot. A car was parked in front of the first bay, and its driver was walking toward the office.

"Guess that's my cue to get back to work." Presley hugged Dash again, smiled at Bryce and rushed for the office.

"Better get back to it too." Isaiah excused himself, going to the car directly behind us. He must have been working on it earlier because there was a pair of coveralls on the hood, identical to Emmett's.

He stepped into them, hiding his jeans and black T-shirt

away. He zipped them up, then turned his back to us, bringing his hands together where we couldn't see them, slipping off his ring.

Isaiah shoved his hand into a pocket. "I'm going to—"

"What did you just do?" Draven cut him off, pointing to Isaiah's pocket. "What's in there?"

My heart dropped. The entire garage stilled as Draven's bark echoed off the walls.

"What's in where?" Dash asked, walking closer.

"There." Draven pointed to Isaiah's pocket again. "Did you just take off a ring?"

I slid my hand behind my hip, but I wasn't fast enough.

Bryce's eyes widened at me. "You got married?"

I winced at the volume. "Yes."

"What? When? Why?" She fired the one-word questions like bullets. "You just met."

Isaiah and I had decided to tell people it was love at first sight. We'd acted on an impulse and were rolling with it. We both figured that the less we elaborated, the less likely someone would catch us in a lie.

But even our simple explanation was hard to remember when I was being stared down by a star reporter, my long-lost father and a trio of bulky bikers.

"We got married." Isaiah came to my rescue, striding over to take my hand in his. He gripped it tight to hide the shaking in my fingers. "We connected. I asked Genevieve to move up here. She agreed. We decided not to mess around and just make it official."

"You're married." Bryce looked between the two of us, dumfounded.

I pulled strength from Isaiah's grip and found my voice. "We're married."

"After meeting for one day?"

"That's right," he answered.

"No." Draven huffed. "I'm not okay with this."

"Well, it's not really your decision, is it?" I shot back.

"You're my daughter."

Anger and frustration were on constant simmer beneath my skin. Mom, her lies and secrets, had put me into this mess. She wasn't here to bear the brunt of my resentment. Draven was the last parent standing, and if he wanted to act like my father, he'd get the force of my emotions.

"Considering I met you three days ago, I'd hardly say that gives you a right to pull the father card." The words were harsh, but I didn't wish them back, even when he flinched.

"Genevieve." Bryce reached for my free hand. "What's going on? I know the kidnapping was extreme, but this? This is extreme too. You guys hardly know each other."

"You and Dash are getting married and having a baby," Isaiah said before I could respond. "And you met, what, six weeks ago? I think you know as well as we do, time doesn't matter."

"You're right." Dash came to her side with Emmett and Leo flanking behind. "And it's not our business."

Bryce crossed her arms over her chest and narrowed her eyes. I'd seen that look before, when we'd been huddled together at the base of a tree as our kidnapper stood by with a gun.

She'd been fierce about escaping. Just like she'd be fierce in finding out what was really happening with me and Isaiah. Nothing Dash or anyone said would change her mind.

"Will you excuse us?" Bryce stepped forward, taking my elbow to haul me across the garage to a quiet corner.

I glanced over my shoulder at Isaiah. He stood alone, facing Draven, Dash, Emmett and Leo. Four against one weren't good odds but Isaiah wouldn't break.

We had too much riding on our secrets.

"What is going on?" Bryce hissed. "You guys have been acting strange all week. You go back to Denver, which I get. We got kidnapped, for Christ's sake, and almost died. But then you show up here and move into Isaiah's apartment without any explanation. Now you're married?"

I blew out a deep breath. "Something happened with me and Isaiah. He's . . . special. I've never felt anything like this for another person in my entire life."

It was all truth. Or half-truth. Every word was a vague version of what had really happened. Maybe if I stuck to these half-truths, I'd be able to pull this show off.

She raised an eyebrow. "Really?"

I was sweating. Why was it so hot in here? "Really."

Before Isaiah, I had never owed another person my life.

"Are you sure it's not like—I don't know—post-traumatic stress from the kidnapping?"

"He makes me feel safe." It was another true statement—a full truth. "Right now, that's what I need."

The single most terrifying moment of my life was when I'd been grabbed from behind in my motel room.

I'd flown to Montana to visit Mom's grave on a Saturday. I'd worked for Reggie that morning, then driven to the airport and boarded the plane with a heavy heart. I'd thought about canceling the trip a hundred times but needed to see Mom's grave with my own eyes.

I needed to know her body had found a place of peace.

The flight to Bozeman arrived late and I checked into a motel near the airport, planning to rent a car the next morning and drive the two hours to Clifton Forge.

Wearing black silk pajama pants and a strappy green sports bra underneath a long-sleeved white top, I left my room for two minutes to get a water from the vending machine, leaving the door to my room propped open by the deadbolt.

When I returned, I locked myself in, thinking I was safe and alone. But a man cloaked in black stepped out of the bathroom and grabbed me by the hair. He pushed me to the floor and duct taped my hands behind my back. My bare feet were bound at the ankles. Then he hauled me over his shoulder and carried my writhing body to the parking lot, where he shoved me in the trunk of a car, right beside Bryce.

The two of us cried in silence; the gags the man had wrapped around our heads kept us from screaming. He took us into the mountains and marched us into the woods. My feet had surrendered to countless bleeding cuts by the time we reached the cabin.

But he didn't take us into the cabin like I'd expected. Instead, he pushed us against a giant pine tree, where we sat in the dark, shivering and nearly hypothermic, terrified that we wouldn't see another sunrise.

As dawn encroached, he hauled me to my feet and cut the tape that bound me. He untied my gag. Then he forced me to hold an unloaded gun to Bryce's temple while he snapped a few pictures.

He bound me again, forgoing the gag, and was *kind enough* to remove Bryce's too. That was when she told me about Draven—that he wasn't Mom's killer, but in fact, my father. He was being framed for Mom's murder.

In any other situation, I wouldn't have believed her, but there against that tree, as death loomed over us, Bryce had no reason to lie.

The next time the killer untied my hands, it was to hold the gun to Bryce's temple again, only this time a bullet was loaded into the chamber.

He planned to set me up for her murder, knowing Dash would take revenge in the form of my life.

Instead, Dash had saved us. He'd saved me. Whether that was his intention or not, I was still grateful that he'd thwarted our kidnapper's plan. All because Dash had come for Bryce.

In a hail of gunfire, we ran for our lives—Bryce into the trees and me toward the cabin.

I should have run the other way.

"I know it seems crazy," I told Bryce. "But this is the right thing for Isaiah and me."

"Then why was he sleeping at the motel?"

Damn small-town gossip. I was going to have to remember that people around this town noticed everything.

"We didn't want to stay together until we were husband and wife. We, uh . . . didn't have sex before the wedding." Or after. As long as she didn't dig too deep and find out that Isaiah had stayed there on our wedding night, we were safe.

"So that's it. You're married and living above the garage."

I nodded. "That's it."

"Hmm." She frowned. "Have you talked to Draven since the cemetery?"

"No."

"Well, buckle up." Her gaze drifted over my shoulder. "Because here he comes, and he does not look happy."

CHAPTER FOUR

GENEVIEVE

"I'd like to talk to you." Draven didn't ask, he demanded.

I squared my shoulders and jutted my chin. Call it years missed of daughter-to-father defiance, but he wasn't going to order me around.

He held my stare for a long moment, then his face softened. Was he cracking a smile?

"Is something funny?" I snapped.

"You've got steel, girl."

No, I had pain.

And at the moment, I was desperately trying to keep from adding more to the pile. I was clinging to this calm, collected façade, hoping it would keep people at arm's length. Because if one more person hurt me, I might crumble to pieces.

"What would you like to talk about?" I held my expression neutral. "Because if it's about me and Isaiah, that is none of your business."

He frowned.

I doubted many people told Draven to mind his own business. If not for the rage burning in my veins, I wouldn't have had the guts to stand up to a man who held himself with such unwavering confidence and command.

Every movement he made appeared deliberate. He didn't fidget with his fingers, and his eyes didn't wander. Except there was something different about how he stood with me as opposed to the others. He seemed . . . nervous. His anxiety clung to the air.

If I wanted the upper hand, it was mine to take. Only, I needed him. I had questions and he was the man with answers.

"Ten minutes," he said. "Please."

"Fine," I muttered, then turned to Bryce. "I'll take you up on that coffee any time you're free."

"That would be great." She put her hand on my arm for a brief moment, then left me and Draven alone. She was about five steps away when she stopped and glanced back. "Congratulations on your marriage."

I smiled. "Congratulations to you too."

When she rejoined Dash, he cast Draven and me a flat glare, then dismissed us completely to escort Bryce to the office.

Isaiah's gaze met mine from across the room. His was full of silent concern.

I gave him a small shrug, then braced to address Draven. "Do you want to talk here?"

"Let's go outside." He held out a hand toward the parking lot.

I nodded, crossing my arms over my chest as I followed him into the sunshine and around the back of the garage.

The field behind the shop was a graveyard for old car

parts. They littered the ground, from the exterior wall of the garage to the fence that bordered the property in the distance. The field had the potential to be a nice space, if not for the overgrown grass and abundance of rusted metal.

Draven led me to a wide cement pad with two picnic tables and a barbeque grill draped with a black cover.

I glanced around before taking a seat. Past the garage, at the end of the parking lot, there was a dark, ominous building situated in a grove of trees. The windows were boarded up and the doors were locked with a thick chain and padlock. All it was missing was a neon sign on the roof that blinked *Keep Out*.

"That's the clubhouse."

"Okay." Was "clubhouse" supposed to mean something to me?

He took a seat across from me, resting his elbows on the table's smooth wooden surface. "How much do you know about me?"

"Next to nothing. Bryce says you're my father. I'm inclined to believe her, but I'd like a paternity test."

He winced.

A paternity test? Where had that come from? The thought hadn't occurred to me until now, but I wanted that test regardless. It would crush my heart into tiny pieces if Draven wasn't my father. Not because I'd grown fond of him in particular, but because if he wasn't, I'd never find my real father now that Mom was gone.

"I'll set it up," he promised. "What else?"

"There's not much else. I came home from work one day this summer to a cop car parked in my driveway. The officer told me that my mother had been murdered in Clifton Forge, Montana."

The words came out in a dull, numb stream. I didn't want to think about how many tears I'd cried that day. How my heart had broken at the officer's words. So I stayed the robot, spewing details like I was talking about someone else's life, not my own.

"I planned her service," I said. "I made sure she was buried in the plot here where she'd asked to be laid to rest. Then I got in touch with the chief of police."

"Marcus."

"Yes." Though I called him Chief Wagner. "He told me what he could about the investigation, and that a man named Draven Slater had stabbed my mother seven times and left her to bleed out in a motel room alone."

He gulped. "Oh."

I was pulling no punches. "Bryce came to Denver to ask me some questions. We talked mostly about Mom because she said she wanted to write a memorial article about her."

Was that true? I'd forgotten about the memorial until now. Bryce had seemed so genuine in her desire to give Mom closure. I'd latched onto that idea with an ironclad hold and told her all the wonderful things about my amazing mother.

That was before. Now I wasn't so sure half of what I'd told Bryce was real.

Bryce had eaten cookies with me as I'd cried over Mom. She'd sat by my side and looked at the old photos and mementos I'd collected from Mom's home before putting it on the market.

I hoped she'd been sincere.

Did I even want her to write that article for the paper? *Not really.* When we went for coffee, I'd ask her to delay the piece, assuming it had been real in the first place. Besides, would the people of Clifton Forge even care about a woman buried in the local cemetery?

Mom's burial request had been a footnote in her last will and testament. She'd purchased the plot years ago.

I hadn't known she had such a fondness for the town where she'd gone to high school. All my life, I'd thought of her in the context of Denver. Even after she'd moved to Bozeman for her job, in my mind, her home was in Colorado.

I'd visited her in Bozeman a few times. The town was fancier than Clifton Forge. It catered to tourists and college students, but it had suited Mom. She'd seemed happy.

So why had she come to Clifton Forge and ruined everything?

Before asking questions, I finished catching Draven up on my side of things so he had some context to provide me answers.

"I kept up with Chief Wagner," I said. "I learned that you were released on bond and they hadn't scheduled the trial yet. He gave me the name of the prosecutor, who I talked to briefly before getting passed off to the victim witness advocate on the case. Then, when I was ready, I flew to Montana because I wanted to visit Mom's grave. That didn't work out so well for me, did it?"

His shoulders sagged. "I'm sorry. You should know this is all my fault."

"Oh, I do." Whenever I needed to place blame, it landed on Mom and Draven.

His gaze met mine, begging for me to cut him a break.

No fucking way.

"Think I'd better start at the beginning." He blew out a long breath. "I've known your mother since we were kids.

Went to high school together. She was a year younger and best friends with my wife—my girlfriend at the time."

My heart rate spiked. This was it. Now I'd find out why. Why me? Why Mom? Did I want to know? The way Draven spoke—his voice raw and his words dripping with sorrow—this would not be a cheerful tale.

I already knew the ending.

It was time to fill in the gaps and learn why Mom had been ripped away from me and why she'd lied to her daughter for twenty-something years.

"You good?" Draven asked.

I nodded. "Keep going."

"After high school, Amina left town. Chrissy and I got married. Life went on and I didn't think much of it when your mom and Chrissy lost touch for a while. Then she came up to visit. Did it about once every summer. Chrissy liked it. She loved showing off the boys and bragging about our kids to her friend."

"Wait. Boys?" My eyes bulged. I wasn't aware Draven had other children besides Dash.

"I've got two sons. Dash is the youngest. Nick is the oldest. He lives in a town called Prescott about three hours away. You'll meet him one day."

Great. I didn't need two brothers who hated me. "No rush."

"Nick's a good man." Draven shot me a glare. "So is Dash. This is . . . you took them by surprise too. They're adjusting."

"Aren't we all?" I deadpanned, then waved for him to keep talking.

He blew out a long breath. "Chrissy stayed home with

the boys. I ran the garage, and I was the president of a motor-cycle club."

"Like *Sons of Anarchy?*"

"That fucking show," he grumbled.

Was that a yes? I waited for further explanation, but he gave no indication he'd give me one. But the clubhouse made sense now. As did some of the information I'd gleaned from Chief Wagner when I'd asked about my mother's murderer. The windows were boarded up because their club was no more.

"Didn't your club break up?"

He nodded. "The Tin Kings disbanded about a year ago."

"Why?"

"Reasons. Things I won't get into with you."

"More secrets." I huffed, clenching my jaw tight. I was so goddamn sick of the secrets. Theirs and mine.

"I'm not telling you because I'm trying to hide it. Truth is, it's not safe. The less you know, the better."

"Safe?" I growled. "Two months ago I was safe. I had a good life and a mother who loved me. I hadn't been . . ." I stopped and took a breath. "It's too late for safe."

"I'm so—"

"No." He didn't get to say he was fucking sorry. "Continue."

"The club put a strain on my marriage. I loved Chrissy more than life. The boys too. But I . . . I lost myself. Chrissy and I hit a rough patch. Your mom was up for a visit, came to a party at the clubhouse and we—"

"Stop. Don't say it." If he said it out loud, I wouldn't be able to forget the words.

These people were destroying *my* mom. They were

tainting her good memory. *My* mom wouldn't have partied with a motorcycle club. *My* mom wouldn't have conceived a child in that filthy, rotten building. *My* mom wouldn't have had sex with her best friend's husband.

But she had.

My heart ached for *my* mom. She'd been the best person in the world. She'd been my mentor and hero. She'd been the woman I'd wanted to be.

Except I hadn't known her at all.

Every detail, every mention of her name felt like she was dying a second time over. Someone had stolen the life from her body. It might not have been Draven, but he was killing her all the same. He was slaughtering her memory.

"She was in love with me," Draven said.

"Does that make it okay?"

"No."

No, it was certainly not okay. Nothing about Mom's life seemed okay.

"I made the worst mistake of my life that night."

This time, *I* winced.

That statement hurt more than I'd thought it would. If not for that night, I wouldn't be alive. He might have regretted it, but I was sure Mom hadn't, because she'd had me.

"I—fuck." He slid his hand across the table, not touching me, just extending. "That didn't come out right."

"I get it. You had a wife. Kids. You screwed your wife's friend and got her pregnant."

"I didn't know. Amina never told me about you. Not until the night she was killed."

"She never said anything about you either." In that, we

were together. Mom had kept secrets from us both. "What happened with your wife?"

I hoped she'd divorced him and found a man who was loyal.

"She died," he whispered. "She was murdered by a rival club. It's my fault she's dead."

"Why? What did you do?" I asked but I knew the answer. "Reasons, right? Things you're not going to tell me because it's for my own good."

"Yeah."

"Was that why Mom was killed? Because of your former club?"

Not even Chief Wagner had been able to explain the motive behind her death. He'd suspected it was a crime of passion involving a known criminal, but without a confession, we'd never know.

"Probably. She came to town, called me out of the blue. She invited me to the motel to talk. I figured she just wanted to catch up. It had been a long time since I'd seen her. Not since that night at the party."

"She never came back to Clifton Forge?"

He shook his head. "Amina loved Chrissy. She felt horrible about what we did. We promised never to tell Chrissy, and then she left."

"Did you tell her? Your wife?"

"No." He hung his head. "Things between us got better. We worked it out. She was the love of my life, but the guilt ate at me. I was going to tell her, confess it all and beg for forgiveness, but she died before I could muster the courage."

She died not knowing her husband was a cheat and her best friend a whore. Maybe that was for the best. Chrissy Slater would have hated Mom—and me.

The pieces clicked. "That's why Dash hates me. He knows what you did."

"Don't know if I'd say hate."

"It's hate. And that's why."

"My son loves his mother, even in death." He gave me a sad smile. "She was an incredible woman, my wife. He is punishing me for cheating on her, as he should. You're getting some of that backlash. It's not you, it's—"

"My existence. It's simply because I'm alive."

"He'll come around. He's a good man. Not sure how, with a father like me, but my children are good people."

"Because of their mothers."

He closed his eyes, letting that slash burn.

He'd get no mercy, not today.

"Back to my question. Why was Mom killed? Meeting with you doesn't seem like enough of a reason."

"We're not sure. Amina came that night to tell me about you. We talked for hours. I was pissed at first that she'd kept you from me, but I understood. We kept talking. One thing led to another and . . ."

"Oh, God." I cringed. "Please don't."

I didn't want the mental image of my parents hooking up in a motel room.

"Sorry." He ran a hand through his hair. "She, uh . . . told me I could meet you. That she'd help negotiate that introduction. We were both nervous, but she seemed relieved too. Like she'd been keeping it from you for so long that it had eaten at her too."

Maybe it had, but she still should have told me.

"I left her at the motel the next morning and came to the garage," he said. "Your mom promised to call after she told you about me. Then the cops showed up and hauled me in for her murder. I don't know who did it, but someone's setting me up to take the fall."

"Who?"

"Probably a rival club. One of our old enemies."

That explained the vest worn by my kidnapper. It had been black, like the rest of his clothing, except for the white patch stitched on the back. "The Arrowhead Warriors?"

Draven stiffened. "Yeah. Where'd you hear that name?"

"The man who kidnapped us? It was on his vest."

"Cut."

"Whatever. So because of your motorcycle club, my mother was viciously murdered and I was nearly killed."

"I'm sorry." He held my gaze. "I want to tell you it's over, but there's a chance you're in danger. The cops found a body in that cabin in the woods after it burned down. It might have been the guy who took you. It might have been someone else."

This wasn't over.

The man who'd burned to death in that cabin had not been my kidnapper.

And I was still very much in danger.

Dash was glued to Bryce. They were all being careful. If for some reason I got even the slightest inclination that was not the case, I'd say something to ensure her safety. Until then, I was staying quiet.

"And if I'm in danger?" I asked. "What do you expect from me?"

"Be cautious about going places alone. Avoid it if you can. Take your *husband*." His dark eyes narrowed, his expression harsh.

Draven saw straight through my façade. He knew this marriage was a sham.

"Doll?" Isaiah walked around the corner of the garage, saving me from Draven's scrutiny.

Doll? Oh, right. That was me.

"Hey, baby." Ugh. While Isaiah's *doll* sounded endearing and sweet, like he called me that every day, my *baby* sounded forced. Maybe because I'd never called anyone baby before. I'd had three boyfriends in my life, two lovers. None had been recent—I'd been too busy to date—and none had earned *baby* status.

Isaiah came to my side of the table, standing close enough to put a hand on my shoulder. "Just wanted to check on you."

"Draven and I were talking, but we're done for today."

I wasn't sure I could hear any more. I swung my legs over the seat, standing beside Isaiah. I threaded my fingers through his, marveling at the surge of strength that passed from his body to mine.

I took a step but paused. "Bye, Draven."

"Bye, Genevieve."

Isaiah led the way around the building, not stopping as we continued past the shop's doors. He kept his grip firm as we took the stairs to the apartment. Was it for show? Or did he know how much I needed him to keep me anchored?

I was about to pull my hair out and scream.

Why? I still didn't have a good answer. Why had Mom been killed? Why had she waited all this time to tell Draven about me? Why was this happening?

Even Draven didn't know.

Isaiah opened the apartment door, only releasing my hand when we were inside. "Are you okay?"

I went to the couch, sinking down on the edge and dropping my head into my hands. "No. My brain might explode."

The couch shifted as he sat by my side. His hand cupped my knee, but he didn't speak.

Isaiah was a man of few words, something I was learning. Mostly, he seemed to communicate with gestures so small, most people probably overlooked them.

"Thank you for coming to rescue me. I don't know if Draven had more to say but I couldn't take it any longer. I'm confused and overwhelmed and . . . sad. I miss my mom and wish she were here. I want to talk to *her* about all this. Not him."

"Is that what you and Draven talked about?"

"Mostly."

I spent the next ten minutes giving him the short version of my conversation with Draven. He filled in some blanks where he could, mostly information about the club he'd learned through observation in the garage.

After Draven had stepped down as president of the Tin Kings, Dash had taken on the role. Both Emmett and Leo had been members too. When the club had disbanded, they'd kept their jobs at the garage. Draven had officially retired, though he still worked in the office most days.

With the exception of the kidnapping, the guys had tried their best to shelter Presley and Isaiah from anything related to the former club.

"Draven suspects that the body they found in the cabin wasn't the kidnapper," I told Isaiah.

"That's a good thing. Everyone seems to be watching out."

"And no one went to the cops?" I'd been worried that Bryce would report our kidnapping, but given that no officer had come to question me about it, I assumed we were safe.

Isaiah shook his head. "Not that I know of. I don't think

the guys want to bring the cops into this. They want to deal with it themselves."

"That's a good thing." We didn't need the police asking questions about that cabin.

At some point, I'd have to call Chief Wagner and the victim witness advocate again. I'd been talking to them regularly up until the kidnapping.

Or maybe I'd let small-town gossip work in my favor. They had to know that Draven was my father. Living above his garage, they'd eventually realize I no longer thought he'd killed Mom.

"If for any reason Dash stops hovering over Bryce, we have to tell them. No matter what."

"Agreed." Isaiah nodded.

"Until then, we keep it to ourselves."

He dropped his gaze. "I hate this."

"Me too. The secrets are eating at me."

"Same."

Maybe the two of us should talk about it. Maybe we should hash it out, just to make sure we'd made the right choice in the heat of the moment. But I worried that once some of the information was set free, it wouldn't want to return to its cage.

"I better get back to work." He stood from the couch and I did too, following him to the kitchen. It was the smallest kitchen I'd ever seen—the L-shaped cabinets formed a miniscule line. But it had the necessities.

I went to the cupboard next to the fridge, where I'd put my baking supplies, and lifted out a sack of flour, a jar of sugar and a bag of chocolate chips.

Isaiah paused by the door. "What are you doing?"

"I need to bake cookies. They're our only hope."

He didn't smile but the darkness in his eyes disappeared for a fraction of a second. "Save one for me?"

For him, for what he'd done for me, I'd make cookies every day. Of course, I couldn't say that. It was far too intimate and comforting for our fledgling marriage.

Instead, I winked. "No promises."

CHAPTER FIVE

ISAIAH

"Incoming."

I was lying on my back on a creeper, ready to duck under a rig, but I stopped at Draven's word.

He walked toward the parking lot. Dash, Emmett and Leo set their tools aside to follow. I hopped up and did the same.

How Draven had heard, I wasn't sure, but the rumble of motorcycles drifted down the road, preceding a long line of bikes. The men riding them wore dark shades and matching black leather cuts.

Fuck.

The instant Dash spotted them, he rushed to the office door. "Bryce! Lock up. You and Pres get out of sight."

My eyes shot up to the ceiling. Genevieve was upstairs baking cookies to soothe her broken heart. *Stay put, doll.*

She might get curious about the noise and come out, but I was betting she'd take one look at these men in the same style vest as the man who'd kidnapped her and be halfway back to Colorado before nightfall.

Leo walked to a tool bench. To an outsider, it didn't look like he was in much of a hurry, but it was twice the speed of his normal stride. He pulled his keys from his pocket and unlocked a drawer I hadn't opened before—I didn't have the key—and pulled out three pistols.

My stomach dropped. *Not again.* The last time there had been guns in this garage was the day we'd ridden into the mountains and my life had been turned upside down.

Leo tucked one gun into the waistband of his jeans, covering it with his T-shirt, and carried the others over, handing them off to Dash and Emmett behind their backs. Draven had hung around the garage after his conversation with Genevieve. He bent and pulled a pistol from his boot.

All I had was a goddamn three-eighths-inch wrench.

"I should have taken Bryce out of here," Dash said. He normally didn't work on Fridays, but after they'd come down to announce their engagement and the baby, he'd decided to spend a few hours with Emmett and Leo, designing the new custom project they'd be starting in a couple weeks.

He might not want to be here, but I was sure glad he was. There were a lot of Friday afternoons when it was only me finishing up for the day while Presley was in the garage. I wouldn't have had a clue how to handle thirteen bikes pulling into the parking lot on my own.

The men parked in a long row, stretching the distance of all four shop doors and effectively blockading us into the shop. The only way to our own bikes, parked along the fence, was past them. Genevieve's car and Presley's Jeep, both parked in front of the office, weren't an option either.

My skin crawled.

We were trapped.

The roar of the bikes was deafening. It echoed off the

walls and floors, bouncing off concrete and metal. None of the men shut them down. They sat on them, their legs planted wide on the asphalt for balance, and stared at us, a wall of dark eyes and noise.

It was intimidating. Was that what this was about? Intimidation and fear? If the other guys were nervous, they didn't let on. Dash and Emmett had their arms crossed over their chests. Leo had a hand in his pocket, casual like this happened every day. Draven looked bored.

I held perfectly still, every muscle in my body locked. The weak man in a group fidgeted. The weak man avoided eye contact and let his nerves get the better of his control. Which was why the weak man suffered first—a lesson I'd learned my first week in prison.

The standoff continued and my ears throbbed until, finally, the man astride the center bike held up his hand and the engines were turned off. Silence descended as the rumbling floated into the clouds.

The same man swung off his bike, rolling his shades into his hair. Only three other men dismounted as the others remained on their seats. Those four walked to Draven, offering no smile or friendly greeting. Their guns weren't tucked behind their backs or hidden under clothing. They were holstered on hips and against ribs, the weapons on display for the world to see.

"Tucker." Draven didn't extend his hand to the leader. "You guys need some work done on your bikes? We'll cut you a group discount for all thirteen."

"Got some questions for you, Draven."

"Did you lose my phone number?"

"Me and the guys wanted to get out. Pretty summer day.

Haven't been to Clifton Forge in a while. Forgot how nice it is this time of year."

Draven cocked an eyebrow. One subtle gesture and Draven had control. Show up with thirteen men, he didn't care. This was his territory. "Your questions?"

"A couple weekends back, we had some trouble at our property on Castle Creek. Asked around, put some feelers out and heard a rumor that some of your bikes were spotted heading in that direction at the time of the trouble."

"A rumor?" Dash scoffed.

One of the other men lifted a shoulder. "Or traffic cameras."

My heart stopped. If they knew we'd gone up there, what else did they know? When the fuck was I going to catch a break? I hadn't thought much about who owned that cabin. I tried my best not to think about that cabin, period. Just my luck it had belonged to another motorcycle club.

"Heard you had a fire. Lightning, was it?" Draven asked.

"Investigator called this morning. Arson."

"Bad luck." Dash whistled. "Any idea who'd light it up?"

Sweat dripped down my coveralls.

Tucker leveled his gaze on Dash. "The Kings used to love lighting fires. Was it you?"

"Nope."

"We have no reason to burn down an old cabin, Tucker," Emmett said, his voice calm and steady.

"You sure?" Tucker shot back. "We've seen each other more in the past month than we have in a year. You guys keep asking questions about that woman's murder. Maybe you didn't believe me when I said we didn't have shit to do with it."

"We didn't burn down your cabin," Draven said. "We

went up there because someone wearing your Warrior patch took my daughter and future daughter-in-law. Traced him up there. Went to get the girls. Didn't set foot in that cabin. Sure as fuck didn't burn it down."

Tucker stepped closer to Draven. "One of my men was in that cabin. Now he's dead and I want to know who killed him."

Draven stood an inch taller than Tucker and he rose to his full height. "It wasn't us. We got the girls and got them the fuck out of there. We tried to find the guy who took them but he vanished. Like Emmett said, we have no reason to burn down your cabin or kill one of your men. Because, after all, the guy who took the girls wasn't your man, right? Just like it wasn't your man who killed that woman in the motel?"

Damn, Draven was good. He'd pinned Tucker into a corner and the only way out was to back down or admit one of his men had kidnapped Bryce and Genevieve.

"I want answers," Tucker demanded.

Leo scoffed. "Join the fucking club."

"Listen, Tucker." Dash held up his hands. "We don't want trouble. But someone took my pregnant fiancée from her home. If it was one of your men, we'll find out. And he'll pay. But burning down your cabin doesn't do anything for us. We're not at war here."

"We got history, Dash. Not a good one."

"I get it." Dash nodded. "You don't trust us, and we don't trust you. Do what you have to do to find out who killed your man, but I'm telling you, whatever trail you find won't lead back here."

Yes, it would.

Had we left a trail?

Tucker shot Draven and Dash a scowl, then turned and

strode back to his bike. He started his first, the signal for the others to follow suit. Then as quickly as they'd come in, they were gone.

When the rumble from their pipes was no longer in the distance, I let out the breath I'd been holding.

"Fuck." Dash growled, raking a hand through his hair. "That's just what we need, Tucker and his men thinking we're out to get them."

"What did he mean you used to love lighting fires?" I asked.

Emmett sighed. "We—the Kings—burned down their clubhouse a while back."

Shit. No wonder they'd come here first after learning it was arson.

"I'm going to go check on Bryce and Presley." Dash marched to the office door, banging on it and calling Bryce's name. She opened it, wide-eyed, and slammed into his arms.

Dash tucked her into his side and they rejoined our huddle. Presley followed close behind. He gave Bryce and Pres a recap of what had happened, not sparing them any details even though it was so closely linked to old club business. Maybe Dash figured arming them with information was the best way to keep them safe. Tucker and his men had only been here for about three minutes, but it had felt like hours. And if they'd come once, they could come again.

"Everyone is careful," Draven said, looking at Presley. "Everyone."

"We thought there was a chance that the guy in that cabin was the kidnapper," Dash said. "But if Tucker is telling the truth . . ."

"It wasn't him," Bryce answered, looking to Dash. "The man in that cabin wasn't the one who kidnapped us."

Relief coursed through my veins. Now that they knew the kidnapper was out there, they'd be careful. And Genevieve and I didn't have to explain ourselves.

Yet.

"Tucker has sworn all along that it wasn't the Warriors who killed Amina," Emmett said. "It feels like the truth."

"Agreed," Draven muttered.

"This isn't good." Dash let loose an angry growl. "Things would have been easier if the guy in the cabin was our killer. But he's still out there. Now we've got the Warriors sniffing around. Just what we don't fucking need. Goddamn it, I'm mad I missed that bastard."

When we'd gone to rescue Bryce and Genevieve, Dash had taken a shot at the man who'd been holding Genevieve captive. At the time, he'd been under the impression Genevieve was going to kill Bryce. Yeah, he'd missed the man in black.

But he'd also missed Genevieve.

"The fire." Leo's forehead furrowed. "Our guy must have gone back to the cabin and killed the Warrior. Burned the place down. Which means we and the Warriors have the same enemy."

"No. It means"—Draven returned his pistol to his boot—"that this guy is setting us up. Again. He's positioning us to take the fall for killing a Warrior. It means he's hoping Tucker will solve his problem and take us out before we discover his identity."

Dash pinched the bridge of his nose. "This actually might work to our advantage. Let's see what kind of traction the Warriors get finding him. Because right now, we're stuck."

"Be careful," Draven repeated. "Let's get back to work."

We all nodded, then broke apart. But I didn't go back to my oil change. I ran up the stairs, taking them two at a time, to check on Genevieve.

The door was locked. "Genevieve, it's me."

Footsteps came running. The door flew open and she peered over my shoulder to the parking lot. "Are they gone?"

"Yeah." I nudged her into the apartment, closing the door behind me.

It didn't take more than two minutes for me to rattle off everything that had happened.

"So everyone knows the kidnapper and Mom's killer is still out there?" She closed her eyes. "Thank God. I've been worried about Bryce."

"No more grocery store trips alone, okay?" Dash wouldn't let Bryce out of his sight. I'd be sticking close to Genevieve too.

"Okay—no, wait. Shit. I got a job today."

"You did?"

She nodded. "Jim, Draven's lawyer, called me. I don't know what Draven told him but he offered me a job without an interview or anything. I start Monday."

"Great news."

"It's going to make it harder to not be alone. I won't have Bryce's flexibility on office hours."

Bryce was part owner of the newspaper and worked with her father, the editor in chief. She didn't have to be at the paper to write. And Dash, unlike me, wasn't tied to a punch card. Those two could come and go as they needed.

"It would be easier if I could stay here all day, but I need this job," she said. "Until I sell my condo in Denver, I can't afford not to work."

At some point, we'd have to discuss how we were going

to handle money, not that I had much to share. But today wasn't the day to divide utility and grocery bills. "We'll figure it out," I promised.

Maybe I'd follow her to and from work every day. I could check in with her more often. *Whatever it takes.*

I'd do everything in my power to keep her safe until we woke from this nightmare.

But damn, it would help if we knew who we were fighting.

———

THE NIGHT after the Warriors visited the garage, I barely slept. Too many worst-case scenarios plagued my mind. I woke up stiff, sore and restless.

The couch was comfortable enough for an hour or two watching TV, but after seven hours of tossing and turning, I could pinpoint where the frame's boards had worn down the cushion stuffing and where the seats sagged from use.

Genevieve had the bed and I wouldn't take it from her, but the floor was mighty tempting.

Normally, my Saturday mornings were spent lazing around. I'd spend the morning in bed, catching up on sleep. I'd drink an entire pot of coffee while channel surfing. I wouldn't bother getting dressed.

Except Genevieve was in my bed, and she probably wouldn't appreciate me walking around in only my boxers.

So what the hell was I supposed to do on Saturdays now? Were we supposed to spend the day together?

We'd done okay in short bursts of conversation this week, but tension was rife in the apartment. We ate dinner together, both of us doing our best to chew without noise. I'd stifled numerous moans of pleasure as I'd devoured a few of her cookies. We danced around who would use the bathroom first. And when the lights were off, neither of us dared make a move in our beds.

That was only for a few hours each evening.

An entire day was daunting, and the shop downstairs called my name.

I stood from the couch, stretching my aching back, then walked to the bathroom for a shower. When I came out, Genevieve was pretending to be asleep like she did each morning.

Her breathing was faster than it was at night. Her face muscles were taut. And her eyes stirred behind her eyelids. Still, I was grateful when she nuzzled deeper into the pillow.

It gave me a chance to escape the apartment without the fear of making eye contact or accidentally brushing up against her in the kitchen.

Come Monday morning, there'd be no escape. We'd have to figure out a morning routine to get us both to work on time.

But not today.

I wouldn't leave Genevieve alone, but that didn't mean I had to stay in the apartment.

While I'd been in the shower, I'd brewed a pot of coffee. With a steaming mug in hand, I went to the garage and unlocked the shop door with my key. I hit the code to deactivate the alarm, then flipped on all the lights.

The smell of grease and metal filled my nose. The air was stale from the night, so I walked to a panel on the wall to open up the first bay door, letting in some fresh air.

The natural light glinted off the tools hanging on the wall. I inhaled a deep breath of the morning breeze, closing my eyes and letting it spread through my lungs. Most people in Montana took for granted the abundance of clean air. Then again, most people in Montana hadn't spent three years in prison.

I set my coffee mug on a workbench and walked to my bike parked outside. I released the kickstand and pushed it into the garage.

I'd been fixing up this Harley since I'd bought it over a month ago. It was ten years old and the previous owner hadn't treated it with much respect, more like a dirt bike than road bike. But the price had been reasonable, and the machine had potential.

After weeks of tinkering on it in my spare time, it was almost good as new. A few more adjustments and it would fit me perfectly. Leo had promised me one of his famous paint jobs once everything was as I wanted it.

Since I had an entire Saturday to burn, I got to work.

Lost in the machine, I didn't hear Genevieve enter the garage until she cleared her throat behind me.

I glanced over my shoulder, and my eyes forgot their manners. They tracked her from top to bottom in a perusal that stirred feelings—and body parts—that had been dormant for a long, long time.

It was her legs. My God, she had sexy legs. She was wearing white shorts cut close to the apex of her thighs. The bright cotton was a stark contrast to what seemed like miles of tan skin. Her tee was a pale sage green with a neckline that dipped low enough to make my mouth water. Her hair, floating over her shoulders in chocolate waves, didn't do a good job at hiding her nipples, which were peaking through her bra and shirt.

"Um . . . hi." She pulled her hair over her breasts.

My eyes snapped to hers, catching the flush of her cheeks, before I turned to the bike and hung my head. *Fuck.* The tension between us was only going to get worse if I drooled over her every day. "Sorry."

"No apologies, remember?"

I nodded and stood, and this time when I gave her my attention, I kept my eyes on her face. It wasn't much easier to keep my body's reaction to her in check with the glossy sheen she'd swiped on her lips. "What's up?"

"The moving truck is almost here with my boxes." She waved her phone. "They just called."

Not almost. They were here. A large delivery van pulled into the parking lot. I waved them in as they backed up toward the stairs. Then we spent the next two hours hauling boxes into the apartment.

When we'd first opened the van, I'd made the mistake of thinking Genevieve hadn't sent much stuff from Colorado. But now that the boxes were piled and crammed into the apartment, I realized just how small the space was.

"Thank you." She swiped a bead of sweat from her brow. "That would have taken me forever alone."

The van drivers hadn't lifted a damn finger as she'd hauled box after box upstairs. Or as I'd hefted two at a time. They'd been hired to drive, not move. That hadn't stopped them from gawking at her legs each time she'd come down the stairs. *Fuckers.*

"I'm going to go down and lock up the shop. Then I'll help you unpack." Though there was no way all that stuff would fit. We'd be tripping over boxes for a year.

"Oh, that's okay. I can do it myself."

She'd given me an out. I could get the hell out of here and avoid her for a few more hours, but there was no way I'd be able to focus on my bike knowing she was working her ass off alone.

"We're going to have to learn to stay in the same space at some point. Maybe even get comfortable with one another to the point where we don't pretend to be asleep when the other one is awake."

She winced. "Noticed that, did you?"

"We're married. Or pretending to be. We expect people to treat us like a married couple, so . . ."

She sighed. "I guess we'd better learn to act like it."

"Yeah." Starting with a Saturday of unboxing.

It took me a few minutes to lock the shop. When I returned, Genevieve had a chocolate chip cookie in her mouth and one on a napkin she'd set aside for me.

I ate it in two bites. "Good cookie."

"Thanks." She went to the plate where they were stacked, taking out two more from underneath the plastic wrap.

"Where do we start?" I asked before inhaling the second cookie.

"Most of these are clothes. How about the closet?"

"Let me clear some space." I didn't have much, just a few button-down shirts and my nice pair of jeans. I hauled them off the hanging rod so she could have the entire thing.

"What about you?"

I shrugged. "I'll fold these and put them in a drawer. You take the closet."

Today, we'd get her moved in so she wasn't living out of the suitcases in the corner. And after today, maybe it would sink in.

This wasn't temporary. I lived with Genevieve. I was married to Genevieve. There was no sense mourning a single life or my own space. The reality was, we were in this together.

I finished another cookie, then dug out a pair of scissors from a drawer in the kitchen. I picked one box marked shoes —safe enough—and cut open the tape. The box was full of Genevieve's bras and panties.

An image of her wearing the bra on top popped into my head. It was pale pink lace without padding. Her nipples would show through.

My mouth went dry.

"What's that one?" She came to my side and peered into the box. "Oh."

I shook my head, forcing the mental picture aside, and cleared my throat. "According to the label, shoes."

"Not shoes." She giggled, covering her mouth with a hand as her cheeks turned pink.

Her laughter gave life to the apartment. So did the cookies. Maybe this place would feel like a home with Genevieve here, not a box that bore an uncanny resemblance to a prison cell, minus the bars.

Genevieve swiped the underwear box away and kicked it toward her suitcase. Then we opened the next box in the stack, this time finding shoes. She put things away as I opened and collapsed boxes. I ate five more cookies as she did her best to shove her wardrobe into the closet. There were ten boxes to go but the rod was crammed full.

"This is a pitiful excuse for a closet." She frowned. "But it'll do for now. At least I have clothes to wear at work this coming week. I'll have to get a rolling rack or something. Is Amazon Prime a thing in Montana?"

"My mom uses it all the time."

"Your mom lives here?" Her jaw dropped. "In Clifton Forge?"

"No, in Bozeman. That's where I grew up."

"Oh. Does she"—her hand flung between us like a ping-pong ball—"know about us?"

"Not yet." And I wasn't telling her anytime soon. "What's next?"

Genevieve didn't seem to mind that I shut down discussion of my mother. She scanned the boxes, her gaze landing on a set of plastic totes stacked in front of the couch. "Most of the stuff in those tubs was from Mom's house. Pictures and mementos. She loved taking pictures, but that was before the digital age, so they're all prints."

Her voice broke. The pain she hid so well most days swallowed her up. The anger she clung to fell away and her eyes flooded. With everything that had happened, I'd forgotten she'd just lost her mom—her only real parent.

"Would you mind if I put up a picture of her?" Genevieve asked, blinking away the tears.

"Not at all."

She went to the couch and sat on the edge, dragging a tub closer. As she opened the lid, curiosity got the better of me and I joined her on the seat. Her frame crumpled as she reached in for the photo on top.

"That's her?" I asked, looking at a picture of two smiles. I'd seen Amina's picture in the newspaper after her murder, but she was much younger in this one. Genevieve sat on her lap, laughing as Amina held her daughter close. "She's beautiful."

"She was." Her fingers skimmed her mother's face. "She would have hated this for me."

It was the brutal reality.

My mother would hate this for me too.

I stretched into the tub, reaching for a bundle of pictures wrapped in a rubber band. But as I leaned in, Genevieve did too. Our arms brushed, the heat from her smooth skin radiating across mine. A zing reverberated through my chest, hot like the spark of metal grinding on metal.

"Sorry." We both turned to apologize. Our noses brushed.

My gaze dropped to those glossy lips. All I had to do was lean in a fraction of an inch and capture them. One fast spin and I'd have her beneath me on the couch, her breasts heaving against my chest.

The desire to kiss her sent me reeling backward, scrambling off the couch for the kitchen. I grabbed another cookie from the plate and shoved the entire thing in my mouth.

The only sweetness of hers I'd have on my lips would be from these cookies.

I didn't get to kiss Genevieve. I didn't deserve that kind of beauty.

Not after all the ugly I'd caused.

CHAPTER SIX

GENEVIEVE

"See ya." Isaiah lifted his chin as we parted ways on the bottom stair.

"Bye." The keys in my hand rattled as I waved. I took one step for my car but stopped when the office door opened with a whoosh behind me.

"Off to work?"

Every morning it was the same question.

I turned. "Yep."

Draven had been here to see me off each day this week. I wasn't sure what time he arrived, I never heard his motorcycle drive in, but without fail, he would lurk in the office and emerge as Isaiah and I hit the last step.

"Be careful. Watch out for anything suspicious."

The same question. The same warning. Five mornings in a row.

"She's careful." Isaiah came to my side and threw his arm over my shoulders.

After a week of practice, I was getting better at melting

into his side. The first morning, he'd caught me by surprise and I'd stiffened like a board.

Pretending to be in love with someone was not easy. An actress, I was not.

"It's worth repeating," Draven said, his eyes narrowing at us. His scrutiny was beginning to unnerve me, but Isaiah and I had held fast.

I slipped my hand around Isaiah's waist, smiling up at his face. He hadn't shaved this morning and the scruff on his jaw caught the sunshine, making the bristles appear lighter than his normal dark brown.

He was so handsome—too handsome. The two of us made a cute picture, but not the breathtaking one he deserved. Because it wasn't real. Our lack of authenticity would always dull our image.

When Isaiah found the right woman, one he loved and who loved him in return, they'd shine brighter than the light from a thousand stars.

His scent enveloped me as I leaned into his side. It was the same smell I'd found on his pillows when I'd moved into the apartment—fresh soap, cedar and his own natural spice. That scent had comforted me the two nights I'd slept in the apartment alone, locked away from the world to cry into his pillow.

Those nights, I'd cried in fear. A murderer was at large. He'd taken Mom's life and wouldn't fail at a second chance to take mine. I'd cried in grief because earlier I'd picked up the phone to dial Mom's number—only to realize that she'd never answer. I'd cried because I'd simply been . . . alone.

Until Isaiah had returned. He chased away some of the fear with his presence, though the grief was always there.

His pillows no longer smelled like him and they no longer caught my tears. The days I needed a cry, I saved it for the shower.

But I had his scent in the morning, when we put on this little show for Draven and pretended to be dreamy newlyweds.

Isaiah tipped his chin down and leaned in close. If not for the darkness and dread in his eyes, I might have believed he wasn't terrified to touch me. "I'll follow you in. Text me when you're ready to come home."

"Okay." I smiled, steeling my spine for what was coming next.

Isaiah and I had been married for over a week and we'd kissed five times. Once at the courthouse and once each morning for Draven.

Today I'd need two hands to count the number of times we'd kissed. That seemed monumental for some reason.

Normally, Isaiah would be the one to take the lead. He'd dip low and brush his mouth against mine as I'd close my eyes and let myself pretend it was real. What woman wouldn't want this gorgeous and sexy man to kiss her before she went to work each morning?

This morning's kiss was no different. I stood on my toes, waiting as he pressed his lips to mine. And then, like all the other mornings this week . . .

Isaiah cringed.

The muscles in his back bunched. His arm around my shoulders tensed. His lips hardened. I doubted Draven noticed. If he did, it probably looked like Isaiah was simply pulling me deeper into his firm chest or maybe that Isaiah was holding himself back since we had an audience.

Only I knew the truth. And that cringe hurt more and more each day.

Was I really so awful?

I broke us apart, sinking my heels to the ground and loosening myself from Isaiah's hold.

"Sorry. Lipstick." I reached for his mouth, using my thumb to wipe away the lipstick I'd left behind. Really, it was to wipe away the kiss. I knew he wanted to erase it, but with Draven standing there watching, he couldn't do it himself.

"Thanks. Have a good day."

"You too, baby." *That still sounds off.* "Bye." I gave Draven a small wave, then went to my car.

Isaiah walked to his bike and started it up. He'd follow me to the office, making sure I made it inside safe. Lunch was in my purse and would be eaten at my desk, and when I was ready to leave for the day, Isaiah would drive over and escort me home.

I'd offered to let him drive my car so we weren't taking two vehicles—mine sat unused in the parking lot all day—but he'd insisted on riding separately.

A weight lifted off my shoulders as I drove away from the garage. Excitement for the day ahead chased away the pain of Isaiah's kiss. For the next nine hours, I wouldn't have to pretend. My mind would be too busy working to worry about Isaiah or contemplate Mom's choices.

For the next nine hours, I'd get lost in my new job.

Jim Thorne was one of three lawyers in the county. Two specialized in corporate dealings, serving the businesses in town as well as the plethora of farmers and ranchers in the area, while Jim handled nearly everything else. Divorce settlements. Custody disputes. Criminal proceedings.

According to Jim, the office was swamped with work, but

he hadn't been advertising an open paralegal position, which explained why it hadn't come up in my search. He'd claimed it was because he didn't have time to train anyone without legal experience. He'd said it was easier to simply do the work himself.

Or maybe he'd been waiting for a paralegal who wouldn't mind that an entire defunct biker gang had him on speed dial because said paralegal was living above said biker gang's garage.

I hated the idea that I'd gotten this job because of Draven, but these days I was a beggar. My bills had to be paid. And like everything else in my Clifton Forge life, this was only temporary.

So I'd taken the job, and Jim seemed overjoyed that I'd come to him with strong experience.

It took six minutes to drive to the firm. I parked in the lot beside the brick building, locked my car and walked to the front door. The chime echoed above my head as I entered and waved at Isaiah idling outside, sending him on his way.

"Good morning, Gayle." I smiled at the receptionist at the front desk as I crossed the dark oak floor. The entire office suite was adorned with taste and class, something Jim made sure to credit to his wife, Colleen.

"Morning, Genevieve. Love those shoes."

"Thanks." I kicked up the heel of one red patent leather pump. These shoes were the spice to my plain black trousers and white blouse.

The click of my shoes was muffled by the carpet in my office. I dumped my purse in a desk drawer and stared at the blank cream walls.

This office had been empty for three years, since Jim's last paralegal had retired. He'd told me to decorate the space at will but decorating was too permanent. I was secretly praying a paralegal position with one of the other lawyers in town would open up before too long and I could sever this connection with Draven's lawyer.

I'd find my own job, *thank you very much.*

Across from my office was a long conference room. Next door was the employee lounge. I stowed my lunch in the refrigerator and filled a mug with coffee, then walked down the hallway that divided the narrow building. I found Jim at his desk in the last office at the end.

"Morning." I poked my head through his door.

"Hi, Genevieve." He grinned, waving me inside. Jim was probably close to Draven's age.

His white smile was striking against his dark bronze skin. His rich, brown eyes radiated warmth and kindness. He didn't seem like a smarmy biker's lawyer, but my mother hadn't seemed like an adulterous liar, so I was keeping up my guard.

"How are you this fine Friday morning?" he asked.

"Can't complain." Well, I could, but not to Jim.

I just wanted to work. A lot. I needed the distraction and the distance from my personal life. My baggage didn't get to come into this office and ruin the biggest chunk of my day. And though I was still wary of Jim, I was grateful for this job, however short-lived.

So far, Jim had given me a lot of rope, which I appreciated. He didn't micromanage my tasks and seemed to enjoy answering my questions.

Smarmy biker's lawyer or not, I'd worked for Jim Thorne for one week and he'd treated me with more respect than Reggie had in years. My job with Reggie had been my first post-college job, and I hadn't known what I'd been missing.

Reggie's arrogance was out of control. He was no hero, something he'd proved when I'd resigned.

Gayle had raved about Jim on my first day of work, making sure I knew she considered him one of the best men around. She told me he was a good man who'd worked hard to build his reputation in a small town.

The fact was, Montana was not a diverse state. Maybe he would have had it easier in a larger city, but he loved this town and it was his wife's home. And for the moment, he was my boss.

"What's the plan for today?" I asked.

Jim relaxed in his chair. "You know, for once, I might try to get out of here and start my weekend early."

"All right. What can I do?"

"Exactly what you've been doing. I have to say, Genevieve, I'm quite impressed." He smiled. "Draven said you were smart and that I'd like you. As usual, he's right."

"Thanks." I forced a smile. Draven barely knew me. How did he know I was smart? Why was he talking about me like he was a doting father? Especially when he hadn't been involved in the slightest with my upbringing. If I was a hard worker, if I knew how to use my brain, it was because Mom had taught me how.

"Have a seat and we'll dive in." Jim spent nearly an hour walking me through the projects he needed me to work on today. It was a lot, but every time he asked if that was enough, I told him to pile on more.

I could handle it. I *needed* it, desperately.

This job would be my salvation for the time being.

"All right." I hefted the stack of files we'd gone through. "I'll get to work."

"Thanks." He smiled, the crinkles beside his eyes deepening.

Jim had a gentle nature, but Gayle had told me during my second day not to let that fool me. For his clients, Jim was a bulldog and his success rate proved it.

No surprise Draven had him on retainer. Bulldog was definitely Draven's style.

"One last thing." Jim stopped me before I could leave, his smile fading. "As you know, your dad is my client."

"Yes."

"The trial won't start for a while, but normally, I'd have you help me prepare motions to suppress evidence and do background checks on any witnesses the state will call. Not this time."

"I understand. It's a conflict of interest."

"I'll be as honest with you as my employee as I am with my clients. Draven knows this is a long shot."

"Oh." I jerked. Why did that shock me? Just weeks ago, I'd thought Draven was the killer.

But a lot had changed. I might know the real killer was out there, but the police didn't. If the prosecution convicted him, he'd spend the rest of his life in prison.

I'd forgotten that the world saw Draven as a murderer.

"I appreciate the honesty," I told Jim. "If there's anything I can do, let me know."

Jim pointed to the stack of folders in my arms. "You're doing it. When I have a big case, normally everything else gets done at night or not at all. It might not seem like you're helping, but by you keeping things going around here, it'll give me time to focus on your dad's case. Keep it front and center."

"I'll do my best."

I spent the remainder of the morning in my office, cranking through the tasks Jim had assigned me. I filled every free moment, never once taking a break, because if I stopped, even for a moment, I'd think about Mom or Draven or Isaiah. I didn't want to think about them. The only exception was when my timer dinged on my phone every hour and I texted Isaiah my one-word check in.

Okay.

He didn't respond. But I knew if he didn't get that text every hour, he'd race this way.

Jim popped in shortly after lunch. "I'm taking off. Thanks again."

"Have a great weekend."

He waved, then said goodbye to Gayle, leaving the two of us alone.

When the door chimed behind him, I pulled the can of pepper spray from my purse and left it on my lap as I worked. Draven had handed it to me on Monday when he'd met us before work. Gayle was a stout woman, a bulldog in her own right, but I doubted she'd be able to stop a killer if he stormed into the firm.

Would staying alone get easier? Or would I spend the rest of my life looking over my shoulder, clutching cans of pepper spray?

I forced the fear away, focusing on work. When five o'clock rolled around, I texted Isaiah that I was ready to leave, collected my things and met Gayle at the door.

"Have a nice weekend, Gayle."

"You too." We stepped onto the sidewalk and she locked the door, tucking her keys in her purse. "Glad you're here, Genevieve."

"Thanks."

Gayle took off in the opposite direction, preferring to walk the five blocks home in the summer months, as I went to the parking lot. A black motorcycle was parked behind my car. Its rider's haunted, magnificent eyes were hidden behind dark sunglasses.

"Hey."

Isaiah's rugged voice sent a shiver down my spine. "Hi. How was your day?"

"Fine. You?"

"It was a busy day." I walked to my car, forgoing the door to lean against the trunk. I wasn't in a hurry to get to the apartment and hole up. I wanted a few moments for the sun to kiss my face. "Jim talked to me about Draven's trial. I forgot with everything else happening that most think he's guilty. And I feel like I'm playing catch-up, that everyone is ten steps ahead."

Isaiah swung off his bike and came to lean against the trunk. "Want me to tell you what I know? It isn't much, but maybe it'll help."

"Please." Maybe together, we could make sense of what was happening.

"The police have the murder weapon. It was a hunting knife with Draven's name engraved on the side. Had his prints. And they know he was at the motel."

Those were things I'd learned from Bryce's newspaper. I'd forced myself to read the stories about Mom's murder earlier in the week.

"A guy broke into the clubhouse and stole that knife," Isaiah said. "Emmett caught it on surveillance. Bryce ran a story a few papers ago showing the guy breaking in. She speculated that he could have stolen the knife. She'd hoped it would cause a stir, that maybe people in town would start to question the investigation, and it would force Chief Wagner to dig deeper."

"Did it?"

He shook his head.

"Damn." I didn't blame the chief. He had his killer and there was no need to chase down improbable leads. Especially when the daughter of the victim called from Colorado every other day, begging for justice.

"You should go back and read through all the papers," Isaiah suggested.

"I already did," I said with a sigh. "It still feels like I'm missing big chunks of what happened. Do you know anything else?"

"That's it." He shook his head. "I've been on the outside too. I know you're not sure how to deal with him yet, but the person with the most information is Draven."

"Yeah," I muttered. I wasn't ready for another lengthy discussion with him yet. First, I'd start with Bryce and see if she knew more than what had been printed. "What do you think will happen if Draven goes to prison?"

Or when?

My entire life I hadn't known my father. I'd just found him and was . . . adjusting. If he was successfully framed for Mom's murder, he'd disappear again.

"Dash won't let this go," Isaiah said. "He won't stop until he finds the real killer."

"How?"

Isaiah sighed. "I don't know, doll."

Doll. There was no hesitation in the word. It was becoming habit—one that chased away a sliver of the tension between us. Maybe after enough *dolls*, we'd chip away all the awkwardness and find a friendship underneath.

This would be easier if we were friends.

"Dash is determined," he said. "Bryce, Emmett and Leo are too. They don't want the real killer to go free, and now that they know he wasn't the guy who died in the fire, they'll push harder."

I shivered at the mental image of the cabin on fire but pushed it aside. "Do they have any leads?"

"No idea. I've mostly stayed out of it. Except when . . . you know."

When he'd rescued me and tied our fates together.

"We have to talk about it at some point. The cabin," I whispered, glancing around the parking lot. I knew we were alone but felt the need to double check whenever the topic came up.

"Nothing to talk about." His frame locked. "I killed a man."

"And I started a fire."

Two crimes that had bonded us forever. Though I wished they were reversed. Killing that man had taken a part of Isaiah's soul. It would haunt him along with the other demons torturing his heart.

"I need to go to the grocery store," I said, changing the subject.

"I'll follow you."

I pushed off the trunk, going to my door, but paused before opening it. "Would you help me?"

"At the store?"

"No. With something else."

I wanted to set my ghosts free. I wanted to set *us* free and give Isaiah the chance to find a woman he would kiss out of love, not obligation. A woman who would help him battle those demons and bring some light into his life.

He deserved freedom. We all did.

"What?" he asked.

"I want to find the man who killed my mother."

"Okay. But we might never find out," he warned.

"I know. But I have to try."

CHAPTER SEVEN

GENEVIEVE

I stood from my desk and stepped toward the door. The hallway was empty. Gayle sat at her desk working while Jim had left for the courthouse hours ago.

The stack of work on my desk was done, and I had two hours before I'd text Isaiah to go home.

It had been three days since I'd told him I wanted to find Mom's killer. And in those three days, I'd devised a plan.

A plan I was keeping secret for the time being.

I sat in my chair, angling the screen of my computer so if Gayle barged in, she wouldn't see what I was doing. Then I pulled a notepad from my purse and opened it to the first page, writing a name on top.

Draven Slater

I flipped to the next page.

Dash Slater

Then the next.

Emmett Stone

Leo Winter

Presley Marks

With the exception of Isaiah and Bryce, each person at the garage had a page.

I'd fill the empty lines with notes from background and criminal checks. I'd pull a report from the LexisNexis database for property addresses, aliases and anything else I could get my hands on. Then I'd add more names to my notebook.

Next I'd dig into other members of the former Tin King motorcycle club. And after that, I was turning my attention to the Arrowhead Warriors.

Because somewhere, hidden, was a killer. The only weapon I had to find him or her was information. So I was exploiting my resources at the firm to get it.

I spent the next hour clicking through public records and database reports, scribbling notes as fast as I could write. I was in the middle of jotting down Emmett's long list of properties when my pen stopped on the page.

Emmett shared most of the properties with his mother. Had they been joint investments? Or had Emmett inherited them when his father had died years ago? If it was the latter, why wouldn't all ownership have gone to Emmett's mother? I wasn't familiar enough with Montana's property and estate laws to know how inheritance defaulted after death.

I blinked.

I wasn't familiar with a lot of Montana's laws.

My fingers dove for the keyboard, pulling up a search engine for the state's legal code. Then I typed in *spousal privilege*.

The words on the screen blurred as I read them once, then twice. The third time through, my stomach pitched and I shot out of my chair, racing to the bathroom. My knees cracked against the tile floor as the contents of my stomach erupted into the toilet.

I coughed, my head dizzy, as I wiped my mouth dry and sank onto the cool floor.

"Oh my God." I dragged a hand through my hair.

How could I have been so stupid? How could I have missed this? I'd assumed Montana's law on testimonial privilege followed the federal regulations.

But it didn't.

Isaiah and I had gotten married for nothing. A court could call me in to testify against him, and unless I lied under oath, I'd be bound to tell the truth. Maybe there was a loophole. Maybe if the DEA or the FBI got involved, this would fall under federal jurisdiction, but the likelihood was slim.

My stomach rolled again.

Everything, the marriage, the lies, it had all been for nothing.

"Genevieve?" Gayle knocked on the door. "Are you all right?"

"Fine," I choked out. "My lunch isn't settling very well."

"Oh no, honey. I'm so sorry. You'd better head on home."

Home? Where was home?

Because as of right now, it didn't have to be Montana. I could walk away from this. I could annul my marriage to Isaiah and get the fuck out of Clifton Forge.

I pushed myself up off the floor, holding onto the wall as I shuffled for the sink. I splashed my face with water. I rinsed out my mouth. And then I took a long, hard look at my wedding ring.

It was a sham. This entire thing was a sham, for nothing.

I'd been in such a panic after the cabin, I'd made some assumptions to protect Isaiah. I'd made a mistake by not verifying them sooner. But with Mom's death, the move and being thrust into the Slater family, I'd been too distracted.

My eyes turned up to the mirror.

What would Mom do?

The mother I'd known and loved, *my* mother, would stay. Not because the law had trapped her into a marriage, but because she'd made a promise. I'd vowed to stand by Isaiah's side and see this through.

So I was going to do what my mother would have done. I'd keep this to myself since it was my mistake to bear, and I'd keep my promise to Isaiah.

Besides, to find Mom's killer, I needed to be here in Montana. If I ended this marriage with Isaiah, everyone would question why I was still living in Clifton Forge.

I rinsed my mouth once more, then returned to my office, closing down my computer and stowing my secret notebook in my purse. Then I texted Isaiah that I was ready to leave.

It didn't take long for the sound of his motorcycle's engine to echo outside.

"Ready to go home?" he asked when I met him in the parking lot.

I looked into his eyes, those beautifully haunted eyes, and my stomach stopped churning. This was the right thing to do.

For Isaiah.

"Yeah." I nodded. "I'm ready."

CHAPTER EIGHT

ISAIAH

"Ouch. Son of a bitch." A pan clanked in the sink. I rushed out of the bathroom to find Genevieve in the kitchen, her hand under a stream of water. "What happened?"

She hung her head. "I burned my finger."

I was beside her in a flash, my hands diving into the cold water to retrieve hers and assess the damage. There was a pink spot on her index finger, but it didn't look serious.

"It's fine." She wrenched her hand out of my grip and returned it to the faucet.

I wasn't sure how she'd burned her finger. With the mood she was in, I wasn't going to ask either.

One month had passed since Genevieve had told me she wanted to find her mother's killer. Like I'd warned her, there just wasn't anything to find—something she was struggling to accept.

As the days of August drew to a close, she'd become more and more frustrated. The two of us had spent hours talking with Bryce and Dash. We'd gone over everything that they'd found since Amina had been murdered. Twice.

Genevieve had even spent a few hours with Draven, getting his point of view. There were things about the motorcycle club that none of them had wanted to share. We didn't push. And at the end of it all, we were just as stuck as everyone else.

She kept studying this notebook, poring over the pages. I wasn't sure what she'd written down, but she'd always close it with a huff and shove it into her purse, angrier after reading through her notes than she had been before.

Bryce didn't offer her much comfort either. If anything, those two would get together and spin each other up. They met at least once a week for coffee while Dash and I took turns standing guard. Mostly, they talked about Bryce and Dash's upcoming wedding because Bryce had surprised Genevieve and asked if she'd be matron of honor. But there were times when their conversation turned to the murder investigation or the kidnapping. The two of them would storm out of the coffee shop fuming mad.

No matter how much we talked about it, no matter how many times they looked at the events from one angle or another, there was no trail to follow.

The man who'd killed Genevieve's mother was in the wind. He'd get away with murder and kidnapping, leaving Draven to take the fall.

Draven's trial was set for the first week of December. Genevieve would come home spouting updates from Jim and legal jargon I didn't catch about motions and hearings. I'd learned the basics during my own experience with the justice system, but Draven's situation was different—he'd pleaded not guilty.

We all dreaded the trial. Once it started, it would be nearly impossible to get the police and prosecutors to consider another suspect unless we handed one to them on a silver platter. Hell, they were as closed-minded about it now as ever.

Genevieve was losing hope. It was washing away faster than the water down the sink's drain.

She kept her head down, glaring at the pan as she let her finger cool.

"Still hurt?" I took her hand out of the water again. This time she didn't jerk it away.

"It's fine." Her shoulders fell. "It stings."

"What happened?"

"I was boiling water for pasta and when I picked up the pan, the water sloshed. It was a stupid mistake because I wasn't paying attention."

In the last month, I'd caught her staring into space a dozen times, totally lost in thought.

"I'm so . . ." She growled, pulling her hand free and stalking away from the sink. "Mad. I'm so mad."

I preferred Mad Genevieve over Sad Genevieve.

When she'd moved here, there had been times when she'd been so close to tears. She'd tried to hide them in the shower each morning. Amina's death, the kidnapping and this marriage had taken their toll.

But I hadn't seen tears lately. Instead, her eyes were fixed in a constant glare, and she barked at inanimate objects. Yesterday she'd scolded a hook in the bathroom for not holding her towel the right way.

"I get it." If I were in her position, I'd be pissed too.

"I wish we had something, anything, to go on."

There were no clues left at the clubhouse about the man

who'd broken in and stolen Draven's knife to kill Amina. The Warriors had disappeared since their surprise trip to the garage. They were either waiting to catch us all by surprise, or they were stuck too.

If they found out that Genevieve and I had been the ones in that cabin, we were already dead.

"Let's get out of here. Stop thinking about it for a day."

She stopped pacing. "Where do you want to go?"

"Leo's coming in today to paint my bike. We're going to work through the design. Come down and help. See how it turns out."

"Okay. Can we grab some lunch?"

"Sure."

"Give me five to change." She walked over to the new dresser and pulled a pair of denim shorts from the middle drawer. She disappeared into the bathroom while I dried the pot in the sink and put it away.

I leaned against the counter, waiting for her to emerge, and took in the place. It was cramped, for sure, but not uncomfortable. Since her belongings had arrived, Genevieve had spent most Saturdays organizing the apartment. She'd shuffle things around for hours, attempting to make space. The UPS guy delivered some sort of container or storage piece about every damn day.

But she'd done it. The boxes were gone to the recycling bin and everything had its place.

Her clothes hung in the closet and on a rolling rack pushed against the wall beside the bed. There was a new dresser that had arrived in a flat box. She'd assembled it two Saturdays ago while I'd been in the shop. I'd planned to do it for her, but she'd finished before I had the chance.

She didn't need help—or maybe didn't want it. It was

strange to live with a woman so self-sufficient. Though my only comparison was Mom. My older brother Kaine and I were always doing jobs for Mom. Fixing a gutter. Hanging a shelf. Mowing the lawn or touching up some paint.

Shannon had been like that too. She wouldn't try to open a stuck jar of spaghetti sauce. She'd just hand it over with a smile.

Not Genevieve. Last week she'd fought with a jar of pickles for ten minutes before it had been too painful to watch and I'd taken it from her, opening it with a pop.

Had she said thank you? No. She'd scowled and told me she'd almost had it.

Genevieve was self-reliant, a woman who needed no confidant or companion. I suspected it was a new thing since her mother's death. Amina had let her down, epically. Maybe Genevieve was sheltering herself to avoid future pain. Or maybe she was proving to herself she could stand on her own two feet. That she could survive this.

Whatever the reason, living with her was an adjustment.

Not in a bad way. Just an adjustment.

But as roommates went, she was the best I'd ever had—that was, if you considered cellmates as roommates. Living with Genevieve was easier than living with Mom too.

Mom worried too much. She pitied me too much.

Genevieve's bath products cluttered the shower. There was always makeup residue on the sink and strands of her hair on the floor. But I'd take that messy bathroom over a cellmate who snored or punched me while I slept for no damn reason other than he could.

"Ready." She came out of the bathroom no longer wearing her pajama pants but shorts and a plain gray tank top. She slipped on some flip-flops and grabbed her purse.

My eyes zeroed in on her long legs and I swallowed a groan. We'd been living together for weeks. Wasn't it supposed to get easier? When would she stop being that beautiful woman naked in my shower and start being just . . . Genevieve? My roommate who happened to have my last name?

Kissing her every morning before work wasn't helping. I'd stopped counting because the higher the number climbed, the more frustrated I was that each was more excruciating to bear than the last.

Every morning I had to fight my own goddamn tongue from tasting her lower lip. Just like today I had to force my eyes away from those legs.

"What do you feel like eating?" she asked.

I swallowed hard. "Sandwich work for you?"

"Is the grocery store deli okay? I need to pick up a few other things too."

"Fine by me." I held the door for her and as we walked down the stairs, I dug my bike's keys from my pocket. "Lead the way."

"You're not going to ride with me?"

"No."

She blinked. "Why not?"

Ghosts. But it wasn't something I had the guts to explain. "I want to take the bike out before Leo gets here, make sure all the tweaks are done," I lied.

"Oh. Should I ride with you?"

I shook my head. "No space for groceries."

That, and I didn't ride with other people. I hadn't for six years. I definitely didn't drive other people, not even Mom. If Mom and I went on a trip to visit Kaine in Lark Cove, we took two vehicles, even though it was a five-hour trip.

The one and only exception was the day I'd driven Genevieve off that mountain. It was the only time another person had ridden with me on the bike because there hadn't been another choice.

"Fine," she muttered, taking her keys from her purse.

I followed close behind her car as she weaved through town and parked beside her at the store. We walked into the store, not speaking and definitely not touching. We stood a foot apart at the deli, both assessing the premade sandwich and salad options.

My insistence on riding separately hadn't helped Genevieve's mood, but a grumpy wife I could handle.

A dead one, I could not.

"Oh, hey, guys."

We both spun around at Bryce's voice. I stepped toward Genevieve, instantly closing the gap between us. She slid her arm behind my back. We'd perfected this move—the smashing of our bodies together so it looked like we were newlyweds.

"Hey." Genevieve smiled.

I looked past Bryce. Dash wouldn't let her come here alone, would he? "Where's Dash?"

"He's lost in the ice cream aisle. I came to buy some veggies to balance us out. What are you guys up to?"

"Picking up some lunch," Genevieve said. "Then Leo is coming over to paint Isaiah's bike. We were going to watch."

"That sounds like fun. What color?"

"Probably black."

"Ah." Bryce nodded. "I should have expected black."

All the bikes in the shop were black. Some had flames on the sides. Others had words. Leo's was actually a deep, shimmering bronze with a gold pinstripe design, but unless you were up close, it looked black.

Bryce tucked a lock of hair behind her ear, her rings catching the light. "Do you guys want to come over for dinner next weekend? We'd love to have you over."

"Uh." Genevieve flinched. Or maybe that was me. "I don't know if that's such a good idea. Dash and I aren't exactly . . . friendly."

They also didn't speak. Dash addressed Genevieve only when absolutely necessary.

Genevieve pretended it didn't bother her, but I saw the hurt cross her eyes when he dismissed her.

"He'll be on his best behavior," Bryce promised. "And I think it would be good for him to get to know you. He'll see that you're amazing and he's being an asshole."

The woman wasn't wrong on either count.

"Are you sure?" Genevieve asked.

"I'm sure. Please? I'd love to host you guys before I have this baby, and I'm consumed by all things motherhood."

That was still months away, but Bryce was not leaving this store with no for an answer.

"Okay," Genevieve agreed, forcing a smile.

"Great. Let's plan for Saturday. I might have pictures of the wedding from the photographer by then. She said it would only take a week. Maybe you can help me pick which one to frame."

Bryce and Dash had gotten married last weekend. It was the one Saturday Genevieve didn't spend secluded in the apartment. Instead, she spent the day with Bryce at a local salon, getting her hair and makeup done. I stood watch outside for hours until they emerged, dressed for the ceremony.

Genevieve's sleeveless black dress molded to her torso and twirled around her hips as it floated to her toes. She stepped out of the salon and stole my breath. I had trouble paying attention to the wedding with her standing beside the altar. I made myself look away to watch Dash and Bryce exchange vows.

The wedding wasn't an extravagant affair, but I hadn't been to one nicer. It was held at dusk on the bank of the Missouri River, which flowed past the edge of town. The reception and party had been at Dash's favorite bar, The Betsy.

Genevieve and I did our best to play the loving couple. We hugged. We held hands. We danced. Hour after hour of pretending. By the time we got back to the apartment, we were both worn out.

And I was strung as tight as a rubber band. I told her the smell of The Betsy had bothered me, then took an ice-cold shower.

Dinner at Bryce and Dash's house would be painful, but we could survive an hour or two. We'd stick to hand-holding and hugs, the simple, friendlier touches that were easier to compartmentalize. Like this hug in the grocery store. It didn't matter that I liked when Genevieve slid her hand around my back and held tight.

"Can we bring anything to dinner?" Genevieve asked.

"Nope. I have it all covered."

Dash emerged from the frozen-food aisles, searching both ways for Bryce. When he spotted us, he raised his hand. Two pints of ice cream were in his other.

"Okay, guys. I'd better get my veggies so we can get home before that melts. See you this week?"

"Yep." I nodded.

Bryce came to the garage to work in Dash's office every morning. Sometimes, they'd stay all day. Others, they'd leave in the afternoon so she could spend some time at the newspaper. Until she was safe, Dash wouldn't leave her alone.

Dash walked by us to join Bryce, who was rummaging through heads of lettuce. He lifted his chin as he passed. "Hey, Isaiah."

"Hey," I said.

He didn't pay Genevieve any attention. None. He didn't say hello. He didn't look her in the eye, though he rarely looked at her period. He acted like she didn't exist.

I put my arm around Genevieve's shoulders, pulling her close, mostly to keep myself calm. His attitude toward Genevieve wasn't fair, and it sure as fuck wasn't deserved. It was getting harder and harder to stay quiet, but if I said something, I risked getting fired and evicted from our apartment.

"We have a week to get sick so we can get out of this dinner," Genevieve muttered.

"Flu?"

"No, something that's longer lasting. We need to buy ourselves at least a month."

"Ebola?"

"Perfect." She giggled, the sound shooting straight to my heart. And my groin.

Christ.

After I ordered a sandwich and she ordered a salad, we picked out the other things on Genevieve's list and got through checkout as quickly as possible, wanting to avoid another run-in with the Slaters. The drive home was fast. It only took me a minute to open the garage and we sat on a couple of the rolling stools to eat our lunch.

"What do those tattoos mean?" Genevieve asked, using her fork to point to my hand. "On your knuckles."

I stretched out my fingers, taking in the tattoos that decorated each finger. The line and dot designs sat between the base and middle knuckles. I'd gotten each in prison and all at the same time. My hands had hurt for days and been tough to use. The black ink was fading and the detail was sloppy, but someday I'd have them cleaned up and sharpened.

"They're constellations." Some fit between the knuckles. Others dipped down to the softer skin between my fingers.

"Why constellations?"

I turned my attention to my sandwich. "For someone I used to know who loved the stars."

Shannon had tried to teach me the constellations. She'd point them out, rattle off their names, but the only two I'd ever been good at finding were Ursa Major and Orion.

I didn't search for them now. I had them on my skin, a part of me forever. It was too painful to look up into the night sky and know she wasn't alive to see it because of me.

Before Genevieve could ask more about the tattoos, Leo's motorcycle rolled into the parking lot.

"Maybe we should have gotten him lunch," she murmured.

Or breakfast. As Leo slid off his shades, he gave her a sleepy grin. He'd probably spent his night at The Betsy and woken up with whatever woman had won his attention at the bar.

"Hey." I shook Leo's hand.

He winked at Genevieve. "How are Mr. and Mrs. Reynolds today?"

"Doing all right," I answered.

"Give me a bit to mix up a color." He clapped me on the shoulder. "Then we'll get this going."

He disappeared into the paint booth. It was adjacent to the last stall in the garage so we could push cars and haul in parts easily. That booth was Leo's domain. Like the rest of the garage, he had top-of-the-line equipment and his tools were a dream.

Not long after Genevieve and I had finished eating, Leo came out with a plastic cup in his hand, stirring the liquid inside with a paint stick.

"Check this out." He came close and lifted out the stick, letting the paint drip into the cup and the color shine. "I know you said black but this color would be fucking awesome."

Like Leo's bike, to the naked eye, it would appear black. But it was actually a shadowed blue. He'd added a shimmer, like on his own bike, and when the light caught the glimmer, it resembled a million diamond flakes attached to the velvet midnight sky.

"That's so pretty." Genevieve met my gaze, hers silently pleading with me to pick that color.

"I like it," I told Leo.

"Sweet. Let's hit it."

We spent the next few hours getting the parts ready. I'd already had the tank and other pieces he wanted to paint primed. We detached them from the bike and hauled them into the booth. Leo finished prepping them, making sure they were clean and smooth, then suited up and kicked us out.

It took Leo less than an hour to paint the bike. When he came out with a smile on his face and a mask dangling around his neck, I knew before seeing it that the blue had been the right choice.

This bike had been the right choice.

Damn, I was proud of finishing it up. Of doing it myself, with my own two hands. It felt good, sharing a piece of it with Leo and sharing the day with Genevieve.

We left the parts to dry, said goodbye to Leo, then returned to the apartment.

"Thanks," Genevieve said when we were inside.

"For?"

"For taking my mind off stuff today. For following me around town and making sure I'm not alone. Especially at the grocery store. It's depressing to always go by myself."

"Happy to." After a month of grocery shopping with her, I wouldn't want to go alone either. It was an adventure with Genevieve, a race. She walked through the sliding doors and turned into a power shopper. It was like she timed herself to see how fast she could cross off all the items on her list.

Genevieve crossed the apartment and fell backward on the bed, her long hair spreading out on the gray quilt that had been in one of her boxes. It was a hell of a lot nicer than the faded brown comforter I'd slept under for years.

That comforter and the bed itself had moved with me from Mom's. She'd bought it for me when I'd gotten out on parole. Maybe she'd just wanted to upgrade the bed in my room. Or maybe she'd known that I'd spent three years on a cramped, piece-of-shit mattress and no pillow. Mom worked hard for her money and she'd splurged.

Genevieve had dressed it up with that soft quilt and a pile of pillows. It was inviting—the bed, and the woman lying on top.

Her toned legs dangled over the edge. She hummed as she closed her eyes, her face relaxed and peaceful.

She dazzled. The first time I'd called her doll, it had been a slip. I'd figured a pet name like honey or sweetie would help convince people this was real. I'd planned on one of those. But doll had come out instead because she was flawless.

I stood by the door, unsure of my next move.

The weekends were tough for us. We'd been working long hours, so during the week, idle time was easier. Genevieve would cook dinner when she got home. I'd clean up. She'd read for a couple of hours, and I'd watch TV. Then we'd call it an early night. We'd fallen into that routine and it worked.

But we hadn't found a routine for the weekends. There was more time together and these were the moments when the awkward crept in.

Genevieve sat up on her elbows. "Do you mind if I watch TV?"

"No." I walked to my designated area—the couch.

She reached for the remote on the nightstand next to the bed and flipped on the TV, scrolling through the guide. It sat on a cart beside the door, adjacent to the new dresser. The screen wasn't big but nothing larger would have fit in this apartment.

"I was thinking of doing a Harry Potter marathon. Would you hate me if I watched them? They're really good. Mom and I read the books together."

She glanced at the framed photo of Amina on the nightstand and a flash of pain crossed her face. Genevieve was furious at Amina, but when she put that anger aside, there was deep, suffocating pain waiting. I wished I had some advice on how she could move past it, but considering I lived with that crippling pain and guilt every day, I had nothing to offer.

If watching Harry Potter movies lessened the sting for a few hours, I wouldn't deny her.

"Go ahead. I've never seen them."

"What?" She gaped. "You're kidding."

"Nope."

"We're watching them," she declared. "And ordering pizza for dinner."

"Sounds good." The television was better than silence.

I angled myself on the couch where I could see the TV. For it to be comfortable, I needed a pillow. But Genevieve had taken to making the bed with my pillow too in case someone stopped by for an unexpected visit. I shifted, attempting to find a good spot to relax. But damn, my back hurt. A month sleeping on this couch had taken its toll.

"Come up here."

"Huh?" I glanced behind me to the bed.

"It's easier to see the TV. Come up here."

To the bed? Even to watch a movie, that seemed too intimate. If I weren't so stiff and sore, I would have declined. As it was, I swung my legs off the couch and toed off my boots. Then I walked over, hesitating by the mattress.

She rolled her eyes. "If you keep standing there, you're going to miss it."

I sat down, swinging my legs up and relaxing back. *Oh, hell.* Returning to the couch would be brutal.

"Better, right?"

"Yeah." Better was an understatement.

We watched two in a row before pausing to order dinner. The movies were definitely geared toward kids, but

Genevieve promised they'd get darker and more intense. When the pizza delivery arrived, we were halfway into the third movie.

"You read all these books?" I asked as we hit pause to eat some pepperoni slices.

"Yep." She swallowed. "They're really good. Do you read much?"

"I used to." I hesitated before adding the next part. "In prison."

"Oh." Her gaze dropped to the mattress. We hadn't bothered getting up, instead eating on our laps. "How long were you in prison?"

"Three years."

"Did it ruin reading for you? Prison?"

"Don't know. I haven't read anything since."

Her eyes were so open and captivating. When I met her gaze, I expected either pity or judgment. People who knew why I'd gone to prison pitied me. Those who didn't, condemned. But instead of either, I found curiosity.

"Want to find out? We could read Harry Potter together. Or any other book."

How could I say no to those pleading eyes? "Yeah, okay."

A smile transformed her face. It was the first true, unrestrained smile I'd seen from Genevieve. She'd been stunning before, but with that smile . . . my heart skipped.

"Should we stop watching the movies if you're going to read the books?"

"Nah." I'd read the books later. For now, I wanted to keep watching, because if we shut off the movie, I'd have to go to the couch. I wasn't ready to leave this bed or Genevieve's side.

It was the first time in a long, long damn time I'd truly been at ease.

She did that. I glanced around the apartment, spotting a candle on the kitchen countertop. There was a tiny potted aloe plant in the windowsill.

She'd made this a safe space. For us both.

We finished eating and hit play on the movie.

And when I fell asleep on the bed beside her while the fifth movie played, I slept without bars closing in on me and the scream of a dying woman echoing in my dreams.

CHAPTER NINE

GENEVIEVE

"Remind me why we agreed to this?" I asked Isaiah as we stood on the sidewalk outside Bryce and Dash's house. They lived at the end of a quiet road, far from neighbors and bordered by an open field.

"Did we have a choice?"

"No." I glanced behind me, wishing I could get back in my car.

It was parked on the street along with Isaiah's bike. As always, he'd refused to ride together to dinner. His excuse this time was his headlight. It had been flickering or something and he wanted to test it out. I'd baked cookies to bring over so riding with him was out. It wasn't dark yet, but I expected on the drive home later, there would be no flickering headlight in my rearview mirror.

Why wouldn't he ride with me? I was a good driver. I'd never been in an accident and my driving record was spotless. If he preferred to drive, I'd gladly surrender the wheel.

"How was your mom?" I asked, hoping to delay this dinner for one more minute.

Isaiah's mom had called him right before we'd left the apartment. He'd ducked outside to talk to her privately. "She's good."

"Have you, um . . . told her about me?"

He sighed. "No."

"You'll tell her eventually, right?" Or was I going to remain a shameful secret?

Isaiah lifted a shoulder.

What the hell does that mean?

We'd been married for a month. Soon, it would be two. What if this marriage lasted years? I couldn't imagine it would be easy for him to tell his family that he'd married a stranger. He'd have questions to answer and concerns to appease. But was I really that bad?

My heart, already black and blue, wasn't going to hold up if the punches kept coming.

I didn't press Isaiah for an answer. His shoulders were bunched and his jaw locked. He was the king of clamming up and shutting people out. Especially his "wife."

Bryce spotted us from a window and waved. I clutched the plate of cookies in my hands, plastered on a smile and walked toward the front door.

I loved spending time with her, and had this been a girls-only dinner, I would have looked forward to it all week. Helping her plan her wedding had been a blast. I hadn't been in a wedding before—excluding my own—and she'd included me in every detail. I'd thrown myself into my tasks, reveling in the flowers and the dresses and the bridal magazines. I tucked ideas into the far corner of my mind in case one day, I got a real wedding too.

But tonight wasn't only Bryce and me. How was I going to avoid Dash in his own home? Not only was he a jerk, he was arguably worse than Draven at scrutinizing our marriage.

"We're going to have to amp it up tonight. I think Dash suspects something. Maybe kiss me a few times."

Isaiah's lip curled. It was faint, a ghost of a movement, but I caught it.

I tried not to take it personally.

It wasn't like I didn't dread kissing him too, though I feared it for a different reason. I feared how much I looked forward to those chaste kisses each morning before work. I feared the hitch of my breath and the race of my heart. I feared the way I craved more than just a brush of Isaiah's perfect lips.

"We don't know each other. They're going to see right through us," I whispered, my eyes locked on the wooden door. It was stained a dark honey, matching the beams and gables.

Their home was something out of an HGTV episode, and for a reason I didn't have time to dissect now, that made me more nervous. We were about to step into their beautiful home and taint it with our lies.

"We'll be fine." Isaiah's hand found mine, his fingers threading with my own. They were rough and calloused and long. And they were strong. I borrowed a teaspoon of their strength as the door swung open.

"Welcome!" Bryce smiled. "I'm so glad you guys are here."

"Come on in." Dash shook Isaiah's hand, then reluctantly looked at me, muttering, "Hey."

"Hi." I handed him the plate of cookies. "These are for you."

"Thanks." He stared at the cookies like they were poisoned.

Asshole.

My half brother was an asshole.

Why was I here again? Before I could sprint for the car, Isaiah pulled me through the door.

Bryce took the plate from Dash's grip, shooting him a glare, then smiled. "Oh, I love these cookies. Thank you for making them."

"You're welcome." I unlaced my hand from Isaiah's and followed Bryce to the kitchen, taking in their home as I walked, the inside as beautiful as the outside. "What can I help with?"

"Nothing. Dash is going to grill the steaks. I've got veggies ready and a salad. We're all set."

Dash and Isaiah came in behind us, Dash opening the fridge. He took out one amber bottle, twisting off the top. "Beer?"

"None for me," Isaiah said.

"No, thanks." I didn't drink if I was driving. And these days, I was *always* driving. "If you want to have a couple beers, I'm sure we can leave your bike until tomorrow. I'll drive home."

He dropped his voice. "I don't drink."

The words were for me, but Dash heard them. He leveled me with his gaze. "You didn't know that?"

Shit. A wife should know that her husband abstained from alcohol. And the reason why.

Three minutes into this dinner and it was already a disaster.

"Dash, knock it off," Bryce said, then sent me an apologetic gaze.

I stayed quiet, unsure of what to say. I didn't owe Dash an explanation and maybe he'd drop it.

His hazel gaze hardened to granite. *Or maybe not.*

My palms were sticky. My heart crept into my throat. And Dash didn't so much as blink.

How could Bryce live with this guy? Why would she marry him? He was terrifying. I felt like I was on the wrong end of a flamethrower.

Dash lifted an eyebrow, reminding me that he'd asked a question—one he expected me to answer no matter what his wife said.

"No," I choked out, holding Dash's stare. My tan wedges were screaming my name, but I didn't drop my gaze to the floor. "We don't really know each other yet."

"We're still learning." Isaiah threw an arm around my shoulders, the touch my excuse to look away. "Bet you guys are too. You and Bryce met a few weeks before Genevieve and me, right?"

Bryce snorted. "Very true."

I swallowed a laugh. Isaiah might as well have told Dash to shove it.

Isaiah hadn't commented much on Dash's attitude toward me. I knew he was toeing a tough line as Dash's employee, and I didn't fault him for staying out of the drama. But I should have known he'd have my back.

I leaned into his side, looking up to mouth, "Thanks."

"I like that we don't know everything about one another," Bryce said. "It's fun to learn something new every day."

Bryce was smiling, but there was a sharp edge to it—a silent reprimand, and Dash's frame fell ever so slightly.

Did he feel outnumbered, three to one? Would that work in my favor? Or would he fight harder to come out on top?

Dash didn't strike me as the type to lose. My stomach knotted as I worried things were about to get worse.

"Any word from the Warriors?" Isaiah asked Dash, changing the subject.

He shook his head. "Nothing. Not a sign either."

"I've been keeping up on Ashton news," Bryce said. "I reached out to the newspaper over there to introduce myself, and they've been sending me their weekly editions. The only news connected to us was the Warrior's funeral."

Bryce used her position as co-owner of the newspaper to keep us all informed. She spent time the rest of us didn't have reading the news from neighboring counties, and she knew more about the happenings around town than anyone else.

I'd been combining all of the information she'd collected with research of my own.

And so far, nothing had jumped out at me, but I wasn't going to quit. I'd pulled files on every single living Tin King member and had begun collecting names for the Warriors.

It was a slow process, but I had time until Draven's trial. If Jim had noticed that each day I spent my lunch hour glued to my screen and notebook, he hadn't commented.

Turns out, he wasn't smarmy at all.

He was actually the most understanding and supportive employer I'd ever had. He praised me constantly, thanking me for doing the job he was paying me to do. It had taken me weeks to realize the man was utterly sincere and nothing about his appreciation was because of Draven.

Work had become such an enjoyable part of my day that I'd stopped checking the job service website for openings at the other firms in town.

Besides, I had all the connections I needed at the moment to keep digging.

The first Warrior I'd researched had been the one from the cabin.

Weeks after our kidnapping, the authorities had released a statement on the fire, including the identity of the man who'd died in the cabin. His name was Ed Montgomery and he'd been thirty-three. Even thinking his name gave me chills.

Ed had lived in Ashton, a town about three hours away that the Arrowhead Warriors called home. Because the fire in the cabin had burned so long and so hot, the police had been forced to confirm Ed's identity through dental records.

He hadn't been wearing a Warrior cut that day. Our kidnapper had, but not Ed. I could still picture Ed's clothes with extreme clarity. Faded jeans. Black hoodie. Heavy boots. I'd never forget the sound of those boots. The thud was the soundtrack to my nightmares. When I was alone, when fear got the better of my common sense and I let terror swim in my veins, those boots echoed with every beat of my heart.

But Ed was dead—a charred corpse. For that, I was eternally grateful.

"It's been a month." Isaiah's forehead creased. "What are the chances the Warriors have ruled us out?"

"It's a toss-up," Dash said. "The Warriors lost a man. They might be quiet, but they won't stop until they have justice. All we can hope is they realize it wasn't us."

I dropped my eyes to the hardwood floor because avoiding Dash's gaze was the easiest way to hide our lies.

"Any updates from Jim on the case?" Bryce asked.

"No." I shook my head. "He keeps me out of it."

"And you should stay out of it." Dash pointed at me with his beer bottle. "Jim's a good lawyer. He knows what he's doing and we can't have anyone mess it up."

My mouth fell open. "Are you insinuating that I'd purposefully interfere with Draven's trial?"

"Don't know." He sipped his beer. "He was the reason your mother was killed. Maybe this is your vengeance."

"No." I gritted my teeth. "I want the real killer to pay."

That was why I was here. The only things keeping me in Clifton Forge were my promise to Isaiah and my desire to find Mom's killer. Dash might be my relative, but he could go fuck himself. And when I did leave someday, he'd never hear from his *sister* again.

"Dash," Bryce hissed. "Knock. It. Off."

"Gotta ask the question, babe. We don't know anything about her and she's in a position of influence."

"You're being a dick," Bryce fired back.

"It's fine." I stood straighter, taller, shrugging out of Isaiah's hold. Dash needed to see I could stand on my own. "My mother was murdered. We have that in common. Would you have been satisfied if the person who murdered her got away with it?"

"No."

"Then we have that in common too."

He almost looked angrier, knowing that we shared some similarities. My heart raced as I waited for his reaction. Those stone-cold eyes didn't waver. Then he shifted his attention to his wife, his anger vanishing in a blink. "Sorry."

It was an apology to Bryce, not to me. Still, I tasted victory.

"I'll go start the grill." Dash kissed Bryce's forehead, then nodded for Isaiah to follow.

When they were out of earshot, I blew out a long breath. "Wow."

"Grr." Bryce closed her eyes, bracing her arms on the island. "I'm so sorry, Genevieve. If you want to leave, I would totally understand."

"But then he'd win." And I was not letting Dash win.

"I told him to relax tonight, to stop acting like this. It's not . . . he's not this guy. But did he listen? No. And trust me, when you do leave later, he's going to get one hell of an ass chewing."

"Thanks for that."

"I'm sorry," she repeated.

I waved it off. "I can stand my ground."

"Yes, you can. He'll push hard to see how hard he *can* push. Don't let him win."

"Trust me, I won't." I was treading carefully around Dash. He wasn't just my brother; he was Isaiah's boss and our landlord. I'd let him get away with the glares and the underhanded comments. But like tonight, when he crossed a line, I was no longer staying quiet.

"Can I change the subject?" I asked. "There's something I've been meaning to ask you."

"Of course." She stepped closer.

I took a fortifying breath. "When you came to Colorado, you said you were writing a memorial for Mom. Was it a ruse? Or did you mean it?"

The color drained from her face. "That wasn't a ruse. I know reporters who would use it as an excuse for information, but I wouldn't have lied about that."

"Okay." I relaxed. "Have you written it yet?"

"Most of it. I was waiting to publish it, hoping we'd be able to prove Draven innocent first. Then I was going to ask you to read it. But we don't have to wait. I can run it whenever you're ready."

"I'm not," I confessed. "Not yet."

"Then it'll be there if and when you are." She gave me a sad smile. "How about a tour?"

"Absolutely." I sighed, hoping the awkward moments for this night were over.

We spent the next thirty minutes wandering through the house. I envied their space. I envied their doors. I envied that her living room didn't also double as the bedroom.

Bryce and Dash's basement was bigger than Isaiah's apartment. He and I were living on top of one another, something most newlyweds would likely enjoy. For us, it amplified an already complicated situation.

"Will you find out if you're having a boy or girl?" I asked as we stood in their home office. They would be converting it to a nursery and moving the office downstairs.

"We're not sure yet. Dash wants it to be a surprise, but I like to plan. We're battling it out at the moment."

"I like the idea of a surprise." I ran my hand over a soft, cream baby blanket she'd folded on the desk.

"I'm trying not to be nosy, but my curiosity is a beast of its own. Will you guys have kids someday?"

I should have anticipated Bryce's question. I'd always heard that once you were married, people immediately began asking if kids were next. "Um . . . maybe."

Telling Bryce *no* would only lead to more questions. I couldn't exactly tell her that Isaiah and I didn't and wouldn't be having sex. *Maybe* was a safe deflection. Another half-truth.

Bryce led me from the office across the hall to the master. I refused to look into the walk-in closet for fear I'd die of envy. I should have avoided the master bathroom too.

"I'm so jealous of your double sinks. And a shower where you actually have room to bend over and shave your legs."

She scrunched up her nose. "How's it going at the apartment? I've never been up there."

And I—awful friend that I was—hadn't invited her in. I'd correct that mistake soon. "It's crowded and small. Next time we're both at the garage, come up and I'll give you the tour. It takes twenty-three seconds if we do the long version."

"How long do you think you'll stay there?" she asked as we walked away from the bathroom.

"I don't know." My resolve broke and I glanced into her closet. "Ugh. Your closet is a dream. I wish I could fit all my clothes in one spot."

"You guys could move. Rent something bigger."

That would require Isaiah and me to talk about the future. We'd been so busy adjusting to this new life that neither of us brought up anything past the upcoming week. Maybe because we were both still hoping this would end, sooner rather than later.

"My condo in Denver sold," I told Bryce as we returned to the kitchen. "I'm closing on it next week so that gives us more options."

At the moment, I didn't have any desire to buy property in Clifton Forge. A purchase was too permanent. But I might change my tune after another few months in the apartment.

"Options for what?" Dash asked as the guys rejoined us inside.

"A bigger place," Bryce answered for me. "With a decent closet and bathroom."

"But we're not in a hurry," I rushed to add. I didn't want Isaiah to think I was miserable. Maybe I had been at first, but the misery had faded. Day by day, it was getting easier.

"Yeah." Isaiah nodded. "We're good in the apartment for now. Though I wouldn't mind making some updates, if that's okay with you."

"Fine by me," Dash said. "What are we talking about here?"

"There's about two feet of dead space beside the closet. I was thinking of framing out some shelves. It would give us more storage space. And the whole place could use some paint."

My heart swelled. Isaiah didn't care about storage space or paint. But I did. He'd change what he could about the apartment for me.

Dinner turned out to be tolerable, despite the rocky start. Dash didn't talk to me, but the rudeness was gone. Maybe Bryce had been right. If I stood my ground, he might not like it, but he'd respect it.

Maybe the attitude had been a test to see if I'd leave.

We spent the meal talking about Clifton Forge, its stores and popular restaurants. Bryce hadn't lived here for long, she'd only moved earlier in the year, but with her job at the paper, she'd done a better job getting out to explore.

Isaiah and I shared a look when we were each halfway through our steaks. By staying hidden in the apartment, we were missing out.

"Who wants a cookie?" Bryce asked, scanning the table of empty plates.

"Me. I only ate two earlier." Isaiah stood, taking his plate to the kitchen. Normally, he ate five.

"I'll get them." Bryce followed, leaving Dash and me alone.

I glanced up from my plate, finding his stare waiting. I dismissed it, looking past his shoulder and into the living room beyond us. There were photos framed on the fireplace mantel, and I abandoned my seat and wandered over.

The largest photo was of Bryce and Dash from the wedding. They were smashing cake into each other's faces. The next photo was of Bryce's parents. The one after that was a photo of Dash and Nick standing beside two motorcycles with their arms around each other's backs. Nick had a beard; otherwise he and Dash looked alike.

They both resembled Draven, and we all had his dark brown hair.

I'd met Nick at the wedding. I'd been prepared for another angry, resentful brother, but Nick had been a pleasant surprise. He'd been kind as he'd introduced himself, shaking my hand. His wife, Emmeline, had hugged me without hesitation and introduced me to their two adorable children as Aunt Genevieve.

Nick hadn't spent much time with me since he'd been Dash's best man, but he'd escorted me down the aisle, and as the two of us stood for Bryce and Dash, he'd given me a genuine smile or wink whenever I met his gaze.

Being tied to the Slater family wasn't all bad.

When I came to the next picture, I froze. It was an older photo, the colors muted and the print quality dull. I'd never seen this woman's face before but she was no stranger.

It was Chrissy Slater.

She was beautiful and her smile lit up her eyes.

Goddamn it. *How could you, Mom?*

Loving Draven wasn't an excuse to betray her friend, not

like this. Was that the reason Mom hadn't dated anyone in Denver? I couldn't remember a time when I'd stayed home with a babysitter so Mom could go out with a man. Had she loved Draven all this time?

I feared the answer was yes, and that love was the reason she was dead.

Chrissy had loved Draven too. She'd also paid with her life.

"You hate me for her," I whispered, sensing Dash behind me.

"Yes."

"Fair enough." I was the living, breathing reminder of our father's adultery. I turned away from the photo. "I'm not my mother, but I loved her. I don't agree with what she did, but she was my mom. Maybe one day you'll see that I'm a victim here too."

Dash said nothing. His eyes stayed on the photo of his mother as I slipped past him, joining Isaiah and Bryce in the kitchen. They were both chewing a cookie.

They each ate two more as I ate one.

Dash refused.

Did he know Mom had called them Chrissy's cookies? His mother had given my mother the recipe.

And now it was mine.

Dash's sullen mood clouded the air, so Isaiah and I thanked them for a lovely evening and slipped into the dark night, each driving our vehicles home.

"We survived," I breathed, tossing my keys onto the kitchen counter in the apartment.

"Yeah." Isaiah unzipped his jacket. His cheeks were red from riding in the cool night air.

"Am I a bad driver or something?" I blurted.

"Huh?"

"Am I a bad driver? I've never been in an accident or gotten a speeding ticket. But you won't ride with me. Do you think I'm a bad driver?"

"Oh." He toed off his boots. "No, you're not a bad driver."

"Then what is it?"

Silence.

"Isaiah?"

Silence again. He set his boots beside the door and padded to the bathroom.

I stared blankly at the door as he closed himself inside. The water turned on. The toilet flushed. And I waited, wondering what the actual fuck had just happened.

Isaiah came out of the bathroom in only his boxers. I gulped at the sight of his washboard abs, then walked to my dresser to get my own pajamas.

"Do you want to watch something?" He picked up the remote for the TV.

"Not really."

He turned it on anyway.

I went to the bathroom and got ready for bed. When I emerged, he'd already shut off the lights and made up the couch. I slid quietly into the bed and stared at the ceiling.

Hello, tension. The television's volume was low, but it couldn't chase away my unanswered question. I didn't dare ask again. I'd only get more silence.

The light from the screen bounced off the walls. A car raced down the street outside.

"Sorry," Isaiah whispered, barely loud enough for me to hear.

"It's fine," I muttered. "Like I said before dinner, we don't know each other."

"No, we don't."

And with those words, I knew that wasn't going to change.

CHAPTER TEN

ISAIAH

"Lunch!" Presley hollered into the shop. She'd been teasing us all about buying a dinner triangle so she didn't have to yell.

Emmett set his tools aside with a clank. Dash slid out from beneath the car in the third bay. Leo popped up from the opposite side, shedding his gloves.

I was almost done with a belt change on a Honda sedan. My sandwich could wait ten minutes.

Dash, Emmett and Leo had spent the morning working on restoring a '61 Lincoln Continental. They'd been cutting out the swiss cheese floor, and though the whole car was rusted, it was salvageable. The owner had given Dash a huge budget and free rein to make it a collector's dream in two months. They'd jumped right in.

Meanwhile, I was doing oil changes, tune-ups, tire rotations and a slew of other general maintenance activities. I was putting in my time, working from the bottom up. Dash knew I wanted to get in on the rebuilds, and I trusted he'd make it happen eventually.

For now, I tackled the jobs Pres put on the board and kept the routine work rolling.

"Isaiah, are you coming?" she called from the office.

"Be there in a few. I'm almost done here."

"Okay."

Over the past month, lunch had become something of an event at the garage. When I'd first started here, I'd packed a lunch. All the guys had. We'd eat whenever we were hungry, usually standing in the middle of the shop, shoving food in our mouths and wiping crumbs on our jeans.

But since the kidnapping and since Bryce had taken over Dash's office as her own, the dynamic in the garage had changed. She and Presley pulled us together more often. The lunches had started out randomly; someone would forget to pack something so we'd all order from whichever restaurant was delivering. Then random became regular.

It was early October and the last time I'd packed a lunch had been before Genevieve and I had gone to dinner at Bryce and Dash's place last month.

Every day we'd congregate in the office for lunch. We'd talk about nothing as we ate sandwiches or pizza or tacos. We paid for our own meals, and while it was more expensive than a peanut butter and jelly, I could afford it since I didn't have rent and Genevieve and I split the other bills fifty-fifty.

Some days, I didn't mind eating inside the office with everyone. Others, it was too much.

Before prison, I'd thrived in the center of a group. I'd lived for the noise and excitement of my rowdy friends getting together for some fun. Most of them I'd known since kindergarten. Most of them, not wanting to associate with a convicted felon, had forgotten my name before I'd even been sentenced.

There were a couple guys who'd reached out after I'd been released and had moved home with Mom. I'd ghosted their calls until they'd stopped altogether.

I didn't need their pity.

The guys, Presley and Bryce didn't judge my past because they didn't know it. Dash knew I'd been convicted of manslaughter, Draven too. But the details behind it were not something I shared.

When we were working in the shop, the guys didn't ask me personal questions. Lunch was a whole different story. Though I'd escaped it so far, it was only a matter of time before Bryce wanted to know more about my life. I'd deflect, like I'd done with Genevieve.

And I'd alienate them, like I'd done with Genevieve.

My stomach growled and I hustled to finish the job. As I was washing up at the sink, a cold wind blew into the garage. A flurry of snowflakes fell on the pavement, only to melt a moment later.

The snow had already hit in the mountains, and with it flying this early, winter was likely to be a bitch.

Not that I minded the snow.

The first winter of my parole, I'd spent a lot of time on Mom's deck, looking over the smooth, snow-covered yard. There was peace in the snow. A clean blanket, it erased the death of fall. Maybe I'd brush off a picnic table in the barbeque area behind the garage and take my lunch breaks out there this winter.

On the days when the office felt too much like a cage.

"Hey, Isaiah."

I shut off the water, turning from the sink as Bryce came over. She lifted up a lunch sack with my name on it.

"Thanks."

"Sure. I didn't want it to get soggy."

I'd ordered the cheesesteak and after about thirty minutes, the bread tended to soften. I ate it anyway. Soggy bread was better than any meal I'd had in prison.

Bryce didn't return to the office, but took a round, rolling stool a few feet away. She tucked her fingers into the sleeves of her sweater.

Guess we're eating lunch together.

I pushed over another one of the stools and tore into my brown paper bag. "Did you eat?"

She shook her head. "I ordered chicken salad, which seemed like a good idea at the time, but the smell got to me. Apparently, this baby only likes red meat."

My cheesesteak was divided into two aluminum-wrapped sections. I held up one half. "Want it?"

"Would you mind?"

"Bring me your chicken salad later and we'll call it a trade."

"Deal." She tore into the sandwich and took a huge bite, moaning as she chewed, then swallowed. "Genevieve said you're from Bozeman. I didn't know that."

"Yep." I dove into my sandwich, already wishing I'd gone into the office when Pres had called. Questions were easier to dodge in a group. One-on-one with Bryce? I was fucked.

"That's where I grew up."

My jaw stopped. My shoulders stiffened. Did she know? She couldn't know, right? "Small world."

"Especially in Montana. How old are you?"

"Thirty-one."

"Oh. I'm thirty-five. We just missed each other in high school."

There was only one in Bozeman. "You might know my older brother. Kaine Reynolds?"

Her eyes bulged. "Kaine Reynolds is your older brother?"

"Uh . . . yeah." *Shit.* Why had I said that? I was a goddamn fool. I'd opened the door wide open to my past.

A blush crept up Bryce's cheeks and a grin spread across her face. "Kaine was a year older than me, but I knew him. I think *all* the girls knew him."

No shock there. Most girls in high school and middle school had been in love with my brother. Kaine had an effortless kind of cool. He didn't have an awkward bone in his body. Where I'd had a miserably awkward teenage phase, Kaine had skipped it.

He'd been the kid who wasn't in anyone's clique because he'd had a clique of his own. He'd never needed a bunch of friends like I had. Or used to. He was content alone.

I'd stopped at nothing to be the center of attention in high school. I was the kid who took every dare. The boy who started fights when necessary. The class clown teachers dreaded to see on their roster.

That was before Shannon.

Now I was more reclusive than Kaine had ever been.

"I had the biggest crush on him," Bryce admitted.

"Most girls did."

"How's he doing?"

"Good. Happy. He lives in Lark Cove, up by Flathead Lake, with his wife."

"Glad to hear it." She smiled. "Next time you talk to him, tell him Bryce Ryan says hello."

"I'll do that." I took another bite, chewing furiously,

wanting to keep my mouth full so we didn't get into more about my life.

Maybe I'd dodged that bullet. Bryce didn't seem to know anything about the accident. Hopefully, she wouldn't go digging.

I'd come to Clifton Forge to escape my past, not talk about it. There were too many ghosts in Bozeman. Too many bad memories. Here, for the most part, no one cared.

Except Genevieve.

She'd been quiet lately and standoffish. I'd hurt her feelings last month when I'd refused to answer her question and I hated myself for it.

She deserved to know what kind of man slept on the couch beside her every night. But every time the window presented itself, I couldn't bring myself to speak.

She'd judge me, rightly so. Coward that I was, I didn't want to see fear or judgment in her eyes—not from her. Or worse, pity. Genevieve knew I'd been in prison, but she'd never asked for what crime. Ever since the cabin, she'd put me on a pedestal. She thought I was a good man.

I wasn't.

But damn, it was nice to feel worthy for a change. To be worthy of a woman like Genevieve was nothing short of a miracle.

I wasn't ready to throw a miracle away with the truth.

A car door slammed out front. Outside, a black Chevy Blazer had parked in front of the office. It was probably another simple job. Maybe someone wanted to get a jump start on ordering snow tires.

I'd swallowed my bite and set my sandwich aside, ready to go out and greet the customer, when I looked up and my heart dropped.

"Mom?"

She didn't hear me. She was on her way to the office.

I hustled through the shop, dodging parts and tools on my way. "Mom!"

Her head whipped around, and a smile brightened her face. "Hi."

"Hi." I pulled her in for a hug, and she kissed me on the cheek. "What are you doing here?"

"It's been months since I've seen you. You're always so busy working when I call. I took the day off and thought I'd come for a surprise visit. You can show me the bike you've been working on. Maybe after you're off, we can go out to dinner."

"Uh . . . sure." All things that would normally be fine.

Except for the fact that in a matter of hours, my *wife* would be home.

Shit. Genevieve had asked me if I'd told my family about our marriage. I'd dodged that question because I still hadn't told them.

Mom and Kaine were the past. Genevieve was the present. I was doing everything in my power to keep the two from converging. It would be too painful, for all of us.

When Mom learned that I'd kept my marriage from her for months, she'd be destroyed. What the fuck was I doing? I should have called her from the motel on my wedding night. Hadn't I hurt her enough?

Maybe if I got to Genevieve first, introduced her as my girlfriend, we could spare Mom's feelings. Genevieve would be pissed, but in the scheme of things, the scales weren't balanced. I could suffer Genevieve's disappointment. I wouldn't pile more on Mom.

"I'm pretty busy right at the moment." I took her elbow,

turning her back to her car. "What if you went shopping? Killed a couple of hours. I'll try to get off early. Downtown has some nice places. A good coffee shop too."

"Perfect." Mom beamed. Suzanne Reynolds was pure sunlight. She was as go with the flow as a person could get. She had the cool vibe down and had definitely passed it to Kaine.

Mostly, she loved her sons. Even after all that Kaine and I had put her through, she adored us.

My mission in life was to avoid causing her any more stress. If that meant pissing off Genevieve, I'd take the hit.

"Sorry, Mom," I said. "I wish I could get off now, but—"

"Don't be sorry. I knew you'd be working when I decided to visit. I'm going to explore and see your new town." She stood on her tiptoes to kiss my cheek again. "It's good to see you."

"You too." I wrapped an arm around her shoulders.

We were almost at the Blazer's door, almost in the clear, when a voice came from the shop.

"Hello."

Damn it. I'd forgotten about Bryce.

She came our way, her hand extended. "I'm Bryce Slater."

Introductions were unavoidable. "Mom, this is my boss's wife. Bryce, this is my mom, Suzanne Reynolds."

"Oh, hi." Bryce's face lit up. "It's so nice to meet you."

"Nice to meet you too." Mom clasped both of Bryce's hands in her own. It was how she always shook, like she was giving your hand a hug.

"Are you visiting?" Bryce asked.

Mom nodded, taking my arm and hugging it. "Yes. I

thought I'd surprise Isaiah. I haven't been to Clifton Forge before."

"That's so great." Bryce looked to me. "You should take the rest of the day. I'm sure Dash won't mind."

"I'll ask him if I can get out early, but I need to finish up a couple of jobs first." And call Genevieve. "Mom's going to go shopping and grab a coffee."

"Oh, well, if you're heading downtown, you should swing by Genevieve's office. I'm sure she'd love it."

Fuck. My. Life.

Mom's forehead furrowed. "Who's—"

"She's working," I told Bryce, taking Mom's elbow and pushing her to the Blazer.

"Isaiah," Mom scolded. "What's the matter with you?"

"Nothing. I'm just in a hurry to get this work done so I can meet you for dinner. And I don't want you to miss out on any of the shops. Some of them close early."

"Okay. Fine." She scowled at me, then looked past me to Bryce. "Lovely to meet you."

"You too." Bryce stared at me like I'd lost my damn mind.

Maybe I had—three months ago when I'd married a stranger at the courthouse.

Mom was seconds away from getting in the car. Her foot was on the running board and her hand on the door to step up.

Then Genevieve's Toyota rolled into the parking lot.

"Fuck," I muttered.

"What was that?" Mom asked.

"Nothing." I hung my head, sucked in a deep breath and looked up. "Better get down. Genevieve's here."

"Who?"

"Genevieve," I spoke quietly so only she could hear. "Someone I want you to meet."

Mom side-eyed me, no doubt because Genevieve was clearly a female's name. The last time I'd introduced Mom to a woman had been years ago. Before Shannon.

Genevieve parked in her spot beside the office and climbed out of the car. When she waved, there was a pair of shoes in her hand and her feet were bare. "My heel broke. I came home to get a new pair."

I frowned. "You should have called me."

"I'm fine." She waved a hand up and down her body. "Unharmed. Jim escorted me to my car and you can follow me back."

We'd talk about her leaving without texting me later. "Come here a sec. I'd like you to meet someone."

Bryce stepped closer, her eyebrows coming together. "They haven't met yet?"

"Mom's never been here," I explained. "And we've been busy and haven't gone to Bozeman yet."

"Ah." Bryce nodded. "Then this will be exciting."

If exciting meant painful.

"What's up?" Genevieve walked over on her toes, trying to keep the hems of her black slacks from dragging.

I sucked in a deep breath. "Genevieve, meet my mom, Suzanne Reynolds."

"Oh." Genevieve covered her gasp with a smile. "Hi." She held out her right hand but had forgotten the shoes. "Shoot. Sorry." She tossed them on the ground, wiping her palm on her pants and extending it again. "It's so nice to finally meet you."

"You too." Mom was smiling outwardly, but her eyes

darted to me. She had no idea who Genevieve was. Why would she?

Genevieve caught the confusion in Mom's stare. A flash of pain crossed her eyes, but she blinked it away because Bryce was standing watch. "Isaiah has told me so much about you, Suzanne."

A total lie, but Genevieve was playing the part. I'd thank her for it later if we survived.

"I'm sorry." Mom shook her head. "Am I forgetting something?"

"No." I put my arm around Mom's shoulders, holding her tight. "Mom, this is Genevieve. My wife."

The second the word was out of my mouth, Mom's body flinched like she'd been punched. "Y-your wife?"

"She didn't know?" Bryce whispered to Genevieve.

"We wanted to tell her in person," Genevieve lied—God, I could kiss her for it.

"I'm sorry, Mom." When would I get to stop apologizing to her for my mistakes? "I should have told you on the phone but—"

"You're married?"

I nodded. "Yeah."

"How long?"

"Since the end of July."

"Oh." Her chin dropped as she let it sink in. When she looked up, there were tears in her eyes.

"Don't be upset. We wanted to tell you in person and—"

"You're married. Oh, Isaiah." She took my face in her hands and smiled. "This is just . . . wonderful. You're happy?"

Happy? Never. But if Mom thought being married had made me happy, I'd go along with it. "Yeah, Mom. I am."

She threw her arms around me and laughed. "I didn't think we'd ever get here. Not after Shannon."

At Shannon's name, Genevieve stiffened. Everyone was getting surprised today.

"I'll leave you guys alone." Bryce smiled at Genevieve and disappeared to the office. *Now she leaves?*

Mom let me go and wiped her eyes. She reached for Genevieve's hand. "Thank you. From the bottom of my heart."

Genevieve simply nodded.

"What a surprise," Mom said. "I didn't expect to come to Clifton Forge today and gain a daughter."

Another flash of pain crossed Genevieve's face. She wasn't ready to be another woman's daughter, not when she was still mourning her mother.

"Mom's going to stick around for dinner," I said. "We can all go out once you get off work."

"That sounds nice." Genevieve bent to pick up her shoes. "I'd better swap these out and get back to work. See you tonight, Suzanne."

"I can't wait." Mom waved as Genevieve headed for the stairs.

"Mom, can you hang out for one sec?"

"You go. I'll head out and do some shopping. Call me when you're off work."

"Okay." I kissed her cheek. "See you soon."

I took the stairs two at a time, flying up to the apartment. Genevieve was dropping her shoes inside the trash can.

"Sorry," I breathed. "She surprised me."

"It's fine." Genevieve wouldn't look at me. "I thought by now you would have told her, so it took me by surprise too. I mean, you never said you told your family, so I don't know why I'm shocked. It doesn't matter. It's fine."

It wasn't fine.

I crossed the room and put my hands on her shoulders, spinning her to face me. "I should have told her."

"Why didn't you? Are you ashamed of this? Is that why?"

Christ. I'd fucked this up too. "No, not at all. Mom's had a rough few years, with me in prison. I wasn't sure how to tell her. And I wasn't sure how she'd react. I don't want to cause her any stress."

"I get it." Genevieve sighed. "It'll be fine. We'll go to dinner. Pretend to be the loving couple with her too. It's no big deal."

"Thanks. It means a lot. *She* means a lot."

Mom was the one person who'd always stood by me. Even when it had cost her years with Kaine, she'd taken my side.

I didn't deserve her either.

"I'd better get going." Genevieve stepped out of my hold. "I have a lot to finish up if we're going to dinner. I'll try to get off early."

"I'll follow you to the firm."

She nodded, stepping away to go to the closet and get a pair of shoes.

I closed my eyes and let my head fall. As introductions went, that could have been much, much worse. It could have been the disaster I'd imagined.

Now I just had to make it through dinner. I was counting on Mom not mentioning Shannon again, hoping she would be too consumed with getting to know her daughter-in-law to talk about the past.

Genevieve stepped into a pair of black heels, making her a couple inches taller. Then she crossed the room, passing a stack of paint cans by the dresser.

I'd already built the new shelves around the closet and this weekend, we were painting.

Genevieve had picked four different colors. One for the bathroom, another for the ceilings, another for an accent wall, and the fourth for everywhere else.

She'd be an angel to Mom over dinner, and for that, Genevieve wouldn't have to lift a brush. I'd paint this entire place for her, twice if she asked me to.

"Thanks," I repeated.

"Sure." She wasn't looking at me again as she walked to the door. She turned the knob but paused and let it go, the spring recoiling with a click. "Who's Shannon?"

My chest tightened. "A memory."

"Will you tell me about her one day?"

A lie would have been easy. I could promise *maybe*. But Genevieve had earned the truth.

"No."

CHAPTER ELEVEN

GENEVIEVE

"Hey." Isaiah closed the door behind him and tugged off his boots.

"Hi," I muttered, not taking my eyes off the brush.

In the week since his mother had visited Clifton Forge, painting had become my escape. If I wasn't at work, I was here with a brush or roller in hand. So far, I'd painted all of the apartment's ceilings.

Getting the tarps set up each night was a huge pain in the ass, but I would not sleep at the Evergreen Motel, where Mom had been murdered. Bryce had warned me that the other two motels were rumored to have bed bugs. So I covered and uncovered like it was my job.

We slept with the window and door open, fans blaring so we didn't suffocate from the fumes. The trip to the bathroom in the morning was frigid, but nothing a hot shower couldn't chase away.

Today, I'd graduated to walls. First up was the accent wall behind the bed. Tomorrow night I'd tackle the bathroom. Over the weekend, the rest of the walls would provide me with an excuse to avoid Isaiah.

I had a blister on my index finger from the roller's handle. I had paint speckled on my face and arms. The chunk of hair above my left eyebrow was streaked with indigo blue. But if not for this painting, I would have gone crazy.

"How was your day?" Isaiah asked.

I shrugged, not bothering to turn around and look at him. "Fine."

Jim had escorted me to my car after work each evening, saving Isaiah a trip downtown. So I'd skipped my lunch hour all week and left an hour earlier than normal so I could paint. My research had hit a dead end. Unless the Warriors wanted to give me a full roster of their members, I'd dug into all of their known affiliates without any leads.

Painting was distracting me from that too.

By the time Isaiah came up from the shop, I was in the thick of it.

"What can I do?"

I'd already pushed the bed into the middle of the room and covered it in plastic. My paint tray was full. The baseboard trim was taped so I could cut in the edges tonight. I had an extra brush with my supplies, but I didn't want his help. "Nothing."

Isaiah sighed and opened the fridge to take out a Coke— just like he did every evening after work. The cans in the cardboard box shifted to fill the empty space as he popped the top and gulped.

Why did Isaiah like Coke? No idea. It was the only thing I'd seen him drink besides water. Did he like the carbonation? Was it the sugar? Why didn't he drink alcohol?

He wasn't telling.

And I wasn't asking.

"Feel like dinner?" he asked. "I could eat pizza."

I did not want pizza. "Fine."

"Or cheeseburgers?"

"Pizza." I had no plans to eat that pizza with Isaiah. It would reheat better than a cheeseburger. Or I'd eat it cold. My painting had saved me from dinner conversation all week. The last meal Isaiah and I had eaten together had been with his mom.

Suzanne Reynolds was a nice woman. All through dinner, she'd found excuses to touch me, like a pat on the hand or a touch on the shoulder when I said something she liked. She smiled a lot. She laughed easy.

Like Mom used to do.

Would Mom be smiling now? Would she be laughing if she knew how her lies and secrets had landed me here? Was she looking down on me, watching as I repainted this dingy apartment that I shared with a man who hadn't even bothered to tell his sweet mother that he'd gotten married? Or fake married.

Whatever.

"Pepperoni?" Isaiah asked.

Ugh. We'd had pepperoni last time. I. Was. Over. It. "Fine."

His gaze was hot on my neck as he waited for more, but that one word was all he was going to get. Finally, he muttered, "'Kay."

Why should I talk when he didn't?

"Would you like me to roll while you cut in?" he asked.

"No."

Isaiah had offered to paint the entire place after his

mother had left town. Suzanne had driven back to Bozeman after our dinner, calling two hours later when she made it home safely. Isaiah had waited up for her call, then he'd promised to paint after work each night.

Since I got home an hour before he was done downstairs, I started before he had the chance to stop me.

The only reason he wanted to paint was because I'd made his mother laugh and had let her ask me question after question, answering without hesitation. I didn't need any more guilty favors. If I wanted a white ceiling and a wall the color of midnight, I'd make it happen myself.

Why count on people when they'd only disappoint? Or leave? Or die?

"Genevieve." Isaiah's voice was low, my name soft and gentle as it trickled off his tongue. No one spoke my name like Isaiah.

My anger ebbed. "What?"

"Would you look at me?"

I huffed and pushed up from the floor where I was crouched to paint the edge near the baseboard. I kept my face flat, expressionless, and turned to meet his gaze. He was closer than I'd expected. I'd thought he was still in the kitchen, but he stood at the foot of the bed.

"Are you okay?" He sounded genuinely concerned.

"I'm fine."

"I'm getting that word a lot. You seem mad."

I gritted my teeth. Why was he asking? It wasn't like he really cared. "I'm busy."

"Maybe you wouldn't be so busy if you let me help paint."

"I don't need help."

He pursed his lips. "Fine."

"Fine." *Fine* was my word. I said it better anyway.

Isaiah planted his hands on his hips. "Is this how it's going to be now? I get the silent treatment every night? Can't we at least be civil?"

Seriously? I saw red.

My paintbrush rocketed toward his head.

He dodged the actual brush, sidestepping it with an easy sway. But the paint spattered across his black T-shirt. He wiped a streak with his finger, staining his skin. "What the fuck?"

"You don't get to lecture me on the 'silent treatment'!" I shrieked, air quotes flying. "Your mom is a sweet, lovely woman."

"So?" His forehead creased. "You're ignoring me because my mom is sweet?"

"No, I'm ignoring you because you didn't tell that sweet, lovely woman about me. I'm mad that I had to lie to that sweet, lovely woman. I'm frustrated that I'm in this position in the first place because of *my* mother, who was once sweet and lovely too but now she's dead."

His shoulders fell. "Gene—"

"Don't."

I was on a roll, and damn it, I wanted to get it out. For once, I wanted to set some of this anger free because keeping it trapped inside was eating me alive.

"I'm mad *because* I'm mad. It's all I feel most days and I can't even grieve my mother because the anger trumps everything else. Bryce wants to publish a memorial article about Mom, but I can't stand to read it. I don't want to remember how great she was because in here," I touched my heart, "she isn't great. It feels . . . wrong. Because if she was so great, then I wouldn't be painting this apartment, hoping it will feel just a little more like the home I've been missing since some bastard butchered her at the Evergreen Motel."

Isaiah took a step my way, but I held up my hand, stopping him before he came too close. If he crossed the invisible line between us, anger would dissolve into tears.

There was more to release before the crying began.

"I'm mad because I got shoved into the back of a trunk. I'm mad because someone *took* me. I'm mad because he's still out there, and I'm scared to go anywhere alone. I'm mad because this crappy apartment is one of the only places where I feel safe. I'm mad that I've gained five pounds because I bake cookies from my mom's special recipe every other day since those stupid cookies make me feel like my mom was great."

My throat began to close and my nose stung, but I kept going. If I didn't get it out, he'd never know. And tonight I had the courage—I needed him to know.

"I'm mad." A tear dripped down my cheek. "I'm so mad at her. And I can't be mad at her because she's gone. So I'm going to be mad at you instead. I'm mad that you have a sweet, loving mother. I'm mad that I learned more about you from her over dinner than I have in the months we've been married. And I'm mad that you don't tell me anything."

Another tear fell and I reached up to swipe it from my cheek. I hated that I was crying and that Isaiah was seeing me break. My rant stained the air a putrid gray and humiliation shoved the anger aside. *Oh my God. I'm a psycho.*

My cheeks burned.

I wanted my paintbrush. I wanted to get back to work and forget this had ever happened. Damn it. Why had I thrown it?

"Will you hand me my paintbrush?" I whispered, refusing to meet his gaze.

"No."

"Please?" My voice sounded tiny and fragile. Weak.

"I don't want you to know about me."

I gasped. *Ouch*. I'd just poured my heart out and he'd taken it in his hands and squeezed it to bits. Was I really such a monster? Why was opening up to me such an impossibility?

I blinked, another tear falling. How much more could I take until the pain swallowed me whole?

"Fuck. That's not what I meant." Isaiah sidestepped the bed, leaning down to snag my hand. He pulled me to the edge of the bed. We sat, the plastic tarp crackling under our weight.

I picked at a dot of dried ceiling paint.

Isaiah hooked his finger under my chin. "Look at me."

He really did have pretty eyes.

So sad, but so pretty.

"That's not what I meant." His shoulders sagged. "I don't want you to know about me, because I don't think you'll like me much when you do. I want you to like me."

"Oh." And now I was the jerk who had been so self-absorbed with her own grief that she'd missed Isaiah's shame. *Shit*. "Sorry. We're quite the pair."

"Yeah." He dropped his gaze to my lap, taking my left hand and rubbing a speck of paint from my ring.

"I'd like to know you," I said. "At least a little. This might go on for years. We can't pretend to be married outside these walls and be strangers inside. Maybe we could be . . . friends."

I was short on friends in Clifton Forge. My girlfriends in

Colorado called sometimes. I'd call them other times. But with every passing week, they were getting on with their lives and I was getting on with mine. Soon, we'd drift apart because we had nothing in common.

They all thought I'd gotten swept up in a whirlwind romance. Most thought I was crazy, and though they'd never admit it, I think they were waiting to welcome me home when it fell apart.

They weren't wrong.

Isaiah nodded. "Friends."

"Good. I like your mom." Despite my earlier meltdown, it was important he knew that.

"I'm glad. She's . . . she's the best person I know."

"Will you tell me more about your family?" At dinner, his mom had talked endlessly about Isaiah and Kaine, her two sons. But there'd been no mention of their father. "What's your brother like?"

"He's a good guy. He builds custom furniture that's more like art than tables and chairs. He's always had that kind of raw talent. I used to get jealous of how things came so easily to him. I'd probably hate him if he weren't the second-best person I knew."

"And he lives in Montana?"

Isaiah nodded. "In a little town called Lark Cove. It's different than Clifton Forge. Sits right on a lake."

"Why did you pick Clifton Forge over Lark Cove? Did you not want to be close to your brother?"

"The job. Dash's garage is pretty well-known and not a lot of places will hire an ex-con."

I forgot most days that Isaiah had been in prison. That his record would follow him for the rest of his life. "And your dad?"

145

"I didn't really know him. Mom divorced him just a few months after I was born. They were already separated. I was an accident."

"We have that in common," I muttered.

"I honestly don't remember him much. Couldn't tell you what he looked like. Can't even think of the last picture I saw of him. Weird, right?"

"No, not really." People were more easily forgotten than anyone wanted to think, certainly about themselves.

Would I forget Mom one day? I didn't want to. Angry as I was, I didn't want to forget her smile. Maybe if I kept enough pictures around, I'd never lose her.

"Anyway," Isaiah continued, "he worked for a company that did a bunch of overseas development. They ended up moving him to Asia. He'd call. I remember Mom taught me to use the phone when I was little so I could say hi. But he didn't visit more than once or twice a year. He'd send me gifts on my birthdays and Christmas. Then when I was eight, Mom sat Kaine and me down and said that Dad was sick. He died eight months later."

"Oh my God," I gasped. "What was it?"

"Pancreatic cancer."

"I'm sorry." I put my hand over his.

He lifted a shoulder. "I was just a kid. When it came to the stuff that a dad should teach a boy, I had Kaine. He taught me how to ride my bike. How to throw a ball. And a punch."

He had a tight-knit family, sort of like mine. Given his shock at Suzanne's reaction to the news of our marriage, Isaiah must have expected them to go ballistic at our out-of-the-blue relationship. I could see why he'd kept it from them. It wasn't about me. He didn't want to disappoint them.

I bumped his shoulder with mine. "Thanks."

"Welcome." He bumped it back.

"Why did you think I wouldn't like you?" Nothing he'd told me seemed bad. I didn't care what his family situation was. Look at mine. His was tame compared to the tale of my origin.

"Those were safe questions, doll."

"Oh."

Maybe he'd expected me to ask about Shannon again. But I'd gotten the hint last week. That was a no-fly zone.

Who was she? His ex-girlfriend? Or . . . ex-wife? Had he been married before? All these questions I wanted to ask, but they didn't seem safe. And he was talking—finally talking. I was worried that with one wrong question, he'd shut me out.

"How about this? What *should* I know about you?"

He leaned forward, dropping his elbows to his knees. "Not many people here know I was in prison for three years. I don't hide it. Won't deny it. But I'm not broadcasting it either."

"I can understand that. Will you tell me why you went?"

He stared at the door.

Second after second ticked by. The tension that normally came when Isaiah ignored a question wasn't there. This was different. He was ashamed. It pulsed off him in guilty, thick waves. It was hurting him. He was enduring it, because I'd asked for an answer.

"You don't have to—"

"I killed someone."

I froze. "Who?"

"A woman and her unborn baby."

I flinched. I didn't want to, but it happened involuntarily.

He hung his head.

This couldn't be real. Isaiah wouldn't kill a pregnant woman. It had to have been an accident, right? The Isaiah who'd saved my life wasn't a murderer.

He was kind and reserved and thoughtful. I refused to picture this man as a cold-blooded killer.

Wait, was that why he didn't drink? Did the woman's death have something to do with an addiction? He hadn't spent long in prison. Three years plus parole was common for manslaughter. So it had to be an accident. Maybe drunk driving?

Or drugs?

My mind whirled with the possibilities but stopped when a loud pair of footsteps echoed up the stairs outside. That staircase was better than any doorbell. No one could sneak up here unnoticed.

Isaiah was off the bed in a flash, striding to the door. He opened it just as our visitor knocked.

"Dash." Isaiah waved him inside.

Dash strode in and scanned the room.

I stood from the bed, wishing his first visit to our apartment wasn't when it was covered with paint supplies. The brush I'd thrown at Isaiah was on the edge of a plastic drop cloth—thank God—not the carpet.

"What's up?" Isaiah asked, closing the door.

"Got some news," Dash said. "The Warriors are making a move. Tucker called me today and said they're coming over Saturday and expect a meeting."

My heart dropped. No. *Nonononono.* Had they learned that Isaiah and I had been in that cabin?

"About?" Isaiah asked.

"The fire. They've spent time trying to figure out who

started it but haven't had any luck." He turned to me. "They want to talk to you and Bryce about the guy who took you."

"We don't know anything," I blurted. "We told you everything."

"Now you'll tell them."

"Why?"

"Because." He scowled. "We're cooperating with them. The last thing we need is a war that we'll never win. These guys don't play by the rules. They kill first and ask questions later."

I gulped. "So what do we do?"

"You tell them what you know." He pointed at my nose. "And it better be the exact same story as the one you told me."

CHAPTER TWELVE

ISAIAH

"I don't like this place," Genevieve whispered as she huddled closer to my side.

"Me neither."

We'd just walked through the front door to the Tin King clubhouse, where we'd be meeting with the Warriors.

I tightened my grip on Genevieve's hand. It had become something of a habit for us—linking hands. At first, it had been the easiest way to show the world we were a couple, far less stressful than a kiss or even a hug. But then it had evolved. It had become . . . more. We were united. We were a team. We were in this together, until the end.

After months of reaching for her, months of winding her dainty fingers through mine, her hand had become a shelter.

We both needed the comfort today.

Waiting two days for this meeting with the Warriors had been agonizing. Genevieve was so keyed up, she'd hardly slept. Something I knew as fact because I'd hardly slept. Last night, I'd finally had enough of the two of us shuffling in our respective beds. I'd gotten up and flipped on the TV. We'd already finished the Harry Potter movies, so I'd restarted them from the beginning.

I still hadn't read the books. Maybe Genevieve was right. Maybe prison had ruined reading for me. If we survived this mess, I'd pick up a book and find out.

This morning had been stressful at best. With nothing to do but wait, Genevieve and I had painted. She'd relented and let me help. When Dash and Bryce had arrived, followed shortly by Draven, Emmett and Leo, we'd met them in the parking lot and followed them to the clubhouse.

I hadn't given a lot of thought to this building. From the outside, it was fairly unassuming. It sat abandoned at the far end of the lot, shadowed by a copse of trees. The leaves had turned and most had fallen into the overgrown grass around the dark-stained building.

The windows were all boarded up with sturdy sheets of plywood. Whoever had done it had used screws, not nails, and secured the boards from the inside, not out. There'd be no way to pry them open. To break in from the outside, you'd have to shatter the dirty glass first, then use a saw to cut your way in.

Escaping from a windowless building would be impossible. Years ago, I wouldn't have thought a thing of it, but prison had a way of changing a man's perspective.

Now, I always looked for an escape.

After following Dash inside, none of us spoke. We stood in the open room behind the doors, waiting as he and Emmett flipped on the lights.

It wasn't the musty smell that made my skin crawl. It wasn't the stale air, thick with an undercurrent of booze and smoke. It wasn't the dust on the pool table or the spiderwebs on the bar. My heart was racing and my palms clammy because we were trapped. There was only one visible way to get out of this clubhouse—to get Genevieve out—and that was through the door at my back.

"We'll meet in here." Leo waved us through a set of double doors directly across from where we were standing.

Genevieve clutched my hand with both of hers as we shuffled into the room.

"This is the chapel." Draven ran his hand over the long table that ran the length of the space. "This is where we held our club meetings."

Genevieve's wide eyes took in the room, the grip on my hand tightening. It looked like a normal conference room and didn't smell as bad as the outer room. The leather from the black high-backed chairs seemed to chase away the stink from the bar. The scent of lemon polish filled my nose. While the rest of the place was dusty, someone had recently been in here to wipe the table and chairs clear of dust.

"We'll all sit on this side." Dash pointed to the opposite side of the table. We'd be able to see the front door, but it made escaping more difficult. Between us and the exit would be the Warriors.

Maybe Dash didn't expect a fight. Maybe this really would be a simple meeting. But the knots in my stomach would only vanish when it was over and we were outside, breathing free.

Genevieve slipped her hand from mine and walked to the back wall of the room. It was lined with pictures of men in black leather vests. Some stood in front of motorcycles. Some were riding. In every picture, there were smiles.

The smiles threw me. These pictures made the Tin Kings appear friendly. It made the club look fun. Maybe they'd smiled right up until the moment they'd put a bullet through some person's skull.

There'd been a guy in prison, Beetle, who'd been in a motorcycle club. He'd been assigned to the cell two down from mine. He was as far from a beetle as a man could get—Bear would have been more appropriate. Beetle had killed three men with a lead pipe in less than five minutes. Beetle never smiled.

My mind couldn't connect that kind of violence and the men I'd been working alongside at the garage. Dash, Emmett, Leo—they were good men. But they were in a few of the hanging pictures. They'd worn the cut. I was kidding myself that they hadn't been ruthless men.

Maybe, despite the masks of our normal lives, there was a streak of evil in us all.

After three years of living in a place where Beetle was one of the tame, I hadn't thought twice about taking a job at a garage that was known to have ties to a former MC. I knew not to believe the smiles.

For Genevieve's sake, I hoped she believed every single one.

She lingered over the photos for another moment, then stepped to a flag hanging between the frames. It was the Tin King patch. A skull was in the center. On one side, it was decorated with bright colors and jeweled adornments. On the other, the silver stitching made the face seem like metal. Flames licked the black background.

Genevieve cocked her head to the side, trying to make sense of it. If its purpose was to strike fear into the hearts of their enemies, I suspected that it had failed. It was too artsy. But if it was to make a statement, to be something a person could see once and remember for a lifetime, I'd call it a success.

"Take a seat." Dash was already in a chair at the head of the table. Bryce sat in the first chair on our side. Next to her was Draven, followed by Leo and Emmett. Which put Genevieve and me at the end of the row.

I pulled out her chair, letting her sit beside Emmett. I trusted that if something went down, he'd help protect her.

"Can we go over this one more time?" Bryce asked, letting out a shaky breath. "I'm nervous."

Dash covered her hand with his own. "Nothing to be nervous about."

She rolled her eyes. "Says the man who has a gun in his boot and another in the waistband of his jeans."

Fuck. Should I have brought a gun? The day I'd gone to the mountain to rescue Bryce and Genevieve, Dash had given me a gun. He hadn't asked for it back. I hadn't returned it either—having it close made me feel safe, and it wasn't like I could go buy one of my own. It was hidden in a box on one of the new shelves I'd built in the apartment.

"Tucker agreed to bring only a few guys," Dash told Bryce. "Nothing like the last time. That was an intimidation play."

"So is this," Emmett muttered, shaking his head. "I don't like the way he demanded this meeting."

"I don't either," Dash agreed. "But we don't have a choice. The sooner he realizes we're telling the truth, that we don't know shit, he'll be gone. And I, for one, would really like to get rid of at least one threat."

Draven nodded. "Agreed."

"We don't know anything," Bryce said.

"Tell him that, babe. Let him see the truth in your eyes."

Her face paled. "Okay."

Genevieve turned her chair, her worried eyes meeting mine. *What if he does see the truth?*

I took her hand.

The room went quiet, the only movement the rise and fall of breathing chests. It reminded me of nighttime in prison, when the air went still. Some nights it stayed quiet and I'd find a few hours of sleep. Others, I'd stay up listening through the night, waiting for the worst and wondering how the other inmates were able to sleep.

About a year into my sentence, I'd heard a rustle from a few cells down. A man who'd only been in prison for ten days had used his bedsheet to hang himself. His cellmate had slept through the whole thing.

"Are we allowed to come to the trial?" Emmett asked Draven, breaking the silence.

"You are," Draven answered. "But don't. You've got better things to do."

Time was running out. December was approaching rapidly and once the trial started, no one expected it to last long.

Genevieve was hesitant around Draven. The two didn't spend time together and hadn't spoken about Amina since the day he'd pulled her aside after we'd announced our marriage. But he was there every morning to greet her before work. He'd left an opening for another conversation should she decide to take it.

Unless we found the man who killed Amina, Draven would go to prison. She'd effectively lose another parent.

If Draven was sentenced, I'd do everything in my power to keep Genevieve from visiting him in prison. She was too pure to set foot in that place.

Draven would probably handle prison better than I had. He'd go in hardened. I'd gone in numb. I'd been easy prey for beatings in the yard because I just hadn't cared. I'd welcomed the physical pain—it was nothing compared to the pain on the inside. I'd deserved it, every hit and kick. Every broken rib and black eye.

The first time Mom had come to visit me, I'd been covered in bruises and my lip split. She'd cried the entire time. I'd asked her to stop visiting, but whenever she insisted, I made sure to cover my face before letting the animals have their fun.

The beatings had eventually stopped. I wasn't a fun target anymore, and thankfully, I hadn't attracted the kind of attention that came in the shower stalls. Not like the guy who'd hung himself ten days into his sentence because he'd been raped five days in a row.

Maybe Draven would get lucky and be in maximum security. Maximum was like living in the Four Seasons compared to the Super 8 of minimum.

The rumble of motorcycles cut through the silence. The tension in the room spiked and everyone moved at once.

Dash stood in a flash, striding out of the room. Bryce put her hands on her growing belly and closed her eyes. Leo took out the gun from his boot and set it on his lap, hidden beneath the table. Emmett and Draven shared a look, hardened their expressions and sat taller.

What the hell had I gotten into? What had I brought Genevieve into?

I should have told her to run that day. To run to Colorado and never look back.

All eyes were glued to the door as boots boomed in the front room. Dash appeared first, followed by five men.

I recognized Tucker plus three other men from the day the Warriors had surprised us at the garage. The fifth was new.

They were wearing the Warrior cut with the plain, white arrowhead stitched on the back. I caught a glimpse of it as one guy stretched across the table to shake Emmett's hand.

"What's up, Stone?" the man asked, calling Emmett by his last name.

Emmett stood. "Same old."

Leo remained seated but he had a grin on his face. "Welcome to the party."

If I didn't know him better, I'd say Leo looked like he was enjoying this. He was good at putting on a show.

"Draven." Tucker shook his hand. The gesture made the side of his cut flare out, revealing a gun holstered to his ribs. "Heard your trial kicks off in December."

"Yep," Draven said, resuming his seat.

"Have a seat," Dash ordered, taking his position at the head of the table. He sat straight and tall in the chair. This meeting wasn't his idea, but it was his meeting and he was in command of the room. "Tucker, you wanted to talk with my wife and sister."

Genevieve's hand jerked. Dash had never acknowledged her as his sister. The only reason to call her that today was to exert power. He was making it clear that she was under his protection.

"That's right." Tucker steepled his fingers under his chin, covered with a dark goatee speckled with gray. He had to be close to Draven's age. The skin on his cheeks was weathered from the sun and wind. He'd probably spent his life on a bike, riding every second of the spring, summer and fall, much like Draven.

"Take care with your questions, Tucker," Dash warned.

Tucker's eyes flashed annoyance, but he nodded before turning his attention to Bryce.

Good. It was better if Bryce started. She was calmer than Genevieve, maybe because she wasn't hiding anything. Whatever nerves Bryce had brought to this table were buried deep. There was defiance in her gaze now. She was facing an adversary head-on and had no plans to lose.

"Normally I ask the questions." She smirked. "Mind if I take the first one?"

Tucker nodded. "Shoot."

"How stuck are you?"

Draven grinned. Emmett stiffened. Dash frowned at his wife for taunting the Warrior president.

But Tucker didn't take offense. He smiled, flashing white teeth. "Pretty fucking stuck."

"Welcome to the misery," she said. "Whoever took us was good at covering his tracks. And I'm guessing since you're here, you really were telling the truth. You didn't kill Amina Daylee and you don't know who did."

Genevieve's breath shuddered at her mother's name.

Tucker nodded. "That's what I've been telling you."

Bryce leaned her elbows on the table. "So what do you want to know?"

"Tell me about how he got you."

"I came home after dinner with my parents. My place was dark. He came up behind me, hauled me out of my house, taped up my wrists and ankles, gagged me and shoved me in the trunk of a car."

"What kind of car?"

"A black sedan. No markings. I didn't get a look at the plates."

"Did you?" Tucker's gaze swung to Genevieve, who shook her head. He eyed her for a long second, and damn if she didn't just hold it.

There was more strength to her than people recognized, including herself. She wasn't bold about it like Bryce, but when it mattered, she had nerves of steel.

"Where'd he nab you?" Tucker asked Genevieve.

"My hotel room in Bozeman," she answered.

Tucker's men sat in utter silence. One of them kept a firm stare on Genevieve that stoked my temper. I shot the creepy bastard a warning glare. He only raised an eyebrow and went back to staring at Genevieve.

"What did he look like?" Tucker asked Bryce.

"He was covered. Head to toe. I'm not sure why. If he was going to kill us, why not reveal himself? I thought that was strange, unless he was worried that we might get away—which we did."

"Tell me about that," Tucker ordered. "How'd you get away?"

"He wanted to make it look like Genevieve killed me. Then Dash would kill her. So he pushed me to my knees, untaped Genevieve's hands and made her put a gun to my head. Dash and the guys got there before he could make her pull the trigger."

"Why not kill you both himself?"

"I haven't the slightest." Bryce shrugged. "He said it was to win an old war."

Tucker hummed, his attention shifting to Dash. "How would that win an old war? We settled our disagreement years ago. I don't give a fuck if you kill your sister."

Genevieve flinched. The man across the table grinned.

Sick fuck. I might have taken some hits in prison but I'd

159

delivered them too. If he wasn't careful, I'd leap across this table and beat him within an inch of his life.

"Now you know why nothing makes sense to us either," Dash told Tucker. "Maybe he figured we'd assume Genevieve was working with the Warriors. Not gonna lie, that thought crossed my mind. Maybe he thought we'd retaliate against your club. If she had died, there'd have been no one to deny it."

"Retaliate?" Tucker scoffed. "You'd all be dead in a minute. You can't stand against us."

Draven leaned forward. "Don't underestimate the power of revenge. The last club that did was wiped from this earth by my own hands."

That had to be the club that killed Chrissy Slater, and Draven had taken his revenge.

"Can we get back to the discussion? I've got places to be on a Saturday." Leo reclined deeper into his seat, pretending to be bored. Meanwhile, beneath the table, his gun was pointed at Tucker and his finger was on the trigger.

"You escaped," Tucker said to Bryce.

"Dash fired a shot at him. It gave me and Genevieve a chance to run."

"Where'd you run?" Tucker asked.

"Away from the whacko with the gun," she deadpanned. *Smart-ass.*

Tucker wasn't amused this time. "Be specific."

"You mean like north or south? I don't fucking know. I ran downhill. I was frozen and too busy trying to stay on my feet to chart my direction against the sun."

"And you?" Tucker twisted his chair to address Genevieve.

She sat perfectly still. "And me, what?"

"Where'd you run?"

"The other direction so I wouldn't cross paths with the guy who took us."

"To the cabin?"

"Yes." Her voice was so resolute, not a hint of fear.

"How'd you get in?"

"Through the front door. Most cabins have those. Doors."

Christ, these women. Bryce's attitude was contagious, and neither of them would be bullied.

"Then what?" Tucker asked.

"I crouched beside a window and watched outside. I saw the man who took us going up the slope into the trees. When I lost sight of him, I got the hell out of there."

She didn't rush her words. Her statement was cool and calm. And complete bullshit.

"Did you see anyone inside?"

"No."

Tucker narrowed his eyes but stayed quiet.

"Then what?" The man who'd been staring at Genevieve spoke up. That's when she finally noticed his stare. He was talking to her breasts. He licked his lips.

"W-what?" she stuttered. It was her first sign of weakness.

"I found her and we got the fuck out of there," I answered.

"Nothing else?"

"Nothing." I narrowed my eyes and kept a firm grip on Genevieve's hand.

"How do we know this isn't all a lie?" Tucker asked. "Maybe you didn't believe me when I said that we didn't kill that bitch in the motel. How do I know this kidnapping isn't just a story you made up to cover the fact that you killed one of my men?"

Genevieve's hand twitched at Tucker's *bitch*.

"Enough." Draven's voice resonated in the room. Dash might be at the table's helm, but Draven had just as much power from his chair. "You'll talk about Amina with respect. And what you heard here is the truth. We both know these girls aren't lying."

"What the hell are you expecting to find, Tucker?" Dash asked. "One of your guys is dead. We didn't kill him. Or is there something more? Something you're hiding? What exactly was one of your guys doing in that cabin, anyway?"

Tucker's jaw ticked. "Not relevant."

"Seems relevant to me," Emmett said. "We're sitting on our side of the table telling the truth. What's yours? Maybe we're done sharing until you do the same."

"Not maybe." Dash stood. "We're done."

Draven stood next, holding out a hand to help up Bryce. When she was on her feet, she crossed her arms. Then Leo stood, the gun held tight in his hand. Emmett stood next, followed by Genevieve and me.

In total, we outnumbered them. We'd probably lose a fight but being on the side of the line with bigger numbers was never a bad place to be.

"This is the truth?" Tucker asked, still seated beside his men.

"Yes," Bryce and Genevieve said in unison.

"Any proof?"

Bryce rolled her eyes. "We didn't exactly have a chance to carve our initials into a tree."

Tucker rapped his knuckles on the table, then stood. The others rose with him. "Appreciate the info."

They left the room in a single-file line. None of us moved as we waited for their motorcycles to start.

Dash left first, hustling Bryce out of the room. We joined him outside on the wide concrete slab beyond the front door in time to see the Warriors speed from the parking lot in a flash of black and a cloud of noise.

"Fuck." Dash ran a hand through his hair, then pulled Bryce to his side, dropping a kiss to her forehead. "Good job, baby. But can you please, for fuck's sake, keep the sass under control?"

She shrugged. "I can't help it."

Dash huffed, then looked over Bryce at Genevieve. "You did good too."

Genevieve blinked. "Oh, uh . . . thanks."

She'd done amazing. No one here even knew how hard that had to have been—they never would. The truth was between the two of us and a dead man.

"We're outta here." I hauled her away from the club-house, not loosening my grip on her hand until we were safe in the apartment.

"Phew." She put her hands to her hair, wide-eyed and dazed. "We got married so we wouldn't have to turn witness to the cops. I guess we should have thought about others too."

"No shit." The cops, at this point, were the least of our problems. I put my hands on her shoulders. "Proud of you."

"I'm glad it's over." She fell into my chest, sliding her hands around my back. When we hugged, it was normally her into my side. Front-to-front holds were chaste at best. This was lasting, like she needed to be here for a hug. My arms didn't quite know where to settle. On her waist? Her shoulders? I didn't want to drop them too low, too close to her ass. I decided on one at her shoulders and one just below her ribs.

Genevieve fit against me, her soft curves molding to my stony lines. And she was warm. God, she was warm. I'd forgotten how it felt to hold a woman. To sink into a woman's hug. I dropped a cheek to her hair, taking the comfort she was offering.

It ended too soon. Genevieve broke away. "I'm glad we practiced."

"Me too."

"Do you think they believed us?" she whispered. The attitude and confidence she'd worn in the clubhouse slipped away. Her dark, beautiful eyes filled with fear.

"I sure hope so."

Otherwise this would never end.

And it *had* to end.

I had to let her move on with her life. I had to get her free of this obligation.

She needed to leave this town and fade into a memory.

Before I forgot that I didn't deserve her.

CHAPTER THIRTEEN

GENEVIEVE

"What's the plan for today?" Isaiah asked from the couch. "Want to hit the first coat on the walls?"

"No," I groaned into my pillow. The last thing I wanted to do today was paint.

Sleeping this Sunday away sounded like a much better plan. I was tired and . . . awake. Maybe I could sneak in an afternoon nap.

After meeting with the Warriors yesterday, I'd had a hard time calming down. I'd been sure they'd return to call me a liar.

Isaiah had done his best to assure me that I'd been believable, but doubts had kept me from falling asleep. Had they heard my voice shake? Had they heard my toes bouncing on the floor? Had they noticed how hard it had been to keep firm eye contact?

The courage in Bryce's voice had given my confidence a boost. She'd been like that on the mountain too, arrogant in the face of our kidnapper. Dash called it sass. I called it survival—the sheer will to live.

I wasn't much of a liar, but I'd had a lot of practice these past few months. I hoped it was enough.

"Can we skip the painting today?" I yawned. "Watch movies and do nothing?"

"Fine by me." He sighed, shifting and flopping into a new position on the couch. Given the number of times he'd turned from one side to his other last night, Isaiah hadn't slept well either. He had to be uncomfortable on the couch. His legs were too long and his shoulders too broad, yet he'd slept there without comment for months.

"Starting tonight, I want to sleep on the couch."

"Huh?" He sat up, the blanket dropping off his bare chest. "Why?"

"Because it doesn't seem fair for me to have the bed all the time." I was twisted sideways with a pillow bunched under my cheek. It gave me a perfect view of Isaiah's inked skin, especially the black pattern that ran down the side of his neck, across his shoulder and to one of his rounded pecs.

It had taken me weeks of stolen glances to identify all of Isaiah's tattoos. They were all black. Each one was a pattern. There were no faces or words. They stretched across his smooth skin, molding to the muscle beneath.

"I don't mind the couch," he said.

"Please, let's switch. It will make me feel better."

"Can't do it, doll. I'm good here." He sank into his pillow, stretching his arms over the arm of the couch. Then he tucked his hands behind his head and stared at the ceiling.

I hugged my pillow closer, studying the definition in his arms. They were strong, the muscles large, but with long, sweeping lines. One muscle would rise, then disappear beneath another. His shoulders spanned beyond the width of the couch. When Isaiah raised his arms, they sometimes looked like wings.

Wings decorated in black.

"Did you get all your tattoos in prison?" I asked.

"No, only my fingers and part of this one." His finger trailed down the tattoo on his neck. "It's against the rules to get tattoos in prison, but a bunch of guys did it anyway. My third cellmate did them for me at night. I'm probably lucky I didn't get sick or something because he did it with pen ink and a paperclip he'd sharpened into a needle."

I grimaced. Isaiah rarely talked about prison. When he did, it was only little things. But the bits and pieces were enough for me to know I probably didn't want to hear the full story. If he ever wanted to tell it, I'd listen. I'd cry, but I'd listen.

"The one on my neck wasn't as big. It used to end here." He lifted up and pointed to a spot on his collarbone. "When I got out, I went to an actual artist and had him fix it. Eventually, we expanded it. And I got the rest."

He raised his arms, stretching them high so I could see the tattoos on his forearms. He also had tattoos on a calf, his ribs and his left foot.

I'd never had a desire for a tattoo, but after spending so much time with Isaiah, I'd begun to appreciate their artwork. Maybe I'd get one if it was something unique, like his. "Did they hurt?"

"Yeah, they hurt. The ones I got inside were the worst and they took forever because he could only do a little at a time. The one on my neck took him almost three months. But I didn't care. It wasn't like I was going anywhere."

"Why the black?"

"That's the color pen he had. When I got out, I decided to keep going with the black."

"What does that one mean?" I asked. "The tattoo on your neck."

"Nothing really. It's just a pattern. The guy wanted to try it out. He was good but it wasn't like he had actual tattooing equipment. So it's a lot of simple stuff with blurry lines. I've had it all touched up since, but at the time, I didn't care. I told him to experiment."

"Why?" If I got a tattoo, I'd want it to be special. Why would you get a tattoo and go through the pain if it didn't mean anything?

"Pain," Isaiah whispered. "I wanted the pain."

"Oh."

Since my meltdown, I hadn't asked Isaiah for more information about the pregnant woman's death. We'd been consumed with anxiety over meeting with the Warriors. And I'd been a coward. I wasn't sure I wanted all the answers.

Were the tattoos a punishment for what he'd done? A way of atoning? Because prison sounded rough enough without adding self-inflicted misery to the mix.

Though I suspected Isaiah was punishing himself to this day.

His beautiful eyes were so haunted at times. They didn't flicker or spark. In the beginning, I'd thought it was because of his time in prison, or of what had happened at the cabin.

I was likely wrong on both counts.

There'd been a few moments lately when I'd begun to gather hope. Isaiah didn't laugh or give flashy smiles, but he'd show me a rare grin. There were never teeth visible and it was barely an upturn of his lips, but it stole my breath every time.

He'd grin whenever I had cookies out for him when he came up from the garage. He'd grin when I did his laundry. He'd grin on the nights when he'd come up and find some new purchase for the apartment. Was he happy here with me?

Should I even be asking myself that question?

Isaiah wasn't mine to keep forever. Eventually he'd move on to find someone who made him truly happy. The selfish part of me loathed the idea of a different, future Mrs. Reynolds who'd get more than subtle grins.

I very much wanted to be the person who put a smile on Isaiah's face, just once before this was over. Before I was the ex-Mrs. Reynolds and I missed him from my life.

"Thank you for yesterday," I whispered.

"For what?"

"For holding my hand. I don't think I would have gotten through it if you hadn't been there." Not only had lying to criminals been terrifying, replaying the kidnapping never got easier. The image of Bryce on her knees as I held that gun to her head was one that would haunt me for years.

"No need to say thanks." Isaiah sighed. "You wouldn't have had to go through it in the first place if it weren't for me."

I huffed. "It's not *your* fault."

He sat up and leaned forward on his knees. The tattoo of a tree—twisted and gnarly—ran down his ribs. The branches wound up his shoulder and dipped over his back. Some limbs twisted across his pec. "Whose fault is it then?"

"My mom's," I answered immediately. "If there's a person to blame, it's her."

"V." He closed his eyes.

169

V. No one had ever called me *V.* I loved it when Isaiah spoke my whole name. I loved the one letter even more.

Isaiah opened his eyes and met my gaze. "She wouldn't have come up here to meet with Draven if she'd known what it would do to you. I know you're mad and you have every right to be, but don't stay mad."

Guilt raced through my veins and closed my throat. He was right. I was mad. I was furious. And if Mom were here, she'd apologize every minute of every day.

But she wasn't here. Maybe being angry, placing that blame, was my way of keeping her close. When there was no more anger, she'd truly be gone.

Isaiah stood, stretching his arms above his head. He was a beautiful distraction from the pain in my heart. He twisted and turned his torso, stretching out his back. His abs flexed and the V of his hips cut sharp. I didn't linger on the bulge in his boxers—much—and drank him in.

Whoever got him next was a lucky woman.

Isaiah folded the blankets on the couch into a neat square. Then he stacked them on the pillow, bringing them to the base of the bed, where I'd put a cheap trunk. He tossed them in, then met my gaze. "A lazy day?"

"Let's be sloths."

He grinned.

Isaiah Reynolds really was something. I smiled back and let the butterflies flutter in my stomach.

"I'm going to take a shower."

"'Kay," I breathed, ignoring the pulsing in my core at the thought of Isaiah stripping off those briefs, pushing them down his hips and over his thick, bulging thighs and standing to reveal his—

And that's enough. I buried my face in the pillow so he wouldn't see my red-hot cheeks.

Isaiah padded toward the bathroom, but the sound of footsteps on the stairs had him stopping and me sitting up like a rocket.

We didn't get visitors. The last one had been Dash and look at what he'd dragged to our doorstep. So who would be here on a Sunday when the garage was closed?

Isaiah crossed the room in his underwear. He flipped the deadbolt and cracked open the door. "Oh. Hey."

My heart settled. That wasn't a *hey* for someone not welcome here.

He opened the door wider, stepping out of the way to let Draven inside.

"Uh, hi." I had my comforter clutched to my chest. I was wearing only a thin tee and sleep shorts. I'd gotten used to Isaiah seeing my nipples peeking out beneath my pajamas, but Draven? I wouldn't be getting up to greet him.

"Morning." Draven's eyes alternated between me in the bed and Isaiah dressed in nearly nothing. He squirmed.

For appearances, having him walk in on us during a sloth-like Sunday morning was excellent. We looked like a married couple who'd spent a lazy morning in bed. Thank God for that trunk and the fact that Isaiah couldn't start a day without a shower.

"Is something wrong?" Isaiah asked. "Did you hear from the Warriors?"

"Oh, uh . . . no." Draven glanced around the apartment. "You're painting? Looks nice."

"Genevieve gets the credit."

Draven kept inspecting the walls, looking anywhere else

than at my face. Isaiah looked at me. I held up my hands. He jerked his chin at Draven, urging me to talk.

Ugh. "Fine," I mouthed. "Was there something you needed?"

Draven looked at his boots. "I was wondering if you'd like to go out for breakfast."

"Ohh-kay," I drawled. "Why, exactly?"

"To talk. Thought maybe while I was a free man, I'd get to know you some. If you wouldn't mind."

It was interesting how he'd phrased the request. *He* wanted to get to know *me*. Not get to know each other.

My feelings toward Draven were confusing at best. I was under the impression he struggled with all his kids. According to Bryce, Draven and Dash had been close once. Then Dash had learned of Draven's affair with Mom and their relationship had been shattered. Bryce had mentioned briefly that Draven and Nick had gone through a rough patch as well. But at the wedding, they'd seemed to get along fine. Mostly, Draven had doted on Nick and Emmeline's kids.

Breakfast would only last an hour or two. The desperate look on his face, the silent plea, was hard to dismiss.

"All right. May I have fifteen minutes to get ready?"

He nodded. "Take your time. I'll wait in the office downstairs."

The moment he was out the door, I flopped backward on the bed. "Do you want to take the first shower before we go?"

"We? I think that invite was just for you."

I sat up on my elbows. "What? You have to go with me. I need you there."

"You need me?"

"Duh. We're a team."

Isaiah stared at me, dumbfounded. Why was he surprised? We hadn't dealt with anyone alone up to this point. I wasn't going to start now.

"So?" I tossed a hand toward the bathroom. "You or me first?"

His eyes softened. "I'll go first."

Fifteen minutes actually took thirty by the time we were dressed and downstairs. Our awkward family caravan to the diner downtown was led by Draven in his truck, me in my car and Isaiah following on his bike.

The place was packed for a Sunday morning. Most people were dressed in nicer clothes than my black yoga pants and pale purple hoodie. They'd probably already been to church while I'd been lying in bed, salivating over Isaiah's tattoos.

As we followed the waitress across the black and white tiled floor, the people we passed cast Draven sideways glances. A few leaned in to whisper behind his back. They narrowed their eyes. They hugged their children closer.

I gritted my teeth to keep my mouth closed.

He was innocent. The urge to defend him nearly won out when I heard a man say the words *death sentence* to his wife. But I held my tongue, glad when we reached a red booth along the far wall.

Draven took one side while Isaiah and I took the opposite. We ordered coffee and water, then focused on our menus.

The eerie whispers made the hair on the back of my neck stand on end. Conversation in the restaurant had all but stopped.

I slapped my menu down and shot glares at anyone who dared meet my gaze.

Did these people not believe in innocent until proven guilty? Hadn't they read the paper? Bryce had done her best to show there was reasonable doubt in Draven's case, but maybe it was too little too late. Without proof he hadn't killed Mom, there'd be no changing minds.

Clearly, if I was sitting here with him, it was worth pondering. I mean, it was my mother who'd been killed. Small-town gossip had no doubt spread about Draven's daughter working for Jim Thorne. And here I was, about to share omelets and pancakes with the accused man. Didn't that make people wonder?

The two men at the table across the aisle from us were blatantly staring. Judgment was written all over their faces.

"What?" I barked.

Their eyes whipped back to their plates.

When I turned to face our own booth, Draven was holding in a laugh.

"People need to mind their own damn business," I said loud enough that our surrounding tables would hear. "And it's rude to stare."

I picked up my menu again, flipping it over to the breakfast side. It took me seconds to pick my breakfast.

"I'm getting pancakes. What are you having?" I asked Isaiah—anything to not acknowledge that I'd just snapped at two strangers in an effort to defend the father I barely knew.

When I looked up, his vibrant, green-gold gaze was waiting. He wore a black baseball cap today. It hooded his eyes, making his eyelashes stand out and the chocolate ring around his irises pop. And he wore the grin.

It stole my breath.

"Pancakes. And the Denver omelet."

I leaned closer, brushing my arm against his. I was glad

Draven was here and that we were in public. Maybe it was because of yesterday's stress, but I was feeling oddly clingy with Isaiah today. He didn't seem to mind. Since we were in public, I could pretend he was a real husband. I could believe that grin was for me.

Day by day, I was falling in love with the lie.

The waitress came over and delivered steaming cups of bitter coffee. I loaded mine up with cream and sugar while Isaiah and Draven sipped theirs black.

"How's work?" Draven asked. "Do you like Jim?"

"He's the best boss I've ever had," I admitted. It was true. "I, um . . . thank you. For helping me get that job."

He shrugged. "I just made a phone call. You got yourself the job."

Modesty was not something Draven wore often. It suited him.

"Has he told you much about my case?"

"No." I shook my head. "He's trying to respect the personal situation here, which I can appreciate. He expects that if there's something you want me to know, you'll be the one to tell me."

"That's fair. Jim's always been fair. He's one of the few people in the world I trust. And you know, I've never lied to him. He's defended me the best he could while staying true to the law, even the few times when he knew I was guilty. He kept me from trouble with the law."

That wasn't exactly what I wanted to hear about my new mentor. But I'd learned the last few months that my sense of justice—of right and wrong—had been naïve. Unlike the diner's tiled floor, there was no clear line between black and white. If there were, then Isaiah would be in prison.

So would I.

"And what about this time? What are Jim's chances?"

"Not good." Draven sighed, running a finger over the rim of his coffee mug. "This time, there's no settlement to pay. No loopholes."

"But you're innocent."

"No." Draven lowered his voice. "I'm far from innocent."

Was he giving up? He sounded like the jury had reached a verdict already. Draven didn't seem like the type of man who'd go down without a fight.

The man who'd done this was still out there. Didn't Draven want to know who it was?

The man who'd killed Mom might have disappeared already, but there was a chance he could come after any one of us. We all assumed framing Draven was his end goal, but what if it didn't stop there? What if he was lying low, waiting for Draven to be punished before he resurfaced? This unknown enemy of ours might try to kidnap me again. He might go after Bryce. He might go after any one of the former Kings—Dash or Emmett or Leo.

If Draven went to prison, the bastard won.

"It's not fair."

"Life's not fair." Spoken like a parent. Draven looked up from his mug. "Do you believe I didn't kill her?"

"I wouldn't be in this booth otherwise."

Under the table, Isaiah's hand found my knee. He knew this wasn't easy for me.

"What was the best birthday present you ever got?" Draven's question came out of nowhere, until I remembered the purpose of this meal. He wanted to get to know me.

"One of those little kid cars. Mine was a pink convertible that Mom bought me when I was five. I'd seen it on TV and begged for it. It was the Barbie brand and probably cost her a fortune at the time, but I'd wanted it so badly."

Mom hadn't spoiled me. Normally I'd get one gift from my Santa list, a book and some clothes. Maybe that was why the convertible stood apart from other birthdays and other Christmases. She'd splurged.

I'd driven that car around our driveway and up the neighborhood block until I could barely fit in the seat.

"Your birthday is July sixteenth, right?"

I nodded. Mom must have told him.

"That's . . ." Isaiah trailed off.

I nodded.

Our wedding day.

He dropped his chin. To Draven, it probably looked like he was studying his coffee cup. But I knew he was berating himself for missing it. How could he have known? We'd been strangers.

Later, I'd tell him it wasn't a big deal. I hadn't wanted to celebrate my birthday this past year anyway, not without Mom.

"Where'd you go to college?" Draven asked. "Your mom mentioned you were top of your class."

"University of Denver. I got my undergraduate degree in political science at the same time I got my associate to become a paralegal. I thought some work experience would set me apart in law school. And I needed the money. I didn't want to be too far in debt when I started law school."

"Smart."

"Hard. It was hard. There wasn't a lot of time for fun." And luckily, I had a skill to fall back on. Or else I might have been waitressing in this diner.

We talked more about my life in Colorado. Draven asked

question after question. I gave answer after answer, both for him and Isaiah, who listened with rapt attention during the meal. Finally, when my stomach bulged and we'd had our fill of coffee, Draven paid the bill and we walked outside into the fall air, loitering on the sidewalk.

Draven took out a pair of sunglasses but didn't shield his eyes. "Before this is over, before I go away, can this become a thing? Sunday breakfast?" He was so sure he'd be proven guilty. Or maybe he was preparing himself for the inevitable.

I nodded. "Okay."

"Thanks. See you tomorrow." He waved, turning for his truck.

"Wait." I reached for him but didn't touch. "Can I ask you something?"

"Yeah."

"Did you love my mom?"

The question had been at the back of my mind since our first conversation at the picnic table. I wasn't sure why it mattered. Maybe because I wanted to feel like I'd come from something other than a drunken party.

His shoulders fell. "I've only loved one woman in my life. And that was my wife."

It wasn't a shock, but it stung nonetheless. I was a mistake. He'd said it himself. "But Mom loved you anyway."

"Wish I had taken better care of her feelings, but I didn't know. Not until it was too late."

I sucked in a deep breath, finding the courage to ask about one more thing. As I'd been digging into the details of what had happened, I'd read Bryce's newspaper stories. I'd filled pages and pages in my notebook about people related, even loosely, to the motorcycle clubs. Everything I found jived with what he'd told me months ago. It wasn't until I'd had some time to let it sink in that one thing had begun to bother me.

Draven had had sex with Mom before she'd been killed.

Why?

Chrissy had been gone for more than a decade. Had something blossomed between Mom and Draven?

When Mom had moved to Bozeman for her job, she'd started dating a guy—Lee. I'd been proud of her. I'd worried about her living alone in a new town and hoped dating would help her meet new people. She hadn't told me much about Lee other than it was casual.

Had she kept it casual on purpose? Had she always been in love with Draven? Had her trip to Clifton Forge been a last-ditch effort to try and win him again?

I'd never know the answers to those questions, but I could find out why Draven had slept with Mom.

"Why did you have sex with her?"

He ran a hand over his beard, blowing out a deep breath. "We were talking. Reminiscing. One thing led to another and well . . . she asked me to."

Damn. Mom had been a pity screw? My heart ached for her. She'd loved him, too much. Why couldn't she have just let him go? Why? We wouldn't be here if she had just moved on.

"I cared for her," Draven added. "Always."

But that wasn't enough.

"That's all I wanted to ask." I was done with the questions and certainly with this topic.

"See you next Sunday?"

I nodded, not risking another word.

Draven waved, leaving me and Isaiah on the sidewalk. I

felt dizzy. Heartache and disappointment and fear and sadness swirled, threatening to kick me off-balance.

"You okay?" Isaiah's arm came around my shoulders.

"No." I fell into his arms, holding on to him the way a wife held on to her husband.

We were still in public. The patrons of the diner only had to glance up from their breakfasts to see us beside the street.

So for the next few minutes, when I needed his embrace and to make believe love didn't always end in disaster, I was going to live our lie to the fullest.

CHAPTER FOURTEEN

ISAIAH

"It snowed." Genevieve stared out the window, looking at the parking lot.

I pulled a sweatshirt over my head and walked to stand by her side. "More like dumped."

Given the thick white layer on the staircase's railing, we must have gotten three inches. We'd had small flurries over the past month but any snow that stuck melted away days later. As usual, there'd been a skiff on the ground for Halloween last week.

But as of this morning, winter was here.

"Bet we'll have a quiet day at the shop." Not many would want to venture out to have their vehicle serviced on a day like this. Most avoided the roads if possible on the first major snow of the year.

There'd be a handful of fender benders today caused by idiots going too fast on slick roads. People forgot over the summer what it took to drive on ice and snow. The tow company in town would be busy until it thawed next spring.

Dash had asked me last week if I knew how to pop out

dents and dings. My experience before working here had been centered entirely around engine work. This week, he and Emmett were going to teach me some body basics. I'd start with the easy stuff, and maybe one day I'd get to help on the customs.

"Guess your bike is in the garage for now."

"Yeah," I muttered. I had an older truck—not the cool kind of old—that I drove in the winter. Now that I'd spent months on the bike, I was dreading starting up the '96 Ford and being trapped inside a cab for the next five months.

"What did your brother want?" Genevieve spoke to the glass, her gaze mesmerized by the snow outside.

Kaine had called right before she'd disappeared into the bathroom to get dressed for the day. She was wearing an olive sweater that draped over her shoulders but fit snugly across her hips. She'd paired it with a tan skirt and leather boots that ran up to her knees.

I'd never met a woman who dressed like Genevieve. Her clothes were sophisticated without being snobby. She was down to earth but had so much class. She put effort into her style, taking the time to add little touches like jewelry or scarves that set her apart. When she walked into a room, heads turned.

And she was stuck with a guy like me.

Every day I thought about letting her go. All I'd have to do was walk into the police station and confess, and she'd be free to live a better life than the one here in this cramped apartment.

But I couldn't walk away.

The painting was done. Genevieve had made this place nicer than it had ever been. It was warm and stylish, but it would never be good enough. Not for her.

Neither would I.

My eyes ran down the back of her sweater, following the loose curls in her hair that cascaded to her waist. My gaze raked over her ass, the perfect shape of her hips and the skirt that tapered at the knees, framing her tight curves.

Fuck, but she was sexy. I hadn't found a woman sexy in years. The only women I saw in prison were those who'd visit other inmates. And once I was out, I'd been too fucked up to think about a woman. Hell, it had taken me months to get used to sleeping in a regular bed again.

Or sleeping at all. For three years, I had guarded my nights by not sinking into a deep slumber. I'd figuratively slept with one eye open.

Finally, about four months after being home with Mom, the years of exhaustion had caught up with me, and I'd let myself truly fall asleep.

Then, I'd slept for days.

Mom had been worried I was sick or dying, but I'd just explained that I was tired. The burden of prison memories was mine to carry alone.

Things were easier after that. I'd found a job at a local lube shop. The owner was a friend of Mom's and had broken company policy to hire me as a favor. I'd worked. I'd gone home. I'd slept.

I didn't meet women because I didn't want to meet women. Shannon wasn't on my mind as often as she'd once been, but I thought of her. I remembered her—another burden to carry. No woman's beauty or grace had compared to her memory.

Until Genevieve.

Nothing in the world could have prepared me for Genevieve. She'd crept up on me, consuming more and more of my thoughts, day by day. And then she'd stolen my dreams.

A month ago, I'd woken up with a raging hard-on, dreaming that she'd come to the couch and straddled me in one of those short sleep shirts she wore sometimes. The dreams hadn't stopped since. Tonight, I'd dream of hiking up that tan skirt.

I was waking up earlier so I had time to get off in the shower and staunch some of the ache. I'd started wearing pants for sleep, anything to help hide my erection as I went into the bathroom every morning. She didn't need to know a man who was supposed to be her friend couldn't control his cock during a dream.

"Isaiah?"

My head snapped up from her skirt. "Sorry. What?"

"Your brother?"

"Oh." I rubbed the back of my neck, embarrassed she'd caught me staring at her ass. "He wanted to invite us to Lark Cove for Thanksgiving. I told him I'd check. But if you don't mind, I'd like to go."

"Sure." She nodded. "That sounds nice."

"Are you sure? You can stay here."

Her eyebrows came together. "Do you not want me to go?"

"No. That's not it. I just wasn't sure if you wanted to stay. Maybe do something with Draven."

"Oh." She shook her head. "No. I think Nick and Emmeline are coming up. He should spend time with them and their kids before . . ."

Before the trial.

Draven's case had been moving at a snail's pace, which

was a good thing. It gave us more time to find the real killer—if a miracle happened and a new lead surfaced.

Since the meeting with the Warriors last month, we hadn't heard a thing. It seemed . . . too easy. So we maintained our guard. I followed Genevieve to work every day. I went to follow her home each evening. As Bryce's pregnancy began to show, Dash became even more protective, and she went nowhere without him now.

The vibe in the shop had shifted this past month too. There wasn't as much teasing or banter. The air was heavier. It arrived each morning with Draven and lingered long after he'd left the office for the day.

Hope was waning. Dread was winning out.

Genevieve had been so steadfast and determined to find Amina's killer, but as the days had gone by and no new information had surfaced, the wind had left her sails. That notebook of hers appeared less and less. Not only would there be no vengeance for her mother, she was also going to lose her father.

Over the past month, Draven had come each Sunday morning to the apartment to take Genevieve to breakfast. I hadn't gone since the first time, making excuses so the two of them had some time alone.

Genevieve's heart was thawing toward Draven. She was softening with every encounter. Maybe she was even growing to love him. His incarceration was going to devastate her, whether she wanted to admit it or not.

"I'd better get to work." She sighed. "I've got a busy day."

She was pulling more and more from Jim, doing whatever she could to make his life easier so he could focus on Draven's case.

Jim would do his best to paint Draven and Amina as

reunited lovers. He would tell all the truths. The two had been affectionate and there was no motive for Draven to kill her, especially since they shared a daughter.

But the prosecution had the murder weapon. They had Draven at the scene. They had everything they needed to convict an innocent man.

"Let me start the cars and warm them up." I pulled on my boots and a coat, then took my keys and hers off the hook she'd hung beside a coat rack. "Be back."

I went outside, the snow muffling my steps down the stairs and on the pavement. I swept off Genevieve's car first and started it up, cranking the defrost and heat. Then I did the same for my truck. With them clear, I went back inside to find Genevieve on the couch, her shoulders slumped forward.

"What's wrong?"

"Nothing." She stood, wincing as she did. "I'm just sore today."

"Probably because you slept on the couch."

She'd insisted for a month. I'd refused for a month.

Then last night, she'd finally had her way. I'd been in the bathroom, brushing my teeth. When I'd come out, she'd already been tucked in on the couch, curled up and fast asleep. She'd looked so peaceful, and I'd left her there instead of carrying her to the bed.

I should have moved her.

But I hadn't been able to make myself pick her up. Carrying her to bed felt too intimate. So I'd told myself she'd get the couch for one night, then I'd take it back. I'd slept in the bed with the smell of her vanilla lotion and lavender shampoo on the pillow.

No surprise she'd been in my dreams.

"I'm taking the couch from now on."

She stretched her back, planting her hands on her hips and leaning back. "No, I'm fine. I'll get used to it."

No, she wouldn't. If I found her there again, I'd get over my own shit and put her in the bed. "Better wear a coat. It's cold."

"Okay." She shuffled to the coat rack and pulled off a black wool dress coat. Her eyelids drooped as she shrugged it on and tied the belt around her waist. The woman was dead on her feet.

"Maybe you should stay home. Sleep."

"I can't." She waved it off. "I'll be fine."

Her steps were sluggish as she trudged down the stairs. She cut through the snow, following my tracks to her car.

Should I drive her? Drop her off and pick her up? *Yes.* I reached out a hand to stop her but pulled it back.

Fuck me, I couldn't do it.

There was no way I'd be able to put her in the passenger seat.

Shame pulled heavy on my shoulders as I followed her to the driver's side door. This was just one of many reasons Genevieve didn't need me in her life. She might think she needed me, but she didn't.

How were we going to make the drive to Lark Cove? I hadn't thought that far ahead when I'd accepted Kaine's Thanksgiving invite. That trip would be hours. Driving separately wouldn't work this time. I didn't have an excuse to give.

Shit. Maybe I should cancel and blame it on the roads. But Kaine had asked me to come and I wouldn't say no to him. Not after he'd finally let me back into his life. He wanted to meet Genevieve and it wasn't possible for him to come down here. Piper was about six months pregnant, they had two-year-old twin boys, and they needed to be in their home.

Which left me with no choice. Somehow, I'd get Genevieve to Lark Cove and suffer through the many miles to do it.

"I'll text you when I'm ready to come home."

"'Kay." I closed the door for her, then walked to my truck.

The drive through town was uneventful and quiet. There weren't many cars out yet and those that were took the roads carefully. I idled outside the firm as Genevieve parked in the lot. I waved as she disappeared inside, then went to the garage and got to work.

As expected, it was a slow day. Emmett and I flipped a coin to see who'd take the one oil change we had on the schedule—I lost. Then we watched Leo do some freestyle pinstripes on the Lincoln in the paint booth. The man had a damn gift.

I barely blinked as he created orange and red flames set against gleaming black on the car's tail fins. I was so consumed with his brushstrokes, I nearly missed my phone vibrating in my pocket.

Genevieve's name flashed on the screen. It was only two o'clock in the afternoon.

"Hey," I answered, stepping out of the booth.

"Will you come get me? I don't feel good."

"Be there in five." I walked for the office door, not wasting even a second to punch out. With the snow and freezing temperatures, we'd cranked the heat in the shop and kept the bay doors closed, only opening them to pull a car inside or back it out.

"What's up?" Presley asked from her desk.

"I need to go get Genevieve."

"Everything okay?"

"She's sick." And I shouldn't have let her leave this morning.

I whipped the door open and stepped into the cold, jogging for my truck. The snow had returned. The wind had picked up, turning the loose flakes into miniature ice daggers that bit into my cheeks as I climbed into the truck.

The streets were slicker than they'd been this morning. I took a corner too fast and the end of my pickup fishtailed. I eased off the gas a bit even though all I wanted was to speed to the firm. I parked on the street, leaving the engine running as I hustled inside.

Genevieve was leaning against the reception desk. Her face was pale, her eyes red. She wore her purse like it weighed fifty pounds.

"I'll take it." I slipped the handbag from her shoulder, slinging it over mine.

"Feel better," the receptionist told Genevieve while giving me a once-over. I hadn't come inside their office before.

"Thanks, Gayle," Genevieve murmured. "See you tomorrow."

"No, she won't," I corrected. She was getting a long night's sleep and staying in bed tomorrow. She was so weak she could barely lift her feet. I pressed a hand to her forehead. "You're hot."

She gave me a little smile. "Is that why you were checking me out this morning?"

"Come on." I opened the door for her, ushering her outside.

"Brr. That's miserable." She shivered. "Will you dig my keys from my purse?"

"I'll drive."

Like I should have done this morning. There was no way she was getting behind a wheel on these roads and with her being sick. I led her to the truck and opened the door to help her inside.

The moment I closed her in, my stomach dropped.

Fuck, I couldn't do this. How was I supposed to do this?

You don't have a choice.

Genevieve had to get home. And I sure as fuck couldn't call someone to come and help. How many questions would that raise? Why couldn't I drive my wife home from work when she was sick?

I swallowed the bile that had risen in my throat and sucked in some oxygen, forcing the panic away. Then I walked around the truck, one step at a time, and climbed inside, focusing on each individual action.

I shut the door. I buckled my seat belt. I went to turn on the key but remembered the truck was already running. I put my foot on the brake. I shifted into drive.

Step by step.

I focused on driving. And not once did I look over at Genevieve. When she shifted, I blocked out the movement from the corner of my eye. I watched the road. I kept both hands on the steering wheel.

And at the one and only stop sign on the way home, I sat there, checking left and right, then right and left again, just to make sure no one would come sliding through the intersection.

Finally, when we pulled into the parking lot and I eased into her space by the office, I breathed. I blinked. I pried my fingers off the steering wheel and shut down the truck. Then, only then, did I look over at Genevieve as she leaned against the door, nearly asleep.

"Why was that hard for you?" she whispered.

Because you're you.

She was important. She was special and precious.

And I had the power to destroy her.

I avoided answering by escaping into the frigid cold. I rounded the hood and opened her door, catching her as she nearly fell out. "Whoa."

"Sorry. I'm a little dizzy." She swayed as she found her feet. There was no way she'd make it up the stairs.

I picked her up and cradled her in my arms. "I've got you."

"I can walk."

"Liar," I teased.

She let her forehead drop to my shoulder. "I hate it."

"Being sick?" I asked, jerking my chin when I caught sight of Presley in the window to the office.

"No. Being a liar."

"I was joking, doll."

"I know. But it's still true."

At the top of the stairs, I had to set her down to get the keys out of my pocket and open the door, then I scooped her right up again.

I let all reservation fly out the window as I carried her to bed. I set her down on the edge and knelt to unzip her boots. I helped her shimmy out of her skirt and into a pair of my sweatpants. I pulled her sweater over her head, leaving her bra on as I grabbed a T-shirt from the closet and yanked it over her hair.

"I'm going to go and get you some medicine." I yanked the covers back and guided her underneath.

"There's some NyQuil in the bathroom." She cuddled into the pillow I'd slept on last night. "Under the sink. It's probably expired but it'll do."

I hustled to find it. It was a month past expiration, but it had to be better than nothing. I came back, helping her sit up to take a swig.

"Blech." She stuck out her tongue. "Water."

"On it." I got her a glass and helped her take a drink. "What else?"

"Will you lie with me?" Her eyes were closed. She'd be out in minutes.

"Sure." I kicked off my boots and pulled off my sweatshirt. It smelled like metal from the garage and the wind from outside. Then I lay on top of the covers as she burrowed beneath.

"Thank you for coming to get me."

"No problem."

"I hope you don't get sick too. I'm probably contagious."

"I'll be fine." I tucked a strand of hair behind her ear. "Sleep."

She nodded. "I'm glad we're friends."

"Me too. Now sleep."

"You're my best friend." She spoke with her eyes closed, almost as if she were dreaming. She was definitely delirious from the fever. "I haven't had a best friend since fifth grade. Her name was Mandi. We had brass heart necklaces. You know, where one person has half a heart and the other has the other half."

"Yeah. Now go to sleep."

"Who's your best friend?" she chattered on.

"You," I admitted. Maybe if I answered her stream of crazy questions, she'd fall asleep.

"No, before me."

"Kaine."

"Your brother doesn't count. He's family. Otherwise I would have said my mom. Who else?"

I gulped. The truth would lead to more questions but I wouldn't lie—not to her. "Shannon."

Genevieve's lashes lifted. Those dark eyes, so beautiful, sank right into my soul, stirring feelings I'd thought were buried in Bozeman. "Who's Shannon?"

"Go to sleep, doll. Please?"

She nodded and closed her eyes. The questions stopped. Her breathing evened out. And when I knew she was out for good, I shifted on the bed to make myself more comfortable.

I took out my phone and texted Presley that I was done for the day. She texted back that she'd clock me out and let Dash know.

Genevieve would probably sleep for hours. She'd be fine if I went to the shop, but I wasn't leaving her alone. Not today. So I closed my eyes and let myself drift to sleep.

I dreamed of a woman with dark brown hair and a gorgeous smile she didn't use often enough. I dreamed of her whispering in the dark that she needed me.

I dreamed of my wife.

Until that dream turned into a nightmare, one where Genevieve sat limp in the passenger seat of a car as blood trickled down the side of her mouth.

And those expressive eyes I loved lost all their light.

CHAPTER FIFTEEN

GENEVIEVE

I stared out the window of the cabin, taking in the surrounding forest. The evergreens towered above us. The forest floor was dusted with a thin layer of snow. And even though I couldn't see it through the trees, I pictured the lake in the distance, long and wide and deep blue.

The town was smaller than Clifton Forge. Cozier. Coming here was the escape I'd needed. Here, there weren't motorcycle gangs—former or current. Here, the memory of my mother's murder seemed further away. Here, maybe Isaiah would finally open up to me about what had been bothering him for weeks.

"Remind me why you picked Clifton Forge? Because Lark Cove is gorgeous." Like, *I want to live here instead* gorgeous.

"I went where there was work." Isaiah kept his head down, studying the coffee table. Eye contact over the past three weeks had been nearly nonexistent.

"I like this cabin."

He lifted a shoulder. "Yeah."

"Better than the last one we were in together."

That got his attention. He looked over at me on the opposite end of the couch. My heart would have soared at a grin. I would have taken a frown. I was desperate for any reaction other than that fucking blank stare.

Gah! Why? I was about to leap across the couch and strangle him with my bare hands until he surrendered and told me what had happened when I'd been sick.

I remembered him coming to get me from the office. I remembered the massive surge of anxiety emanating off him as he drove me home. And I remembered him putting me to bed.

My nasty fever had taken two days to break. When I'd emerged from the haze, the Isaiah who'd grinned was gone. In his place was the shell of my friend. It was worse than it had been even in the early days of our marriage.

It had only gotten worse on the drive to Lark Cove.

Isaiah had asked me to drive. I was happy to, thinking maybe with some time trapped in the car, he would finally relax enough to tell me what was wrong. The road trips I'd taken with Mom as a kid had been filled with nonstop conversation. But this was hour after hour of silence. Even with the radio on, the quiet screamed.

His hands stayed braced on his knees the entire trip, his tattooed knuckles white as he gripped his legs. I made the mistake of looking at him once and asking if he was all right.

Eyes on the road.

Those were the only words he spoke to me besides *turn left, next right* and *keep going straight.*

By the time we reached Lark Cove, I was nearly in tears.

Where was Isaiah? *My* Isaiah? I thought we'd learned to rely on one another. Or had it just been me leaning on him this entire time? Did I give him no comfort? No strength? Would he ever trust me with the truth? There was only so much prying I could do. At some point, he had to put his faith in me, like I'd done with him.

Was it the holiday in general that had set him off? Did Isaiah not like Thanksgiving? He hadn't seemed anxious around his mom, but was there something going on with his brother? Maybe this trip was causing him stress.

I convinced myself Isaiah hated turkey and stuffing and pumpkin pie. After all, I hadn't done anything wrong except catch a bad cold. His attitude had nothing to do with me at all, right?

Wrong.

I pulled into Kaine and Piper's driveway behind Suzanne's Blazer and hadn't even shut off the car when the front door to their home opened. A man who had to be Kaine stepped out. He held two boys in his arms, both squirming and waving and laughing. Kaine smiled.

Isaiah smiled.

An actual, full smile, so stunning that tears flooded my eyes. The smile transformed Isaiah's face. He looked years younger. He was a thousand times more beautiful. The joy at seeing his brother broke through his cloud of sorrow—then faded as quickly as it had appeared.

When he unbuckled his seat belt and glanced at me, the sullen mood came roaring back.

I put on a brave face, hiding the fact that he'd just cracked my heart.

The trip was long and we arrived at twilight. We hurried to haul our things inside before dark, then went through a flurry of introductions with Kaine and Piper and their twins.

Suzanne wrapped me in a hug, strong and tight, that nearly crushed me. It was the hug of a mother.

I wasn't ready for those yet, not even from my mother-in-law.

So I focused on the kids, playing with them on the carpet before dinner.

Kaine was quiet, like his brother. Every now and then, he'd look at me with an odd expression like he wasn't sure where I'd come from. I caught the same look from Piper.

Everyone knew something I didn't. Something big.

What? What was it? Maybe I should have added Isaiah's name to my research notebook after all. But I wanted so badly for him to be the one to tell me. I wanted at least a piece of our relationship to be true and honest.

Except this was just another weekend to pretend. Isaiah held my hand when they were around, but there was no desperation in his grip.

We ate a delicious dinner after arriving, then escaped to this cabin, the home that had been Kaine's before Piper had moved in next door and the two had gotten together.

I slept in the bed, Isaiah on this couch. He made sure to get up early and stow away the blanket and pillow. Not wanting to wake the other house if they were still asleep, we'd spent the past hour on the couch, drinking coffee, barely speaking a word.

I stared at the forest and occasionally his profile.

Isaiah was memorizing the wood-grain pattern of the coffee table like there'd be a quiz later.

My first Thanksgiving without Mom would be hard enough this year without those blank stares from *my husband*. We were in a strange—yet breathtaking—place with people I'd met yesterday, and the ache I had for Mom's presence was nearly unbearable.

The holidays would be excruciating this year. Not once in my twenty-seven years had I spent a Christmas or Thanksgiving without my mom.

Thanksgiving had been her favorite while I'd preferred Christmas—presents and all. Our Thanksgiving tradition was to spend the entire day in the kitchen, preparing a feast. Often, it was only the two of us there to eat and we'd have leftovers for a week.

There'd be no cooking for me today. I'd offer to help out of politeness and pray my assistance was declined. And I'd endure Isaiah's silence like it didn't bother me in the slightest.

Something had flipped a switch in Isaiah, but what? Had I said something when I was sick that had upset him? I wished I could remember. Damn my stubbornness, I wouldn't ask either. He'd only shoot me down.

"I'm going to get dressed." I stood from the couch. "Then do you want to go over?"

He nodded, his eyes glued to his empty mug.

What did I do? Tell me. Please. What did I do?

He stared at the table.

I'd lost him.

My heart broke. My feelings toward Isaiah, the ones I wasn't ready to acknowledge, shattered.

I disappeared into the bedroom at the back of the house and pulled on some jeans and a sweater. I swiped on some deodorant, having showered last night. With my hair braided and hanging over one shoulder, I came out of the bedroom with my shoes in hand just in time to see Isaiah open the door.

"Morning." Kaine slapped him on the shoulder and stomped his boots dry on the mat as he came inside. When he spotted me, he said, "Morning, Genevieve. How'd you sleep?"

"Great," I lied. "Thanks again for having us."

"Glad you could make it up." Kaine ran a hand through his dark hair, pushing it off his forehead.

There were similarities between the Reynolds brothers, but they weren't mirror images. Kaine's hair was longer and his face was covered with a dark beard. They had the same eyes, only Kaine's were happy and full of life. Whenever he'd spotted Piper from across the room last night, they'd brimmed with love. It was the same when he'd looked upon his boys.

Kaine ducked to the window in the living room that over-looked the front of the cabin. Outside, Gabe and Robbie were playing.

There wasn't as much snow here as there was in Clifton Forge, but both boys were decked out in head-to-toe snow gear. Bibs. Puffy coats. Boots. Hats with earflaps. Mittens. All I could see were chubby cheeks, red noses, bright eyes and shining smiles.

They were the perfect picture.

Those twins made me want a pair of my own someday. A family that was mine. A love to fill the open void.

"Piper wants a Christmas tree," Kaine said. "I told the boys we'd go hunting for one. Want to come along?"

"Sure." Isaiah nodded, standing side by side with his brother. They were both about the same height, an inch or two over six feet tall.

"Genevieve?"

I'd never been Christmas tree hunting. Mine always

came from whatever church or youth camp stand was set up in the grocery store parking lot in Denver. Yes, I wanted to go. A new adventure sounded like a wonderful distraction.

But the one person who made Isaiah seem happy was his brother. Maybe if I wasn't around, he'd have some time to actually enjoy it and not feel the need to pretend with me.

"You guys go ahead. I didn't bring enough warm stuff to go traipsing through the mountains."

"Piper has lots of stuff you could borrow," Kaine offered.

"That's okay. I'll go over and see what I can do to help."

Isaiah took our coats down from the hook beside the door. I quickly pulled on my boots, then stood as he helped me into my coat. It probably looked sweet, a husband helping bundle up his wife.

Except Isaiah took care not to touch me, not even to brush my sweater with his knuckles. Kaine didn't notice, but I did.

"Do you want a tree?" Isaiah asked as he zipped up his own coat and pulled a beanie over his head.

"Could we even get it home?"

"We can hook it to the top of the car."

"That would be nice." Now that my painting project was done, I was out of things to keep me busy at night. Decorating a tree would occupy at least one night and give me a task to block out Isaiah's cold shoulder.

Kaine led the way outside and I followed, Isaiah closing up the cabin behind us.

"Koda!" Gabe laughed as he fell off the dog's back. The loose snow puffed up around him.

When I'd walked into Kaine and Piper's place last night, I'd gasped at the dog trotting down the hallway to greet us. I'd sworn it was a wolf.

Not a wolf, just a dog. Unless you asked the twins, who treated Koda more like a furry horse.

The second Koda's back was free, Robbie launched himself at the dog, scrambling to climb up. Koda sidestepped, causing Robbie to crash to the ground beside his brother. Then the dog licked their tiny faces, causing a fit of laughter that echoed through the trees.

Kaine chuckled, picking up an ax leaning against a post at the top of the porch stairs. "Come on, boys. Uncle Isaiah is coming with us."

The twins squealed in unison, struggling to stand with their thick clothing.

Kaine walked to them, patted Koda on the head, then helped his sons up, one by one.

I glanced at Isaiah, opening my mouth to wish him luck, but stopped when I saw the expression on his face.

"You're smiling." The whisper slipped out. The smile disappeared. That would teach me to keep my mouth shut. "You like being here, don't you?"

"I'm glad to see Kaine happy. He deserves it."

"And you don't?"

"No." Isaiah took the stairs and joined his brother and nephews without a backward glance.

Standing on the top step, I wrapped my arms around my waist. He believed he didn't deserve happiness down to the marrow of his bones.

Would he punish himself forever for his sins? Wasn't prison enough? Was this about Shannon, whoever she was? In the back of my mind, I knew the answer.

Shannon.

She was the key to his misery. Who was she to him? Did he love her still?

If he'd just open up a little bit, maybe I'd know how to help him. Maybe I'd know why he was this way and ease some of his pain—or at least stop resenting him for it.

I was his wife, after all. I'd always thought some other woman would come along and be the one to heal him. She'd be the one to put light in his eyes. But then months had passed. Feelings had grown. He didn't need another woman to break through his walls.

Isaiah needed me.

I waited until Kaine, Isaiah and the boys were off on a trail that headed deeper into the trees, then made my way across the trodden path that linked the cabin to the main house.

With a brief knock on the front door, I smiled as Suzanne opened it for me.

"Good morning!" She wrapped me in a hug, practically pulling me inside the house. "How did you sleep?"

"Great," I lied again. Every time, it was harder to keep the truth from leaking out. Wasn't lying supposed to get easier with practice?

I followed Suzanne into the kitchen, inhaling the scent of sage, fresh bread and turkey. "Good morning." I smiled at Piper. "It smells amazing in here. Can I help with anything?"

Say no.

"Thanks." She smiled, taking a sip from a mug. "And nothing. We're taking a break. The turkey's in the oven so we have a couple of hours. We'll do the rest later."

"Would you like some coffee?" Suzanne asked, going to a cupboard to take down a mug. "Or hot chocolate?"

"Coffee would be lovely. Thank you."

We all took our drinks into the living room off the kitchen, sitting on the comfortable sofas that filled the space.

"We're so glad you could come up here." Piper splayed a hand over her pregnant belly. "We've been anxious to meet you. I told Kaine we should go to you but he's been so busy in the shop. He's got orders for the next two years solid."

"He made this?" I ran my hand over the handcrafted wooden coffee table.

"Yep." Her smile was prouder than Suzanne's.

"It's exquisite." Though the piece that had really caught my eye was their dining room table. It was walnut, stained a dark brown that brought out the natural pattern of the grain. There were a couple of places where it looked as if I could reach into the boards and tickle the striations.

"I'd always hoped that Isaiah would want to work with Kaine," Suzanne said. "They'd make such a great team. Both are so good with their hands. But . . ."

I waited for her to continue, but she simply gave me this look, like she expected me to know the reason they didn't work together. She expected me to know about my husband's past when I did not.

The conversation turned to the twins and their excitement about having a baby sister. I refilled my coffee once more before excusing myself for the bathroom.

I was just coming down the hallway when Piper's voice caught my ear.

"Is he doing okay?" she asked Suzanne. "He seems . . . off. Maybe it's just me. Kaine thought he seemed fine, but I don't know. Maybe I'm just being hormonal."

My heart jumped into my throat. They had to be talking about Isaiah. Could they tell we weren't in love? Did Piper suspect our relationship was a fraud?

"He has his ups and downs." Suzanne sighed. "It's still hard. But I'm glad he has Genevieve. I mean, it has to mean something that he's finally opened up. The marriage was a surprise, but I'm taking it as a good sign. I didn't think he'd ever get over Shannon, but the way he looks at Genevieve, there's love there."

No, we were just getting too good at lying.

Suzanne spoke about me like I was some sort of savior. Would she hate me when Isaiah and I ended our marriage? Would she realize I'd caused more harm than good?

I wanted to change that. I wanted to help.

"Do you think he'll ever get over the accident?" Piper asked.

So it had been an accident, as I'd suspected.

"I don't know," Suzanne said. "I think when he comes here and sees Kaine happy, it helps. Maybe when he realizes that Kaine has forgiven him for Shannon, he'll finally forgive himself. I'm more worried about what happened in prison. He won't talk about it. I hope he confides in Genevieve."

Nope. Not a word.

Wait, what was I doing? I was intruding on their conversation. Sure, they probably would have had it if I were still sitting beside them on the couch because they expected I knew about Isaiah's past. They thought I knew about Shannon.

I hated eavesdropping, straining to soak up every word.

I hated that Isaiah was so lost in punishing himself he wouldn't confide in me.

God, I wanted the truth. I'd promised myself I wouldn't dig into Isaiah's past. Was this better? Hearing it rather than reading it? If I stood here long enough, I might get a taste. But guilt seeped into my veins and made my insides slimy.

Isaiah would confide in me when—if—he deemed me worthy.

I took a step, ready to head for the kitchen and make some excuse to change the subject. Hell, I'd even do some cooking if it changed the subject. But then Suzanne spoke again and my greedy ears devoured every one of her words.

"I pray with everything I have that he holds on to Genevieve. That they last. When he and Shannon got together, they were so worried about hiding it from Kaine until the baby was born. Then he finally proposed and . . . she died. I don't want him to have a love disappear again."

My stomach plummeted. My hands came to my ears, covering them up. It was information overload and I didn't want to hear another word.

Shannon was the pregnant woman he'd killed. Maybe I'd suspected it for a while, but to know it was true didn't make it easier to hear.

This was Isaiah's nightmare. He'd killed his fiancée.

And their baby.

CHAPTER SIXTEEN

ISAIAH

"Hey, guys," Dash called into the garage from the office doorway. "Take a break. We gotta talk."

I grabbed a rag to wipe my hands. There was some grease that would only come off with Fast Orange, but since Leo and Emmett didn't bother stopping at the sink to wash, I didn't either.

Dash was sitting in the chair across from Presley's desk. Her seat was empty and her car wasn't out front. Dash had probably sent her to the bank or post office before calling us in. He'd stopped sheltering us from these conversations—we were long past pretending Presley and I weren't at risk or that we didn't know something bad was going on. Though at times, he kept Presley on the fringe unless she was in danger.

Dash's elbows were balanced on his knees. In the chair next to him, Bryce had her arms crossed and her jaw was locked tight.

"What's up?" Emmett asked, taking one of the chairs along the window.

Leo stayed standing. So did I, taking up the space next to him to lean against the wall.

"Dad called ten minutes ago," Dash said. "Prosecution's done presenting their case."

"Already?" Leo asked.

"Yeah." Dash sighed. "They wrapped up faster than Jim had hoped. Now it's his turn to present."

Shit. Did Genevieve know? She had to know. She just hadn't texted me.

It had been two and a half weeks since we'd gone to Lark Cove for Thanksgiving, and in that time, we'd hardly spoken a word, though she'd been a constant worry on my mind.

I had to find a way to set her free.

God, I would miss her, but this marriage, this fake marriage, was killing us both.

We were as cold to one another as the mid-December air. The quiet, I could live with. That wasn't hard for me to endure.

Except every now and then, I'd catch her staring at me. Watching. When I'd meet her gaze, hers would be full of pity.

I fucking hated pity.

Those pitiful glances had started after Thanksgiving. If I had to guess, Mom or Piper had said too much. Had they told her about the accident? Had they told her about Shannon?

As pissed as I was that they'd talk to Genevieve about family business, I couldn't exactly blame them. No doubt they thought she already knew.

Bringing it up with Genevieve wasn't an option. If they hadn't told her, it would only lead to more questions. I was sick to death of the questions. Of the secrets. Of the lies.

Of the pity.

All the reasons we'd done this in the first place be damned. Living this way was eating me alive. And keeping her tied to a man like me wasn't fair to Genevieve. She deserved more.

It was time to let her go. It was time to break this off. I'd deal with the consequences.

It was time to plan an exit strategy.

"What now?" Emmett asked.

"Nothing." Bryce huffed. "We have nothing. No leads. No information to go on. Whoever kidnapped us has disappeared. Whoever Amina was dating, that Lee guy, he's gone. And it pisses me off."

Dash put his hand on her knee as it bounced. "We always knew this could happen."

"That's not good enough, Dash." She stood from the chair and paced the room. "What happens when this guy decides it's your turn next? Or Emmett's? Or Leo's? We're helpless. He's out there, watching as his master plan unfolds. Draven will go to prison. And the rest of us will look over our shoulders for the rest of our lives. We can't live like that."

Her chin quivered, her arms cinching tighter around her ribs. Dash was out of his chair in a flash, pulling her into his arms as her forehead dropped to his shoulder.

"She's right." Leo blew out a deep breath. "Draven goes to prison and this guy wins. And if this really is about some old war with the Kings, we're all next."

Even I wasn't safe. I'd never been a Tin King, but I'd been on that mountain too. "What can we do?"

"We've tried everything. Every damn thing." Emmett ran a hand over his hair.

"I think we need to push harder to find Amina's

boyfriend." Bryce stepped away from Dash, sniffling. She wasn't a crier so seeing her like this was odd. Maybe it was the pregnancy hormones, but she was cracking.

"The boyfriend's a ghost," Emmett said. "A dead end."

"But he's all there is," Bryce insisted. "He's the only person in Amina's life we haven't tracked down. And doesn't that seem suspicious? She'd been seeing this guy and she dies, then he just disappears?"

"Maybe they broke up before she died." Amina had hooked up with Draven in that motel. For Genevieve's sake, I hoped Amina hadn't cheated. Again. "That would explain why he never showed up. Maybe she'd already called it off, so she was free to hook up with Draven."

Bryce nodded. "Maybe. But we won't know anything until we find him."

"How, babe?" Dash plopped back down in his chair. "All we have is a first name. Lee is not exactly unique."

"And Genevieve has racked her brain," I said. "She can't think of anything else."

"What about Amina's things?" Bryce asked. "Did Genevieve find anything in them that might have been Lee's?"

"No. Nothing."

"Damn it," she muttered.

A car door slammed outside, drawing our attention. Genevieve stomped from her car to the stairs. The look on her face was blank, her eyes turned down to the shoveled cement.

"Be right back." I hurried to the door, just in time to stop Genevieve before she'd gotten past the fifth step. "Hey. You didn't text me to come get you."

"No, I didn't," she snapped. "For once, I wanted to drive myself home."

"You heard about the trial."

"Yep."

"What did Jim say?"

She sighed. "The prosecution has a strong argument and things aren't looking good. They had three officers present. The witness who saw Draven come and leave from the motel. A fingerprint expert for the knife. A crime lab tech for the DNA and blood. It's done, so I decided to take the rest of the day off."

"You okay?"

"Fantastic," she deadpanned. "Draven will go to prison for murdering my mother. Life's grand."

"We're just talking about it." I tossed my thumb over my shoulder to the office. "Come on in."

"No, thanks."

"Please? You're not the only one who's upset."

"Fine." She grumbled something else under her breath before sulking down the stairs. She gave me that goddamn pitiful look as I opened the door for her, waving her in and out of the cold.

"I'm sorry, Genevieve." Bryce stood to give her friend a hug.

"Me too." Genevieve unwrapped the scarf around her neck and took a chair next to Emmett.

"We were just talking about what we could do," I told her as I sat by her side in the last open chair.

"Nothing." She shook her head, digging in her purse for her notebook. "There's nothing to do. I've been over and over things. I've researched every single person who could have been involved and there's nothing to find."

"You've been what?" Dash asked, sharing a look with Bryce.

"Researching." Genevieve waved the notebook. "Criminal records. Background checks. Personal information. I've looked into all the known associates of the Tin King Motorcycle Club, you included, and whoever I could find linked to the Warriors."

The room went silent.

I blinked, my eyes glued to that notebook. Was my name in there? Was that how she knew about me? Had she known all along?

My pulse raced with a mixture of fear and anger that she'd kept this from me. When had she been doing this?

"Why didn't you tell me?" Bryce asked.

"Because." Her shoulders fell. "There's nothing, so what does it matter?"

Emmett held out his hand. "Mind if I take a look?"

She clung to her notebook for a second, then sighed and handed it over.

He flipped through the pages quickly, nodding as he went. "I'm impressed. You've got nearly everyone in here. Us included."

Genevieve took the notebook back and looked at Bryce. "Except you. And Isaiah."

The air rushed from my lungs. So she hadn't dug into my past. She'd respected my privacy even though she wanted to know so badly. She'd waited, giving me time, and hoping I'd open up.

Damn.

"You went behind our backs," Dash said.

Genevieve held up her chin. "Yes, I did. Because I didn't know you."

Dash shot her a glare and opened his mouth, but Bryce spoke over him. "I think it was smart. I would have done the same thing. I just wish you had found something."

"Me too," Genevieve muttered.

"I still feel like your mom's boyfriend might lead us to a clue."

Genevieve nodded. "So do I. Mom was always so vague about him. She always brushed him off as casual, which would make sense if he was a Warrior. She wouldn't want to pull me into that."

And clearly Amina had a thing for bikers.

"Did you find any mention of a guy named Lee?" Emmett asked. "Because I've done my own research and can't find a damn thing."

"Nothing." Genevieve ran her thumb along the notebook. "Maybe some of you can look through the names. None of the Warriors I found are named Lee, but maybe I missed someone."

"I'll do it." Emmett nodded.

"When you went through her stuff, you didn't see anything that might have been his, did you?" Bryce asked.

Genevieve shook her head. "Nothing jumped out at me. I could go through it all again. Just to double-check."

"Do it," Dash ordered, the frown still on his face. "What about her stuff? Was there anything missing?"

"I didn't exactly take an inventory of my dead mother's things."

"Then do it now," Dash barked.

I took a step forward, ready to step in, but Genevieve noticed and held out a hand, stopping me.

"Why?" she asked Dash.

"Because maybe he took something of hers. Jewelry or a

trinket, or I don't know. Something valuable. If he pawned it in town or even in Bozeman, we might be able to track it down."

"Oh," she muttered. "Okay."

"Any word from the Warriors?" Leo asked.

"Not a word," Dash answered. "Which normally would be a good thing, but my gut says we'll be hearing from Tucker before too long."

"You don't think he believed us?" Genevieve asked.

"I think his hands are tied too. He wants to know who killed his man. That's the same guy we're looking for. We're not stopping. Neither will he."

Fuck. Would this ever go away?

At least twice a week I woke from that damned repeat nightmare. Genevieve was in her car in the passenger seat. The grill of a truck was smashed against the broken glass of her window. Her eyes were lifeless and blood oozed from her mouth.

Would that be her fate? Would she die too if she stayed here? Enough was enough. It was time to free her from this shit and let her get on with her life.

The best place for Genevieve was far, far away from me. She wouldn't leave willingly, not until she knew I was out of danger. Maybe if we found the man who killed her mother, we'd be able to convince the Warriors he'd also killed their man. Then she'd be safe to leave too.

I'd help her go through her mother's things and pray we found a clue.

"Do you think it's worth me digging through Amina's finances again?" Emmett asked Dash.

"Again?" Genevieve asked before Dash could answer. "Do I even want to know how you can do that?"

"Probably not." Emmett shrugged. "I didn't find anything the first time. Might be worth a second look."

Genevieve stood from her chair, taking her scarf and purse. "I'll let you guys know if I find anything."

She was out the door before anyone could respond. There was a sheen of tears in her eyes.

"Do you need me the rest of the day?" I asked Dash. "The job board is clear. I was just cleaning up."

"Nah, go ahead. It's dead. I'll finish up."

"Thanks." I went back into the shop, unzipping my coveralls and stripping them down to hang on a hook for tomorrow. Then I went to the sink and scrubbed my hands, doing my best to get the grease off.

My cuticles were cracked, the tips of my fingers raw. They were normally rough but the air this time of year was so dry, I took extra care. Presley had put a bottle of lotion next to the sink for us to use and I slathered some on, dug my ring from my pocket and slid it on, then ventured upstairs to the apartment.

Genevieve was on the couch when I walked into the apartment. Her knees were pulled up to her chest. Her arms were wrapped around them, hugging them tight.

"You okay?"

"Fine."

She wouldn't be *fine* until this was over.

I kicked off my boots, stacking them on the mat so the snow wouldn't follow me into the apartment. Then I crossed the room, taking a seat on the couch beside her, one cushion away.

"Why didn't you tell me about your research?"

She lifted a shoulder. "Because there wasn't anything to

tell. And it was something I could do on my own. I just need-ed . . . I needed to try."

It made sense now why she'd been so frustrated. She'd been searching for clues and coming up empty at every turn.

"I've been thinking about something." I ran a hand over my jaw, loosening it. I'd been thinking about this for weeks, but the words were like molasses.

"What?"

"As soon as the trial is over, once we know what will happen with Draven . . ." I blew out a deep breath. "I think you should go."

"Go?" She blinked. "Go where?"

"Away. Get out of this town. Get out of this life."

"What?" She let go of her legs and turned to face me. "What about you?"

"I'll be fine." And if I wasn't, it wouldn't be her problem anymore. "The cops didn't find anything. I doubt they will. They probably aren't even looking."

"And the Warriors?"

"If they decide to retaliate, it would be best if you were already long gone."

Her mouth fell open. "So . . . we just call it quits?"

"Yeah."

She stared at me for a long moment. The surprise on her face faded. Her shoulders fell. "Am I that hard to be around?"

"The truth?" I swallowed hard. "Yes."

She flinched.

It was unbearable to be around her, knowing she'd even-tually leave. It was exhausting to keep her at arm's length when all I wanted to do was hold her close.

"We never should have started this," I whispered.

Genevieve pushed off the couch and marched for the bathroom. The door slammed, its boom shaking the walls.

I dropped my head to the back of the couch. *Done. It's done.*

And I was a bastard for hurting her.

There was a small spot on the ceiling Genevieve had missed when painting. It was no bigger than a dime, but the off-white of the old paint showed if you caught it from this angle. She'd fix it if she knew, but I wouldn't say a word. I wanted that spot to remember the months we'd spent together.

Genevieve might be upset now, but she'd see this was the right call. Eventually, she'd be relieved that my shackle was no longer around her ankle.

The bathroom door whipped open and the wounded Genevieve who'd been on the couch had disappeared. She pounded across the apartment in her bare feet, stopping right in front of me. "What's the real reason you're doing this?"

"It'll be better if we end this now."

"I don't believe you." She held her chin high. "I have opened up my heart to you. I've told you everything about my mom. About how I'm really feeling. I laid it all out there. I cut myself open and let you see the ugly mess inside. You're the one person in the world who gets the real me. Why can't I have that from you?"

I stared up at her beautiful, flushed face and stayed quiet. Silence was my armor. Because if *I* cut myself open, I'd never be able to sew the wounds shut.

"That's it?" she whispered. "Isaiah, I want to help. I want to be there for you like you are for me. But you have to talk about the accident. If not with me, then someone. I see this guilt. This pain in your eyes and it kills—"

"Who told you about the accident? Or did you look it up?"

She blinked. Her face paled.

"Did you?" I demanded, louder this time.

"No. I didn't look it up. I-I was—"

I was off the couch in a flash, my heart pounding. The movement forced her to take two steps back. "Someone told you. Who? Was it Mom? Because she had no right."

"She didn't tell me anything." Genevieve held up her hands. "I overheard her and Piper at Thanksgiving. I shouldn't have eavesdr—"

"No, you shouldn't have. That's none of your fucking business. That's between me and my family."

"Then don't take me to meet your family," she yelled. "Don't blame them for assuming you'd tell your *wife* about your fiancée. That you were going to have a baby. That she died in an accident and you're blaming yourself."

She had it all wrong. She saw me as a tragedy. No, I was a killer. "You don't know what you're talking about."

"Exactly!" She threw her hands into the air. "I don't have a fucking clue what I'm talking about because you—" She poked a finger in my chest hard enough to leave a red mark. "You don't tell me anything."

I clamped my mouth shut.

Her nostrils flared as she did the same.

We stood there in a soundless standoff. If she was expecting me to talk, she had to know I wouldn't—couldn't.

Finally, her fuming breaths slowed. Her furious gaze chilled. "You're right. What am I doing here? It doesn't even matter. I was wrong about the law."

"What? Say that again."

"The law. I was wrong. Montana doesn't have testimo-

217

nial privilege like I assumed, which means this marriage was doomed from the start."

My head was spinning. Was she saying that we didn't have to get married? That it wouldn't protect us? How long had she known?

Why had she stayed?

"Slow down, I—"

"So you're right." Genevieve huffed. "We're strangers. I call you my husband. You call me your wife. But we're strangers. Hell, you even cringe when I kiss you."

This woman was making no sense. I didn't cringe when I kissed her. "What are you talking about?"

"I'm talking about this." She took my face in her hands, pulling me down for a kiss.

The softness of her lips, her subtle taste—I tensed.

I always tensed.

It was the only way to hold myself back.

She let me go and pointed at my face. "There. That. You look like you're about ready to crawl out of your skin because I kissed you. And you know what? I hate you for it. *I hate you for it.* Because I look forward to every single one of those pretend kisses even though you look like—"

I crushed her lips to mine. I wound my arms around her back and hauled her to my chest. I ran my tongue across her bottom lip. I moaned into her mouth as she let me dip inside for a taste. I kissed her the way I'd wanted to kiss her for months.

Genevieve had the power to destroy me completely. My life would be in ruins when she walked away. This kiss wouldn't change the future.

I shoved those thoughts away.

And I kissed my wife.

CHAPTER SEVENTEEN

GENEVIEVE

I saiah had kissed me. He *was* kissing me.

And damn, he tasted good.

I leaned into the kiss, drinking him in. I shuddered as his rough hands roamed my curves. I relaxed in the hold of his strong arms.

Any moment now he'd push me away. He'd retreat behind those sky-high walls and any chance I had at breaking through would evaporate into thin air. So I savored his kiss—every wet lick, every sharp nip—praying it would continue for just one more minute.

Isaiah let a groan loose and it hummed into my mouth and down to my center. My hands were between us, my fingers splayed over his T-shirt, pressing firm into the warm, taut muscle beneath. I risked a move and let my hands drift lower. His abs really were as hard as they looked.

His lips broke away from mine and my eyes snapped open. I expected to see horror or disgust. Instead, his gaze was pure lust. The colors darkened, the outer ring of chocolate seeping into the green and gold swirls as Isaiah framed my face.

I held my breath.

Would he kiss me? Would he tell me to go?

I wasn't ready for this marriage—sham marriage—to end.

"What do I do?" he whispered.

"Kiss me," I whispered back.

He dipped his head, tilting mine just where he wanted it. The first kiss had been a release. A test. But what came next was so full of heat and power, it left me dizzy.

Isaiah's tongue slipped between my lips, caressing against mine in long, languid strokes. He shifted his hips forward, letting me feel the arousal behind his zipper.

I moaned, my knees weakening. We were moving in a slow shuffle that felt more like swaying in place until I realized Isaiah had taken us to the bed.

My racing heart skidded to a dead stop.

Was that where we were going? Sex? My core clenched. I wanted Isaiah more than I'd ever wanted a man in my life, but was this smart? We'd been fighting minutes ago. He'd asked me to leave.

His fingers dropped from my face and drifted down my neck. They pressed into my skin, branding me with his touch as they slipped lower. In one large hand, he cupped my breast through my sweater, filling his palm.

My breath hitched. My head lolled and I arched into his grip. *Don't think.* I shut off my brain, the common sense and worry. I would not overthink this and sabotage the one good thing I'd felt in months.

Isaiah was kissing me. We had no audience. We had no ulterior motive. This kiss was mine.

And so was he for the moment.

I reached for the hem of his shirt, lifting it above his navel to feel his warm skin underneath. The touch caused Isaiah's muscles to bunch even tighter, but it wasn't a cringe. This was tension from a lover's touch. It was anticipation that I'd slide my fingers into the waistband of his jeans. The moment my nails raked over the line of hair below his navel, our kiss took on a whole new intensity, his tongue plundering instead of exploring. Our mouths fused.

I went for the button on his jeans, needing both hands to flip it open. Isaiah used his other hand to palm my ass.

"Genevieve," Isaiah warned, breaking away from our kiss.

No. My spirits crashed. I'd gone too far. I'd pressed too fast.

"I want to," I blurted. My eyes pleaded with his. "Once. Just once."

Isaiah studied my face, a crease forming between his eyebrows. Then, after what felt like hours, he nodded.

I stood on my toes, smashing my mouth against his. My palms skimmed over his short hair for a brief moment before moving in a frenzy to pull up his shirt. With it raised between us, I tugged at the zipper on his jeans. He met me step for step, until my sweater was stripped over my head and the black lace of my bra rubbed against his skin.

He reached behind his head and yanked off his T-shirt before coming back to me, cupping one breast while the other went to the side zipper on my trousers. They fell into a puddle at my bare feet.

Then I was up and moving, my lips ripped away from Isaiah's as he hoisted me by my thighs.

My center was pressed against his erection, the dull ache becoming a pulse that couldn't be ignored. I wrapped my arms around his shoulders, holding on as he laid me on the bed, his nose running along my neck as he dragged in a deep breath of my scent.

Then his tongue went back to work, licking like my skin was made of melting ice cream. Isaiah's hands went to his jeans, pushing them over his hips. I looked down to see those black boxer briefs I'd grown to love. They contained his straining bulge but just barely.

He lifted off me, grabbed one of my hands and hauled me up to a seat. Then he flicked the center clasp on my bra, replacing the lace with his hands.

"Oh, God," I moaned, my head rolling loose the moment he had my nipples pinched between those calloused fingers. I squirmed and lifted my hips, desperate to feel his thick cock pressed against my panties.

He shifted us deeper into the bed, settling his weight into the cradle of my hips and forcing my thighs apart. My bra was stretched behind me from one elbow to the other. My knees were up and bent, my legs splayed open. It was a wanton position, no holds barred. I closed my eyes and offered my body for his taking.

Isaiah drew a long, cool line with the tip of his tongue from my collarbone through the valley of my breasts. Then he stepped away, leaving me cold and breathless. The bed shook as he retreated.

My eyes stayed closed. My breaths came in heavy pants. Was he coming back? If he quit on me now, I would have to flee this apartment. Mortification would demand I disappear forever.

His knee hit the bed and a relieved cry nearly escaped my lips. I dared to crack open my eyes. They widened when I saw a hot and very naked Isaiah coming my way.

Good God, he was gorgeous. He was all inked skin strung over tight, bulging muscle. A work of art and beauty.

Isaiah looked in the mirror and saw everlasting broken pieces, but maybe my broken pieces would fit with his. Together, maybe we'd make a whole.

My hands went to my panties, pushing them down as my hips lifted off the bed. Isaiah's eyes were glued to my pussy as I bared myself, kicking the black lace to the floor and shedding the straps of my bra.

He swallowed hard, tearing his eyes away to meet my gaze. "Fuck, I don't deserve you."

"Take me anyway."

We were a blur as he captured my mouth in another scorching kiss. I was lightheaded and shaking as he positioned himself at my entrance and rocked us together.

I gasped at the connection. I was almost too full, the emotion too much. Sex had never been like this, threatening to consume me whole. I leaned into it too, taking Isaiah's face in my hands to kiss him again as he started moving in deep, slow thrusts.

The build of my orgasm was like a brewing thunderstorm, the clouds billowing, the lightning looming, until there was no choice but to relish the downpour.

"Isaiah," I moaned as my orgasm broke.

He groaned my name, dropping his head into my hair as his body trembled against mine. A sheen of sweat covered us both as he poured his release inside me. And then he collapsed, dropping to give me his weight as we both rode out the aftershocks.

I clung to him. He clung to me. His arms slid beneath my back, wrapping me up tight.

We'd both needed that connection for far too long.

"We didn't use a condom." He sighed, sliding out. He flopped into the empty space beside me, staring at the ceiling. It was cold without his body on mine. "Goddamn it. Sorry. I don't even have any."

"I'm on the pill. And I'm clean. I haven't been with anyone in a long, long time."

"Me neither."

What about Shannon? Now was not the time to think of her. Not here in this bed. Not when for a few minutes, he was mine.

I rolled out of bed and walked to the bathroom on wobbly legs to clean myself up. I expected to find Isaiah on the couch when I emerged, those walls snapping back into place. When I came out wearing nothing, my steps faltered to see him in bed beneath the covers.

My side was turned down and waiting.

"I'm not ready for it to be over." He cast me a longing glance. "Not yet."

Me neither. I smiled and padded to the bed to crawl in beside him.

We curled together. My head rested on his chest. His hand closed over mine on his stomach. Our legs intertwined.

The pieces fit.

————

"HI." My face flushed as I came out of the bathroom the next morning.

"Hey." Isaiah turned from his seat at the table that separated the kitchen and the couch. There were only two chairs and the table barely held a large pizza. But we'd been sharing meals there for months.

224

He'd dressed while I'd been in the shower. He had on a pair of faded jeans and his normal black T-shirt. His feet were bare.

I inched my way across the apartment, wishing we could have stayed in the bubble from yesterday. We'd stayed in bed all evening, alternating between sex and sleep, until I'd drifted off into a dreamless slumber. As the morning light had snuck through the windows, reality had come crashing back. I'd woken up to find Isaiah on the couch. He'd moved sometime in the night.

"So . . ." This was the most awkward morning of my life. Worse than the first morning he'd stayed here after we'd gotten married. "Should we talk?"

He sighed, nodding to his coffee cup.

Coffee. Coffee would be good.

I went to the pot, busying myself by filling a cup and then mixing in some creamer, using the menial tasks to avoid direct eye contact.

Why had I asked him to talk? I didn't want to talk. I wanted to escape this apartment and go to work, where I could lose myself in paperwork and research, where I would try not to think about sex with Isaiah.

Mind-blowing, marriage-shattering sex.

Shit. I was stupid.

The one thing I'd been able to count on these past few months was Isaiah. He was my new constant, even with his hot-and-cold behavior. He might be sullen and somber, but he was always there. His friendship was the most important relationship in my life.

After last night, I could kiss it all goodbye. But conversation couldn't be avoided. And before we talked about the sex, we had to address everything that had come before.

"Do you really want to call this quits?" I asked, watching my spoon swirl in the tan liquid in my cup.

"Yes."

Don't cry. I wasn't going to cry. Yet. I'd wait until I was in the safety of the bathroom at the office.

At first, I'd been so focused on leaving Clifton Forge, I hadn't noticed how it had crept up on me. But it was home. This apartment was my sanctuary. I loved my job and wasn't ready to give it up yet. Coffee dates with Bryce and Sunday breakfasts with Draven had filled a gaping hole in my heart.

And at the center of it all was Isaiah.

"Why?" I whispered. Was he miserable here?

"For your own sake."

I took in those tormented eyes and my heart squeezed. Had sex made it worse? "I don't understand. Why do you see yourself as such a monster?"

"Because I am."

"You're not. Do you think I would have stayed when I didn't have to if I thought you were a terrible human being?"

I'd stayed because there was so much good in him, even if he didn't see it himself.

"Isaiah, I stayed. For you."

"You shouldn't have." His Adam's apple bobbed. "I killed Shannon."

"But it was an accident." Right? They called them accidents for a reason, because no person was at fault.

"You only got a piece of the story from Mom."

"Then tell me the whole story. Please?" I begged.

Isaiah stood and rubbed the back of his neck as he paced the open space in front of the couch. "I don't like to talk about it."

"Either you tell me, or I'm left guessing. I've been

guessing for months. Do you really think the truth is worse than anything I've imagined?"

He went to the couch, collapsing onto the edge. "Shannon was my best friend. I met her after she showed up on Kaine's doorstep one morning and told him she was pregnant."

I jerked, the coffee sloshing over the rim of my mug. "Kaine?"

He nodded. "They met in a bar. Hooked up. Went their separate ways. She came back when she found out she was pregnant."

"Oh." It hadn't been Isaiah's baby.

"She moved in with Kaine but they weren't together. But Kaine wouldn't have had it any other way. He didn't want to miss anything with the pregnancy. They dated for a while. He even asked Shannon to marry him, but they didn't love one another, not like that. She turned him down."

My heart was in my throat as he spoke. His voice was laced with so much pain and regret, it made breathing difficult.

"They didn't work as a couple, but as roommates, things were pretty good. The excitement for the baby just drowned out everything else. Mom was over the moon. I was looking forward to becoming an uncle. And Shannon, she would have been a good mother. The best. No matter where she went, she had a pregnancy book in her purse. I think she'd nearly memorized the thing by the time she, uh . . . died."

"How?"

"I killed her."

He kept saying that, but it made no sense. He wasn't a murderer. He was a protector. A good man with a broken heart.

"How?" I needed details so I could prove him wrong.

"She was there all the time. At Kaine's. And he was my brother. My best friend. So I hung out at his place a lot too."

"You fell in love with her?"

He stared blankly across the apartment. "She smiled all the time. And she loved me. She chose me, not Kaine. Not many people did that."

"Did Kaine know?"

Isaiah shook his head. "No. We didn't want to tell him until it was the right time. He was so focused on the baby, building a bassinet and helping narrow down names, we didn't want to take that from him. It was his baby, not mine."

I put a hand over my aching heart. How hard had that been for him? To see his brother's child growing inside the woman he loved?

"When she was about eight months' pregnant, she told me she wanted to move out. That she wanted us to find a place to settle together. I was still nervous about telling Kaine, but Shannon had such faith that we'd make it work. 'Our beautiful unusual family.' That's what she called us."

His eyes were glassy. A tear slid down his cheek and he wiped it away. "I didn't want to just move in together. I wanted to marry her so I asked her to dinner one night. Got down on one knee and proposed. The restaurant cheered. Shannon cried."

My heart thundered. My throat burned at the mental picture.

I bet he'd laughed. I bet he'd smiled. It was strange to think of him happy and in love, something I hadn't seen with my own eyes, but I could imagine it as clearly as I saw him hunched on the couch.

He wasn't that man anymore.

Shannon's version of Isaiah had died with her.

"I had three beers to celebrate when I should have stopped at two. I wasn't hammered but I shouldn't have had that last beer. On the drive home, I was teasing her about how I'd have to get her ring resized after the baby because her knuckles were so fat. They weren't. We were laughing. I had one hand on the wheel and I leaned over because I wanted to kiss her. We didn't get to kiss much because we were too worried Kaine would find out."

I closed my eyes, bracing for the rest. I didn't need him to continue. The rest was easy to assume with near certainty. But Isaiah kept talking, the story no longer for me, but for himself.

Had he told anyone since the accident? A cellmate in prison? Or had he held it inside all this time?

"I blew through a stop sign going forty in a twenty-five and got T-boned by a truck going thirty. That's what the police report said. All I know was it felt like we got hit by a train. I got knocked around. The truck pushed us clear through the intersection. When I got my bearings back, Shannon was . . ."

Gone.

She'd died. And the baby too.

A tear fell down my cheek, landing on the floor by my foot.

It all made sense now. Why he was so relieved to see Kaine happy. Why he didn't drink. Why he acted so tense and miserable when he was in the car with me.

This accident had altered the path of his life.

I set my coffee aside and went to the couch. Isaiah kept his gaze forward, even as I placed my hand on his thigh. "It was an accident."

"No, I killed them."

"No, it was an accident," I repeated. "I know the difference. You killed the man in the cabin."

He turned to me, the sorrow disappearing in confusion. "Huh?"

"You strangled him to death. You killed him."

He blinked. "Yeah. So?"

"So? Did you love him? That man?"

"No."

"Do you feel guilty for killing him?"

His jaw ticked. "No."

"If you need to claim a murder, claim *that* murder. But don't put Shannon's life on your hands. It was an accident. And from what I can tell, the only person who blames you is yourself."

He studied my face, his expression blank. He'd gone too many years thinking he'd killed Shannon. That he'd killed Kaine's baby. He'd spent too many days and nights blaming himself. I probably wasn't the first person to try and convince him it was an accident.

I wasn't the first person who'd fail.

Until Isaiah decided to give himself a reprieve, he'd never be free to move on from Shannon's death.

"Thank you for telling me."

He faced forward, nodding his head. "Now you see."

"See what?"

"Why you have to go. Because I don't deserve to have you here. Not after what I did. And I've got nothing to give you."

Wrong again. He had love to give. It might not show on the surface, but it was there, peeking out when he looked at his brother. Or hugged his mom. Or played with his nephews. Isaiah was shoving me out the door because he was terrified of the connection between us.

"I'm not leaving. I made that decision months ago and I'm not changing my mind now."

His shoulders fell. "Genevieve, please."

"No. Knowing the whole story doesn't change anything. Just like last night, us being together, doesn't change anything."

Another lie.

Last night, he'd let down his guard.

Last night, I'd fallen asleep in his arms.

And last night, I'd stopped pretending I wasn't in love with my husband.

CHAPTER EIGHTEEN

ISAIAH

"I s this it?" I held up a necklace I'd found at the bottom of a plastic tote.

Genevieve looked up from the tote she'd been digging through and frowned. "No. It's not in this box either."

"Damn. Sorry, V." I put the necklace back where I'd found it.

"I hate that Dash might have been right about this." She put the lid on her tote. "I hate that I didn't think of it myself."

"I know. But you'll feel better if we catch a break."

"I hope so." She sighed. "We'd better get going, or we'll be late."

I nodded, closing the tub to stand and grab my coat. I shrugged it on and helped Genevieve into hers. We collected hats and gloves and scarves and walked outside.

It was pitch black. The stars and moon were hidden by the clouds that had rolled in this morning. The forecast was calling for a light snow, fitting since we were headed for the Clifton Forge Christmas Stroll downtown.

Genevieve gripped the railing as we descended the slippery stairs. "I wish I could remember if I'd packed up that necklace at Mom's house. Maybe she lost it. Or maybe I lost it. Maybe it's in all my stuff in storage."

"You put everything in those totes?"

"Yep." She nodded. "Everything else I left in her house to sell furnished."

"Lee might have taken it."

"Bastard," she muttered. "I liked that necklace and I don't want to think of him touching it. It was the one I wore to my senior prom. It had this dainty gold chain and a small North Star pendant with a white crystal in the center. It probably cost ten bucks but she'd had it forever. At least I have the ones she wore more often."

We'd spent the better part of the afternoon going through those totes, like we'd promised Dash and Bryce earlier in the week. The minute we'd pulled the boxes down, Genevieve had started cataloging jewelry. I was glad she had the task, something concrete to focus on so that rummaging through her mother's things didn't make her as sad.

It worked. Not once had I caught her teary-eyed. Instead, she'd held her face in utter concentration, inspecting everything she touched. She'd searched through every book, every envelope, every item. The necklace was the only thing she couldn't find. And there had been no hint of Amina's boyfriend Lee. Nothing he might have left behind.

We reached the last step and she let go of my arm to walk to the driver's side of her car. "Are you sure about this?"

I took a deep breath. "Yeah."

"I don't mind if you want to drive separately."

"I'll be all right." I opened the door and climbed inside. Riding shotgun was better than driving her around.

She got in and gave me a reassuring smile.

The car was warm and running. I'd come out ten minutes ago to scrape the ice from the windshield and give the seats a chance to heat.

As she pulled away from the garage, I gripped my thighs and stared out the window. I waited for the anxiety.

One block passed, then two. My heart rate was normal. My hands weren't sweating. I wasn't ready to fling myself out of the moving vehicle. *What the hell?*

I looked at Genevieve's profile. I hadn't had the nightmare of her dying in a car crash in two days. Not exactly a feat, but considering I'd had it nearly every night since she'd been sick in November, the break was welcome. And now I wasn't panicking at being in a car with her. Something was off, but I had no complaints.

"What?" she asked. "Do I have something on my face?"

"No."

She stretched to see her face in the rearview anyway.

I faced forward, breathing again. Waiting for that feeling. But it was . . . less. Not gone. I was very aware we were in a car together. This was not relaxing, but I wasn't in a crippling panic.

Maybe it was the sex. Maybe jerking off in the shower for years hadn't been enough to relieve the stress. Or maybe the past two days of peace were because of Genevieve. Because I'd finally confessed.

Whatever the reason, a weight had come off my shoulders. There was a lightness in the apartment too, like we weren't tiptoeing around each other anymore. For the first time in a long time, I could breathe.

"Brrr." Genevieve shivered. "I hope we don't freeze tonight."

"I'll—" *Keep you warm.* I swallowed the words, covering with, "We'll be fine."

Shit. I'd been close to making those types of slips for two days.

We hadn't had sex since that first night. I'd slept on the couch. She'd been in the bed. We didn't avoid touching, but we didn't touch more than we had before either. She'd reach for my arm when we took the icy stairs. We'd brush as we passed one another in the kitchen.

I was afraid to do much more for fear I'd get carried away. But, fuck me, I wanted to touch her. I wanted to be inside her again.

There'd be no avoiding touch tonight. We were meeting Dash and Bryce at the stroll. Emmett and Leo would be there too. We'd be playing the happy, loving couple—though it didn't feel as much like a lie.

Presley was planning to come with her fiancé, Jeremiah. In all the months I'd worked at the garage, I'd never met the guy. From the way Dash, Emmett and Leo talked about Jeremiah, he wasn't well liked, and I wanted to see for myself how he treated Pres.

I got the impression that Jeremiah was stringing her along. He'd asked her to marry him but had been dragging his feet about the actual wedding. I didn't want to make a judgment based on grumbles and rumors, but my gut said if a guy never came to see his fiancée at work, something was up.

Hell, Genevieve and I were pretending, and I picked her up and dropped her off every day. Sure, that was for her own safety, but no one could say I wasn't attached to my wife.

And damn was I ever attached.

"I don't want you to go," I blurted. *Son of a bitch.* Of all the slips to finally make its escape.

"Go where? Here?" She pointed to the grocery store's parking lot, where she'd been about to park. It was where most people left their cars for the stroll since Central would be blocked off. "Where should I park?"

"No. Park here." I pointed her into the spot. "I meant, I don't want you to go. To leave."

"Oh." She gave me a small smile as she put the car in park. "Good. I wasn't going to anyway."

I grinned. *My stubborn wife.*

We hadn't talked about the argument again. We hadn't talked about the accident. I didn't want to talk about either. Maybe we could simply leave it as settled.

Genevieve wrapped a scarf around her neck and made sure the ends of her gloves were tucked into her coat sleeves. She pulled the beanie covering her hair lower over her ears.

I zipped my coat all the way up my neck and got out, meeting her in front of the car. "Yeah, it's gonna be cold as fuck tonight."

She giggled. "We need hot chocolate. Stat."

Her laugh drew me in and chased away the chill. I took her gloved hand in mine. Her nose was already red from the cold. She smiled, a full, bright, white-toothed smile.

I nearly fell on my ass. There was no pity in her gaze, only affection. She looked at me like I'd never told her about Shannon. Like those years in prison had never happened.

Genevieve looked at me and saw the man I'd once been. The man who'd laughed easy. The man who hadn't appreciated his freedom. The man who'd needed a woman like Genevieve to straighten him out—though apparently, I was still that man.

I don't deserve her.

"Ready?" she asked.

I managed a nod as she tugged me along.

As we approached Central, she buzzed with excitement. Her grip was firm on my hand as she urged me to walk faster.

Above us, large garlands streamed from one side of the street to the other. Five of them created a canopy that stretched for blocks. The businesses and shops along Central were open late, some serving hot cider and others handing out cocoa. Groups huddled together. Mothers and fathers corralled hyped-up kids into Santa's line for pictures.

"Wow." Genevieve tipped up her gaze to take in the lights wrapped around lampposts. "This was worth it."

"Worth what? The cold?"

"No." She flashed me that smile again. "Worth moving here. Maybe Clifton Forge isn't so bad."

Before I could respond, Genevieve's attention shifted, and her smile got impossibly wider. She waved at Bryce and Dash, who were wandering our way.

"Hey, guys," Genevieve said, not letting go of my hand to hug Bryce.

I shook Dash's hand. "How's it going?"

"Good. Better if Bryce would stop asking me to get my picture taken with Santa."

"Oh, stop." She rolled her eyes. "One of the guys from the paper, Art, is Santa. I promised I'd stop by and I'm not going to stand in that line and not have my picture taken."

"Or you can just see him at the newspaper tomorrow," Dash said. "Skip the line altogether."

Bryce ignored him. "Do you guys want to get one taken too? All the proceeds go to charity."

Genevieve sandwiched my hand between hers. "Can we?"

"Fine by me."

After going through Amina's things today, I'd been baffled at the sheer number of pictures she'd taken. The tubs had been crowded with photo after photo, most rubber banded into tight stacks. Maybe it was a mother thing, wanting photos of your kid.

In all the time she'd lived here, I couldn't remember Genevieve taking a picture.

She didn't post selfies on social media. She didn't snap pictures of anything in town. I wouldn't mind having a picture of us together, something to remember her by years down the road when she was gone.

Who would she end up with? Genevieve deserved a good man, but I could barely stomach the thought of her in another man's arms.

I shook off the envy, holding her hand tighter as we strolled through the crowd, following Bryce and Dash as they led the way.

Dash seemed to know everyone tonight. He'd wave or jerk up his chin to those we'd pass. He'd nod and introduce Bryce to the people who'd stop, but for his sister, he'd barely spared a single glance.

I bit my tongue as we kept moving toward the Santa line, knowing if I said something, it would ruin the night for our wives.

The only time Dash stopped to have an actual conversation was when an older man with a protruding belly pulled him in for a short, backslapping embrace.

"You hear anything yet?" the man asked.

Dash shook his head. "No. Nothing."

"Goddamn it." The guy kicked at the snow with a heavy black boot. "You call me if you need anything."

"Will do, Louie. Appreciate it." Dash slapped him on the back once more, then nodded for us to keep walking.

When we were a few steps away, Bryce glanced behind us. "Is that the same Big Louie who used to be in the club?"

"Yeah. He used to be a King."

I leaned in to whisper in Genevieve's ear. "Did you look into him?"

"Yes," she whispered back.

"I'm going to have to go through your notebook and catch up."

"So am I," Bryce said, joining in our conversation.

She giggled. "By all means."

"Louie bought the bowling alley in town a while back," Dash told us. "He doesn't come to the garage often, but he keeps in touch with Dad."

We took up our spot at the tail of Santa's line. Kids weaved through their parents' legs as they ran around and played. The scent of a campfire filled the air from where they'd set up a marshmallow-roasting station.

"You want some hot chocolate?" I asked Genevieve and Bryce, receiving two nods. Dash stayed with them while I went to grab four cups from a stand on the other side of the street. I was handing Genevieve hers when a prickle ran up my spine.

My shoulders tensed and I twisted to look behind me. I'd spent three years in prison learning what it felt like to be watched. Someone was staring at me, but who?

I scanned the crowd. Nothing seemed odd. People were enjoying themselves, laughing and talking. The street was packed with people and not one seemed to care about me.

I shifted closer to Genevieve as she gabbed with Bryce.

The hairs were still raised on my arms, my gut screaming, and when I looked at Dash, his eyes were scanning the crowd. He'd felt it too.

Dash put his arm around Bryce, holding her close.

I did the same with Genevieve, tucking her into my side.

"You okay?" She wrapped her arm around me, tipping her chin up.

"Yeah. Just a strange feeling. It's gone now."

"Dash." Emmett's voice carried through the crowd as he strode our way, Leo just a few steps behind.

Their expressions were ice cold and not from the weather.

"What?" Dash asked.

Genevieve tensed as they inched closer to talk so no one around us would hear.

"Leo and I were walking in," Emmett said. "Saw a group of Warriors."

"Fuck." Dash cursed first but it was only a split-second before my own. "Thought maybe we'd catch a break and they'd give up on us."

"Guess not," Leo muttered.

"What do we do?" Bryce asked.

"Nothing, babe," Dash answered. "We keep an eye out. Stay together."

The mood shifted as we stood in line. None of us spoke. We only shuffled forward as our place in line progressed.

"Hey, guys!" We all turned at Presley's happy voice. Her white pixie cut was covered by a slouchy beanie. Her smile faded as she reached our group. "What's wrong?"

"Warriors."

Presley stood on her toes to look around. When her eyes landed on something behind us, she froze.

Three men wearing Warrior cuts over their coats were

talking to a lanky guy with a cigarette pinched between two fingers.

"What the fuck is Jeremiah doing?" Leo barked.

Wait, that was Presley's fiancé? Why was he talking to the Warriors?

"Those are the Warriors?" Presley asked, her eyes widening as she turned to Dash. "I didn't know. Jeremiah told me they were a couple guys he met playing poker. They come over sometimes."

"To your house?" Emmett asked.

She nodded, her face paling. "They didn't wear those vests."

"Goddamn it." Dash rubbed his jaw. "So they haven't been lying low. They've been here this whole fucking time."

"Do you talk to them?" Leo asked Presley.

She shrugged. "Sometimes."

"About what?"

"Nothing. I don't know. One of them asked me where I worked. They talked to me about the wedding. It wasn't anything important. Mostly they came over, hung out for a while and then Jeremiah went out with them."

"Did he know they were Warriors?" Emmett asked her.

She closed her eyes. "I don't know."

Genevieve stiffened at my side. We'd been fools to think they'd believed us. Convincing as she was, Genevieve had lied to their faces. Either the Warriors knew, or they suspected.

When they found out, I was a dead man.

"We're up." Bryce nudged Dash for their turn at pictures. They smiled but neither's reached their eyes.

When it was time for Genevieve and me to go up, I didn't want there to be strain in our faces. This might be the only picture the two of us would have together. So right before we were ushered in for our pictures, I took Genevieve's face in my hands. "Block them out."

"How?"

I dropped my lips to hers, letting the kiss linger for a long moment. I savored the soft feel of her lips and the smell of her hair.

When we broke apart for our picture, she had a rosy glow on her cheeks and a little smile on her face. Picture or not, I'd remember that look until the end of my days.

Even if that end was right around the corner.

———

"I'M AN ICICLE." Genevieve's teeth chattered as we hurried to the car.

The seats were going to be cold inside, but a breeze had picked up as we'd left the stroll and I was ready to get her out of its path.

We weaved through the cars in the grocery store's full parking lot. An overhead lamp cast a glow on the trunk. Genevieve beeped the locks.

My steps slowed. "What the fuck?"

Genevieve gasped and her hand flew to her mouth. "What is that?"

"Give me the keys." I took them from her. "Stay here."

She didn't listen. As I crept closer to the car, her hands clutched the back of my coat.

There was a small animal on the trunk of her car. Dead. A baby pig. Its throat had been slashed and its blood was freezing to the car. It hadn't been there long because some of it still dripped onto the snow.

"Oh my God." Genevieve spun away, burying her face in my chest. "Was it them? The Warriors?"

It had to be. Who else would do this? My eyes were glued to the animal as I pulled off a glove and dug my phone from my pocket. I pressed Dash's name.

"Hey," he answered. "I can't talk right now. Someone broke out the window to my truck."

Not someone, the Warriors. Dash and Bryce hadn't parked at the store. They were on a residential side street. The Warriors had been busy searching for both vehicles. "Someone sent us a message too."

As I told him about the pig, Genevieve burrowed into me deeper.

"Take a picture," Dash ordered. "Clean it up. Then get the fuck out of there."

I ended the call without another word and took Genevieve's hand, pulling her toward the store. "Let's go."

"Where?"

"Get some garbage bags. Clean it up, then home."

She nodded, picking up her steps to match my pace. The color had drained from her face.

The store was deserted save for a lonely cashier reading a book at the checkout line. He rang up our garbage bags and we hustled for the car.

"Get in," I ordered.

"I can hel—"

"Get. In. Lock the doors."

She didn't argue, going to the driver's side, shutting herself inside and clicking the locks. She started up the car as I took a picture, then wrapped the pig in two garbage bags.

I wiped off as much blood as I could, but the car would

need a wash. Then I took the bags to a Dumpster beside the store, ignoring the signs to keep out.

With it disposed, I jogged to the car and got inside. My gray gloves were wet and stained with blood.

"What are we going to do?" she whispered, gripping the wheel.

"We hold tight. We stick together." If the Warriors knew, they would have done much more than kill a pig. They were intimidating us. They were trying to force a confession. We had to stay strong until there was no other choice. "This was just a scare tactic."

Her worried eyes met mine. "Mission accomplished."

CHAPTER NINETEEN

GENEVIEVE

It was funny how time moved at different speeds. Weeks and months went by in a flash. Years drew to a close and new ones dawned with the flipping of a calendar's page. But seconds could stretch on for an eternity.

Jim had walked into my office with news eons ago. In reality, it had only been a minute since he'd told me Draven's fate was now in the jury's hands.

"It's over?"

He nodded from the chair across from my desk. "It's over. I did the best I could. Now we'll wait for the jury."

My eyes flooded with tears as I stared at the top of my desk. "How long do you think they'll deliberate?"

"I have no idea. The longer the better."

"What if they come back with guilty?" Which they likely would. "Is there any reason to appeal?"

"I've already called a friend of mine who handles criminal appeals. She's going to take a look. But unless I screwed something up, which I don't think I did, we've got nothing."

So after the jury reached their decision, Draven would

go to prison, presumably for the rest of his life. He'd be punished for my mother's murder while she rested in the cemetery with no justice.

I swiped the tears away. Every time I swallowed the lump in my throat, it crawled right back up. "What do we do?"

Jim gave me a sad smile. "I'm afraid there's nothing to do. You still have a little time. Make the most of it."

Maybe a day. Maybe a week. But time was running out for Sunday breakfasts with Draven at the diner. Time was running out for me to know the man who'd slowly become so important to me.

"Would you mind if I left a little early today?"

"Of course not." Jim stood. "Enjoy the weekend."

"Thanks. And, Jim?" I stopped him before he could leave my office. "Thank you for trying."

He nodded, his shoulders falling. "I wish I could have done more."

"You did all you could do."

Jim had worked tirelessly on Draven's case, but the evidence was stacked against Draven and evidence was impossible to ignore.

There hadn't been much for Jim to present. He'd brought Emmett in to verify that he'd taped the recording of the man breaking into the clubhouse. He'd speculated the knife was stolen and had brought in a fingerprint expert to discuss how fingerprints could be falsified.

Draven kept telling me how Jim was doing an incredible job and that praise had given me a false sense of hope.

We'd all begun to hope.

Bryce had invited Isaiah and me to her house for Christmas. Draven had been there. The judge had come down

246

with the flu and the trial had been delayed for a few days, plus they'd taken off for the holiday.

Nick and Emmeline had driven from Prescott with the kids, who'd stolen the show. They'd opened the mountain of gifts laid out for them, ones from Draven, Dash and Bryce. Isaiah and I had gotten them presents too—a remote-control car for young Draven and packs of stud earrings for Nora.

We'd eaten a feast of both turkey and prime rib. And for maybe the first time, I'd felt part of this family. Dash hadn't had much to say to me, per his normal behavior. But Bryce's affection and love had made up for his cold shoulder. Nick and Emmeline's had too. Why couldn't Nick be the brother who lived in Clifton Forge?

Tell me all about your life, little sister.

He'd sat on the couch beside me and we hadn't moved from that spot for an hour. He'd peppered me with questions, much like Draven did during our breakfasts at the diner.

Christmas, like Thanksgiving, had been hard without Mom. I'd woken up and cried in the shower that morning. But Isaiah had been there. I'd leaned on him, his steady presence never far away.

None of us had talked about the Warriors. None of us had mentioned the kidnapping or Mom's murder. We hadn't spoken about Draven's trial.

Because we'd hoped it would end in our favor.

False hope.

To the world, Draven was guilty. It was just a matter of time until a jury made it official.

Tears threatened again as I collected my things and pulled on my coat and scarf. I rifled around the bottom of my purse for my keys and phone. I brought up Isaiah's name,

247

ready to call him to escort me home, but hesitated. It was close to closing time and he'd been so busy at the garage. I hated bothering him when I was sure he was trying to wrap up the day.

They'd been working on a new car at the shop, one Nick had brought over at Christmas.

Nick and Emmeline had a garage in Prescott called Slater's Station. Unlike Dash's garage here, Slater's Station wasn't the only shop in Prescott. The oil changes and tune-ups were mostly handled at the other garage, which meant Nick's shop specialized in custom work. Jobs that took months, not hours.

He specialized in restoring cars and motorcycles, much like Dash did, but based on the banter that had been tossed around the Christmas dinner table, I'd gleaned that Nick was good at his job. Really good. So while the Clifton Forge Garage needed mechanics like Isaiah to do the more routine maintenance work, Nick specialized in restorations.

Dash had built up that side of his business too, but with the regular jobs that came in daily, they couldn't solely focus on *the fun stuff*, as Isaiah called it.

Except Nick was overbooked. Dash already had one restoration going, so adding in a second meant Isaiah was able to help.

He came home to the apartment each night with a grin. A grin that seemed to be widening, millimeter by millimeter, each day. Isaiah had even started laughing. Well, not exactly laughing. There were no teeth showing. He didn't throw his head back and let loose. But there was a deep, strong rumble in his chest. A grinning chuckle.

He was probably watching and observing Dash, Emmett

and Leo right now, soaking up everything they were teaching him.

I didn't want to pull him away from that, even for twenty minutes.

Jim could walk me to the parking lot.

I put on my gloves and shut off the light to my office. With my purse slung over a shoulder, I walked down the hallway. "Hey, Jim? Would you mind walking me to my car?"

Probably a strange request from an employee to her boss, but Jim knew why we were all being cautious. I wasn't sure how much Draven had told him, but it was enough that he immediately abandoned his chair and put on his coat.

I hadn't told him about the baby pig. Mostly, I was doing my best to block that image from my mind because there wasn't anything to do.

We'd been threatened. Message received. We were all on constant guard.

"Bye, Gayle." I waved to her as I passed the reception desk.

"Bye," she said before answering the phone. She gave her normal greeting, then looked to Jim as he caught up to me at the door. "Oh, hi, Colleen. Let me see if he's free."

Jim held up a hand. "I'll be right back."

"Sorry," I said as we hustled out the door.

"No problem at all. Colleen will chat with Gayle." He walked me to the corner of the building. "See you Monday."

"Have a good weekend." I waved and hurried to my car, glancing over my shoulder to see Jim waiting by the building until I'd opened the door and shut myself inside. Jim turned to go inside.

I'd put in the key and was about to turn it when a dark figure appeared by my window.

"Ah!" My scream was cut short when the door was ripped open.

I hadn't locked it.

My hands fumbled, pulling hard on the handle, but he was too strong. One moment, I was in my car, the next I was being hauled out by my hair. "Nooo—"

He slapped his gloved hand over my mouth.

I twisted and fought, trying to squirm away, but he had a grip on me that was so terrifyingly familiar I wasn't able to breathe.

Not again. *Oh, God, please, not again.*

I threw my elbows, flailing to connect with his ribs. I let my legs go limp, forcing him to adjust his hold on my hair, hoping I'd slip in his hold. White spots broke across my vision as he hauled me up by my roots.

Tears dripped down my cheeks as it felt like my scalp was detaching from my skull. I couldn't drag in enough air with his hand over my mouth, and my head went fuzzy.

But I fought.

With weak limbs and a racing heart, I fought, hoping and praying someone would see me this time. I wasn't in a quiet hotel after midnight. I was in broad daylight, standing in a parking lot.

I thrashed my head as well as I could with his hand restraining my hair, desperately trying to get his hand off my mouth.

One good scream. That was all I needed. One good scream and maybe I'd scare him away.

I opened my mouth, ready to bite down on his palm,

when the sound of a voice broke through the thunder of my pounding heart.

"Genevieve!"

The grip on my hair was gone. My knees crumpled to the snow and I fell forward, catching myself with the heels of my hands right before my face collided with the metal frame of my car.

I sucked in a deep breath, my lungs burning as the oxygen seeped in. My legs were Jell-O. My arms shook. I didn't have the strength to stand up and get out of the snow, but I didn't have to.

Isaiah's strong arm gripped me by the elbow as he hauled me into his arms. "Are you okay?"

I nodded, a stream of tears flowing down my face and into his coat. "No."

"I've got you." He kissed my hair and held me tighter. "I've got you."

My eyes squeezed shut as I held tight, letting my nerves settle. It took a while to get the shaking in my limbs under control, but once I was solid, I took a deep breath and loosened my grasp on Isaiah.

Except he didn't let me go.

"I'm okay."

He held me closer.

"Isaiah, I'm okay."

He took one last breath of my hair, then let me go. Not entirely. Just enough to lean back and look me up and down. "Are you hurt?"

"My hair." I put my fingers to my scalp, sure I'd find blood when I pulled them away, but they came back dry. "My head hurts but that's all." And I'd nearly had a heart attack.

"What happened?"

"Nothing. I don't know. I was ready to come home, and Jim escorted me out. I got in my car. The parking lot was empty. And then he was just . . . there, yanking my door open."

"Fuck. He must have hidden."

"Did you see him?"

Isaiah nodded. "Only the side of his face. But I saw his patch."

My stomach dropped. "The Warriors?"

"Fuck." Isaiah pulled me into his chest, muttering the curse again.

"Genevieve." Jim was coming around the corner of the building. "Are you all right? I heard Isaiah yell."

"Someone came after her," Isaiah answered for me.

"What?" Jim rushed over. "Are you hurt? Should I call for an ambulance?"

"I'm okay," I choked out as his hand rested on my shoulder.

"I should have waited." He hung his head. "I'm so sorry. You got in the car and I—"

"It's okay, Jim. It's not your fault." I looked up at Isaiah. "He came out of nowhere. He must have been watching and waiting for me to leave. He had to know you normally come and meet me."

Isaiah's jaw ticked. "Let's get out of the cold. We'll talk at home."

"Okay." I nodded and turned. Jim's hug was waiting.

"I'm sorry."

I relaxed against his shoulder. "I'm okay. Promise."

He squeezed me for a second longer, then spoke to Isaiah. "Take care of her."

"I'll die trying." Isaiah's voice, those words, soothed the rest of my ragged nerves.

As Jim let me go, I sat in my driver's seat, hesitating to swing my legs inside.

"Just grab your purse, V. We'll come get the car tomorrow."

"But . . ." The last time he'd driven me home, he'd gone cold for weeks.

He waved me out. "Come on."

"Okay," I agreed, not wanting to be inside my car at the moment. I yanked my purse from the passenger seat and retrieved the keys from the ignition.

Isaiah took my arm the moment the door was closed and locked, keeping a firm hold on me as we walked to his truck. The driver's door was open, the engine running.

"How'd you know to come here?"

"Draven called the garage." His eyes filled with concern. "Said the jury is out for deliberation."

"I know. Jim told me."

"I wasn't sure if he'd tell you or not, so I came in case you needed me."

I let my head fall against his shoulder. "I always need you."

And always would.

Where would I be if he hadn't thought to come here? In another trunk? I shivered, fear creeping in. The Warriors probably didn't believe in trunks. They seemed more like the live-burial type.

"Was this another scare tactic?" I asked as Isaiah opened the passenger door for me. "Or would he have taken me?"

He sighed. "I don't know, doll. Could have been."

Since the pig incident, I'd been constantly looking over my shoulder. We both had.

"Why me?" I whispered as Isaiah buckled my seat belt. "I'm not affiliated with the club. Before this summer, I'd never set foot in Clifton Forge. Why would they want me? I'm a no one to them. Unless . . ."

"They can't know about the cabin. There's no way." Isaiah leaned into the cab and dropped his forehead to mine. "We'll figure it out."

"How?"

"Together."

I closed my eyes, relaxing into the warmth of his touch. I dragged in a breath of the cab and his comforting scent.

Isaiah leaned away and cupped my cheeks, staring into my eyes like I was something precious. He dropped a soft kiss to my lips, then closed me inside the cab, rounding the hood for his side.

He put his hands on the wheel and froze.

"I can drive," I offered.

"No." He tightened his grip. "I can do it."

We didn't move. Beside me, he was waging an internal battle to put the truck in reverse.

"You won't hurt me," I whispered.

He looked over and the raw emotion on his face, the vulnerability in his eyes, broke my heart. "I might."

"You won't."

After a few long moments, he put the truck in reverse. Then we made our way to the garage, Isaiah barely breathing as he drove.

But we made it. Safe. Unharmed.

Together.

We'd won today's battle, but the war was far from over.

CHAPTER TWENTY

ISAIAH

I peeled my hands off the steering wheel and shut off my truck. Then I breathed.

We made it. I ran a hand over my face, shaking away the anxiety.

Driving Genevieve home today was easier than it had been the day she'd been sick, but only by a fraction. Even though I hadn't had that fucking nightmare since I'd started sleeping in bed with her, it was still screwing with my head.

Maybe I should have risked a glance at her—just to see that she was alive and breathing. Would it ever get easier? Probably not. I didn't deserve for this to be easy.

Genevieve opened her door first and gave me a sad smile. "Let's go up."

I nodded and climbed out on shaking legs. Adrenaline streamed through my veins, both from the drive and seeing that motherfucker's hands on her. I shoved that image away before I went into a rage.

Someone had come after Genevieve. *My wife.*

We clung to one another as we climbed the stairs home. I

255

helped her out of her coat and shook off mine. She left her shoes on and the spiked heels dug into the carpet as she crossed the room and sank onto the couch.

Fuck, I could have lost her today. That guy could have taken her. He could have strangled her beside her car and left her lifeless body in the snow. Maybe he'd wanted to do to her what he'd done to that baby pig.

What would I do without her? Losing her would destroy me. She was the best thing to come into my life in years, and if protecting her from this meant I spent the rest of my days in prison, I'd go tomorrow.

"V," I whispered.

Her eyes were glassy when she met my gaze. We were both thinking the same thing. "We can't keep this a secret anymore."

"No." I joined her on the couch and my hand found hers. "We need help, doll. The secrets aren't worth it if I can't keep you safe."

"Everyone will know what happened."

"They won't tell." It had taken me months to fully understand the loyalty these people had to one another. As we'd watched Draven's trial progress, as we'd shared our lunches and our lives, as we'd turned old wrecks into works of art, I'd gotten a glimpse of the brotherhood Dash and Emmett and Leo had had in the club.

They wouldn't betray us. I saw that now. We could tell them the truth and they'd safeguard it with their lives.

Genevieve clutched my hand. "They'll know our marriage isn't real."

But it was real, wasn't it? Somewhere along the way, this marriage had become the most real thing in my life.

"We'll deal with it," I said. "We'll figure it out."

She fell into my side, her cheek resting on my shoulder.

I shifted, wrapping an arm around her and pulling her close. "Let's wait until the garage closes. Wait until Pres goes home. She doesn't know everything that's happened with the Warriors lately, and I think Dash wants to keep it that way."

"Especially if the Warriors are trying to get to us through Jeremiah."

While we trusted Presley implicitly, Jeremiah was a different situation. And Pres didn't need to be put in the middle. We worried enough about her, sending her home each night. She'd assured us that the Warriors were gone and she was safe.

But she was Presley. We worried.

Genevieve and I leaned into one another, settling deeper into the sofa as we waited. I closed my eyes and blocked out the world beyond our door. I hugged my wife. I pretended the illusion was true—that Genevieve and I had met and fallen in love on the same day. That I was just as head over heels in love with her now as I had been on day one.

Maybe I was.

But it was time for the illusion to come to an end.

I kissed the top of her hair as she breathed me in. We were both savoring these last moments.

Until the sounds from the garage began to dull.

And our time was up.

AN HOUR LATER, when the garage was closed for the night, everyone was in our apartment. No one had hesitated when I'd asked them up.

Though it was only six o'clock, it was dark outside.

Daylight in a Montana winter was as short-lived as phone calls had been in prison. The black window matched the mood.

Draven, Leo and Emmett were shoulder to shoulder on the couch. Bryce and Dash were at the table, while Genevieve and I sat on the end of the bed. This was the most people I'd venture to guess had ever been in this apartment. We wouldn't have to speak loudly to hear one another across the room.

"What are we doing here, Isaiah?" Draven asked.

"Something happened today," I said.

Dash sat straighter. "What?"

"Someone came after Genevieve."

The room exploded.

Not in the typical explosion where people shot out of chairs and began pacing. Not a soul moved. But the tension and anger and fear that detonated into the air was an explosion, nonetheless.

"When?" Draven asked through a clenched jaw.

"After work," Genevieve answered, telling them about leaving early. She shuddered as she described how the man had dragged her from her car. As she spoke, her hand drifted to her hair where, beneath those brown locks, I was sure a nasty bruise was blackening.

"Did you get a look at him?" Dash asked.

"Yes." Genevieve nodded. "I've never seen him before. Dark hair. Brown eyes. But he wasn't one of the men I found in my research, so I don't know his name."

"He was wearing a Warrior cut. I only got a look at him from behind. When I got there, I shouted, and he ran to the back of the building. Disappeared. He never did turn so I could see his face."

"Fuck," Dash spat. "Tucker thinks it's us."

Genevieve's hand found mine on my knee. She squeezed it, then gave me a sad smile.

This was it. The end.

No more secrets.

"There's something you guys should know." I blew out a long breath. "We lied to you. About what happened in the cabin."

Dash's face turned stone-cold, his expression harder than I'd ever seen it before. Bryce's jaw dropped. Emmett and Leo shared a wide-eyed look. Draven frowned but didn't seem surprised. Maybe he'd known all along.

"I ran to the cabin. You guys know that already," Genevieve said. "The door was unlocked so I slipped inside. I thought I could hide there. My feet were hurting so badly, I knew I couldn't run fast or far. It was dark inside, but there was a light coming from the far back corner. You wouldn't have even seen it unless you'd gone inside, so I walked that way, hoping maybe it was a back exit or something. It was a stairwell."

Dash scoffed. "And let me guess, you went down."

"No." She shot him a glare. "I went the other way, toward a room. I was looking for a way out so when I saw it was just a room, I almost turned and left. But then I saw it was full of bags. All plastic. All tiny. And all of them were filled with something white."

"Drugs," Bryce guessed. "The Warriors were using that place to store drugs."

"They're dealing now?" Leo asked.

Draven shook his head. "Doesn't seem like Tucker's style. He wants the money from the suppliers but knows getting involved in distribution would put a target on his back. They're not dealers. They're the muscle and the guns. But maybe they added a service. Instead of just running protection routes on shipments, they're doing some storage too."

Protection routes? For drugs? Was it something the Kings used to do?

Did I want to know that answer?

No.

"Keep going," Dash ordered Genevieve.

She nodded, her grip on my hand tightening. "I backed away, wanting to get the hell out of there. But as I turned, this guy came up from the basement. He was in a daze. His eyes were glassy. He was high as a goddamn kite."

"Maybe those drugs were the Warriors' personal stash," Emmett muttered. "And he was assigned to watch over them."

Draven leaned forward, his eyes glued to Genevieve. "What happened next?"

"He smiled at me." She shivered. "He said, 'Looks like the boys sent me a present.' And then he came at me. He tried to kiss me. He licked my cheek. He put his hands all over me."

I clenched my jaw, not wanting to think about it.

"I fought him off as best I could," she said. "I tried to run for the door, but he was strong and I'd been in a trunk and tied up beside a tree all night. I was exhausted. He grabbed me and ripped at my shirt."

The other men in the room sat stiff. Bryce gasped, sad eyes and pain etched on her face.

While she'd run from their kidnapper into Dash's arms, Genevieve had run from one hell to another.

"He would have raped me." Genevieve swallowed hard.

"Probably killed me too. He punched me in the stomach and told me to stop fighting. It knocked the wind out of me and I collapsed."

That's how I'd found her. With a man pinning her to the floor, tearing at her clothes. He'd gotten her pants off past her hips. Her panties too. She'd been bare, exposed and helpless.

I'd only caught a glimpse of Genevieve as she'd run toward that cabin and it had been from behind. The first sight of her face—in person—had been on that floor.

I'd never forget the look on her face, the sheer terror as she gasped for breath, all while her bare ass writhed on a dirty floor because she was trying to get her most precious place away from a man who had no right to touch it.

"I ripped him off her," I told the room, trying to block out the image of her.

So far, I'd been able to keep that image locked down tight. I did my best to never think of the cabin. Now that we were airing our secrets, would I have a new nightmare tonight? Instead of Genevieve dying in the passenger seat of a car, would I see her on that dirty fucking floor?

"I hit him a few times, tried to keep him down, but he kept coming." The guy had gotten a few hits in of his own, mostly to my ribs. Nothing broken, but they'd hurt for a couple days. So had my hands from punching him.

"Did you kill him?" Dash asked.

"Yes." The word hung in the air. "He was in a blind rage. Had to be the drugs. I knocked him down and got my hands around his throat."

Then I'd strangled him.

When his arms and legs had fallen limp to the floor, I'd stopped.

I could have stopped sooner. I *should* have stopped

sooner. Maybe Genevieve and I would have been able to call the cops then, explain it as defense of another.

But I didn't. I fucked up.

I held his neck, squeezing the life out of him, until he was gone from the world.

"I'm not sorry." I met Draven's eyes. I wouldn't be sorry for taking that man's life. "He wasn't wearing a cut. I didn't know he was a Warrior. Not that it would have mattered. I would have killed him all the same."

Draven nodded. "You did the right thing."

"Yeah," Dash, Emmett and Leo echoed.

My shoulders fell, a relief settling that I hadn't felt in months. I'd needed someone to tell me it was right. I thought it was, but my judgment was so fucked up, what the hell did I know? Genevieve never blamed me for it. She never looked at me like I was a killer.

"He would have killed you both. If not then, later." Dash ran a hand through his hair. "The Warriors take their revenge. It's what we would have done as Kings too."

Genevieve shifted her grip, lacing our fingers together. Maybe everyone was good with that being the end of the story, but they needed to know the rest, so I gave her a small nod to continue.

"Isaiah was worried he'd go back to prison. At the time, we weren't even thinking about the Warriors. We were worried about the police."

Because normal citizens didn't fear their actions would lead to retaliation from a motorcycle gang. They feared jail time, as they should.

The realization that I'd killed a man, that I'd go back to prison, had dropped me on my ass on that cabin floor.

I can't go back there.

262

I'd chanted those words, over and over, as my options had raced through my mind. Suicide had been at the top of the list. Because I wouldn't survive another day in prison, let alone a life sentence.

I wasn't like Draven. Prison wouldn't harden him. It wouldn't scare him. He'd weather it like he had life, with a deadly gaze that would take him to the top of the inmate hierarchy. He was cold and hard enough to survive.

It was a good thing Genevieve had some of her father's strength or I wouldn't have pulled myself up off that floor.

She'd sprung into action, standing and righting her clothes. Then she'd rushed to my side, shaking me out of my stupor.

What's your name?

That question, her voice, had broken through the fear.

Isaiah.

She'd looked me dead in the eye. *Thank you, Isaiah.*

Fuck, but she was too good for me.

"We knew someone would eventually come looking and find the body," Genevieve told the room. "My fingerprints were everywhere. I knew if the cops found us, they'd take Isaiah back to prison for saving me."

Maybe we could have run, but instead, I'd killed him. An ex-con who'd gone to prison once for manslaughter wasn't going to get a light sentence on another charge.

"I found a lighter. It had fallen out of the man's pocket," Genevieve said. She'd picked up that silver-plated lighter and an idea had washed over her face. "The fire was on me. I started it by the fireplace, thinking an investigator would think it was a regular fire that had gotten out of control. And it was close to the body."

I hadn't been surprised when the place had gone up like

a torch. It was an old wooden cabin with logs for walls. It had burned like gasoline on a barbeque.

"We watched it for a few minutes, making sure it was roaring," I said. "Then we got out of there."

We'd run to where we'd parked the bikes. I'd held Genevieve's hand, helping her traverse the forest floor. On one step, she'd cried out and that's when I'd taken a good look at her feet. I'd made her climb on my back and carried her the rest of the way.

Emmett and Leo and Draven had been searching for the girls' kidnapper and their bikes had been parked beside mine. They'd assumed we'd left right behind Dash and Bryce. They'd assumed the kidnapper had doubled back to the cabin and started the fire as a distraction.

"What'd you do with the lighter?" Draven asked Genevieve.

"I dumped it in a trash can at the airport after Isaiah dropped me off."

"Good girl." The pride in his voice was unmistakable and she blushed.

Odd as it was to be proud of someone for covering up a murder, I was proud of her too. If not for her fast thinking, I'd be done for.

"We stopped about halfway from the cabin to town," I said. "Waited to make sure the fire was reported and didn't burn up the forest. When we saw a forest service truck race by, we made a plan."

Genevieve shifted, inching closer to my side. "If the fire wasn't enough to destroy the body, the only person who could testify against Isaiah was me. And the only person who could testify that I started the fire was Isaiah. So I suggested we get married. I took a chance that depending on the evidence, a prosecutor would have a hard time proving we'd done anything beyond a reasonable doubt."

She paused, taking a moment. I assumed she'd tell them about the law, that we hadn't had to get married after all, but she didn't and my heart swelled. She kept that secret for us alone.

No one else needed to know she'd stayed for me.

Because I knew.

"You got lucky," Emmett said. "That fire was hot enough that it burned up that body and destroyed everything but bone. The hyoid wasn't broken so no one could tell he'd been strangled."

Nods bobbed around the room.

"Isaiah took me to Bozeman so I could fly home and pack," Genevieve said. "Then I came back, and we got married."

When I'd watched and waited for her plane to take off, I'd figured there was a fifty-fifty chance I'd ever see her again. I wouldn't have blamed her if she'd run away and never come back. But then she'd texted me, as promised, when she'd left Denver.

We'd been waiting for the other shoe to drop ever since.

"Fuck." Draven ran a hand over his beard. "Wish you would have told us the truth."

"I didn't know you," Genevieve said. "Any of you. All I knew was that I'd come to Montana to visit my mother's grave, thinking you were the man who'd killed her. I get to Bozeman and someone kidnaps me. Then Bryce, a reporter who I'd only talked to once, tells me that you're my father and you didn't kill Mom. I get away from my kidnapper only to get sent into another hell. Isaiah rescued me and I owed him my life. I wasn't sure who to trust, so I chose him. And I made a promise. If I could keep him out of prison, I'd do it. As for the rest of you, you were strangers."

"We weren't worried about another motorcycle club," I added. "We were worried about the cops."

Draven let the words sink in, then nodded. "I get it. You still should have told us."

Maybe. But it was too late to change things now.

"That's it?" Dash asked me. By rights, that question should have gone to Genevieve, but Dash, that stubborn son of a bitch, wasn't letting her in. And it was his loss.

"Yeah. That's it."

The tension in the room had eased some as we'd told the story. Now that it was over, the room went quiet. The tension returned, this time with an undercurrent of anger, mostly coming from Bryce.

She shot out of her chair—as fast as a pregnant woman could stand—and marched for the door.

"Bryce." Genevieve stood. Bryce turned. "I'm sorry."

"You lied to us." Bryce's voice shook. "After all that we went through that night, you lied to *me*. I get why you did it then, but why keep doing it? You were my matron of honor. We're *friends*."

"I'm sorry," Genevieve repeated. "I didn't know if I could trust you."

Bryce planted her hands on her hips. "Do you know now?"

"Yes."

"Good." Bryce changed directions, coming to Genevieve and pulling her into a hug. "No more secrets. We'll never survive this if we don't stick together."

There was so much truth in that statement.

"I'm sorry that happened to you," Bryce whispered.

"Me too."

The women broke apart and returned to their seats. The moment she was seated on the end of the bed, we clasped hands.

Together. As we had been from the beginning.

Maybe this marriage was fake and everyone knew it now, but that didn't mean we weren't fighting on the same front.

"Now that you all know what really happened"—I looked to Draven—"what's the plan?"

CHAPTER TWENTY-ONE

GENEVIEVE

W*e keep our fucking mouths shut.*

That was the plan we'd all decided on.

And over the next week, we did just that.

Dash and Draven worried that if we admitted to the truth, Tucker would retaliate against Isaiah and me—maybe others. He'd see the lies we'd told during the meeting at the clubhouse as something organized. Something Dash and the other former Tin Kings had done because of the old rivalry between clubs.

So we stayed quiet. And my pretend marriage was intact.

I wasn't ready to give up Isaiah, not yet. Especially with the jury delivering Draven's verdict tomorrow.

Jim had called an hour ago. The jury had reached their decision and would announce it in the morning.

None of us had expected their deliberation to last a full week. I'd hoped it had meant they were deadlocked. That maybe, just maybe, there was a chance at reasonable doubt.

But the fact was, the only way we'd set Draven free was with a miracle. We had to prove, beyond a reasonable doubt, with refuting evidence to support it, that he hadn't killed Mom.

Until then, today was our last Sunday breakfast at the diner.

I wouldn't be able to eat here again after this.

"Stopped by to see Jim on Friday." Draven shoved a bite of pancake in his mouth.

"You did? When?"

He chased his bite with a sip of coffee. "Lunchtime. You were out eating with Bryce."

"Oh. He didn't mention it."

Draven shrugged. "Wasn't a big thing. Just wanted to drop off his final payment."

I nodded. "I see."

Draven had been busy the past week, preparing for his inevitable incarceration. Once the jury announced their verdict, he'd either be a free man or immediately taken into custody until the sentencing hearing.

He was planning for the latter.

Draven had basically settled his estate, going so far as to clean out his house to put it on the market. February wasn't a great time to list a house for sale in Montana but Draven had been prepared to do it anyway.

That was, until Dash and Nick found out. My half brothers had insisted the house be kept in the family. After all, it had been their mother's home. Chrissy Slater may have passed, but her memory was alive and strong with her family.

My mom's was too.

Besides the house, Draven's life was wrapped up. He was maybe the most prepared man in history to face a verdict.

269

"Jim sure is impressed with you. Doubt he'd be any prouder if you were his own."

"I'm lucky to work for a guy like him. He's taught me a lot. Gives me responsibility and trust. It's the best job I've ever had."

"Ever thought about getting your law degree? Jim said you'd make one hell of a lawyer. Even said since he and Colleen don't have kids, you'd be a great partner."

It would be a dream come true to be Jim's partner at his firm. But it was one of those faraway dreams I wasn't counting on or working toward. No one in Clifton Forge knew I'd once planned to become a lawyer, not even Isaiah.

I poked at my omelet with my fork. "Maybe someday."

"Why not now?"

"There aren't many accredited law schools in Clifton Forge."

"No need for you to stay here."

"How about for Isaiah? I won't leave him to deal with this mess alone."

Draven leaned forward. "When you first told us you two were married, I knew something was up. But then after a while you relaxed together. Tell me honestly, did this become something real?"

"Nothing like putting me on the spot," I muttered, making his lips turn up.

Draven's smile was something I'd seen more often lately. And around him, I smiled easier too. There wasn't some big moment where we'd become comfortable around each other. It had crept up on us the way a cloudy sky would clear to blue when you weren't paying it any attention.

"So?" he pressed.

I picked up my fork, stabbing a strawberry and shoving it in my mouth.

Was this something real? Did I love Isaiah?

He was my best friend. He was there for me every day. When something happened at work that made me laugh, he was the first person I wanted to tell. When I woke up some mornings in a foul mood, he made me coffee with cream because it almost always cheered me up. The chocolate chip cookies I made every week weren't for me anymore—they were Isaiah's.

Was that love?

The only person I'd truly loved had been Mom. She'd told me she loved me often. Daily, especially when I was a kid.

Maybe it didn't count as love until I was brave enough to tell Isaiah.

"I won't leave him." My answer—telling as it was—would have to suffice. Besides, Draven was smart enough to read between the lines.

I was very much in love with my husband, and when it came time to tell someone, Isaiah would be the first to know. There were times when I would have guessed Isaiah loved me too.

Or did his heart still belong to Shannon?

It was odd to be jealous of a ghost.

"So you'll stay here. For how long?" Draven asked.

"As long as it takes."

We went back to our meals, clearing our plates the way we did every Sunday. I'd curse myself in an hour for being too full, but the pancakes were delicious and however they made the omelets, the cheese was gooey and so tasty I couldn't pass it up.

271

I was savoring my last bite when a figure appeared at the edge of our table.

"What the actual fuck, Draven?" Presley shouted, drawing attention from the entire restaurant.

We normally had some attention anyway—presumed murderer and all—but this was more than chaste glances and whispers.

Draven didn't even blink. "Mornin', Pres."

She glared down at him, her fists planted on her hips. Presley wasn't a tall woman. She stood only a few inches above five feet. I was five seven in bare feet, and I towered over her whenever I wore heels. Despite her physical size, she cast an intimidating shadow over our table.

Presley ordered the guys around at the garage, running it like a well-oiled machine. Draven, though technically retired, covered most of the office work because Dash preferred tools versus pens in his grip. Now that Draven was leaving, they'd both spent a month teaching her more about the business.

They'd added her name to the bank accounts. She invoiced customers, paid bills, signed contracts and managed payroll. And last week, they'd christened her with the official title of Office Manager.

Did she not want the job? Had something else happened? Isaiah spoke highly of Presley. I hadn't had a ton of interaction with her other than the rare group activity or in passing, but she was always so controlled and poised. To see her fuming was definitely a change.

I closed my mouth. It had been hanging open, food visible.

"Had to be done," Draven said like the entire room didn't have eyes aimed our way.

What had to be done? What was this about?

"You overstepped," she snapped.

"I did what I should have done day one. You're too good for him, Pres."

Ahh. So this was about Jeremiah. They were still engaged, much to the chagrin of everyone at the garage. Presley had assured everyone that the Warriors didn't come to their place anymore. Jeremiah still met with them, but outside their home.

And though it irritated the guys at the garage to no end that she wouldn't dump his sorry ass, they hadn't told her about the drama with the Warriors.

She didn't know they'd come after me. She didn't know they were a threat. So how could we blame her? Presley was in the dark, taking the side of her fiancé.

"It's not your business," Presley snapped.

"He wants to join the Warriors."

She rolled her eyes. "No, he doesn't. He was hanging out with a few of them for a while, but I haven't seen them in weeks. Besides, he promised me he wouldn't join that club."

"His promises don't hold a lot of water. When's he gonna get around to buying you a ring? Set a wedding date yet?"

Her nostrils flared. "Why are you doing this? Why are you making me hate you right now?"

Draven's eyes didn't narrow like I'd expected. They softened. "I won't be here to walk you down the aisle. Doing my best while I can to make sure the man you meet at the end of it deserves to be standing there."

Presley had asked Draven to walk her down the aisle? A pang of jealousy hit. If I ever had a real wedding, he wouldn't be there to give me away either.

The fury on Presley's face washed away with the sheen

of tears in her eyes. "I know you don't like Jeremiah. He's just . . . going through a phase. Trust me. Please? I'll be fine. And would you stop talking like you're dying?" She slid into the booth beside him, resting her head on his shoulder. "It's not like you're never going to see us again."

"No." Draven's definite tone made Presley sit up straight. "I won't see you again."

My spine stiffened. "What do you mean?"

"If they find me guilty, which they will, I'm going away. You girls are not to visit me." He pinned me with his stare. "I don't want either of you in that place."

"But—"

"Ask Isaiah. Ask him if he'd want you in there. If he says yes, I'll reconsider."

Isaiah wouldn't say yes. There was a shadow in his eyes when he thought about that place. While he'd confided in me about Shannon's death, I knew his time in prison would never be a discussion point for us.

He'd shelter me from its horrors.

Draven would do the same.

I wasn't ready to give up my father.

In a way, Draven had helped me let go of some of the resentment I had toward Mom. He was charismatic. He was brutally honest, even harsh at times. He didn't hesitate to plow past the bullshit and talk about something uncomfortable head-on.

He was a pain in the ass.

I loved him for it.

And I could see how Mom had fallen in love with him too. Not that her actions were right, but I saw why she'd loved him.

Draven had this pull about him, this utter confidence.

Not many men accused of murder would walk into the diner with his swagger. He didn't give a shit what other people thought. The only opinions that held any weight were those of his family and friends.

The fact that Dash wasn't speaking to him was tearing him to pieces.

Draven's love for his late wife was undying. Draven didn't speak about Chrissy often, but he'd mention her every once in a while if he had a story to share. He'd get a faraway look in his eyes that held eternal love. That love was always accompanied by a shade of regret—for how he'd treated her and for how she'd died.

And there was regret in Draven's heart for my mom.

I'd always be disappointed that Mom hadn't been brave enough to tell me the truth. But I understood.

Draven was her mistake. Her crippling weakness.

Maybe that was why Presley was so attached to Jeremiah. He was her weakness too.

"I'm coming to visit you in prison." Presley pushed out of the booth and without another word, walked for the door. But about halfway across the diner, she spun back around, hurrying to our table to bend down and place a kiss on Draven's cheek.

He looked up at her with loving eyes and gave her a smile, and then she was gone again.

"What did you do to Jeremiah?" I asked.

"I, uh . . . *encouraged* him to break it off with Pres. Told him if he wanted to be a Warrior, he'd have a better chance at making it if he wasn't tied to a woman in Clifton Forge."

"Wait. You want him to be a Warrior?"

"I want him out of Presley's life. She knows she's got a good gig at the garage. She likes it there and isn't eager to leave. Ashton and the Warriors are three hours away. Now, maybe the Warriors think they'll gain information through her, but they won't. I trust her completely. And eventually, the distance would drive them apart. I'm hoping if Jeremiah joins the club, it'll be the end for them."

Then for Presley's sake, I hoped he'd join too.

Draven left two twenties on the table after we drained our coffee mugs. Then we pulled on our coats and hats to venture outside. He'd started his truck already—remote start. Isaiah had bought me the same type of kit for Christmas and had installed it on New Year's Day.

We got inside Draven's truck and I buckled my seat belt. When he put the truck in reverse, I looked over at his profile. His eyes met mine and he smiled.

Damn it, I'd miss him. I hadn't realized how much until just now. We hadn't had enough time. We talked about me mostly and not nearly enough about him.

What television shows did he like? What was his favorite book? What was his favorite part about Clifton Forge?

All stupid questions but I wanted answers. But instead of asking those, I went for one that had been on my mind for the past month.

"Are you scared?" I whispered as he drove.

"No." He let out a long sigh. "I'm tired. Tired of fighting. Been doing it for too many years."

Would he have to fight in prison? Probably. I didn't think prison would be an easy end to his life. And damn it, he didn't deserve to fight in there. This wasn't his fault.

While he was inside, I would keep fighting outside. My phone calls to pawnshops hadn't turned up Mom's necklace, but I'd call more. I'd start researching every single resident of

Clifton Forge and Ashton besides. Somehow, I'd find the evidence to set him free.

The garage was in front of us before I was ready, and a sting hit my nose. Emotion clawed its way up my throat because I didn't want to have this goodbye.

"I'm glad I got to know you." Draven reached over and put his hand on my shoulder.

My chin quivered. "I'm glad I got to know you too. Will you write to me?"

His answer was a sad smile. Did that mean no? Would he really go to prison and I'd never hear from him again?

I unbuckled my seat belt as he shut off the truck. We climbed out in unison, the slamming of our doors echoing in the quiet parking lot. He met me in front of the grill.

"Take care of yourself."

I nodded. "You too."

He took a small step forward, his arms lifting slightly.

I'd never hugged Draven. I'd hardly touched the man. But in that moment, I flew into his arms, wrapping my arms around his waist and hugging him for all the hugs I'd missed in my life.

"Proud of you, girl." Draven's whisper hit my ear at the same time the tears fell down my cheeks. "So damn proud."

I smashed my face harder into his chest. "Thanks, Dad."

His arms squeezed tight at the name. "Goddamn, I wish things were different."

So did I.

We stood there, hugging, for a long time, until the sound of boots coming down the stairs broke us apart. I swiped at the tears on my cheeks. Draven sniffled, clearing his throat as Isaiah joined us by the truck.

One look at me and I was tucked into his side. Then he

held out his free hand to Draven. "Appreciate all you've done for me."

"You take care of her and consider the debt paid."

Isaiah simply nodded.

I met Draven's eyes once more, the shade of them the same I saw in the mirror every morning. "I don't want to say goodbye."

"So don't." He winked, then spun on his boot heel and went to his truck.

Isaiah and I stood in the lot until his taillights disappeared down the street.

"You okay?" Isaiah asked.

"No." Today, I wasn't okay. Tomorrow didn't look good either.

But we'd get through this eventually.

And I didn't care what Draven said, I'd see him again. I'd go to that prison and keep learning about my father. I'd ask the questions I hadn't yet. And one day, maybe, we'd be able to set him free.

———

FOOTSTEPS on the stairs outside woke Isaiah and me from a dead sleep.

I sat up with a gasp, blinking my eyes awake as my heart galloped. He beat me out of bed. I whipped off the covers, reaching for the sweatshirt I'd tossed on the floor. The clock on my nightstand glowed two minutes after three.

Who the hell was at the apartment at three o'clock in the morning?

Isaiah hurried to the closet for a shoebox. That box had

been the only thing he'd had in there besides clothes. When I'd done the reorganization, he'd asked to keep it inside.

Because there was a gun inside.

"Isaiah." My worried eyes met his as a knock came at the door.

He held up a finger to his lips. Then he pointed for me to stay back as he padded across the floor.

Goddamn it, why didn't we have a peephole? We needed a peephole. After tonight, we were getting one.

Another knock echoed through the dark apartment just as Isaiah turned the deadbolt. He peered through the crack as the door opened, his foot and knee braced on the backside to slow down anyone who might try and bust inside.

The muscles in his shoulders bunched. "What are you doing here?"

"Here."

I vaguely recognized the man's voice but couldn't place it. My heart raced.

Isaiah opened the door an inch wider to take something from the man outside. "What is it?"

"Justice. You're both free." The man's footsteps started down the stairs.

Isaiah slammed the door and flipped the lock. Then he went to the window, watching with the gun still in his hand. The engine outside was barely audible, but it was there. Then it faded as our visitor left.

"Who was that?"

Isaiah set the gun on the table, then stretched for the light switch. My eyes squinted as the room illuminated, and when they adjusted, I spotted the white envelope in Isaiah's hand.

"Who was that?" I asked again as he tore into the envelope.

"Tucker."

My jaw dropped. "Tucker, as in the Warriors' president Tucker?"

He nodded, then pulled a letter from the envelope.

I crossed the room, standing at his side as he unfolded the page.

Isaiah was too tall for me to read over his shoulder and he kept turning so I couldn't read what it said from his side. His face paled. His eyes narrowed at the handwriting on the page.

"Isaiah?"

He kept reading.

"Isaiah, you're scaring me." I tugged on his elbow.

Still, he kept reading. Only when he was done did he turn to me. His face was twisted in agony, his eyes full of sorrow.

"What?" I choked out. "Tell me."

He tossed the letter on the table beside the gun, stopping me as I reached for it. With both hands on my arms, he pushed me backward, away from the paper and to the couch. I sat as he crouched down in front of me, his Adam's apple bobbing while he searched for the words. His hands stayed firm on my arms, braced like he was ready to catch me if I fell.

"It's Draven."

My heart stopped. "What?"

"He's . . . dead," he whispered. "I'm so sorry, doll. He's gone."

CHAPTER TWENTY-TWO

GENEVIEVE

J ustice.

That word had been ringing in my ears for a month and a half.

Draven's death hadn't been justice.

It was my nightmare.

The letter Tucker Talbot had delivered to Isaiah and me had been from Draven. My father had written three—one for each of his children.

Dash had gotten both his own and Nick's. Tucker had dropped them off immediately after dropping off mine.

In them, Draven had confessed to the agreement he'd made with Tucker.

Tucker got the truth. He knew Isaiah had killed the Warrior in that cabin. He knew I had started the fire that had destroyed thousands of dollars' worth of drugs.

And he'd made amends for it all.

Draven had paid Tucker for the drugs with his own money. And he'd paid for that Warrior's life with his own.

My father had sacrificed himself to the Warriors so that Dash, Nick and I would be safe.

According to the letter, Tucker had agreed to stay away from us, to not seek further vengeance. Over the past six weeks, Tucker had stayed true to his word. I'd had my doubts, but Emmett had explained to me a few days after Draven's funeral that an agreement made between club presidents, even a former president, was as good as gold.

We were safe.

It had cost us our father.

It wasn't fair. Draven had fought for us. He'd died for us. He'd stolen our chance to prove his innocence.

Isaiah had told me that Draven had set himself free.

Was that justice?

It sure as fuck didn't feel like it to me.

"Ready?" Isaiah asked as he stood by the door.

I nodded, grabbing my coat and following him out the door. March had come in like a lion with a blizzard worse than any we'd seen so far this winter. The tormented sky, gray and angry, matched my mood.

At the moment, my anger was the only thing keeping me grounded. I'd wrapped it around the torn and shattered pieces of my heart like heavy chains.

When Isaiah opened the driver's side door for me, I got in without a word. Turns out, a marriage can survive on silence. At least, ours did. I didn't have much to talk about, so I didn't bother. Whatever bitter and painful words were on the tip of my tongue would land on the wrong person, so I kept them inside.

The person who needed to hear them was dead.

How could Draven do this in secret? How could he make this arrangement with Tucker?

I can die knowing I did what needed to be done.

That had been one of many infuriating, devastating sentences in his letter.

Well, fuck that. His sacrifice wasn't the only option. We could have worked something else out.

The only person angrier than me was Dash.

If my mood over the past month was gray, Dash's was onyx.

Bryce said Dash blamed himself for not seeing this coming. For not talking to Draven.

Apparently, Dash's letter had explained a lot more than mine. There were pieces included that would stay between Draven and Dash, things having to do with the club that I'd never be privy to.

It came down to one fact: Tucker hadn't believed me. My lies hadn't been convincing.

The Warriors had been set on retaliation. The Tin Kings, former or not, had owed them a life. They'd suspected I'd lied so they'd been set on Dash's life to even the score. Or Draven's.

Tucker's wish had been granted.

The attack on me in the parking lot had been another intimidation play by the Warriors. They'd done it to rattle us into a confession. It made sense now why the man had run away so easily.

In a way, their plan had worked. Isaiah and I had told the truth.

But our timing had been a mistake. Maybe if I'd told the truth in the clubhouse meeting, Draven would be alive. Maybe we wouldn't have had to bury him beside his wife.

Had I known this was how things would end, I would have done everything differently.

This wasn't right. It wasn't supposed to end this way.

This was not justice.

Isaiah walked in on Presley crying in the office at least once a week. Emmett and Leo were withdrawn. Bryce was sad and Dash was, well . . . angry. I could relate.

Did they all blame me? They should. My presence in Clifton Forge had made everything worse.

Since Draven's funeral, I'd done my best to avoid everyone at the garage. To dodge the distraught looks and pity. There'd be no avoidance today.

"Hey," Isaiah said as I raced away from the garage. "Take it easy on the speed. For me."

"Sorry." I eased off the gas pedal, loosening my grip on the steering wheel. "I just . . . I don't want to go."

"I know. But your best friend had a baby and wants you to visit. Can't beg out of this one."

Bryce had given birth to a baby boy last night and had called first thing, inviting us to the hospital to meet him.

Xander Lane Slater.

She'd told me the baby's name months ago. Lane was her father's name. I think if she hadn't already told her dad and seen his excitement at being the namesake, she would have changed Xander's middle name to Draven.

"In and out," Isaiah said as we parked at the hospital in a space marked for visitors.

I nodded. "In and out."

The gift I'd already wrapped was in the backseat. Before I was ready, we were in the maternity ward, walking down the hospital hallway to Bryce's room.

"Knock, knock." The door was open but I entered cautiously in case they were asleep.

"Hey! Come in." Bryce rested on the bed with a little

blue bundle in her arms. The smile on her face erased any hesitation for being here. That and the fact that Dash wasn't in the room.

I went to her side, bending to see the baby. "Hello there, handsome."

His eyes were closed, his dark lashes forming perfect sweeps across his cheeks. A fluff of dark hair peeked out from beneath the blue beanie on his head. His lips were pink and soft and all I wanted to do was cry.

"He's perfect." I smiled at my friend, who looked at her baby like the miracle he was.

Xander was the only good thing to come from these past months. He was a precious gift, to be protected and cherished and loved by his family, even if we were missing one.

A wave of sadness hit, followed by a wave of understanding. The anger I'd held fast for six weeks loosened its grip on my heart.

This was the reason Draven had made his decision. Xander was the reason he'd made his sacrifice. So his grandson would live his life without a shadow looming.

Isaiah set our gift aside and came to my side, squeezing Bryce's shoulder. "Congrats."

"Thanks." Bryce lifted Xander higher. "Want to hold him?"

"Yes." I wasn't sure if she was offering Xander to me or Isaiah, but I didn't give him a chance. I scooped up that baby, cradling him in my arms as I danced him around the room. He scrunched up his nose, not happy with being jostled. "Oh, I love you already. I'm your Aunt V."

I wanted him to call me V, like Isaiah did. Plus, there was no way a small child would manage Genevieve.

"Babe, all they had was chocolate." Dash came through the door, a wide smile on his face. It fell when he spotted me.

"Congrats." Isaiah walked over, his hand extended.

Dash's smile came back as he shook hands. "Thanks, man."

"He's beautiful," I said, looking at Xander.

Dash ignored me, going to Bryce's bed and dropping a kiss to her forehead. "They didn't have strawberry."

"That's okay." She took what I assumed was a milkshake and put it on the tray beside her bed, smiling again at me with Xander.

"So how did things go?" I asked, taking one of the chairs against the wall. Isaiah joined me, sitting close to look at the baby.

Dash perched on the edge of Bryce's bed, rubbing her foot through her blanket as she told us about Xander's relatively peaceful entry into the world. When he started to fuss, I handed him over.

"We'll let you guys be." I bent and hugged Bryce. "Let me know when you're settled at home. I'll bring cookies."

"That would be great." She shifted, gently bouncing Xander. "Thanks for coming."

Isaiah waved goodbye to them both, then followed me out the door.

We were halfway to the elevator when I realized I didn't have my purse. "Shit. I forgot—"

I spun and saw Dash marching our way, my purse in his hand. "Here."

He threw it at me.

I caught it, barely, fumbling it so the contents wouldn't spill on the linoleum floor.

That toss was the last straw.

"What the hell was that?" Isaiah snapped.

Dash didn't respond. He clamped his jaw shut, spun and walked away.

"Stop." My voice carried down the hallway. I handed my purse to Isaiah.

Dash didn't stop.

"Do you want to have this out in the hallway?" I called after him. "Or in your wife's room with your new baby?"

His steps slowed. He turned, squaring his shoulders, planting his hands on his hips. "What?"

"I'm done with your attitude. Done. You don't get to treat me like this anymore. No more glares. No more snapping. No more treating me like a second-rate citizen."

Dash didn't respond. He only shifted his arms, crossing them over his chest.

"I didn't ask to be here. I didn't ask for my mother to be murdered. I didn't ask to be kidnapped. I didn't ask for my father to die. I didn't ask for any of this."

I took a step forward, standing my tallest. Months and months of anger and frustration bubbled to the surface. My hands shook so I fisted them at my sides, not wanting him to see. Then I did my best to keep my racing heart under control and speak with a steady voice.

"I have no family. None. Except for you and Nick. Isn't that a sad fucking fate? All of my family is dead because of some motorcycle club I didn't know existed a year ago. Not the Warriors. *Your* club." I poked at his shoulder. "Yet you act like this is my fault. So fuck you."

He winced.

"Fuck. You." I poked him again, one jab for each word. "I'm not going anywhere. I'm here. You have to learn to live with me. I didn't ask for any of this but I'm here. I'm—"

287

"You're right." He dropped his arms, letting out a long breath. Then he hung his head, rubbing the back of his neck.

I was right? What was the catch? I didn't move. I didn't breathe. I braced for him to deliver a blow that would leave me a shriveling mess. I'd gone for the gusto, but the truth was, I didn't have the energy to keep it up. That outburst had dried up my reserves.

Things had just been . . . hard. Much too hard. And damn it, I was exhausted.

"Sorry," he whispered to the floor.

I blinked. "What?"

"Sorry," Dash said, louder this time, making eye contact.

"Okay." I gave him a sideways glance. What was happening? Was that a real apology?

"I loved my mom."

"I loved mine too."

Dash nodded, then turned, the conversation over. But before he got too far, he spun back again. "I'm angry at Dad."

"So am I. But don't take it out on me."

"He's not here. He did this for me. To save me so I could meet my son." Dash's voice cracked. And I saw, behind the anger, the regret that was torturing him. He hadn't made amends with Draven. And now Draven was gone.

Dash swallowed hard. "Xander will never know his grandfather."

A tear worked free and dripped down my cheek. "No, he won't."

Dash gritted his teeth and closed his eyes. When he opened them again, he had himself under control.

I wished I could say the same. The tears fell freely down my face. No amount of blinking could keep them from dropping.

Dash was blurry as he stepped closer. Three long strides and my brother was hugging me, squishing me to his chest. Shocked by the change, it took me a moment to hug him back. Then my arms found their way around his back.

The embrace didn't last long, seconds really, but in that moment, I didn't feel quite so alone.

Then he was gone. Without another word, Dash let me go and walked back to Bryce's room like his boots were on fire.

Isaiah came and put his hands around my shoulders as I swiped at my cheeks, drying the tears. "Come on, doll. Let's get out of here."

I sniffled as we rode the elevator to the ground floor. I used every moment of the drive home to pull myself together. I feared that once we were inside the apartment, I'd break apart. The hold I had on my emotions was by the fingertips, at best. But when we walked into the apartment and I kicked off my shoes, I felt something I hadn't since the night Tucker had delivered Draven's letter.

Peace.

I walked to the bed, sat on the side and opened the nightstand drawer. I took out the letter and ran my fingers over the black script.

"He loved us. That's why he did it."

"Yeah." Isaiah sat at my side with an arm around my shoulders.

"I wish it hadn't come to this."

We'd told the world that Draven had killed himself. Even Presley thought his death was suicide. Everyone believed the story that Dash had found Draven at home, swinging from a rope.

No one doubted it, not even the police. The world saw

Draven as a coward, a man who'd taken his own life instead of facing the verdict he'd been about to receive.

None of us knew what their verdict would have been.

The truth was, Tucker had killed Draven. He'd hung him inside Draven's own home. Then he'd delivered my letter, followed by the others.

Dash had been the one to find Draven's body, so at least that part was true.

Draven had already staged a suicide note.

"Will life ever be normal?" I whispered.

"For us? Probably not."

I closed my eyes and fell into Isaiah's embrace. He wound both arms around me, holding me as I breathed in the smell of his shirt and soaked in the warmth of his arms. I ran my hands up his back, then let them sink down, lower and lower. My fingers wandered between us, trailing down one of his thighs.

I tipped up my chin, finding his colorful eyes waiting, those swirls darkened with every skipping heartbeat. Then his lips dropped to mine and all was lost.

My worries. My fears.

My heart.

He captured them all with the sweep of his tongue.

We undressed each other, both tossing clothes to the floor as we moved deeper into the bed. Isaiah and I hadn't been together in weeks. Not since . . . before.

We were a mess of kisses and desperation. My hands explored his abs and his firm chest, remembering what it felt like to have his hot skin under my palms. His fingers dug into my spine as they made their way lower to cup and squeeze my ass.

We collided, two people who needed to get lost in a feeling other than grief.

Isaiah laid me on the bed, giving me his weight as his cock nestled between my legs. He paused, locking his eyes with mine. When I nodded, he sank deep, stretching and filling me to the point I was consumed.

My eyes were squeezed shut as he moved, in and out. My hands held on to him with all the strength I had left as he rocked us together, over and over. And then I let go, my orgasm building so fast and hard that I came on a silent scream. A tear dripped down my temple. Isaiah kissed it away before he buried his face in my hair and shuddered through his own release.

We held together until he pulled out and shuffled us both under the covers. Then we found one another again. We didn't drift apart. When many would have pulled away, the hurdles life had thrown at Isaiah and me only seemed to push us closer.

By all rights, I was free to leave Clifton Forge. I could walk away from this life and start fresh. But I'd never leave Isaiah. The life I'd planned to return to in Colorado wasn't my dream anymore.

Isaiah was my dream.

He pulled me tight to his chest, kissing my forehead. "Why haven't we been doing this?"

"Good question." I giggled, feeling lighter than I had in weeks. I lifted up to see his face and what I saw stole my breath.

Isaiah smiled.

Not a grin. Not a turn of one corner of his lips. Not just the crinkles at his eyes. A full-blown, goddamn-my-husband-is-gorgeous smile. Straight, white teeth and everything.

It was a sight I'd never forget.

And I'd put that there. Me. The woman who'd planned to let the next in line have all the smiles.

What a fool. No one was taking Isaiah from me. There'd be no next in line. I was keeping him.

Because I was in love with my husband.

Draven must have known. Otherwise he wouldn't have entrusted Isaiah with my heart. I hoped he'd found his peace. I hoped he'd reunited with his wife. I hoped that if he saw Mom, he'd tell her that I was okay.

Tears fell without my permission, blurring Isaiah's smile. It disappeared altogether when he hugged me to his chest.

And he held me, all through the night, while I mourned the loss of my parents.

While I said my silent goodbyes.

CHAPTER TWENTY-THREE

ISAIAH

"You okay?" Genevieve placed her hand on my heaving chest.

I nodded, my eyes wide as they stared at the dark ceiling. "Just a dream."

A nightmare. I hadn't had it in months. When would it fucking go away? Now it was back, just when I'd started to think the past would stop visiting me in my sleep.

Genevieve shifted closer, resting her head on my bare shoulder. "Want to talk about it?"

"I don't know." I rubbed a hand over my face.

Maybe I'd had the nightmare because we hadn't had sex last night. Normally, we wore each other out before sleep, exploring bodies and making each other come until there was no energy left for dreams. But last night, we'd simply fallen asleep, curled together.

In the past month since Xander had been born, Genevieve had come a long way toward making peace with both Draven's and Amina's deaths. But there was still pain there, nights she'd be shaking so hard in her sleep, it would wake me up. I'd hold her tight and whisper in her ear until she clung to me, using my body to forget. Maybe I hadn't had a nightmare because I'd been so worried about her demons that mine had taken a backseat.

The days were flying by and blending together. The only thing that made them stand apart was sex and Genevieve. I could remember every position, every one of her moans. I could recall with perfect clarity how she'd clenched around my cock five nights ago. And the night before that. And the night before that.

Was it unhealthy that sex had become our coping mechanism?

Probably, but I wasn't going to stop.

Not until she left me and I quit cold turkey.

"Isaiah?" Genevieve lifted up. "What is it that you see?"

I cupped her face with my hand. "You."

"Where?"

"In a car," I whispered. The nightmare was so fresh, I could almost see the trickle of blood on her chin. I wiped at the invisible line. "We get in a crash."

"Oh." Her chin fell. "It's like Shannon."

I nodded. "Yeah."

Genevieve shifted to lie on her back. Her hand found mine beneath the covers. "I've been having the same dream, over and over, about Xander."

I gripped her hand tighter at the confession. Each time I'd woken her from a dream, she hadn't wanted to talk about it. I hadn't pressed, assuming they'd been about Draven. "What happens?"

"The guy who kidnapped me takes him too. We're here, I'm babysitting, and he comes in and rips him from my arms."

294

"Sorry." I turned my cheek on the pillow to meet her gaze.

"He's still out there," she whispered. "With everything that's happened, the kidnapping, Mom and Draven, it's so much. Maybe these nightmares are a sign that I need to get some help. That *we* need to get some help."

"Maybe," I muttered, turning my attention to the ceiling again. "I went to a counselor for a while, right before I got parole."

That counselor had probably helped me qualify for parole. I'd been sentenced to five years and had only served three. It was unlikely my sanity would have survived those last two years.

"Why don't you think it worked?" Genevieve asked. She didn't ask if it had helped, because she already knew it hadn't. She knew I hadn't found peace with my sins.

"Don't know." Telling that counselor everything that had happened between Shannon and me hadn't lifted my grief or guilt in the slightest. The only time I'd felt any relief had been after I'd confessed the accident to Genevieve. "Maybe he wasn't the right person to talk to."

She shifted to her side. Her other hand came to rest over my heart. "It was an accident."

"One that I caused."

"Will you blame yourself forever?"

"Yes." The word hung in the darkness.

There was no letting go of that mistake. There was no forgetting how I'd caused Shannon's death. For the rest of my life, I'd regret my choices that night.

I'd always be sorry.

"Do you think, someday, the past will stop defining who you are?"

Said a different way, Genevieve was asking if I'd ever be happy.

Would I stop living life by going through the motions? Did I deserve to feel joy? Did I deserve a life with her?

I wanted it. I wanted that future more than I'd wanted anything in my life. I wanted to deserve this woman in this bed. I wanted to be a man who smiled because mine seemed to illuminate hers.

But I didn't have a damn clue how to get there.

"I hope so, doll."

"I hope so too," she whispered.

We lay in the dark, waiting and wondering if sleep would come. I doubted it would for me, but Genevieve needed rest. Before she drifted off, I shifted to my side. "Mom's been asking us to come to Bozeman. Would you go with me?"

She nodded, her eyelids growing heavier. "When?"

"Tomorrow?" We didn't have any plans for our weekend. Like most Saturdays, Genevieve and I spent them together.

"Sure." Her eyes fell closed. "I'll drive."

———

AS GENEVIEVE PULLED AWAY from the garage the next morning, the roads were mostly empty. It only took me a minute to settle into the passenger seat and breathe normally. *Progress.* Mile by mile, riding with Genevieve was getting easier. Though me driving her was a feat I'd never master.

The snow around town had melted with the early April rain. The mountains in the distance were still capped white, and they would be until summer. Tomorrow, I was getting out my bike and putting the truck away until winter returned.

It was barely warm enough—I'd be the only idiot on a motorcycle in April.

I scanned the streets as we wound through town toward the highway, something that had become a habit this winter. "Two and a half months and no sign of the Warriors," I muttered.

"Tucker has his justice and is leaving us free. Drav— Dad's plan worked." Genevieve kept her eyes on the road. They were hidden behind large, black sunglasses, making it hard to read her expression. Her voice was flat except for the slight inflection of pain.

Genevieve had stopped calling him Draven whenever his name came up. She tried to call him Dad, even when she was around Dash. It wasn't natural yet, but I hoped one day it would be. And I hoped one day it wouldn't bite when she mentioned his name.

It was too fresh, the wound just stitched. But she was strong. Genevieve would weather this like she had everything else this past year. She'd survive it, though things wouldn't be the same. Her anger and frustration had helped get her through Amina's death. When they'd faded, a permanent bruise had remained on her heart. Draven's death had left another.

She mourned him.

We all did.

Dash had finally cleaned out Draven's office last week. He'd done it on a whim, and with Bryce's help, he'd turned the space into the waiting area. No one wanted to be in there. Presley refused to sit behind Draven's old desk. Bryce wouldn't either. So they'd taken away Draven's desk and donated it to charity. Then they'd bought a couple of couches so customers waiting for their car to be ready weren't in the front reception area with Presley.

Genevieve had started stopping at the office more when she came home from work. She'd been shortening her lunch hours, leaving thirty minutes earlier in the day. Those thirty minutes equated to thirty minutes with Presley and Bryce each afternoon before the garage closed at five.

She wasn't as close to Presley as she was Bryce, but their friendship was blossoming. The three of them leaned on one another, forging ahead through their grief.

"Did Pres text you back?" I asked.

She nodded. "Yeah. She didn't feel like coming along."

Damn it. We'd hoped Presley would take our invite and leave town for the weekend. We were all trying to keep her occupied on the weekends so she wouldn't drive to Ashton. She'd probably left Friday after work.

As Draven had encouraged, Jeremiah had joined the Warriors this past month.

What none of us could have expected was for Presley to stick with him. During the week, when she wasn't at the garage, she was at home alone. When five o'clock hit on Friday, she was on the road to visit him.

Since he'd moved, he had yet to return to Clifton Forge and visit her.

"I don't get it," I muttered.

"Me neither. She could do so much better. And he's not even that good-looking."

I huffed a laugh. "That's what people say about you. *What the hell is Genevieve doing with that guy from the garage?*"

"Oh, please." Genevieve rolled her eyes. "You look in the

same mirror I do every morning. You know you're the hot one in this pair."

"You think I'm hot?"

She slid her sunglasses into her hair, her expression turning serious. "Isaiah, you're the sexiest, most handsome man I've seen in my life. And your heart? When you let me in, you literally steal my breath away."

I blinked. Was she serious? Sure seemed like it. Maybe she didn't see me as a tatted, ex-con loser.

Genevieve didn't expect a response. She turned her attention to the highway because she knew I got twitchy when she wasn't fully focused on the road. She put her sunglasses back over her eyes, protecting them against the glare of the morning sun.

I swallowed the lump in my throat and digested what she'd said. Did she really think I was breathtaking? That I had a good heart? I wasn't anything special, but the conviction in her words, the devotion, made me replay her sentences a few times.

I was a monster, not a savior.

And she thought *I* was the hot one in our pair? Christ, she was delusional.

"You're hot."

She shot me a wry grin. "Gee. Thanks."

"You're the most beautiful woman I've ever seen." True story. Part of what had made it hard to look at her in those early days was that I'd felt guilty. Genevieve outshone everyone living—and those who were not.

"I didn't compliment you so I could get one back."

"I know. I'm saying it because it's true."

She smiled. "Well, thanks."

"You're beautiful," I repeated, just to make sure it sank

in. "You're kind. You're smart. You make the best cookies I've ever tasted. And every time we're together, I can't believe it gets better."

Genevieve's cheeks turned a rosy pink. "I thought it was just me. I haven't, uh, been with anyone in a long time. And even then, I'm not very experienced."

"Same."

"Really?" She furrowed her forehead. "As previously stated, you're sexy as hell. I bet women were crawling all over you."

I chuckled. "When I was younger, yeah. Maybe. But then . . ."

"Right. Shannon. You were with her."

"No." I shook my head. "We were never together."

Genevieve's jaw dropped. "But—"

"We didn't. Not once." Neither of us had wanted to have sex. We hadn't thought it was right, considering she was having Kaine's baby. We'd kissed. We'd held hands. But her body, otherwise, had been for that baby.

Genevieve tapped her fingertips on the wheel like she was counting them. "So before me, you weren't with a woman in—"

"Years." Six of them, to be exact. Genevieve had broken my dry spell. I was sure those first couple of times together, I'd put on a horrible performance. Maybe that was why I'd been trying to make it up to her ever since we'd stopped pretending we didn't crave one another.

"It's been a long time for me too."

"Really?"

She nodded. "I was busy working. I went on some dates but there wasn't anyone who I liked that much."

God, I liked that. I liked that it was us, together. I hadn't

300

even thought to ask her if she'd had a boyfriend in Denver. We'd gotten married and I'd just assumed there was no one she'd left behind. I was really fucking glad there wasn't, that she wasn't pining for someone I hadn't even realized might exist.

Did she think I was still pining for Shannon?

"Genevieve." I waited until she glanced over, until I had her attention for a second. "You stand apart. From everyone."

She faced forward. "Is it bad to say I'm jealous? Because she had you first."

"There's nothing to be jealous about. I loved Shannon, but I'm not in love with her memory."

My heart wasn't hers anymore. I'd given it to Genevieve.

"What was Shannon like?" Genevieve was the only person who said Shannon's name without fear of how I'd react.

"She was sweet. Her parents used to say she'd been a fairy in another life."

She'd been bright and sunny. She'd floated more than walked. But she'd been fragile, like a flower. She hadn't had Genevieve's strength. She never would have survived the things Genevieve had this past year.

Shannon's parents had been like that too. Soft. Kind, but soft. I thought about them often and how they'd coped with losing their daughter. According to Mom, they still lived in Bozeman. Mom had bumped into them at Costco not long after I'd gotten out of prison. Mom had left her cart in the aisle and left the store, not because she couldn't handle the encounter, but because she knew Shannon's parents might not.

It was part of the reason my life in Bozeman had been so confined to Mom's house after prison. It had become a cage of its own. I hadn't wanted to run into old friends or Shannon's family.

I'd worked at a lube shop in the shitty end of town, where the chances of running into anyone from the past were slim. I'd lived dirt cheap with Mom, waiting until my two years of parole were up, then I'd started looking for a job outside of Bozeman.

Enter Draven and the Clifton Forge Garage.

And I'd gotten the hell out of Bozeman before I'd suffocated.

"I never apologized to them," I confessed. "To Shannon's parents."

"It's not too late. Maybe you could write them a letter."

The counselor in prison had said the same. "A letter feels like a cop-out."

I deserved to feel their wrath head-on, not hide behind a piece of paper. Not leave them alone to suffer my words without the chance to retaliate.

"Do you know where they live?"

I nodded. "In Bozeman."

Genevieve opened her mouth but closed it without a word.

"What?"

She stayed silent.

"Tell me."

"No. I'm trying not to push you."

Maybe that was what I needed. She had this way of giving me time. She gave me patience and grace. I didn't deserve any of it, but what she'd said last night had been in my head all morning.

Do you think, someday, the past will stop defining who you are?

The guilt of Shannon's death was permanent. It was as much a part of me now as the tattoos on my skin. But there was a difference between living with the guilt and letting it control my life.

Until recently, there hadn't been much for me to live for. Guilt and shame had been my bed partners. Now, I only wanted Genevieve in my heart while we slept. I wouldn't get there on my own.

"What if you did?" I asked. "What if you pushed me?"

"Then I'd drive you to their house and wait for you in the car."

I swallowed hard. "Okay."

"Okay?"

I put my hand on her leg. "Okay."

When we reached Bozeman, I didn't give her directions to Mom's house. I took us toward Shannon's parents' place instead.

"Do you think they still live here?" Genevieve slowed as we drove through a quiet neighborhood.

At the end of the block ahead, I spotted the two-story green home with the rust-red roof. "Yeah."

Yeah, they still lived there. Because in the yard was a familiar head of blond hair, bent low to tug at a patch of weeds in a flower bed.

Kathy. Shannon's mom.

"Park here," I ordered and Genevieve jerked the car over to the sidewalk, stopping one house down. I pointed to Kathy as Shannon's father, Timothy, came out of the house, wiping at something on his hands. "That's them."

"Her parents?" she asked, taking off her sunglasses.

I nodded, unable to speak or rip my eyes away. Kathy looked up at Timothy and smiled. It wasn't big or flashy, but it was pure. There wasn't a bit of sorrow on her face. What Kathy felt was what she showed. I knew because Shannon had been the same way. She'd inherited that same carefree smile.

Timothy said something to Kathy, making her toss her head back and laugh. They both did. Then he dropped to his knees beside her, put an arm around her shoulders and hauled her close for a kiss on the temple.

Kathy patted his cheek with her garden gloves on. It must have left a smudge because they laughed again as she cleaned him off.

The scene hit me square in the chest. I didn't dare blink in case it vanished. "They look . . ."

"Happy," Genevieve finished.

I nodded, my eyes struggling to believe what I was seeing. Could that be right? How was she smiling? How was he laughing? Hadn't I ruined their lives?

Maybe it was all a show. Maybe they were miserable and putting on a happy face for one another. I guess I'd find out.

I unbuckled my seat belt and reached for the handle, but before I could open the door, Genevieve's arm shot out.

"Don't." She grabbed my elbow.

"Huh?" I let go of the door's handle.

"Don't go."

"But I thought—"

"They let it go." She dropped her hand and turned back to Kathy and Timothy. "They found a way to be happy and made it through the grief. Don't bring it to their doorstep."

My shoulders fell. "I want closure, V."

"I know, baby. But this apology, is it for them? Or is it for you?"

We both knew it was the latter.

Genevieve and I sat frozen, watching them as they weeded. As the long moments passed, as they worked their way around their yard trimming daffodils and tulips, I realized that this was my closure.

They gave it to me by living.

Every moment that passed, every smile they shared, it didn't seem fake. This was no show. They'd lost their daughter. They'd lost their baby granddaughter. But here they were, living.

Mom had told me once that Kaine had found some closure with Shannon when he'd visited her grave. I'd tried it. Twice. Each time, I'd left feeling worse than when I'd arrived because staring at that gray tombstone, I'd known she'd never be back. I'd put her in the ground.

I hadn't needed a grave to give me closure. I'd needed this.

Life.

"They let it go," I whispered as Timothy plucked a flower and handed it to his wife.

That flower was hope that maybe one day soon, I could let go of the pain too and live my life with the woman by my side.

I buckled my seat belt. "I'm ready to go home."

"To see your mom?"

I shook my head. "No. I'll call later and make our excuses. We'll come back to see her another day. Right now, I just want to go home. With you."

"Are you okay?"

I took one last look at Kathy and Timothy. They were walking, arm in arm, toward the house. I committed their smiles to memory, then turned to Genevieve.

She glowed. If my heart left her breathless, then hers

gave me a reason to breathe. Did she know how much she meant to me?

No. Because I hadn't told her.

"I don't want to be fake married anymore."

She flinched. "Oh."

"How about you wear that ring for real?"

Her eyebrows came together. "I don't—what?"

"I don't deserve you."

"Isaiah—"

"Let me finish."

She clamped her mouth shut and nodded.

"I don't deserve you, V, but I can't give you up." If she wanted to go, I wouldn't stand in her way. But if she left, I'd never be the same again.

Genevieve's eyes flooded. "I don't want to give you up either."

A smile spread across my face—it only made her cry harder. "So you'll stay my wife?"

She sniffled, swiping at the tears on her cheeks. Then she leaned over, stretching to brush a kiss to my lips. "Yes."

CHAPTER TWENTY-FOUR

GENEVIEVE

"I want to buy you a better ring."

"Seems like a waste of money since I won't wear it." Isaiah grumbled. "V—"

"This is my ring." I wiggled my finger. "I don't want a different one."

He muttered something else under his breath and went back to the laptop on the table. He'd been searching for an apartment in Missoula for over an hour while I'd been packing.

Three months had passed since our trip to Bozeman— since Isaiah and I had become *genuinely* married. It hadn't happened overnight, but in those three months, the two of us had begun to find our peace.

Together.

Our life wasn't exciting. Isaiah and I worked during the day and spent our evenings in the apartment. An adventure for us was going out to eat on a Saturday night.

There were nights when he woke up from a horrific dream. There were days when I cried over the loss of my parents. But we leaned on one another. We pooled our strength. After all, that was how we'd survived the past year.

And now it was time for a change.

After a long discussion, we had decided to leave Clifton Forge.

I'd spent a solid month studying for the LSAT exam. Thankfully, the time I'd spent studying in Denver hadn't been a waste and the information had flooded back. I'd taken the test and passed and was now a future student at the one and only law school in Montana.

We were moving in two weeks, just in time to arrive in Missoula before classes started.

"Come take a look at this one." Isaiah waved me over to the laptop.

I stood from the box I'd just taped shut and walked to the table, bending over his shoulder to scan the specs and photos for the two-bedroom apartment. "It's a little more than we budgeted, but it's a lot nicer than anything else we've found."

"I'll give them a call. Maybe if we commit to a one-year lease, they'll cut the rent by fifty bucks."

My stomach did a somersault. "Are you sure this is what you want?"

He looked up at me, his gaze softening. "Where you go, I go."

"Okay." I smiled and kissed his cheek, then went back to my packing.

Today, I was trying to put away everything I wouldn't need immediately. Dash wasn't in a hurry to rent this place out after we left, but I didn't want our stuff lying around. We'd leave most of the boxes here until we could get them all to Missoula.

I glanced around the room, taking in the space that had become my safe haven. "I'll miss it here."

Isaiah stood and padded over, wrapping his arms around me from behind. Then he bent to whisper in my ear, "Me too."

"I didn't think I'd love it." Not just the apartment, but this town. Clifton Forge was home. Returning to Denver was a long-lost notion.

"We'll come back," he promised.

"Yes, we will."

Jim had encouraged me to study for my LSAT exam. He'd been the one to push me to finally make it happen. Jim and Isaiah had been the co-captains of my personal cheerleading squad.

Jim had insisted I take time at work to study, helping if I had a question. I think he'd been more excited to get my score than me. Waiting those three weeks had been nerve-racking for us both. But he hadn't been at all surprised that I'd scored well. Neither had Isaiah.

I'd applied to law school and been quickly accepted. The day we'd gotten the email, Isaiah had begun looking for jobs.

The only downside to us moving was that he'd be leaving the garage.

Over the past three months, he'd become more and more involved in the custom car remodels. He loved it, working alongside the guys and making something old new again. He loved the art of it.

Some of that artistic flair that Kaine had for his furniture pieces, Isaiah had for cars. He'd pick me up from a long day of work energized, not tired. He'd wear a small smile on his face.

That smile was the best part of my day.

The best part of my night was falling asleep by his side.

"I better finish up a couple of these boxes." I sighed. "Bryce mentioned she was going to come over today with the paper. I doubt I'll be productive after that."

Isaiah held me tighter. "I'm glad you gave her the okay for the piece."

"It was time."

Today, Bryce had published the memorial article for Mom in the Sunday edition of the *Clifton Forge Tribune*. A year in the making, it was something I'd finally given her the green light to print.

My stomach did another somersault followed by a cartwheel. "I don't know why I'm nervous. I've read it already."

"It's an end. It's okay to be anxious about it."

The tiny lump in my throat that had been there all morning was slowly growing bigger. "I just wish . . ." *So many things.*

I wished there wasn't a need for a memorial article in the first place. I wished there weren't such things as Tin Kings or Arrowhead Warriors. I wished that, instead of packing this morning, I was sitting at the diner eating breakfast with Draven—Dad. I still hadn't gotten used to calling him Dad, even in my head.

I wished for all that and that I still would have found Isaiah. I liked to think that maybe the universe would have put us on colliding paths no matter what, and we would have found one another eventually.

It didn't sit well in my stomach that we were leaving Clifton Forge while Mom's killer and our kidnapper was still at large. But there was nothing to be done but move on with our lives.

We didn't have answers.

And I doubted we ever would.

"What can I help with?" Isaiah asked, letting me go.

"Nothing. I'm just packing up some clothes I won't need." The majority of my dress clothes would be in storage until it was time to work again.

With the money I'd saved from the sale of my condo in Denver, Isaiah and I would have enough money to live on through law school. He'd find a job, hopefully, and his paycheck would cover groceries. My savings account combined with what he'd saved working for Dash would cover rent. If I had to, I'd get a part-time job at a coffee shop or something, but we were planning that at least for the first year, I'd focus on school alone.

"I'm going to see if anything new popped up on the job service."

"Okay, baby." I tipped up my chin, requesting a kiss.

Isaiah rarely denied me. His lips brushed mine and a familiar tingle ran down my spine. I pressed in to deepen it, but right as his tongue slid past my lower lip, a car door slammed outside.

Bryce was here.

I frowned, sinking to my heels, then passed Isaiah to open the door.

"Hey," Bryce said, a newspaper in her hand as she started up the stairs. Her dad, Lane, waved to me from his seat in the car.

She still didn't go many places alone. Neither did I.

"Hi." I hugged Bryce as she reached the landing, then led her inside. We sat on the couch and she handed over the paper. Mom's smile greeted me on the front page. I got lost in that smile. Tears flooded my eyes, blurring the picture and the words.

"Oh, Genevieve." Bryce put her arm around my shoulders. "I'm sorry."

"It's all right." I blinked my eyes clear. "I just miss her."

The anger I'd had at Mom was a memory. Time and love had washed away my resentment.

Maybe because I'd fallen in love with Isaiah, I understood how Mom must have felt about Draven. She'd loved him. She'd made a mistake. And she'd done her best to make amends. I liked to think that if she hadn't been killed, she would have told me about him one day.

I scanned the article, reading words I'd read before. Bryce had emailed the draft to me last week. Something about seeing them in black and white on pale gray paper made them sink in deeper than they had on a computer screen. Holding the article, seeing Mom's chocolate chip cookie recipe on the bottom of the page, made it all too real.

Mom was gone. She'd been gone for over a year.

I'd hold on to things like this paper, to the photos I'd collected, so I'd never forget the loving, bright woman she'd once been.

My fingers skimmed over the page. *Love you, Mom.*

I gave Bryce a sad smile. "Thank you."

"Thank you for letting me write it."

"I'm glad it was you."

She hugged me closer. "Me too. I just wish we could have found the guy who did this to her."

"I was just thinking the same thing."

"Can you believe it's been almost a year since the mountain?" she asked.

"One year tomorrow. Sometimes it feels like it was only yesterday. Then others, like it never happened."

"Same." Bryce clenched her fists. "I hate him. I hate that he got away."

"Maybe he got lost on that mountain and was eviscerated by a bear."

She laughed. "I'm down with that theory."

There'd been no hint of our kidnapper all year. Our troubles had come from the Warriors, who stayed away from Clifton Forge now. The only exceptions were the rare weekends when Jeremiah came to see Presley. In months, he'd only come to visit her a handful of times. Even then, he didn't wear his cut around town and mostly stayed close to her place.

"So, is this okay?" Bryce asked, nodding to the paper.

"It's perfect."

She squeezed my knee, then stood. "I'd better get home. Dash is with Xander and although he knows Dad is with me, he'll get twitchy if I'm gone for too long."

Dash was as protective as ever. Given what had happened this past year, I didn't blame him. Isaiah was the same, and rather than rebel against the hovering, I leaned into it. Bryce did too.

With one last hug, she was out the door. Isaiah stood sentry at the top of the stairs, making sure she was in the car with Lane before he came inside.

"You okay?" he asked, pulling me into his arms.

"No, but I will be." I sniffled the threat of more tears away and held him tighter. "Will you hold me for a minute?"

"No need to ask."

I closed my eyes, relaxing into his embrace. Isaiah was more than I could have hoped for. My heart. My savior. "I—"

The words lodged in my throat like they always did.

Three months of real marriage, and I hadn't found the courage to say *I love you*.

There was no question I was in love with Isaiah, and I was fairly certain he loved me too. So why couldn't I say the words? Why couldn't I tell him? What was I waiting for?

I opened my mouth to try again but nothing came out. So I held him tighter, soaking up this quiet moment, until it was time to break apart and get back to packing.

Isaiah hunkered down behind the laptop to resume his job search. So far, he'd been shot down for everything he'd applied for. His criminal record was difficult to get past for most people. They didn't know him or his good heart. All they had was a checkbox next to *felon* on an online application.

He'd find something. It would take time, but he'd eventually find an employer who wasn't concerned about his past. Dash had made some calls to a few garages in Missoula and we were hoping a glowing referral from Dash Slater would pave the way to a job where Isaiah could work for a few years.

Until we came back.

Dash had already promised Isaiah's job would be waiting.

I spent the next hour packing and organizing. It was nearly lunch and my stomach growled when another car door slammed outside. Actually, two.

Isaiah looked over his shoulder to the door. "Was someone else coming over today?"

"Not that I know of." I pushed up from the floor, meeting him at the door.

He opened it just in time for two police officers to walk up the stairs.

My stomach dropped.

Isaiah's spine went rigid and he reached behind him, searching for my hand. I clutched it with all my might.

"Afternoon," one officer said, sliding her sunglasses off her face. The other stood down a couple of stairs, letting his partner do the talking.

"Hi." Isaiah's grip was so strong it hurt. His shoulders were bunched tight. His breaths came in shallow huffs. He was about to lose it.

"Can we help you?" I stepped next to Isaiah, forcing him over so we could both crowd the doorway.

"Are you Genevieve Reynolds?"

I gulped. "Yes."

"Ma'am, we need to ask you some questions at the police station."

Me? Oh my God. This wasn't about Isaiah. It was about me. I wasn't sure if that was a good thing or bad. My heart was racing but I fought to keep my voice calm and innocent. "What's this about?"

"Just have some questions," the officer answered.

"What's this about?" I repeated.

"Sorry, ma'am. We can't discuss that here. Would you please come with us?"

Part of me wanted to object. They weren't here with a warrant. But if I did, they'd only come back with one. Maybe cooperation was the best way to keep these questions aimed my way and not at Isaiah.

"Am I being arrested?"

"Not at this time."

Not at this time? My throat went dry. How could they know? There was no way, right? Maybe this was about Draven's fake suicide. Maybe they suspected foul play.

"If I come with you, may I drive myself?"

The officer nodded. "Yes, ma'am."

I swallowed hard. "Please give me a minute."

I stepped inside the apartment, practically pulling Isaiah with me. When the door clicked closed, I sucked in a deep breath. My mind was whirling, and concentrating on anything was nearly impossible. I shook it off, going to the kitchen for my purse. Then I slid on the flip-flops I'd left by the front door.

"V, don't go."

"I have to. They'll just come back if I say no." And I would much rather keep the focus on me than Isaiah.

"But—"

"I won't say anything. Trust me. It will be better to cooperate a little. Let's find out what they want before we freak out." Too late. I was already freaking out.

"I don't like this."

I met his panicked gaze. "I don't either. Do you think they . . . that they know?"

"Maybe." His forehead furrowed. "I should go. It should be me."

"No." I rushed him, wrapping my arms around his body. "They want me. I'll go and find out what's happening. Maybe it's about Draven. Maybe they know he didn't really kill himself. But you can't go. They'll know something's up. If I don't go, if I refuse, that makes me look guilty."

He held me so tight I couldn't breathe. Then he let me go to stalk to the door, whipping it open to see both officers there, standing at the ready to escort me to the police station.

I cast Isaiah a glance over my shoulder, then nodded at the officers, following them down the stairs.

Behind me, Isaiah followed in bare feet.

God, what was happening? Why wouldn't they tell me? It had to be something criminal. I wasn't being arrested, but I was a person of interest. If they had some casual questions, they would have asked me at home, not *invited* me to the police station.

My heart was in my throat, my pulse racing, as we stepped off the last stair and I saw their cruiser parked behind my car, blocking it in.

The officers flanked me, walking me toward my car.

I wasn't being arrested but this sure felt like an arrest.

"Wait," Isaiah called. I twisted as he jogged over. He didn't pay any attention to the cops as he took my face in his hands and kissed me, slow and soft. "I love you."

And there it was. The moment I'd most needed to hear those words and he'd delivered. "I love you too."

He dropped his forehead to mine.

"Call Jim," I whispered.

"Okay," he whispered back. "Stay strong."

To keep him safe? He didn't have to worry. "I will."

CHAPTER TWENTY-FIVE

GENEVIEVE

"Hi, Genevieve. I'm Marcus Wagner, Clifton Forge Chief of Police." He stepped through the interrogation room door, closing it softly behind him. Then he came to the table where I was sitting, extending his hand. "Nice to finally meet you."

"You too." I shook his hand.

He sat in the metal chair opposite mine. The table was wide between us, big enough that I wouldn't be able to reach across and touch him without standing. "Sorry to keep you waiting."

I'd been here for almost an hour, sitting in this colorless room alone. The officers who'd escorted me here had given me a Dixie cup of water, then disappeared.

"What's this about?" I asked.

"I've got some questions for you." He gave me a kind smile. "If you don't mind."

Fuck yes, I minded. "Not at all."

This entire thing was off and I had no reason to stay other than that I wanted *my* ass in this chair, not Isaiah's.

And damn it, I was curious.

Being in an interrogation room was never a good idea, especially without Jim present, but I wanted information. Why was I here? The fastest way to find out why I was here was by playing along.

I gave Chief Wagner an innocent smile and sipped from my cup.

I hadn't met the chief before, but we'd talked on the phone after Mom's murder, when I'd been determined to make Draven pay for the life he'd taken.

Oh, how things had changed.

During our phone conversations, Chief Wagner had told me to call him Marcus. He'd given me his personal cell phone number in case I ever needed to talk. He'd reassured me, time and time again, that Draven would be punished for his crime. Marcus's need for justice had seemed as strong as my own.

I'd liked that about him. And I'd liked that his voice had always put me at ease. It had a deep, rich timbre, and now that I could put it with a face, it fit the mental picture I'd built. He was a large man, solid and tall, with a broad chest and barrel of a stomach that could withstand any punch.

Clearly, Marcus kept in shape. He was probably in his late fifties or early sixties but he hadn't let himself go. In a way, he reminded me of Draven. They had the same stature and confidence. They were probably around the same age. Marcus was handsome; the gray by his temples and in his bushy eyebrows just added to his appeal.

He had a wide, thick mustache shadowing his upper lip. It was neatly combed but hid enough of his face that it made reading his expression more difficult. He could scowl under that thing and one might mistake it for a smile.

Marcus studied my face, but the look wasn't intimidating, more curious. It was almost . . . tender. He didn't seem at all angry or on guard.

Shit. Had I misread this entire thing?

"The officers who came over didn't tell me what this was about. Care to help me out here? Because I'm pretty confused about why I had to come to the police station on a Sunday."

"Sorry." He sighed. "They were my two on patrol today. I was running late, otherwise I would have swung by myself. All I asked was that they ask you to come down. I hope they were polite."

"Yes." I nodded. "Very."

Marcus continued to study me and an odd silence crept into the room. It stretched on and on, until my heart thundered in my ears and my palms began to sweat. What did he want? Why wasn't he talking? Why was he just staring at me? Something about the look on his face made the hair on my arms spike.

Was that how he got his confessions? By staring at someone long enough that eventually they spilled their guts?

What are you looking at? What do you want? I screamed the questions in my head. This was worse than sitting across from Tucker Talbot and his creepy biker posse.

I broke. "You had questions?"

Marcus blinked, his gaze dropping to the table for a moment. "It wasn't how I'd hoped he'd pay. He took the coward's way out."

Draven. This was about Draven, not the cabin.

The air rushed out of my lungs.

I hadn't spoken to Marcus since my kidnapping. Why would I? I'd been firmly pulled into the fold at the Clifton

Forge Garage. While I'd been learning about my father, working to prove his innocence, the chief had stayed the course to punish Draven for Mom's murder.

Draven—Dad—hadn't been a coward.

He'd saved my life. And Isaiah's. And Dash's.

But I couldn't exactly say that to the chief, could I? It would fall on deaf ears. Marcus thought Draven was guilty. Rightly so. They had a murder weapon with Draven's prints. They had Draven at the scene of the crime.

Marcus had done his job. He'd found evidence and arrested his suspect.

"As you know, he's my father."

Marcus nodded. "I know."

Everyone knew. This was a small town and the daughter of a victim associating with the alleged killer had spread like wildfire. Add to that a positive paternity test, I'd been a juicy topic. Luckily, not much of that had reached the garage. But I was sure it had reached the chief's desk. I was sure he'd looked for me at the trial, but Jim had thought it best for me to stay away. Marcus had probably heard about my Sunday breakfasts at the diner too.

Jim had actually planned to use my relationship with Draven at the sentencing hearing, hoping it would garner sympathy for Draven.

Bryce had told me that Marcus was revered and respected around town. After the Tin Kings had disbanded, the crime rate had dropped to nearly nothing, and many gave the chief credit for their peaceful community. He was supposed to be an excellent investigator who ran the police force with a firm, honest hand.

So why hadn't he investigated the knife? Bryce had published an article not long after Mom's death speculating a weapon of Draven's had been stolen. Had he ignored it? Maybe he had investigated but there'd been nothing to find.

No surprise—we hadn't found anything either.

"Why am I here?" I asked. And why now? Dad's death was months ago. What was there to discuss?

"Draven killed your mother." His statement, the tone, was full of venom.

"I don't believe that's true."

End of discussion. My allegiance would forever be to Draven. Yes, he'd been a criminal. Clearly, he hadn't gotten along with the chief. But as far as I was concerned, the Draven topic was off the table.

Marcus's jaw ticked. The mood in the room shifted. The tension returned as his stare hardened. He shifted in the chair, its legs scraping against the concrete floor as he fished a bag out of his pocket.

The room spun as he placed it on the table between us.

My mother's necklace lay encased in the clear, plastic bag. It was the necklace I'd been looking for since her death. The necklace I'd described in detail to both pawnshop owners in Clifton Forge and dozens around the state.

How did he have it? Had she been wearing it when she died? Everything else from that horrific morning—her purse, the suitcase she'd had in the motel, even her toothbrush—had been returned to me after the police had deemed it was not part of the investigation.

Was this necklace evidence? If so, why hadn't it been included in any of the trial materials? Jim had let me go through Draven's case file last month. I'd asked him to. Begged, really. I'd needed that piece of closure. There had been *no* mention of the necklace.

"Do you recognize this?" Marcus asked, though he

already knew the answer. I hadn't even tried to hide my wide-eyed reaction.

"Yes. It was my mother's."

The dainty gold chain didn't sparkle underneath the plastic. It was dull and coated in black. The crystal in the center of the North Star pendant had a ring of dirt and grime around the base, like someone had wiped only the large part of the stone clean. Only the center was clear enough to catch a hint of the overhead florescent light.

"Do you remember last summer when that man was burned to death in a cabin in the mountains?"

It took me a moment to register Marcus's question. Then the sinking feeling in my gut nearly pulled me through the floor.

This wasn't about Draven or my mother's murder.

This was about the cabin.

It always came back to that fucking cabin.

"Um, yeah. I think so. It happened right before I moved here." I kept my gaze locked on Mom's necklace, using everything in my power to keep my voice from shaking. I sat on my trembling fingers.

A year ago, I'd spent countless hours rehearsing what I'd say if I was arrested. Over and over I'd practiced, in the shower or as I'd driven to work.

Nothing had happened. I'd gotten complacent. Where were those practiced lines now? Where was the fake surprise?

Marcus touched the plastic bag, pulling it to his side of the table. I wanted to grab it and snatch it back because *damn it*, that necklace should be mine. "That fire's been a cold case for almost a year. The investigators ruled it arson, but we haven't been able to find a trace."

"Okay." I nodded.

"There were some things in the cabin that we linked to the victim. We'd thought this necklace was his as well. But turns out . . ."

I forced my eyes up to meet his gaze. "It wasn't."

How had Mom's necklace ended up in that cabin? I hadn't been wearing it that night. I would have remembered.

I didn't wear jewelry to sleep. The only exception was my wedding ring. I'd been in pajamas, my face washed and teeth brushed, ready for bed the night I'd been kidnapped. Besides, Mom had never given me this necklace.

The last time I'd borrowed it had been—*when?*—in Denver. Mom had lent it to me in college for a third date. That date had gone terribly because the guy had only shelled out twenty bucks for a cheap pizza buffet and thought it was enough for sex. When I'd turned him down, he'd huffed and said *Don't expect to hear from me again.*

Mom had taken me out the next night for a mother-daughter date, with decent pizza, and I'd given her the necklace back. I'd teased her, saying it was bad luck.

That was the last time I'd worn that necklace, I was sure of it.

I'd given it back.

"Any idea how it got there?" Marcus asked.

"No." *Shit.* I should call Jim. I needed to shut up and call Jim. But how did Marcus know this was Mom's necklace?

My spine prickled. That was why I was here, right? Because he knew this necklace had belonged to Mom and he'd brought me in for questioning. Did that mean he knew I'd been in that cabin?

Or was this a tactic, keeping me waiting in this room for an hour before coming in to deliver short, leading questions that would trap me in a corner? I rewound our conversation, replaying my every word and measuring them carefully.

If Marcus hadn't known this necklace was Mom's, I'd told him.

Marcus Wagner was no friend. The chief wasn't on my side.

Which meant I was done talking.

Almost.

"How did you know it was my mom's?"

He held my stare, hesitating to answer. It was like he was assessing me, like he knew I'd just pegged him as the enemy. "A picture in the paper."

Fuck. One of the pictures Bryce had printed in today's paper had been a photo of Mom wearing this necklace.

I was here because Marcus had a new lead on that cabin fire. He sure had acted fast. The paper wasn't even twenty-four-hours old.

Someone had planted that necklace. Someone who'd wanted to blame that fire and murder on me. It was probably the same man who'd killed my mother and kidnapped me and Bryce.

The same person or persons who'd killed Dad.

The Warriors.

"According to your credit card records, you were in Montana the day that cabin burned down. You flew into Bozeman the night before."

The air left my lungs. I nodded.

"Why?"

I took a sip of water from the Dixie cup. Was it telling that I needed water? Did only guilty people drink from those little paper cups? I choked the water down. "I came to see Mom's grave. I hadn't been here yet."

"And did you?"

No. I'd been taken and shoved in the back of a trunk.

But I couldn't tell Marcus about the kidnapping. There was a reason I hadn't gone to the police, and that reason was my husband.

"Genevieve?" Marcus prompted when I didn't answer.

"Am I being charged?"

His mouth set in a firm line. Even the mustache couldn't hide his irritation. "No."

"Then I'd like to go." I shoved my chair back and stood. "I'm not comfortable talking without my lawyer present."

My guess was I'd be back in that chair in a day or two as the primary suspect in an arson and murder investigation.

Law school would have to wait.

My troubles were far from over.

Marcus stood too, picking up the necklace. The bag returned to his pocket as he opened the door, waving me into the hall.

The walk through the bullpen was silent other than our footsteps. Every desk was empty, just like it had been when I'd arrived. The only other person here was the officer stationed up front.

"Quiet day. Do you work on Sundays?" Wasn't that something the chief of police got to avoid?

"Normally, no. But today's the exception."

Spotting that photo had been a surprise to him too.

Marcus reached the door that opened to the exit. He held it open for me, nodding his goodbye.

Then I was free. I could walk right out the front door. So why did I feel like this was all a trick? I was sure at any moment that the chief would summon me back and tell me I'd never be free again.

I quickened my steps, pushing through the exterior door and into the bright sunshine. The moment my eyes adjusted to the light, I spotted the one person I needed most.

"You're here." I rushed into Isaiah's arms.

"Been here since the minute I got off the phone with Jim." He pointed down the sidewalk where Jim was standing, talking on his phone.

He saw me and held up a finger.

I breathed in Isaiah's smell. He'd been standing in the sun, wearing black. There was a hint of sweat beneath the clean-fabric scent of his T-shirt. One inhale and my heart rate slowed.

"You okay?" he asked.

I shook my head. "Not really."

Jim came rushing over and pulled me from Isaiah's arms, giving me a hug of his own. "What happened?"

"Honestly?" I cast a glance at the station. "I'm not sure. Something is off."

An eerie feeling crawled up my skin. The hair on the nape of my neck stood on end, like someone was watching me. I let Isaiah go and glanced around the parking lot. There was my car, Jim's SUV and Isaiah's bike; otherwise it was empty save for a few police cars.

But the niggling sensation wouldn't go away.

I was missing something. We all were and had been for months.

"What?" Isaiah asked. "What is it?"

"I don't know," I muttered.

"Did they charge you? Question you?" Jim asked.

I nodded. "No, and yes. I answered a few but then I refused to continue unless you were present."

"Good," he said. "Next time, don't go at all."

"Sorry. I was curious and wasn't thinking."

"Let's go to the firm and talk it through," Jim said.

"Can we do it tomorrow morning? I'm . . . my brain is fried and I'm an emotional wreck." And before I talked about anything with Jim, I wanted to discuss it with Isaiah.

"Okay," Jim agreed. "But first thing tomorrow morning."

"Eight o'clock."

"Get some rest." He squeezed my arm, nodded to Isaiah and walked to his car.

I wasn't sure what was bothering me, but I wasn't going to figure it out in the parking lot of the police station. So I took Isaiah's hand and whispered, "Let's get out of here."

CHAPTER TWENTY-SIX

ISAIAH

Dash stood beside the office door as we pulled into the garage. His arms were crossed and his face expressionless.

He was pissed.

So was I.

Genevieve parked in her space as I pulled in next to her with my bike. Before she had the chance, I opened her door and held out my hand to help her out. Her feet had just hit the pavement when two other bikes raced down the street, filling the parking lot with their thunder as they rolled in.

Emmett's and Leo's expressions matched Dash's.

I clasped Genevieve's hand and led her to the shop. Dash had already opened the first bay door.

"Did you call them?" she asked.

"Yeah." Dash had been my second call after Jim. Then I'd texted him before Genevieve and I had left the station that we were on our way.

"You good?" Dash asked Genevieve, uncrossing his arms as he came to her side.

For a moment, I thought he'd pull her into a hug. He hesitated, thinking it over, and then she was ripped out of my grip. He wrapped her up, squeezing tight. "Sorry this happened."

She tensed, her eyes going wide for a second, but then she relaxed. "I'm okay. And it's not your fault."

No, the blame was mine.

Emmett and Leo flanked me, standing by as Dash hugged Genevieve. Since she'd called him on his shit, he'd been a different man around her. He'd started acting like a brother. They were adjusting to life as siblings. They didn't have a bond like Kaine and me, but they'd get there.

I was glad she had him. Nick too. They would watch out for her if I couldn't.

Because one thing was certain, if there was even a chance that she'd face charges for what had happened at that cabin, I'd confess in a heartbeat.

Genevieve wouldn't spend a minute in prison.

"Come on in." Dash let Genevieve go. "Let's talk."

We walked deeper into the garage and found Bryce sitting with Xander in her arms. The baby was slugging down a bottle.

Had it just been this morning that she'd come over with the paper? It felt like days had passed as I'd waited for Genevieve outside the station.

Normally, there weren't a lot of places to sit in the shop, just a few rolling stools. If we had to congregate, we went into the office. But a few extra chairs had been dragged in and situated in a circle along with the stools.

There was a mess of tools scattered around the '74 Chevy Nova we'd been restoring this past month. The car's hood was up. Dash and Bryce had probably come here right after I'd called them, wanting to be here when we showed up. Dash must have kept his mind occupied with work.

As soon as we were seated, Leo walked to the wall and hit the button to close the bay door. No one spoke a word until it was lowered.

"What happened?" I asked Genevieve, my hand firm on hers.

She sucked in a deep inhale. "Marcus found my mother's necklace, the one I've been searching for, at the cabin. He suspects, maybe he knows, that I was up there."

"Fuck." My nostrils flared. "Then I'll confess."

"What? No." Her mouth dropped open. "There's no way I'll let you do that. You're not taking the blame."

"It was my fault."

"No, it wasn't. If anyone is going to confess to the murder and fire, it's going to be me."

"Over my dead body."

"Isa—"

"Hold up." Dash cut her off. "Before you both end up confessing, how about we talk this through?"

She shot me a glare, then turned back to our circle. "Good idea."

"Start at the beginning," Dash ordered.

Genevieve nodded. "Marcus has a necklace of Mom's that was missing. The one I told you all about. The one we think her boyfriend stole."

"How did Marcus know it was hers?" Isaiah asked.

"The cops found it when they were investigating the cabin. They thought it was the Warrior's. Marcus only realized today it was Mom's when he saw it in a picture in the paper."

"Oh, shit." Bryce's mouth fell open. "What are the chances?"

Genevieve's tired gaze swung to me. "We were almost free."

I tugged the arm of her chair, dragging her closer. She gripped my hand tighter and rested her head on my shoulder.

Free.

We'd almost been free of this whole thing. We were planning our future. I was looking forward to the move. Genevieve was so excited to start law school. And then this. Our future was on the verge of disappearing before it had even begun.

Was this my punishment? To get a taste of happiness only to have it ripped free before I could sink my teeth in? Maybe I deserved to go back to prison and rot my life away in a cell.

Genevieve would slap me if she heard that thought. She was so certain I'd paid for my sins and then some. Her endless faith astounded me.

I'd actually started to believe we could make it.

I wasn't going down without a fight. Maybe we'd get a miracle and come out of this alive and together. I didn't deserve this kind of happiness, but Genevieve did. And if I was the man who made her happy, if I was her choice, then I'd spend the rest of my life making sure she didn't regret it for a second.

I kissed the top of her hair. My God, I loved her. More than I'd loved another soul.

We'd get through this. *We have to.*

"He planted it." Bryce snapped her fingers, sitting straighter. Xander was over her shoulder and she was patting his back for a burp. "It fits our theory. If the boyfriend was the one who killed your mom and kidnapped us, then he was up there. He had the necklace and planted it during or after the fire."

"But why?" I asked. "He got away with this. Why plant evidence when he was in the wind?"

"There had to be something in that cabin," Dash answered. "Something that could trace back to him. So he put that necklace in there, hoping it would lead to Genevieve instead of him."

"That's a stretch." I shook my head. "Marcus didn't even know it was Amina's until the paper came out today."

"Maybe they were hoping there'd be a fingerprint or DNA or something." Leo ran a hand over his face. "I don't fucking know."

"I think this has something to do with the Warriors," Bryce said.

Genevieve nodded. "That's what I was thinking too."

"All along, we've assumed Tucker was telling the truth. Why?" It was something that had always bothered me. "Because Draven thought he was telling the truth. Draven believed Tucker."

"So did I," Dash said. "He said he didn't have anything to do with Amina's death and I believed him."

"What if he was lying to your face?" I looked down at Genevieve. "Your mom had a thing for bikers, right?"

"Maybe. She had a thing for Draven, that was for sure."

"Tucker." Emmett's voice echoed through the shop. "You think the boyfriend was Tucker. He got jealous when he found out Draven and Amina had sex. Killed her. Found a way to pin it on Draven."

"But why kidnap me and Genevieve?" Bryce asked.

"Maybe he thought you were getting too close." Dash put his hand on her knee. "Asking too many questions."

"That makes sense." She nodded. "But why Genevieve? She's never been a part of this."

"He had to be worried that Mom told me about him," Genevieve said. "Maybe they keep coming after me because he thinks I can identify him."

"But you can't." I huffed. "All along, you've only ever known this boyfriend as Lee."

"Why the fake name?" Emmett asked. "Doesn't seem like Tucker's style."

No, it didn't. I didn't know the guy but giving a fake name to the woman he was banging didn't seem right. "Is he married?"

Dash shook his head. "Divorced. Has two daughters in their late twenties. I see no reason he'd give a fake name."

I shoved out of the chair to pace along the wall of tool benches. "Let's run this through. Assume it's Tucker and see if it gels."

"Okay." Emmett stood too, raking a hand through his hair. "Amina comes here to talk to Draven and they hook up. Tucker must have been following her or found out about it. He goes into a rage, knows there's probably a weapon or two in the clubhouse because that's where we'd always kept shit like that. I'm betting the Warrior clubhouse is packed with weapons too."

"He breaks in," Dash continued for Emmett. "He even had on a patch."

"But not the current one," Bryce jumped in.

"Right." Leo nodded. "Tucker told us the patch the thief was wearing was an old design. One that only old members would have had. Well, there aren't many older members of the Warriors than the president himself."

We were getting somewhere. My heart started to race as I nodded along. The problem was, I hated where we were getting. Tucker was smart. We'd be up against not just one man, but an entire club.

Fuck. If this really was to settle an old war, I didn't like our chances of emerging as victors.

"So he kills Amina. Frames Draven." I kept pacing. "Kidnaps Bryce and Genevieve to shut them up. Why didn't he just kill them in the mountains?"

"That's been bugging me too." Leo frowned. "He had them. Why not kill them and be done with it?"

My stomach knotted. I didn't like the mention of anyone killing my wife. I didn't like thinking about how close I'd been to losing her before I'd even had the chance to know her. From the murderous look on Dash's face, he didn't like hearing how close Bryce had been to death either.

"He wanted Dash to kill me," Genevieve said. "He was set on it. Why?"

"To punish Draven," I answered, coming to the back of her chair. I put my hands on her shoulders. "This entire thing was driven by his hatred for Draven. If Dash kills his mystery daughter, it's not like he can retaliate against his own son."

The room went quiet as everyone thought it over.

"And he planted the necklace because I got away," Genevieve whispered. "He must have known that the police would find it. You guys lost him in the trees. He circled back and planted the necklace. Since he didn't get his way and I survived, he was counting on the cops putting that murder and fire on me."

If he couldn't make Draven suffer by watching his son kill her, then he could watch her be sentenced to prison. In a lot of ways, that punishment was worse.

"Tucker could have killed us at any time," Bryce added. "If he wanted us dead, we'd be dead."

"She's right." Dash nodded, going over to his wife and putting his hand on Xander's head. "When Tucker wants someone dead, they're in the ground."

"And his name isn't Lee," Emmett added.

"Fuck," Leo barked. "It almost works, but not quite. We know Tucker. He's also not the kind of guy to hide behind ski masks and sunglasses."

"My gut says it's not Tucker." Dash growled. "Damn it. But you're right about one thing, Isaiah, this was always about Dad. Goddamn, I wish he were here. He had a way of looking at things from a different point of view."

"What are we missing?" Bryce asked.

"What if it wasn't the kidnapper who planted the necklace?" Genevieve's voice caught our attention. "Maybe I had that wrong."

"Then who?"

She gulped. "A cop. That place would have been swarming with cops."

"Which cop?" Dash and Emmett asked in unison.

"Marcus," she whispered. "He hates Draven."

"No, he doesn't." Dash shook his head. "They always got along. Yeah, Marcus had to arrest him a couple of times, but the charges never stuck. After the club disbanded, they'd meet for drinks every couple months at The Betsy."

It was hard to picture Draven sitting down across from the chief of police at the local dive bar to eat salty popcorn and shoot the breeze over a beer.

"I'm telling you," Genevieve insisted, "there was so much poison in his voice today. He said Draven was a coward for killing himself. And the way he looked was . . . there was something off about it. He *hates* Draven. Loathes him. I'm sure of it."

The room went still except for a gurgle coming from the baby.

"You're sure?" I asked Genevieve. Going up against Tucker would have been difficult. Making an accusation against the chief of police was downright impossible.

She didn't answer right away. Her eyes stayed narrowed and unfocused at a grease spot on the floor.

"Genevieve?"

She lifted her face. "I need to go to the office. I never put him in my notebook. But he could have planted the necklace. He could have framed Draven. It has to be him. Chief Wagner is Lee."

"Emmett, what's Marcus's middle name?" Dash asked.

He shrugged. "No fucking clue."

"I can look it up, but I need to be at work to do it," Genevieve said.

"I got it." Emmett whipped out his phone, typing with fury. We waited as he scrolled and scrolled. "It's not listed anywhere public. I need one of my laptops."

Chairs went rolling as bodies shot to their feet. Following Emmett's lead, we all rushed to the side door and into the summer sunshine. Then we marched to the clubhouse, opening the locked doors so Emmett could disappear to wherever Emmett had disappeared to and the rest of us stood in the open room—waiting.

Xander let out a loud squawk, filling the musty room

with his noise. The echo must have startled him, because his eyes got wide.

"Will you take him?" Bryce asked Dash. "He's getting heavy."

"Sure, babe." He grinned at his son, scooping him up in his arms. "Come here, little man."

I put my arm around Genevieve, pulling her into my side. "You okay?"

"It stinks in here," she whispered. "I can't believe this is happening. What if it's not him? What if I'm wrong? What if—"

"V." I pressed my finger to her rambling lips. "It'll be okay."

"But—"

"You're walking away from this."

Her eyes turned glassy. "But I don't want to walk away from this if you're not with me. Promise me you won't confess."

I gave her a sad smile. "Can't do it, doll."

"I won't lose you too." She closed her eyes, dropping her forehead to my chest. "I love you."

I wrapped my arms around her. "I love you too."

I'd been so hesitant to say those words. The last time I'd told a woman that I loved her, I'd killed her not long after. But seeing Genevieve flanked by two cops had flipped a switch.

What if I lost her? What if I didn't get the chance to say those words?

Life was fleeting. The accident had taught me that.

The *I love you* had come out in a panicked rush. I'd slow them down, every day for the rest of her life.

My wife.

She'd found me. She'd broken through. She loved me.

I wasn't losing her. We'd figure this out or die trying.

We stood there, holding on to one another as we shifted our weight from one foot to another. We waited for Emmett to return. Bryce and Dash stood by the bar, their attention on their son, while Leo wandered around the room, looking over pieces from the past.

His fingers lingered on the rack of pool cues. His hand skimmed the green felt on the table. "We should burn this place down."

His statement caught the room's attention, but before anyone could respond, Emmett came running back into the room.

"It's Lee," Emmett panted. "He's got two middle names. Marcus Ross Lee Wagner."

"Fuck." Dash was on the verge of losing it, but he held it together for the baby in his arms. "He set Dad up. He planned all this. How? Why?"

"Marcus said something to me once," Bryce said. "About a year ago. He said that Draven always came away clean. I didn't think much of it at the time. It was before I knew you guys. But he sounded . . . bitter. Like he'd failed as a cop."

"That's reason enough to take out a personal vendetta." I nodded. "Add in a relationship with Amina—if he was a jealous lover, it's believable. And he's smart. Smart enough to pull it off."

"No wonder he didn't investigate when we printed that article about the knife being stolen." Bryce was fuming, pacing in a fast circle. "The bastard. He stole it himself."

"Now what?" I asked. "We have no evidence. He's the chief of police."

And he'd all but gotten away with murder.

"We have to get him to admit it," Genevieve said.

"Never gonna happen." Leo shook his head. "Never."

"We have to try." She pointed to her chest. "*I* have to try. For my mom and dad. I can't let him get away with this. Maybe if I confront him—"

"Out of the question." There was no way in hell she'd ever be around that man again. "It's too risky."

"Isaiah, it's our only hope." Her eyes pleaded with me. "If Marcus is behind this, there won't be any evidence. He's destroyed it all or made sure it pointed to Draven. The only way to know is if he confesses."

She was right. We were trapped. His confession was the only way we'd be free. "Fuck, I hate this."

"Me too." She took my hand. "But we have to try."

"How?" Bryce asked.

"Torture?" Emmett raised an eyebrow. "We haven't had any guests in the basement for a while. Would be fitting since that was how Draven would have played it."

Dash raised an eyebrow, entertaining the idea.

"No." Bryce glared. "No more violence. There's been enough."

Beside me, Genevieve shuddered. Her face paled as she met my gaze. "I have an idea."

"What?" I asked.

"We're going to do what we've been doing all year. Lie like our lives depend on it."

CHAPTER TWENTY-SEVEN

GENEVIEVE

"I hate this." Isaiah cupped my face, dropping his forehead to mine.

"Me too."

"It should be me going in there."

I shook my head. "It'll never work. It can only be me."

Our plan was to catch Marcus off guard at home. I was going to waltz up to his door and lie my ass off. A half-cocked plan? *Yup.* But it was a chance—a slim chance—at putting an end to all of this.

A chance I was going to take.

The chief of police wasn't going to confess to murder. I gave the likelihood of him admitting to stabbing my mother and shoving me in a trunk slightly above zero percent. But we had to try. What was the alternative? Spending my life in prison? Or Isaiah? Or both of us? *Hell no.*

At least, not without a fight.

So after we'd spent a few hours hashing out the plan at the garage, we'd all gone our separate ways. Dash and Bryce had taken Xander home. Bryce would be at home with the baby while her father came over to stay with them at the house. Emmett and Leo had gone to do whatever Emmett and Leo had to do.

And Isaiah and I had gone to the apartment.

We'd forced ourselves to eat something. I hadn't been hungry at first even though I'd missed lunch. But after a few bites of a ham sandwich, my appetite had returned and I'd inhaled the whole thing.

Isaiah had been too nervous to eat. I'd never seen such worry and fear on his face. We'd sat in a silent apartment, on the couch with our fingers laced, until it had been time to leave. Isaiah had insisted on driving, something I knew he only did when he was really concerned about me.

We'd driven my car across town and had been the first to arrive at the predetermined meeting location.

Two blocks away, Marcus Wagner was in his home. Maybe he was watching television with his wife. Maybe he was already in bed. It was nearly ten o'clock at night and dark. At the garage earlier, we'd decided that the time to act was now. We didn't want to give Marcus any time to talk to a judge and haul me back in for more questions. We didn't want to give him time to settle or recharge. If there was a time to catch him off guard, it was tonight.

My stomach knotted.

"Be careful," Isaiah whispered. "If you see him reach for a gun or—"

"I know." I wrapped my arms around his waist. "We've been through it. I'll be careful. If I think he'll hurt me, I'll run."

"Stay out of his reach. No matter what, stay back."

"I will."

He sighed. "We could go to the prosecutor. Or another

cop. Maybe one of his officers would like a chance to dethrone the chief."

In the garage, we'd tossed around idea after idea. That had been one of them. But without evidence, we were stuck, like we'd been all year. No cop would turn against his boss if he had nothing to hang him on.

"We've talked about this," I said. "If Marcus gets word of that, we'll never win. He'll never talk and he'll push even harder on the necklace." And if he managed to put me in a prison cell, that would be the end. "He's too smart."

"But if he doesn't confess, we're sunk."

I tipped my chin up, meeting his gaze. "How do you feel about Canada? We might have to make a run for it tonight."

He grinned. "If that's what it'll take for us to have a life together, I'm good with Canada."

"We could change our names and live way up north. We'd be like pioneers, living off the grid."

His thumb stroked my cheek. "As long as your last name matches mine, I'm good with that too."

I collapsed into him again, drawing in a deep breath of his smell and soaking in the warmth of his arms. Isaiah had a way with simple words that made me feel cherished. He made me feel special. He gave me a place to belong.

Headlights flashed as the low rumble of an engine drifted across the night air.

I unwrapped my arms from Isaiah as Dash's black truck crept down the quiet street. He parked behind my car, shutting down the engine. Then Dash, Emmett and Leo climbed out. They closed the doors carefully, making sure not to slam them shut.

All three were dressed in head-to-toe black, much like

Isaiah. Dash had a gun holstered on his hip while Emmett and Leo had theirs in hand.

Dash's hazel gaze was cold and deadly. Even in the dark, I could see the menace and calculation behind those eyes. Tonight, he wasn't my brother or the loving husband of my best friend. Tonight, Dash was the cruel and hard president of a motorcycle gang. And he'd brought along his brothers.

Leo pulled his hood over his head. Emmett tucked a strand of hair beneath his beanie.

"Ready?" Dash asked.

No. I nodded anyway. Then I turned to Isaiah, drinking in his handsome face.

I didn't want to do this. I wasn't strong enough. But for him, I'd find the courage. I'd do this for the promise of the life we'd have if we truly set ourselves free.

"Let's get the mic on." Emmett pulled a small box and cord from his pocket. The box went into the back pocket of my jeans, covered by the tails of the plaid shirt he'd told me to wear. The wire was fished up my back, and the small microphone was taped into my collar.

"Say something?" He had a receiver pressed to his ear.

"Uh . . . hi."

"Good enough." He shoved the receiver into his pocket. The red light blinked that it was recording. "Stay within eight feet. Keep him from seeing your back and you'll be fine. Try not to rustle your hair around."

"I could put it up?"

He shook his head. "Down will help hide it."

"Okay. Don't play with my hair. Keep a straight face." *And lie, lie, lie.*

What the fuck am I doing? I was a paralegal, not a spy.

"We'll be here the whole time." Dash put his hand on my shoulder. "Don't worry."

"What if you can't get in?"

"We'll get in." Leo winked at me, then he and Emmett shared a grin.

Was this fun? Because I was not having fun. Maybe their confidence would rub off on me. I could use some—a lot.

"Okay." I sucked in a deep breath. *I can do this.* "Let's go."

Dash squeezed my arm. Emmett and Leo gave me a sure nod. Then Isaiah took my hand as we started down the sidewalk. We walked one block, our footsteps dull thumps on the concrete.

"Emmett, I—"

He wasn't there. None of them were. I scanned the lawns in the neighborhood around us but there was no sign of them. They'd disappeared like ghosts into the night.

"Where'd they go?" I asked Isaiah as my steps slowed.

"They're out there." He tugged me forward. "Don't worry."

I swallowed hard, forcing my legs to keep up with his pace. My footsteps felt off and unbalanced. There wasn't any strength in my strides. Isaiah was basically pulling me along.

"I can do this," I whispered.

"You can do this." He gripped my hand tighter.

We continued toward Marcus's house. At the garage earlier, Dash and Emmett had wanted to do a drive-by to scope the place out. They'd known where Marcus lived but couldn't remember details about the home or property.

So we'd taken one of the old cars from the back lot at the garage, one of the few that actually ran, and crammed inside. It had smelled like rust and dirt as we'd driven across town,

Dash and Emmett up front, Isaiah and me in the back. Leo had stayed with Bryce and the baby.

We'd passed Marcus's house once and Dash hadn't slowed down. He and Emmett hadn't even glanced at the front door. Meanwhile, my face had been pressed to the glass, memorizing every single thing I could about the country-blue rancher in ten seconds.

There was a tan wooden door and a porch swing.

As we approached it tonight, that swing was glowing from the overhead light.

"I'll be right there. Behind that bush." Isaiah pointed ahead. We were four houses away.

"Okay."

Three houses.

"I love you," he whispered.

"I love you too."

Two houses.

My heart raced.

One house.

Isaiah stopped, pulling his hand free of my grip before urging me forward with a gentle nudge.

None of the guys would approach the house until I was already there. They didn't want to risk tripping a motion light while Marcus was inside.

Then while I was talking to Marcus at the front of the house, Dash and Leo would be breaking in through the back door. Isaiah had refused to let me out of his sight, so Dash had made the decision to hide around the side of the house.

I gulped, taking one step after another until I was at the base of the sidewalk that led to the front door. I fisted my hands.

I can do this.

I'd do this for Isaiah. I'd do it for Dad. I'd do it for Mom.

Fuck you, Marcus Wagner.

There, standing right in front of his house, I knew I could do this. He'd stolen my parents from me. If there was a chance I could make him pay, I was taking it.

I *wanted* to do this.

I took one step and caught movement at my side. Isaiah crept onto the lawn between the chief's house and the neighbor's. His pace matched mine as he took care not to get too far ahead.

As I reached the porch, he ducked behind a tall bush, completely hidden from view. The only way Marcus would see him was if he came all the way outside and halfway down the sidewalk.

But he could see me. Isaiah was there, watching. Even from a distance, I'd lean on his strength.

I stepped onto the porch and into the light. Then before I could doubt myself, I shoved my finger into the doorbell button.

A moment later, a light flicked on from inside, illuminating the front bay window.

My hands shook. *Here we go.*

The lock on the door flipped and Marcus filled its frame. He was wearing the same thing he had at the station, a button-down shirt and jeans, but the ends of his shirt were untucked and wrinkled.

"Genevieve?" He narrowed his eyes and straightened his shoulders, already putting up his guard.

Damn it. I was so outmatched. "Hi."

That's what I was leading with? Hi?

We were fucked.

"What are you doing here?" he asked.

There was no point in small talk. Dash had encouraged me to cut to the chase. We were going for surprise, after all. So I shook off my *Hi* and pictured Mom's face.

"You loved her."

He blinked.

"You loved her. And you killed her because she loved Draven."

One step and he was outside, pulling the door closed behind him. I retreated to the edge of the single step of the porch. Like Isaiah had warned, I couldn't let him get too close because Marcus Wagner wasn't afraid to hit a woman.

"What are you talking about?" he sneered, his voice hushed. His wife must be inside.

Time for the lies.

"After you brought me into the station today, I started thinking. Mom had told me about this man she'd been dating. Lee. I didn't know much about him, but Mom made it seem like things were serious. You showed me that necklace and I realized I hadn't really looked through her things since she died. It was too painful."

His eyes widened, barely, but I caught it. *Guilty.* This fucking asshole was guilty.

This bluff was going to work. It *had* to work. My heart raced faster but I did my best to keep calm on the outside.

"I went through her things today," I said. "Her jewelry. Her notebooks. Her photos."

"And?"

"Why did she call you Lee? Was it because of your wife? Did you promise to leave her for Mom?"

Marcus pursed his lips. "I don't know what you're talking about."

"Bryce will be running a special edition of the paper

tomorrow, exposing you as Mom's boyfriend and speculating that you were the one to kill her. She's including the photos I found of you with Mom."

He scoffed. "You're lying."

Yes, I was.

Ironically, our plan was to use a police tactic. I'd pretend I had evidence I didn't have in hopes Marcus would confirm anything to prove his involvement.

He'd basically done the same thing to me earlier today. Maybe Marcus's curiosity would get the better of him too.

I was counting on it, and his arrogance. After all, he'd gotten away with this for a year.

"I guess you'll find out tomorrow when the paperboy tosses your copy onto the sidewalk."

His stare hardened as he inched closer. He was getting too close, something Isaiah was no doubt cussing, but I refused to budge. I locked eyes with his and didn't blink. I didn't breathe. My body was a statue, one he wouldn't be able to ignore.

Even if this failed, even if he hauled me into jail, Bryce was going to run a story. It wouldn't be tomorrow, but it would come as soon as she could pull it together.

She'd do everything in her power to condemn the chief. At the very least, she'd use her newspaper to ensure he was never appointed to his position again. And she'd ensure Marcus's wife had enough doubt in her mind to ask some uncomfortable questions about where he'd disappeared to those weekends he'd been with Mom.

I hated that Mom had been with another married man, but I'd deal with my feelings over that later. Maybe she hadn't known. I'd give her the benefit of the doubt.

I focused on Marcus's stare, on holding this murderer's

gaze. "You should have killed me when you had me on that mountain."

He flinched.

Yeah, asshole. We all know it was you.

"You don't have any evidence."

"I have some," I shot back. "And I'll make sure it's enough."

Marcus leaned forward, almost like he was going to reach for me. But then he shrank, his shoulders falling deep. In front of me, this man—who I'd once thought to be so honest and just—shriveled.

The change caught me by surprise. I staggered back an inch, teetering on the step. What was he doing? Was this a trick? I kept both eyes on him as he dragged a hand down his mustache and retreated to the porch swing.

"I'm tired." He dropped to the seat, his form crumpled. I hadn't noticed those dark circles under his eyes at the station, but now that I looked, he was worn out. Tired.

Ironically, that was the same word Dad had used before he'd died.

A lifetime of fighting had drained them both.

Marcus was guilty. It was clear as day to anyone on this porch. Except I was the only person here, and what I'd gotten from him was not a confession.

I took a step forward, making sure I was out of his grasp but close enough there'd be no missing him on the mic. "Did you love my mom?"

He hadn't confirmed it earlier, but I wanted to know. Maybe because a broken heart was easier to swallow as motive than Marcus seducing Mom only to get at Draven.

"Yes," he admitted. "I always loved her."

"Why'd you kill her?"

He dropped his gaze to the ground. "I assume this is being recorded."

"Yes." There was no point lying. Either he'd clam up and I'd be in the same place as I had been for a year, or he'd give up and talk.

Give up. Please. Just give up.

Wasn't he tired of running? Wasn't he tired of hiding?

"Why?" I asked again, then held my breath as I waited for an answer. My voice dripped with desperation.

He studied my face, much like he had at the station earlier today. "You look like her. And him."

Marcus's face soured and he looked away from me.

"This was about Draven, right?" I asked.

"Why couldn't she just stay away from him? She never stayed away. He didn't want her. He didn't love her. I did. But it wasn't enough. It was never enough."

He wasn't wrong. Mom had been obsessed with Draven. Apparently, Marcus had felt the same for her.

"Why did she call you Lee?"

"We were kids when we met. Teenagers. Her family moved to town and into the place next door. I've never seen a more beautiful girl in my life. That smile of hers—there wasn't another like it."

No, there wasn't. And he'd erased it from the earth.

I held my tongue. I wanted to scream and hit him, to curse him for what he'd done. To strangle him until this monster was gone from the world. But it wasn't enough. He deserved the seventh circle of hell for what he'd done—in the form of a prison cell.

"I was younger than her," he continued. "She'd look at me and I'd run and hide. Took me weeks to work up the courage to introduce myself. Couldn't hardly speak when I did. Said my name so low all she caught was my middle name. But she laughed and from then on only called me Lee."

Marcus stared out into the dark street, a look of love and longing on his face. His wife was presumably inside, yet here he was, pining for my mother.

Even in death.

Had Dad known about Marcus's feelings for Mom? Probably not. Draven had been too busy being in love with Chrissy.

"I lost her for years. She graduated and moved away. We drifted apart. I went to the police academy and came home to work on the force. I got married and had kids. I thought of her now and then, wondered what she was up to. But I left her there, in my memory. And then . . . she was there."

"Where? In Clifton Forge?" I thought she hadn't come back until the day she'd come to tell Draven about me.

"I had a class in Bozeman. I went to dinner with some cops I knew and there she was, eating by herself in my favorite restaurant."

And that was when they must have reconnected and started the affair.

"I was leaving my wife," he whispered.

That was what they all said, wasn't it? I bit back the snark. Though a part of me suspected Marcus would have left his wife for Mom.

"She didn't tell me she was coming here. I wouldn't have known except I saw her car and followed it to the motel." He huffed a dry laugh. "I thought she was here to surprise me. We'd always met in Bozeman and I thought maybe she wanted to see me so she'd come to town. But no. She wasn't here for me. She was here for Draven."

352

He spat Dad's name, that lip curl returning. Even with the mustache, you couldn't miss the disgust on his face.

"She fucked him."

I flinched at the ice in his tone.

"She fucked him," he repeated, leveling his gaze on me. "She had me and she chose him. She always chose him."

"So you killed her?"

Say, yes. Admit it.

"*He* killed her. He should have stayed away from her. If he had stayed away from her, she'd still be alive. I would have made her happy."

Maybe that was true, but we'd never know. "You framed him. Everything you did pointed to the Warriors. Why?"

"It's no skin off my nose if a bunch of biker thugs decide to kill each other."

"So let me guess, you had an old Warriors vest. The chief of police could have taken it from an evidence box without anyone noticing. Maybe you kept it on hand for years, waiting for the chance to get at Draven. And this was it. You broke into the clubhouse and stole Draven's knife. Then you went back to the motel and waited for him to leave. I guess you got lucky it had his prints on it. Though you probably would have just falsified them if they hadn't, huh?"

He didn't confirm or deny it. Even slouched in his porch swing, the chief was being careful with his confession.

"Did you enjoy it?"

"Enjoy what?" he muttered.

"Stabbing her."

"I don't know what you're talking about."

"Did she know it was you? Or did you hide your face like a coward?"

"I'm not the coward." He surged from the seat, sending

me back three feet. "I'm not the one who killed myself to avoid a prison sentence."

I gulped, not allowing myself to cower under his towering height. He was angry—no, furious. Was this the rage Mom had seen on her deathbed? He'd lost it then. Maybe he'd lose it now. Maybe this was the emotional opening I needed to get something, anything, out of him.

I went for it.

"You kidnapped me because you knew I'd find out you were Lee."

His voice dropped. "Like you said, I should have killed you and that fucking reporter when I had the chance."

God, I hoped the mic had caught that. It wasn't a murder confession, but kidnapping and attempted murder were a close second. "Yes, you should have. But you didn't."

And if he hadn't brought me in to talk about the necklace, I never would have thought of him as Lee. Had he even planted that necklace in the cabin? Or had he kept it here this whole time?

"You wanted Dash to kill me. Why?" That question had been the crux of the year.

"He's Draven's son."

That was all the answer he gave.

Did that mean he would have put my murder on Dash too? Probably. He would have arrested Dash for my murder. He would have stolen Draven's son. He would have had it so that Draven's son killed his daughter.

But that hadn't worked, had it? So he'd unearthed that necklace, finally having an excuse to bring me in once Mom's picture was printed in the paper. He'd known for a year that I'd been in that cabin. He'd waited, patiently, to put me away for murder and silence me for good.

Marcus was bitter about Draven's death. Tucker had stolen his vengeance. I fought the urge to laugh in his face.

"How did you know I was coming to town to see Mom's grave?" The only person I'd told had been Bryce. "Were you watching my credit card records or something? Did you see that I'd booked a flight to Bozeman?"

He gave me a noncommittal shrug.

That meant *yes*.

"Would you have come after me in Colorado?"

Again, no answer. I was taking that as a *yes* too.

Marcus didn't know what Mom had told me about him. Had he been living this year in fear? I hoped so. I hoped he'd been looking over one shoulder and sleeping with one eye open, dreading the morning. Because that's how we'd lived this past year.

Besides the necklace, what other things had he taken from Mom's house? Was there a shrine somewhere of her precious belongings that he'd stolen?

"How did you know I was Draven's daughter? Before everyone else, I mean."

"The newspaper. Lane's always been good about giving me a heads-up before anything gets printed. When Bryce wrote that article about the knife and your"—his face twisted in disgust—"father, he told me."

So I'd been on his radar for two reasons, both because I might have been able to identify him and because I was Draven's child. A man he hated.

Marcus had put this elaborate plan in place to ensure none of us survived.

Was Dash next? After Marcus had locked me up for murder and arson, would he have gone after Dash? What about Nick? What about Draven's *grandkids*?

Marcus's quest for revenge against Draven likely knew no bounds. He'd stop at nothing.

All because my mother had broken his heart.

"You killed her."

"Prove it." He turned and walked to the door.

Shit. My recording might create some doubt, but was it enough to convict the chief of police? No way.

He was winning. The bastard was winning and he was walking away. *Fuck.*

"You deserve to die for what you did," I blurted.

His hand paused at the doorknob. "Is that a threat?"

"My father was a great man. He was the love of my mother's life. You were nothing to her. Nothing. She would have stayed with him."

The muscles in his back bunched. He slowly spun around, the door forgotten. "Your father was nothing more than a cheating, lowlife criminal."

"But she still wanted him more than you." I sneered. "She chose the better man. What did she say when you caught her after she fucked him? Did she admit he was better than you?"

"Fuck you."

"Did she tell you that he was stronger than you'll ever be?"

He stepped closer. "Shut your fucking mouth."

"I bet she saw his face when you were in bed with her. Did she ever call out his name while she was with you?" I kept pressing, getting louder and louder, hoping that Isaiah and Dash were close enough to stop Marcus from choking the life out of me when I sent him into a blind rage. "Did she call out his name when you stabbed her? Did she beg for her life?"

"Yes!" His hand flew, hitting me right across the cheek. The sting was blinding, dropping me to my knees. "She begged. She begged for him to save her, but he couldn't. And if I couldn't have her, then he wouldn't either."

My hands clutched my cheek as I blinked the white spots away. My vision returned just in time to see Marcus reach for something tucked behind his back, hidden underneath his shirt.

A gun.

Of course he had a gun. He was a cop and wouldn't answer the door after dark without a weapon.

I ignored Marcus and whipped my gaze to the side. Isaiah was running my way, his own gun drawn.

The shift caught Marcus's eye, but before he could react to my husband, the door to his back opened and Dash flew out, wrapping his arms around Marcus's back and tackling him to the ground. The two landed an inch from my leg, nearly crashing down on my head. Marcus struggled, fighting his way free, but Dash was stronger.

"Are you okay?" Isaiah was at my side, hauling me up and away from the men before they could collide with me.

I clung to him, my breaths coming in heavy pants. "He did it. He killed her."

"Yeah, doll." Isaiah pulled me into his arms, talking over my head. "Did you get it?"

"All of it," Emmett said, coming out of the darkness right behind the porch swing. I wasn't sure how he'd crept behind that tiny shrub without me noticing, but he'd been there the whole time.

Leo came out of the house with an older woman on his heels.

"Marcus?" she gasped as Dash hauled him to his feet. He

had the chief's hands pinned behind his back. "What's going on?"

"Call 911," Marcus ordered. "And our lawyer."

She nodded and disappeared into the house.

"You're going down for this," Dash said through gritted teeth.

"At least I'll take my punishment like a man. I won't off myself like your fucking coward father."

Dash tightened his grip on Marcus, making him wince. "You know nothing about my father."

Red and blue lights came racing down the street five minutes later. By that time, Dash had wrestled Marcus to the end of the sidewalk. His wife was standing on their lawn, her hands clutched around a phone, as two patrol cars skidded to a stop. Emmett was at her back, talking to someone on his phone.

The officers in the patrol cars jumped out and made their way toward Dash and the chief.

A marked police SUV raced in, parking behind the patrol cars. The man inside, dressed in plain clothes, hopped out and pulled the phone away from his ear before shouting, "Hold up."

Had he been talking to Emmett?

The patrolmen, who'd been about to rip Dash's grip off Marcus, froze at the other man's command.

"Who's that?" I asked Isaiah. We were standing by the porch with Leo, who despite the cops swarming, still had a gun in his hand.

No one was paying us much attention. We were the subtext to the main drama up front.

"It's Luke Rosen," Leo answered. "He's the chief's number two."

Luke walked up to Marcus, his eyes hard and his jaw clenched. Luke made no move to release Marcus from Dash's grip. He just stood there and crossed his arms over his chest. "Chief."

"Arrest these men," Marcus spat. "Trespassing and assault. Now."

Luke's eyes tracked to Emmett and he jerked up his chin.

Okay, this was weird. I'd expected all of us to be in a jail cell until we could get the recording to someone.

"What's going on?" Isaiah asked Leo.

"Emmett got the recording to Luke."

My jaw dropped. "Already?"

"They're friends. He called Luke before we came here tonight. Asked if he'd listen in on something."

"So he . . . the whole time?"

Leo nodded. "The whole time."

I looked up at Isaiah. "That means we're free, right? Was it enough?"

"I don't know." He blinked, his mouth dropping as he stared down at the sidewalk.

Luke gave Dash a nod to release Marcus, and then faster than I'd ever seen in a movie or TV show, he snapped cuffs onto Marcus's wrists.

"Good job." Leo grinned, clapping a hand on my shoulder. "I didn't think you could do it, but Dash said if anyone could, it would be you. And he was right. The minute you started pissing Marcus off, got him emotional, I knew you had him."

I couldn't believe it. I blinked at him, not sure what to say. "Thank you?"

Leo nodded and shook Isaiah's hand, then tucked his gun in the waistband of his jeans and walked away. He passed the cops, jerked his chin at Dash and disappeared down the block.

Marcus shouted something as Luke shoved him into the backseat of a police car. His wife, the poor woman, was wailing.

"We're free." The words sounded strange coming out of my mouth. When I looked up at Isaiah, he was shaking his head in disbelief. "We did it."

"No, you did it." He smiled. I lost sight of it as he crushed me in his arms. His chest began to shake and a moment later, I realized he was laughing.

Isaiah was laughing.

It was deep and raspy. Sexy and real. Something I wanted to hear every day for the rest of my life.

"We're free," Isaiah repeated my words, letting me go.

His face was lit with red and blue from the police car. My cheek throbbed and I'd likely have a bruise or even a black eye this week. I blocked it all out. I blocked out everything but my husband.

"I should let you go"—he tucked a lock of hair behind my ear—"but I'm not going to."

"It wouldn't work anyway. Where you go, I go, remember?"

He dropped a kiss to my lips. It was no more than a brush, but it held so much love and promise. Isaiah and his simple gestures. He took the quiet moments, the ones most overlooked, and made the most of them. "I do."

I smiled against his lips. "I do too."

EPILOGUE
GENEVIEVE

Three years later . . .

"Wow." My eyes raked over the white tent. "This is something else."

"They sure cleaned up the boneyard." Isaiah gripped my hand, leading me to our reserved seats.

We were sitting in the second row on the bride's side, the space reserved for family. The white folding chairs were arranged in perfect order. There weren't many of them, but nearly all were filled.

The grass was green beneath our feet. The lot behind the garage that had once been filled with old junkers and spare, rusted parts had gotten a total transformation. It must have taken the guys months.

The old cars had been moved behind the clubhouse. They were hidden by the grove of trees. The grass had been mowed short, surprising us all with the lush carpet that had been hiding underneath years of neglect.

There were flower pots filled with colorful petunias and lime-green sweet potato vines. The trees along the edge of the property had grown considerably over the past three years. Their leaves blocked out some of the bright June sunshine.

"We might actually have a decent barbeque here now." Isaiah glanced over his shoulder at the cement pad and picnic table next to the steel wall of the shop.

I followed his gaze, picturing Dad sitting there. The table was in the same place as it had been years ago when we'd had one of our first conversations. It had been over three years and his memory still brought on the threat of tears.

"He'd be so pissed today," I muttered. "But he would have showed up regardless."

"Just like the rest of us." Isaiah led me to our seats. In front of us, Bryce was wrestling with three-year-old Xander and two-year-old Zeke.

"Sit. Down." Her nostrils flared. "If you two don't stop fighting, I swear—"

"Uncle 'Saiah." Xander launched himself over the back of his chair into Isaiah's arms.

Isaiah caught him. "Hey, kid. Are you being good for your mom?"

"No." He picked at the button on Isaiah's white shirt.

I didn't get to see my husband dressed up much. Normally he was in his garage attire of T-shirts, jeans and motorcycle boots. But this weekend marked two in a row when he'd put on a starched shirt, rolled up the sleeves to show the tattoos on his forearms and pulled on a pair of black slacks. The boots remained.

A rush of heat bloomed in my core. Just like I had last weekend, tonight I'd get to undo the buttons on that shirt and get my hands on all that inked skin.

"So?" Bryce turned in her chair. "How does it feel to be back?"

I smiled at her, then up at Isaiah, who was attempting to teach Xander how to wink. "It's good to be home."

After three years in Missoula, Isaiah and I had moved home yesterday.

Last weekend, I'd graduated top of my class from law school. Monday would be my second first day of work at Jim's firm, this time as a lawyer.

I still had to pass the bar exam, but Jim had ultimate faith I'd make it through flawlessly. For now, I'd be under his wing once more, learning and growing until one day, maybe, he'd pass the practice down to me.

I shifted in my chair, searching the crowd for his kind face. I found it three rows back. He sat beside his wife, Colleen, her blond hair twisted into a fancy knot. They both smiled as I waved.

It was good to be home, surrounded by family again.

Isaiah and I had been alone in Missoula. With my busy class schedule and his long hours working at a small garage there doing routine car maintenance, we hadn't met many friends. On the occasional weekend, we'd drive up to Lark Cove to visit Kaine, Piper and their kids. Suzanne came to Missoula every other month for a visit. She'd sleep in the small guest bedroom and tell me stories about Isaiah from his childhood.

I'd lost my only family when Mom had died, but her death had led me to a new one.

"Hey." Emmett slapped Isaiah on the shoulder as he took the empty seat beside us. "Ready for this?"

"No." Isaiah frowned. "Any chance we can talk her out of it?"

Emmett leaned past us and took in the tent. "It took Dash, Leo and me three hours to figure out that fucking tent. I'm good if she calls this off, but she'd better keep the bar open."

I giggled, looking around again. "Where is Leo?"

"Late as usual." Emmett shrugged, then pulled a Dum Dums sucker from his pocket for Xander. The kid's eyes got wide as Bryce's narrowed.

"That's the fifth one." She shook her head as Emmett handed one to Zeke too. "When they're bouncing off the walls from a sugar high, I'm letting you watch them while *Mommy* enjoys the open bar."

We all laughed, then sure enough, Leo slid into the chair by my side. He leaned over to kiss my cheek, then stretched across my lap to shake hands with Isaiah.

"Is it official? You guys back for good?"

Isaiah nodded. "As of last night."

We'd arrived in town before dark with all of our belongings packed in the back of a U-Haul trailer. Isaiah had pulled it behind his truck while I'd followed in my car.

Every month that passed, Isaiah was getting more and more comfortable driving me around. It was always easier on his bike. Still, for the most part, we drove separately, or I drove him. There was no rush. There was no reason he had to drive. He'd proved over and over that he'd be there in an emergency.

"What's in the shop right now?" Isaiah asked the guys.

"We just brought in this sweet old '66 Dodge Charger," Emmett told him. "There's quite a bit of metal work to do, but it'll be a cool rig when it's done."

"I haven't fabricated anything in a while," Isaiah told him. "I'm out of practice."

"It'll come back," Leo assured him. "Are you guys staying in the apartment for a while?"

"Just for a few weeks, until we close on the house," I answered.

Thanks to Jim's starting salary at the firm and the paycheck spike Isaiah would get being back at work for Dash, we could afford a house. It was a new build, a small starter home on the edge of town, and in three weeks, it would be ours. All we had to do was wait for the builder to paint the exterior and knock out our punch list.

We'd gone to see it first thing this morning.

I was so excited to make it mine I could barely stand it. Though it had been fun sleeping in the apartment last night too. Dash hadn't rented it out in the years we'd been gone. It had become our home away from home, the place we stayed whenever we came home to visit.

Trips to Clifton Forge hadn't happened often in the past three years with my busy school schedule, but we'd managed visits at Christmas and two weeks each summer. We'd spent a long weekend here right after Zeke was born. We'd never missed a birthday party. Isaiah and I had even started going to Prescott once a year, staying with Nick, Emmeline and the kids.

We hadn't started off strong, but the ties that bound us together were strengthening. Dash and Nick had embraced me as their sister. Each year, the three of us met here in Clifton Forge on the anniversary of Dad's death to toast him by his graveside. While they'd go and visit their mother's headstone, I'd do the same with mine.

Marcus Wagner had been convicted of Mom's murder and obstruction of justice. The sheriff from a neighboring county had led the investigation and found evidence stashed away in Marcus's home. The gun he'd used during the kidnapping. The Warrior's vest. And a handful of things that had been Mom's. Those things added to the recording of his confession that the judge had allowed into the case, and the prosecution hadn't had a hard time getting a conviction. Marcus was currently serving a life sentence in prison without the possibility of parole.

Since his sentencing, I'd done my best to forget the man existed.

I had justice for my parents.

The wedding crowd around us rustled, everyone shifting in their seats as whispers drifted from the back row. I turned, wondering what was happening—it was too early to start the ceremony—when Presley marched around the corner of the garage.

Her white gown was hefted into her fists. Her hair was styled away from her face and her makeup was flawless. She was gorgeous. Furious, but gorgeous.

"What's going on?" Isaiah asked Emmett.

"Fuck if I know," he muttered.

As Presley stormed down the small aisle between the rows of chairs, Dash rushed to catch her. He was in slacks and a jacket because she'd asked him to walk her down the aisle. "Pres, don't."

"No." She put up a hand, the dress draping to the grass as she continued walking. "I'll do it."

Presley walked to the altar, nodding at the officiant who stood under the white archway entwined with green vines and white flowers. She squared her shoulders to address the crowd.

No.

We all hated Jeremiah, that was no secret. He'd joined

the Warriors and had moved to Ashton to be closer to the club. Year after year, he'd strung Presley along. He'd promised they'd get married. We'd all thought it was bullshit, but then six months ago, they'd set a date.

So here we were, ready to watch her marry a man none of us liked much. She'd already given Dash her notice so she could move to Ashton. He was in denial, refusing to fill her position at the garage until after she'd left town.

But Presley had made her choice and I'd stuck by her side, even meeting her and Bryce in Bozeman one day to shop for dresses.

I didn't want Jeremiah for her, but I didn't want this either. Not today.

Presley didn't deserve this kind of humiliation.

A flush crept up her face but she kept her chin high. "I'm sorry to inform you all that the wedding has been canceled."

A chorus of gasps and whispers filled the air.

My heart dropped as I searched for Isaiah's hand. He held my grip tight, his molars grinding. Beside me, Leo cracked his knuckles. Emmett's fists were white-knuckled on his knees. The fury emanating from Dash as he stood beside Presley was like a heat wave.

Jeremiah had better not show his face in Clifton Forge for quite some time.

"Thank you all for coming." Presley waved a hand to the tent. "Please take your gifts. I can't—" She shook her head, her eyes turning glassy.

"I got this." Dash stepped up. "You go."

She nodded and bolted to the side, racing away.

Isaiah handed me Xander, standing to chase her. Emmett and Leo were right behind him.

I met Bryce's worried gaze. "What should we do?"

"Get these people out of here," she muttered. "Then either we bring Presley back to the bar, or take the bar to Presley."

The guys were way ahead of us. As Bryce, Dash and I ushered guests to the parking lot, Isaiah, Emmett and Leo managed to snag Presley before she could disappear. They hurried her upstairs to the apartment, Leo grabbed a bottle of tequila from the bar, and they proceeded to line up shot after shot for the wounded bride.

By the time Bryce, Dash and I had taken care of the catering staff, bar staff and deejay, then joined the group in the apartment, Presley was muttering incoherent sentences on the couch, minutes away from passing out. She'd changed into a pair of my lounge pants and a hoodie. She'd cried her mascara down her face.

"A text," she slurred. "He did it in a text."

So Jeremiah had called it off, as I'd feared. *Asshole.* "What did his text say?"

"Hewanz Scarlett."

Scarlett? "Who's . . ."

Presley's eyes drifted closed and she was out cold.

"Okay, never mind," I muttered.

"We'll take her home," Dash said, handing his suit jacket to Bryce.

"No, I've got her." Emmett scooped her up in his beefy arms. "You've got the boys and their car seats."

"I'm going to go find Jeremiah." Leo stood from the couch where he'd been hovering over Pres. When he walked past me, the smell of alcohol on his breath was staggering.

"Not tonight." Isaiah caught him by the arm. "The last thing we need after three years of peace is a fight with the Warriors."

Leo grumbled something under his breath, but he nodded. "Fine. Not tonight. But I'm kicking that guy's ass for doing this to her."

My face paled, something Isaiah noticed instantly.

No. We'd gone so long without trouble, and I didn't want to invite it back into our lives. As much as I would like to see Jeremiah suffer for breaking Presley's heart, I didn't want revenge enough to risk our safety again.

"Leo, I'm driving your drunk-ass home," Dash said.

Thankfully, Leo didn't argue. He just tossed an arm around Bryce's shoulders and made a face that sent Xander into a fit of hysterics.

Zeke had fallen asleep on my shoulder thirty minutes ago.

"See you guys on Monday." Dash took Zeke from me, bending to kiss my cheek. Then he opened the door for everyone to file out.

When it clicked behind him, I blew out a deep breath, walking into Isaiah's arms. "That was bad."

"She'll be okay. Better this than a nasty divorce."

"Yeah." I closed my eyes. "I was looking forward to dancing with you tonight."

He lifted my hand, holding tight to the small of my back, then spun us in a circle. I smiled as he slowed and swayed us back and forth, the only music our beating hearts.

It was home. Here in this apartment, in his arms, was home.

"I'm pregnant."

Isaiah stopped dancing.

I'd found out two days ago and had stalled telling him because of the move. But now that we were here, now that we were home, it was time.

Isaiah and I had talked about having kids. We were both nervous about becoming parents, Isaiah more so than me. He had this lingering doubt that he didn't deserve the love of a child.

But he knew I wanted to be a mother. Deep down, he wanted to be a father. So we'd decided to wait until after school, and I'd gone off the pill two months ago.

"You're pregnant?"

I nodded.

He took my face in his hands. And smiled. "I love you, doll."

Isaiah's eyes had been so haunted once. So dark and lifeless. Tonight, they were as bright as stars. My husband. My life.

"I love you too."

BONUS EPILOGUE
ISAIAH

"Tradition requires we get a tree this weekend." Kaine had his ax in hand as he stood outside the door to the cabin. "The boys are busy playing a game with Mom and didn't want to leave. Grace is helping Piper make a pie, so it's just us."

I grinned. "Let me grab my coat and tell Genevieve."

"I'll wait here. My boots are dirty."

"'Kay." I left the door half open, retreating down the hallway to the bedroom. I peeked inside, finding Genevieve on the bed where I'd left her.

Amelia was asleep by her side.

I took up the space where I'd been resting, the three of us coming to the cabin to put the baby down for a nap.

"Kaine wants to go get a tree," I whispered, running my fingers over the smooth skin of our daughter's arm. "That okay?"

Genevieve nodded and yawned. "Sure. When she wakes up, we'll go over to the other house."

"See you in a bit." I stretched over our daughter to kiss her lips, then climbed off, careful not to bounce the mattress.

I eased the door closed, taking one last look at Genevieve as she smiled at our nine-month-old baby girl.

My heart swelled. Those two were the light of my life.

I was smiling when I joined Kaine outside, dressed in a coat, hat and gloves. The November air was cold but it had yet to snow.

The trip was long overdue. After Amelia was born, we'd stuck close to Clifton Forge.

"Work on any cool cars lately?" Kaine asked as we hiked up the ridge that bordered the back of his property.

"Some. I've kind of become the bike guy at the shop though. It's been fun learning how to piece them together."

"I might have to have you build me one someday. Not sure how Piper would feel about it though."

"Ask for forgiveness instead of permission, right?"

He chuckled. "Spoken like a married man."

We talked about some of my projects and some of his. He told me about the table he'd built Mom for Christmas and the toy box he'd built for Grace. I told him about a motorcycle I was building from the ground up and a Camaro restoration we had in the shop. We hiked and caught up on life, neither of us in a hurry to chop down a tree and neither of us really looking.

When we reached the top of the ridge, the sun was bright against the snowcapped mountains in the distance. The valleys below were a deep green, dotted with a few yellow and orange trees that were clinging to their leaves.

"You've got the view." I stood on the trail, admiring the spectacle.

"Not bad, is it?"

"Not bad at all." I breathed in the mountain air. There

were times I could still taste the prison stink—when I still felt trapped—but up here, free, those days were a lifetime ago.

The demons were growing quiet, more so every day I spent with my Genevieve.

I'd found happiness I hadn't ever expected.

"I don't know if I deserve this life."

Kaine put his hand on my shoulder. "You deserve it, brother. And then some."

Up there, on that ridge, I let my brother's words sink in. They were the same ones that Genevieve told me over and over, when she caught a faraway look in my eyes.

Maybe I did deserve this happiness.

Maybe they were both right.

One thing was certain, I'd never take this life for granted. And I'd never give it up.

ACKNOWLEDGMENTS

Thank you for reading *Riven Knight*! I hope you enjoyed Genevieve and Isaiah's story.

An enormous thanks to my editing and proofreading team: Elizabeth Nover, Marion Archer, Julie Deaton, Karen Lawson, Judy Zweifel, Kaitlyn Moodie and Gwyn McNamee. Thank you to Sarah Hansen for *Riven Knight*'s gorgeous cover.

A huge thanks to all of the amazing bloggers who shout about my books. Thanks to friends and family who made it possible for me to shut myself away and write this book.

And lastly, to Jennifer Santa Ana. For that wonderful day in Texas I'll never forget. I am so very blessed to call you my friend.

ABOUT THE AUTHOR

Devney Perry is a *Wall Street Journal, USA Today* and *#1 Amazon* bestselling author of over forty romance novels. After working in the technology industry for a decade, she abandoned conference calls and project schedules to pursue her passion for writing. She was born and raised in Montana and now lives in Washington with her husband and two sons.

Don't miss out on the latest book news.
Subscribe to her newsletter!
www.devneyperry.com

Made in the USA
Coppell, TX
03 October 2024

38037555R20225